But Why Shoot the Magistrate?

Books by Patricia Sprinkle

Nonfiction

Children Who Do Too Little
A Gift from God
Women Home Alone
Women Who Do Too Much

MacLaren Yarbrough Mysteries

But Why Shoot the Magistrate?
When Did We Lose Harriet?

Sheila Travis Mysteries

Deadly Secrets on the St. Johns
A Mystery Bred in Buckhead
Death of a Dunwoody Matron
Somebody's Dead in Snellville
Murder on Peachtree Street
Murder in the Charleston Manner
Murder at Markham

MacLaren Yarbrough Mysteries

But Why Shoot the Magistrate?

PATRICIA SPRINKLE

ZondervanPublishingHouse

Grand Rapids, Michigan

A Division of HarperCollinsPublishers

But Why Shoot the Magistrate?
Copyright © 1998 by Patricia H. Sprinkle

Requests for information should be addressed to:

ZondervanPublishingHouse
Grand Rapids, Michigan 49530

Library of Congress Cataloging-in-Publication Data

Sprinkle, Patricia Houck.
    But why shoot the magistrate? : MacLaren Yarbrough mysteries / Patricia
Sprinkle.
       p.   cm.
    ISBN: 0-310-21324-X (softcover)
    1. Title.
PS3569.0.P687B8 1998
813'.54—dc21   98–19239
                                                       CIP

Printed in the United States of America

98 99 00 01 02 03 04 /❖ DC/ 10 9 8 7 6 5 4 3 2 1

Cast of Characters

MacLaren Yarbrough—amateur sleuth, co-owner of Yarbrough Feed, Seed & Nursery

Joe Riddley Yarbrough—her husband, a Georgia magistrate and co-owner of YFS&N

Ridd—Yarbrough's older son, high school math teacher and cotton farmer

Martha—Ridd's wife, emergency room supervisor

Cricket (3) and Bethany (16)—their children

Walker—Yarbroughs' younger son, insurance salesman and country western singer

Cindy—his wife

Hubert Spence—MacLaren and Joe Riddley's nearest neighbor and old friend

Maynard—his son, Hopemore museum curator

Dr. Drew Holder—Yarbrough's next-nearest neighbor, a physician

Luke Blessed—Yarbrough's assistant preacher and a friend of Walker's

Amanda Kent—a nurse who lets the wrong person in

Selena Jones—Amanda's friend, also a nurse

Gideon Levy—Amanda's closest neighbor

Victor Davis—Tennessee professor, Amanda's fiance

Lorine Duckworth—a Hopemore society leader and Amanda's best friend

Ronald—her husband, a house painter

Rhonda—their daughter, a beauty queen

Goswami Pandava—founder of Temple of Inner Peace

Charlie Muggins—police chief

Isaac James—assistant police chief

Bailey (Buster) Gibbons—sheriff

Miss Bessie—Luke's landlady

This one is for Judge Mildred Ann Palmer
for friendship,
a role model,
the big idea,
and help with little details.

In a dream, in a vision of the night, when deep sleep falls on men as they slumber in their beds, he may speak in their ears and terrify them with warnings. *Job 33:15*

One

The night of the first murder, a full moon sailed over middle Georgia. Silver light and purple velvet shadows lent lawns, rooftops, and the broad, slick leaves of magnolias a lustre of romance and mystery they didn't generally deserve. The very air pulsed with the glow.

In Hopemore, Georgia—county seat of little Hope County located mid-way between Augusta, Macon, and nowhere—residents slept fitfully. Yard dogs howled. A preacher dreamed strange dreams. And Amanda Kent let the wrong person in.

∞

I woke a little past midnight to hear our three coon hounds serenading the moon. Young Pat, an aspiring Pavarotti, sent notes throbbing into the night. Big Tom

9

added a deeper bass, while old Queen Anne croaked along like an elderly alto who refuses to quit the choir. Just as I raised myself up on one elbow, our beagle Lulu chimed in on soprano. Lulu has a volume any opera singer would envy. That night she had a backup chorus, six pups caroling happily along with no notion they were being sent to new homes in a few days.

I jabbed my sleeping husband in the ribs. "Wake up, Joe Riddley. Go hush those dogs before Maniac calls."

Maniac and Hubert Spence were our nearest neighbors, up the pleasant dirt road Joe Riddley's great granddaddy Yarbrough laid out, back when being half a mile out of town meant living in the country. Since our two places and the old Pickens place up near the highway are still the only houses on the road, nights are pretty quiet except for crickets, owls, and frogs. However, Maniac Spence—named Maynard by his parents but long ago rechristened by schoolmates—was, in his own words, "sensitive and a light sleeper." Any minute now our phone would ring and I would hear, "Miss MacLaren, I hate to bother you so *late*, but could you ask Judge Yarbrough to *do something* about those *dogs*? I simply can't *sleep* with all that *racket*."

Maniac was a champion whiner, and stressed words like hairdressers stress highlighting for women past a certain age. The way he looked as a child—frail white limbs, wide gray eyes, pale yellow hair—I used to wonder if Maniac emphasized words to prove to the world that he was really there. Maybe that's why he came home from New York City with a long ponytail and one gold earring, too.

He'd always hated Hopemore, so I hadn't been surprised when he headed North after high school to study history and stayed there. Until March he hadn't come back but once—for his mother's funeral five years ago, when he was twenty-one.

Still, Maniac was a good son. We had to credit him for that. He gave up a good museum job and came right back when his daddy had a heart attack. He ran the appliance store until Hubert could get on his feet, then after Hubert felt well enough to go down to the store each afternoon, Maniac still worked mornings. He even got permission to spend afternoons cleaning out our little Hope County Historical Museum, which hadn't been kept up for fifteen years, since the last curator died. He nearly drove us all crazy asking if we'd found any war relics in our fields, or insisting that things we used every day were antiques that he needed for displays.

Maniac drove us crazy a lot of ways. Maybe he was just having a hard time adjusting to being back after so many years in New York City, but nothing seemed to suit him. He complained about the heat. Complained about what he called "the utter lack of culture" in Hope County. Complained about southern food being bad for our health—even though folks around here tend to live a good long time. Most of all, he complained about how dusty our unpaved road got his new green Saturn.

Joe Riddley lost his temper over that last one. "Son, this is a *good* road. Your relatives and mine have driven up and down it for over a hundred years. You want a clean car, hose it down each evening." After that, I often saw Maniac out rinsing off his car.

With all the noise our dogs were making that full moon night, I just knew Maniac was reaching for his phone.

Joe Riddley hadn't budged. I jabbed him again. "Go *do something* about those *dogs!*"

"Good gracious, woman, you sound just like Maniac." Joe Riddley climbed out of bed and plodded toward the door, moonlight stripes through our open blinds making him look more like a convict than a county magistrate. I heard him clomp downstairs, then in a minute I heard him shout, "Quiet! Quiet, now!" from our back porch. If the dogs hadn't waked Maniac, that yelling would.

However, Joe Riddley's hounds are so well trained, they stopped mid-howl. Lulu and the pups gave up in a few bars, and quiet reigned again except for crickets, a couple of frogs near our swimming pool, and thumps and bumps below.

Joe Riddley's great-granddaddy built this house five years after General Sherman blazed by and created unprecedented prosperity for the Yarbrough Lumber Company. He built high ceilings, enormous rooms, and a wraparound porch in front and along one side with a rounded curve and a little round pointed roof at the corner. When we took the house over from Joe Riddley's parents back when our boys were small, we screened in the side porch and that curve at the corner, remodelled the kitchen, updated the wiring and plumbing, and put in heat and air conditioning. Over the years we'd repaired the tin roof, slicked things up inside occasionally with new paint and paper, and covered the outside with pale blue siding that didn't need painting. Otherwise the house hadn't changed much. It was lovely and comfortable, but certainly not soundproof.

I could hear every step as Joe Riddley fixed himself something to eat. *Thump*—he slammed the back door. *Squeak*—he opened the bread drawer. *Thud*—he closed the refrigerator. *Smack*—he got a plate from the cabinet and slammed that door. Joe Riddley never shut a door softly in his life. *Scrape*—he opened the drawer to get a knife. *Creak*—he was sitting down at the big round oak table his granddaddy built. Was I going to get no sleep at all?

Still, now that he'd mentioned it, I was a tad hungry myself.

I got up and put on a cotton robe. Living nearly a mile down a dirt road, I *could* go to the kitchen in my gown or even my birthday suit, but we seldom closed our blinds and you never knew who might be outside doing what. That new doctor who bought the Pickens house, for instance, jogged up and down our road at all hours, and a fair share of Hopemore men hunted at night with a fine disregard for the Fish and Game Commission. I prided myself that I looked pretty good for a woman on the sunny side of sixty. I didn't want word to get around that MacLaren Yarbrough was losing her figure.

I found my spouse biting a hunk off the kind of sandwich that makes heart doctors see dollar signs. "What you doin' up, Little Bit?" That's been his pet name for me since he was six and I was four and he blurted out one day, "You're the cutest little bit of a thing I ever did see." Since he was always two years older, and since I stopped growing at five-foot-three while he climbed up past six feet, the name stuck.

"Same thing you are, honey," I told him. "Raising my cholesterol level so I can sleep."

Joe Riddley hadn't bothered to turn on a light. So much moonlight poured through our kitchen windows that moving around was like walking on the bottom of a silvery stream. I found a couple of cold chicken legs and a little potato salad Clarinda, our cook, had tucked in the fridge after dinner, and poured myself a cold glass of buttermilk to go with them.

As I headed to the table, I thought fondly that Joe Riddley might be over sixty, but he was still the handsomest man I knew. He was long and rangy, with high cheekbones, straight dark hair and a permanent tan from his Cherokee great-grandmother. Even in pajamas with his hair tousled, he had a kindly presence about him. An often-convicted thief once confided to me, "Judge Yarbrough treats everybody with dignity, no matter what they done."

I planted a kiss on the back of his neck on my way to my chair. Then we sat in the companionable silence of people who've been happily married for forty-five years and have said everything that needs to be said for the moment. We had no idea what dreadful things were going on downtown.

～

In a hot upstairs apartment, the Reverend Luke Blessed tossed and twisted in sweaty sheets. Luke Blessed (pronounced the old fashioned way, with two syllables) was our new assistant pastor: single and not quite thirty. We adults voted to call him because of his answers to questions about faith and commitment. My sixteen-year-old grand-daughter and her friends voted for his tight brown curls, navy blue eyes, and skill on an electric guitar.

Poor Luke was hot because his landlady insisted, "There's always a breeze upstairs." Her house was on Oglethorpe Street, which runs right through the middle of Hopemore and along one side of the courthouse square. It has our biggest old houses, including three General Sherman's firebrands missed. Maynard's museum is in one. Luke lived in another, belonging to our congregation's oldest, wealthiest member. She created the small upstairs apartment because her children didn't like the notion of her living alone, but while she drove a Lincoln Continental and wore enough diamonds to feed most families for a year, she was well known for pinching pennies where others were concerned. Our pastor search committee was foolish to take what she said about upstairs breezes for gospel truth.

Luke moved into her apartment on a breezy April day. He never complained, but by May he'd bought three fans and opened his windows wide, trying to catch that reputed breeze. On the night of the August full moon, all he'd caught was sticky heat, streaming moonlight, and barking dogs. Anybody might have had fanciful dreams.

Luke described his particular dream to the police the next week. I heard the tape:

I was in a room I did not know. I could see a bed used like a couch over to one side and a lamp with a dark shade on a table beside it. There was a TV in one corner, I think. A tall man was standing in the doorway talking, although I couldn't hear a word he said. At first I thought he was talking to me, but then I realized I was invisible. He was talking to somebody sitting in a big blue chair between me and him. Because of the chair's high back, I didn't know if it was a man or a woman. All I could see was brown hair. Dark brown. The man was tall—six feet, maybe—with great biceps. He had blonde hair and wore a green outfit of some kind. Matching pants and shirt. Maybe golf clothes.

At first they were just talking. Slowly, though, even though he was still smiling, I began to get a feeling of menace, like he was threatening the other person. I got so nervous I wanted to get out of there. That's when I woke up.

According to his testimony, Luke felt so disturbed by the dream that he couldn't stay in bed. Rising quietly so he wouldn't wake Miss Bessie downstairs, he went out to the old sleeping porch Miss Bessie had converted into a kitchen, got himself a glass of iced tea, and tiptoed to his living room up front.

"I thought about going out for a walk," he admitted. "I wish now I had. Maybe I'd have heard something, or been able to do something. But I didn't want to get dressed, so I figured I'd just get a head start on preparing for our young men's Bible study the next Tuesday evening. For half an hour I studied the Book of Daniel, the chapter where Daniel interprets King Nebuchadnezzar's dream. I even decided that knowing we'd be studying that passage was probably what made me dream. After a while I relaxed enough to go on back to bed." He stopped and took a deep shuddering breath. "As soon as I closed my eyes, though, that dream picked up right where I'd left off."

The man across the room suddenly stepped toward the other person. I felt like something was terribly wrong. I tried to shout out a warning, but I couldn't make a sound. I saw him bring one hand from behind him, and he was holding something long. A walking cane, I think. Next thing I knew, he hauled off and hit whoever sat in the chair so hard I saw blood spurt up all over. The person collapsed forward but I couldn't see if it was a man or a woman. All I could see was two hands raised in supplication, but he kept beating and beating. I tried to yell or run, but I was frozen. Finally I woke up, crying.

I knew I couldn't stay in bed any longer. I was afraid I'd keep dreaming. So I got up and spent the rest of the night reading and praying. It was too hot to sleep anyway.

"Hands raised in supplication?" assistant police chief Isaac James would ask Joe Riddley when he came by our office for a warrant to search the Blessed apartment the following Wednesday. "What kind of description is that?"

"A preacher's kind," I told him tartly.

Isaac James is a friendly, thorough bear of a man who played high school football with our son Walker. In the ten or so years he's been coming into our office with warrants and such, Ike and I have become good friends. I make no bones about the fact that I think he's Hopemore's best police officer. He's so good, in fact, that even the racists in this town had sense enough to make him assistant police chief a few years back, in spite of his being black.

However, while Ike and I generally see eye-to-eye on things, on that particular murder case . . .

"Preacher or not, Miss MacLaren, Chief Muggins is certain he went next door and beat that poor Kent woman to death. A psychiatrist up in Augusta says all that folderol about a dream is just his way of confessing." Ike shook his head and rubbed his eyes with one forearm to erase the memory. "I never saw such a mess in my life. Hope to never see the likes again. There wasn't much left but pulp."

Why had a shy, pretty, well-reared girl entertained somebody in her apartment that late at night in her nightgown?

Luke's landlady summed up our collective opinion: "That girl was just asking for trouble, if you ask me."

If so, she got it. What was surprising, considering the ferocious nature of the crime, was that nobody seemed to have seen or heard a thing.

A spirit glided past my face, and
the hair on my body stood on end.
It stopped, but I could not tell what
it was. *Job 4:15–16*

TWO

The first hint Hopemore had that anything was
wrong was Saturday just as the courthouse clock
chimed eleven. Before the last stroke, Police Chief
Charlie Muggins raced up Oglethorpe Street with his
siren blaring.

Joe Riddley and I scarcely noticed. We were in our
little back office at Yarbrough's Feed, Seed and Nursery—me totting up the week's bills and him reading
and answering the week's mail. A minute later, though,
when every siren in town followed, Joe Riddley looked
up from a seed catalogue and said mildly, "Guess they
have to test them sometimes."

I shivered. We don't have but thirteen thousand
people in what our Chamber of Commerce likes to call
"Greater Hopemore." Chances are good that any emergency involves people we know or their relatives. I slid

my feet into my shoes, hurried out onto the sun-baked sidewalk, and peered up the street with all the other downtown merchants.

"Where is it?"

"I can't quite tell. Think it's a fire?"

"I don't see any smoke."

"There goes Hubert. He oughtn't to be out in all this heat."

Hubert Spence left his appliance store and lumbered after the sirens. Hubert had been short on excitement for years, ever since we replaced the volunteer fire department with professionals. He'd loved being our volunteer fire chief.

I'm ashamed to admit that when I saw one last police car squeal to a stop in front of the old Hedrick house two blocks away, I breathed a sigh of relief. The Victorian gingerbread had been cut up into apartments the year before, and was mostly rented to young adults who moved to Hopemore to work. I didn't know a soul who lived there.

I went back to the office with sweat dripping down the back of my blouse, feeling sheepish for being so nosy. "Just somebody down at Hedrick's," I reported to Joe Riddley. "Nothing to do with us."

But I shivered again. Did I suspect, even then, I would live to regret those words?

∽

I returned to my accounts with one ear cocked, hoping somebody would come tell us what was going on. It wasn't likely. Ever since Joe Riddley and I sold off the lumber side of Yarbrough's, our business comes primarily from farmers buying seed and feed in bulk, from landscapers, and from folks putting in gardens or fixing up their yards each spring and fall. By August, Hopemore's so hot you could fry bacon on the sidewalk and so humid you could poach eggs beside the bacon. Anybody with sense stays home. Those without sense play golf.

When the front door did jingle, just past noon, it was our older son Ridd—looking a lot like his daddy did at forty, with less hair. Ridd is a high school math teacher for pay and a farmer for the love of it. He often comes down on Saturdays to help himself to new plants. We don't begrudge him the plants. Ridd's yard is Yarbrough's best advertisement.

"Did you see what was going on down at Hedricks'?" I greeted him.

"Saw a rescue vehicle and every police car in town. Maybe somebody had a heart attack or something."

Joe Riddley tossed another catalogue into his waste-basket. "Can you hang around awhile? I was thinking about taking your mama down to Myrtle's for a bite."

Monday through Friday I pick up Clarinda at eight and drop her off by our house, and she has a hot meal on the table when we get there at noon. Joe Riddley goes on back to the store right after we eat, and I wait and take Clarinda home on my way back. We've done that since the boys were little. I tell people it's because I think one of the best things anybody can do with their money is give somebody else a job. Joe Riddley says it's to make sure we stay well-nourished. He always jokes that I don't know a stove from a sink. I do, I just don't like to cook. Since Clarinda doesn't come on Saturdays, we eat dinner out.

Ridd said he didn't mind keeping the store a while, but wondered, "Why don't you close up and go on home? Nobody's thinking about putting in plants with the heat index over a hundred."

I turned my head so Ridd could read my lips and Joe Riddley couldn't, and word for word I mouthed Joe Riddley's reply. "We need to catch up on the paperwork and read the mail. Might as well stay open in case somebody needs something."

Ridd grinned. His parents had been having that conversation for years.

All three of us knew why Joe Riddley and I went down to the store every Saturday. We went because that store was home. We met there when my daddy went to buy nails from Joe Riddley's daddy when I was four and he was six. We worked there together every Saturday during high school and every summer during college. Our whole married lives we'd shared that office at the back. I re-covered the seat cushions and the chair by the window from time to time—they were currently red plaid—and each year we hung up a new calendar and a few new cartoons, but we'd never carpeted the bare wood floor, painted the natural beaded board walls, or replaced the matching oak rolltops Joe Riddley's parents used. We'd added a fax, copier, and computer, of course. We weren't old-fashioned, we just liked to be comfortable. And we were so used to spending Saturdays in the office, we'd neither one have known what to do with a full day at the house—or so we thought at the time.

Joe Riddley reached for the yellow and green Yarbrough's cap hanging on a nail over his head while I reached for my pocketbook. Our younger son Walker always threatens to bury his daddy in his cap and me with my pocketbook.

"By the way," Ridd said as we headed toward the door, "I've reserved two camping spaces for next weekend. You still okay to leave Thursday? And can I borrow your car, Mama, to go to Dublin this afternoon for some supplies? I want to leave my truck with the dealer to get it checked out before we go." They were heading out for four days' camping and fishing in the Georgia mountains, a family tradition dating from Augusts when Joe Riddley's daddy was a boy.

Joe Riddley nodded. "I'm coming, but Walker says he can't. They have a gig." The three of us exchanged the kind of look families use when words won't do a bit of good.

"I wondered about taking Crick," Ridd suggested. "He's dying to go—"

"What business does a three-year-old have on a fishing trip?" I demanded.

Joe Riddley held up a hand to silence me. "Hold on, Little Bit. If Crick wants to go, it's time we took him. He can swim like a fish, and except for the lake there's no trouble for him to get into." He turned to Ridd. "You tell him his Pop will be proud to have him along."

"And that his Me-mama won't get a wink of sleep while you're gone," I added tartly.

I followed Joe Riddley out to his silver Towncar knowing full well we'd look in by Hedricks' on our way to Myrtle's—even if it *was* in the wrong direction.

❧

We pulled up across the street from a crowd on the sidewalk. They were engrossed in watching a rescue team awkwardly maneuvering a body bag down steep narrow steps from a garage apartment at the far end of the drive. Everybody gasped as the team stumbled, staggered, steadied their load, and managed to get it to the ground in spite of Charlie Muggins, who stood bellowing instructions under Hedricks' two-hundred-year-old live oak. Charlie always reminded me more of a football coach than a police chief.

"See anybody we know?" I asked Joe Riddley, scanning the crowd.

If you ask most people why they like living in Hopemore, they'll say right off, "Because you know everybody." But we don't. Not really. We talk to some folks every day without ever knowing their hidden longings and secret sins. A lot of others we merely know by sight. Still, we know a stranger when we see one. That makes us feel safe.

The day would come when I no longer felt safe. That morning, I was just a little anxious about what kind of disaster had struck, and whom.

I was glad to see Hubert Spence near the back of the crowd. If anybody knew anything, he would. Joe Riddley rolled down his window and called, "What's up, Hube?"

Hubert wiped his forehead with a damp handkerchief and came to the car, his face redder than a man's ought to be five months after a heart attack. "Girl died, so they say." Southern men never personally claim knowledge they haven't gotten by direct experience. Watching a body bag being loaded into a rescue vehicle doesn't count.

I couldn't help thinking how lovely and serene the big gray Victorian house still looked under its canopy of oaks, no matter what had happened inside. Silently we watched the rescue team stow their load and pull out the Hedrick drive. I felt a pang of sadness as they headed toward the morgue. Whoever that young woman was, I was sorry she wasn't still alive to enjoy the fat white clouds sailing high through our hot blue sky.

I might have stayed sad longer, but Chief Muggins distracted me. His car rolled down the drive just as Joe Riddley asked Hubert "How'd she die?" I guess Charlie had lowered his window to say hello. Instead, he answered the question.

"Murdered, Judge. Beat to death. Most brutal thing I ever saw."

I gasped. Joe Riddley's hands tightened on the steering wheel. Of all the crimes in the world, we hate murder most. It cuts short so many possibilities.

"Who was she, Charlie?" I called across Joe Riddley's chest.

Chief Muggins had been perfectly cordial to Joe Riddley, but he glared at me. He has never appreciated the times I've been able to set him straight on a case. Instead of answering my question, he rolled up his window and roared off.

"The way you drive, you'll kill somebody yourself someday," I informed his tailpipe.

Joe Riddley gave a snort of exasperation. "Do you think you two could meet just once without raising your hackles, Little Bit?"

"It wasn't my fault," I pointed out with dignity. "I just asked who the dead woman was."

"Young nurse from Augusta, so I heard." Hubert dabbed his forehead again. His breath came in short wheezy gasps.

Joe Riddley looked at me, and I knew what he was asking. I nodded, even though Hubert isn't one of my favorite dinner companions. He has a habit of belching a lot, then saying "Excuse me" real loud. Mama always taught us never to excuse yourself louder than whatever you'd done. Still, I'd been meaning to have Hubert and Maniac down to supper ever since his heart attack, and I hadn't done it. Taking him to dinner was the least we could do.

Joe Riddley jerked his thumb toward the back seat. "We're heading to Myrtle's, Hube. Wanna join us?"

Hubert opened the back door. "Don't mind if I do. It's too hot to stand around waiting for something else to happen." What did he expect to happen—another murder?

I'd felt queasy watching that body bag, knowing somebody was in it. I felt even queasier once I got a whiff of Hubert. He'd been standing in the sun quite a while, and is one of those men who think deodorant is sissy. I've always thought Hubert goes a long way toward explaining why Maniac turned out the way he did.

Hubert eased himself into the back seat, spread his short legs wide, and asked, "Ready to go down in smoke this fall? Florida has a powerful quarterback."

"We'll cut out teeth on him to get ready for you," Joe Riddley retorted. As you might have guessed, Joe Riddley went to Georgia, Hubert to Georgia Tech.

I didn't pay them any attention. Those two hadn't agreed on a single political candidate, preacher, or quarterback in their lives. Still, they wrangled with the easy confidence of men who've known each other since diaper days, and they were good neighbors. Several acres between Spences' house and ours helped. So did things like Hubert keeping our appliances running for next to nothing and Joe Riddley sending one of our men to plant the watermelons while Hubert was recuperating.

As Joe Riddley made a U-turn and headed to Myrtle's, Hubert leaned forward, smelling as ripe as last week's cantaloupe. "That girl that was killed? I fixed her TV just yesterday."

"Is that a *fact!*" I exclaimed encouragingly, trying not to breathe more than necessary.

"Sure is. Had Maynard run it back last evenin'. Said she was real rude to him." He sank back in his seat without any notion that he'd just offered Maniac as a prime suspect.

However, as Joe Riddley pointed out, "Being in New York so long, looks like he'd have gotten used to that."

"Yeah." Hubert sighed. "I wish Maynard would find him a nice girl and settle down."

I didn't dare catch Joe Riddley's eye. He'd said more than once, "Hubert's never gonna get that boy married off, Little Bit. We're gonna be stuck with him next door the rest of our lives. What self-respecting female would put up with all that complaining?"

"They have any idea who did it?" I asked hastily to change the subject.

"Not that I heard." Hubert wheezed to a close, then offered the standard comfort when murder invades a small town. "Probably some tramp passing through."

None of us really believed it. Tramps are too smart to come to central Georgia in August. And even if one did, why should he single out a woman in a garage apartment on the busiest street in town?

The noontime glare on my window meant I saw not only Oglethorpe Street, but my own reflection. It floated beyond the shield of safety glass, out in a danger zone where a brutal murderer might be hiding inside any one of those brick businesses or gracious big white houses. I knew better than to assume murderers had to live in public housing, unkempt little shacks, or one of the big warehouses that loomed empty and cobwebby down near the tracks. For the third time that morning, I shivered.

❧

Joe Riddley pulled in at Myrtle's sign—*Cooking as Good as Mama Used to Do*. While he parked, I rummaged in the glove compartment for salt. After her husband's bypass, Myrtle declared war on everything that makes Southern cooking good. Instead of fried chicken and green beans simmered with fatback, salt, and sugar until they were soft, she now offered baked chicken and unsalted steamed vegetables. Everybody in town borrowed salt packets from Hardee's or the Huddle House to take to Myrtle's.

"Myrtle ought to change her sign til she gets off this health food kick," Joe Riddley muttered as he turned off the engine.

"If people in this town weren't loyal, she'd have gone out of business." I pulled one last salt packet from inside a map.

"She didn't have to take the shakers off her tables," Hubert agreed. "Those vegetables don't have a speck of taste. Gimme some of that, Mac."

I handed him three little packets, hoping we both wouldn't regret it.

Joe Riddley fished his cap out from under his seat. "Hurry up, you two, before the pie's all gone." He always claims Myrtle makes the best chocolate pie in Georgia. He could be right. Her meringue alone is two inches thick. He always wants me to ask how she keeps it from falling, but I never do. I don't care to know.

That particular Saturday I let Joe Riddley and Hubert go in ahead of me, two old cronies walking a bit creakily. They ought to have looked odd, Joe Riddley six feet tall and Hubert scarcely five foot six, but they didn't. I got a little teary when I noticed how Joe Riddley rested one hand on Hubert's shoulder and opened the heavy door for him.

I took time to repowder my face and run a comb through my hair. Myrtle's might not be a four-star restaurant, but I like to look nice. The mirror showed me looking a little peaky from the heat and the news, so I added more blusher and lipstick than I usually wear, then felt like a painted floozy. I wondered if the murdered woman had been a painted floozy—and what she'd done to get herself murdered.

"That's right, Mac, blame the victim," I said aloud as I headed inside. I often talk to myself. A person needs intelligent conversation *some*times.

Myrtle's was humming with news and gossip—which in Hopemore are sometimes hard to tell apart.

"Raped and like to beat her to death. Now who'd do a kind of thing like that?"

"No sign of forced entry, or so they say. Musta known him and let him in."

"Wearing nothing but a green *nightgown*."

That last fact was what got the most attention. That and the blood.

"Blood *everywhere*. Even on the overhead light fixture, one officer said." With relish the speaker swiped up the last blob of gravy with his last crumb of biscuit.

If that seems like gory mealtime talk, you have to remember that those folks had grossed each other out in elementary school and a lot of the men went through a war together. Besides, we weren't strangers to murder in Hope County. The world being what it is these days, we've had a number of drug-related killings, and magistrates regularly go down to the jail to set or deny bond for husbands who shoot their wives and wives who stab their husbands. I couldn't ever remember a rape-and-beating death, though.

We were just starting our pie when the restaurant suddenly went silent. I looked up to see Drew Holder, one of the new physicians in town, making his way toward the take-out counter. Myrtle immediately handed him a brown bag and he pulled out his wallet.

I'm partial to taller men myself—Dr. Holder wouldn't have made five-ten in his shoes—but he was fortyish and single, with a square face, a strong jaw, and long straight honey bangs, so anybody could see why all the women were watching him. I didn't understand the men, though, until Hubert leaned across the table to say hoarsely, "He examined the body."

Poor thing. Maybe that was why he looked so grim.

Dr. Holder was our neighbor—Hubert's and ours. In April he'd bought the Pickens place up at the top of our road to restore it, after the last Pickens—old Amos—fell off the roof fortifying it against flying saucers. Joe Riddley had stopped by a few times to explain county regulations about what construction debris Dr. Holder could burn and what he'd have to cart away. He said the doctor was working hard at restoring that old house.

All I'd done so far was wave when I saw him jogging down at our end of the road, but as he passed our table on his way toward the door, I waved toward the empty seat in our booth. "Howdy, neighbor. Won't you join us?"

"Hi, Judge, Mrs. Yarbrough, Hubert. Thanks, but I have to get back to work." He lifted a hand to sketch a little salute and hurried out to a black Lexus blocking the door.

"Snooty, isn't he?" a woman at another table asked her companion. "Thinks he's God's gift to women."

"No wonder," said her friend. "Everybody in town with an eligible daughter has invited him to dinner."

Now that might be an idea ...

Joe Riddley looked down at me, then leaned over the table toward Hubert. "You know what MacLaren's thinking, Hube?" he asked softly. "I'll tell you. We don't have an eligible daughter, but MacLaren's just decided that inviting Doc Holder to dinner would be the neighborly thing to do."

Then the Lord said to Satan, "Have
you considered my servant Job?
There is no one on earth like him; he
is blameless and upright, a man who
fears God and shuns evil." *Job 1:8*

Three

After that I couldn't simply call Dr. Holder, casually
invite him down, and bring up the topic of murder when
he got there. I'd have to wait for a good chance. It came
that afternoon after my standing four-thirty beauty parlor appointment.

It was hot and hazy by then, the sky too tuckered out
to put forth the effort to be its usual charming self. The
clouds blended right into the blue and the horizon was
pure white. Definitely too hot to cook, even if I'd been in
the mood, but Ridd and his family always came on Saturday evenings to swim and eat supper. I ran by Bi-Lo
after the beauty parlor and got meat and cheese for sand-
wiches and ice cream for dessert.

As I got in my—or rather, Joe Riddley's—car, I
glanced around nervously. I saw other women doing the
same. We weren't used to having a murderer loose in town.

I came alongside Dr. Holder jogging down the road beside Hubert's cow pond, which is between their two places. He looked a lot more approachable in red shorts and a sweaty white T-shirt than he had that morning in a starched shirt and a three-piece suit.

I rolled down my window. "It's sure missing a great chance to rain, isn't it?"

He jogged in place and swiped sweat off his forehead with a yellow terry cloth band on one wrist. "Sure is. We could do with some cooling off."

"Don't overdo in this heat, now. And drink lots of liquids."

"Thanks." He flicked a bead of sweat from his jaw with one slender forefinger.

I swatted a curious fly away from my open window. "Have you found anything worth keeping among Amos's junk?"

"Nothing but three Indian head pennies and a rocking chair I think I can restore. You wouldn't believe the stuff I've had to chuck out." He picked up a rock off the road and hurled it accurately into the center of Hubert's pond. Did that rock stand for all the junk, or for Amos Pickens and his packrat ways?

"When you get done, the house ought to be wonderful," I consoled him. "It was beautiful when I was little."

He grunted. "Back when the porch had all its banisters, the roof wasn't fortified against Martians, and you could see the house through the bushes?"

"Back then." I indicated the bags beside me. "I'm putting together a simple supper for our son Ridd and his family. You'd be more than welcome. Come swim, too, to cool off."

"Thanks, but I've promised myself to start tearing the kitchen out tonight. I need to get down to studs so the electricians and plumbers can come."

"You have to eat," I insisted. "Come as you are, have a sandwich, and get right back."

He shook his head. "Not tonight, thanks. Maybe another time?"

"Sure. You've had a rough day." I hoped he'd say something about the murder, but he just nodded and jogged in place.

"Good-bye, then. Let us know if you need anything."

"I sure will." He raised one hand in farewell.

I wasn't utterly disappointed. I still had Martha coming to dinner. She probably knew more about the murder than Drew Holder anyway.

I had more than that, if I'd only known. I had the person who would soon be Police Chief Charlie Muggins' favorite suspect.

~~~

As soon as I got inside with my arms full, the phone rang. I could hear Joe Riddley still mowing, so I dropped my grocery bags on the table and grabbed the receiver.

"Mama? You havin' everybody for supper tonight?" It was Walker, our younger son, whom Joe Riddley was describing that summer as "thirty-five going on twelve." He didn't even wait for my answer, since he knew it. "Can you add two more? Our gig got cancelled, so I thought maybe Luke and I could come over to swim and eat."

"Sure, honey. We'll be here."

When Joe Riddley came in from mowing he totally ignored my new perm and asked, "What's the matter, Little Bit?"

"Walker's gig got cancelled. He's coming to supper and bringing Luke Blessed."

"I don't suppose it occurred to Walker to go up to Thomson?"

"He didn't mention it. When they get here, now, you be nice."

Joe Riddley gave me a sour look. "I'll be nice. But Walker's place is with his family. You know that as well as I do." As I started hulling strawberries for the ice cream and he headed up to put on his bathing suit, we heaved identical sighs.

I puttered around getting things ready, muttering to myself. "How can two children grow up in the same house and turn out so different?" Ridd was dependable, easy-going, thrifty, a good husband and daddy. Why wasn't Walker?

Deep inside I blamed Cindy, his wife, whose family breeds race horses up near Thomson and lives in one of those big mansions some people think all southerners have.

Cindy had never worked, unless you count volunteer work, horse shows, hunting, golfing at the country club, and throwing parties. And while Walker did right well selling insurance, it seemed to us like they spent more than he made. "... new cars, expensive clothes, two kids in private schools ..."

When Joe Riddley got restless at night and I'd ask, "Anything the matter?" he'd say, "No, just lying here calculating Walker's probable debt."

Debt didn't seem to bother Walker and Cindy any. Two years back they'd bought a big house out on Academy Street, the kind Joe Riddley calls "a hole in the ground into which you pour new lumber and paint." Cindy hired an architect all the way from Atlanta to tell her what to do with it.

"I could tell her what to do with it," Joe Riddley growled. "Sell it and find a place they can afford to keep up."

Now, Walker was having his mid-life crisis early.

Every Christmas we give each family a thousand dollars, telling them it's an early part of their inheritance we get the fun of watching them spend. Generally Ridd and Martha take a family vacation and Walker and Cindy buy something for their house. That past year, Walker had used every speck of their money for a fancy guitar and western-style clothes. That's when we first heard that he and a couple of old college buddies hoped to become the next country western music sensation.

Not that he didn't have a good voice—he used to sing solos in his college choir. But suddenly he'd started talking in a way that made us wonder why we'd wasted so much money on his education, and spent weekends either practicing or playing Saturday night "gigs" all over the Southeast. Right after school was out, Cindy packed up the children and headed to her mama's. "I can live with a lot of things," she told Ridd and Martha, "but I won't be the grass widow of a country music singer."

As far as we knew, Walker hadn't seen her or the children since. Just went right on strumming and singing songs about how "somebody done me wrong."

I'd done more worrying about that boy in one summer than I'd figured on doing the whole rest of his life.

I was still worrying when Joe Riddley came back down, wearing his red checked bathing suit with a green T-shirt. "You look like a skinny Father Christmas," I told him. I never can get that man to coordinate his clothes.

As usual, he ignored me. Just poured himself a big glass of tea and leaned against the counter. "Say what you will, Little Bit, it seems funny to me for our preacher to be singing in a country western band."

That was one thing on which Joe Riddley and I disagreed. The only good news in the whole Walker mess, as far as I was concerned, was that Luke had recently been asked to join the band. I didn't know Luke well—he was in charge of the contemporary service and we always went to the eleven o'clock—but what I knew I liked. As young as he was, he seemed stable and sensible.

"Luke never misses church, no matter how late they get home," I pointed out, pouring myself a cold Co-cola, "and the church kids brag about him being in the band. I'm proud of how his and Walker's voices blend, too." We'd gone to hear them twice, and I'd been more impressed than I'd wanted to be.

"I'd be prouder, honey, if Walker were a better husband and father."

I sipped my drink, enjoying the tingle it sent up my nose. "Reckon we might be able to put a bug in Luke's ear—a little one—about getting Walker back in church?"

Joe Riddley snorted. "Little Bit, if Walker came to church it would be to sell insurance to the members."

"I don't care why he comes," I told him tartly, "if he'll *come*. We planted good seeds in that boy. God can sprout them if Walker will sit in church one hour a week."

Joe Riddley finished his tea and set his glass in the sink. "Well, if you're gonna put a bug in Luke's ear it had better be a very private bug, or Walker will flat-out kill you."

"Don't talk about killing," I begged. "Not today."

As soon as Ridd, Martha, and their son arrived, I saw how far news of the murder had travelled. Three-year-old Cricket greeted me, "Me-mama! A lady died. Beat to death!" His eyes were wide amber marbles and his honey-brown hair curled with humidity.

I swatted him lightly on the bottom. "Pop's in the pool. Go on out. And you might take a look at the p-u-p-s to see if there's one you like."

"Pups! Pups!" Cricket chanted, running for the door. He'd been begging for a dog, and Joe Riddley had said he could have his pick of the litter. Beagles are good for little children—patient, sweet-tempered, and practically indestructible.

"You car's in the drive, Mama. Thanks. And don't you all go talking about that murder, now," Ridd warned as he set two heavy bags of fresh vegetables on the counter. I eyed them gladly. Joe Riddley and I are too busy selling plants to grow them.

Martha gave me a wink. "Would we do a thing like that? We're just getting supper." Of all the things I like about Martha, one I like best is her voice. It always has a gurgle of laughter running under it.

Ridd looked from one of us to the other and I was afraid for a minute he was going to stay, but Cricket's yell of delight as he hurled himself into the pool sent him running.

Martha stifled a yawn. "Sorry. I worked until midnight last night and seven-to-three today. I'm beat." Martha's an emergency room supervisor at the Hope County Medical Center. During summer, when folks take vacations, her hours are erratic to say the least.

"Have some tea and just sit, then. I've got things under control."

She sank into a chair and drank tea while I arranged meat and cheese on a platter and looked at her contentedly. Martha is as short as I am and even rounder, with straight brown hair and those lovely topaz eyes she gave Cricket. She is comfortable rather than beautiful—wears little makeup and keeps her nails short and unpolished— and I love her like she was my own. She's treated me like a second mother ever since she and Ridd started dating. It's nice to have *one* daughter-in-law who has made herself part of the family.

Walker certainly greeted her like a sister when he arrived, picking up her glass and helping himself. "Don't mind my typhoid," she told him.

"I won't," he agreed, offering the glass to Luke.

"You get your own glass," I told Luke, handing it to him, "and you," I told Walker, "get to *fix* your own. You know we don't wait on people but once in this kitchen."

They looked good together, Walker with my blonde hair and brown eyes and Luke with tousled brown curls and navy blue eyes. Walker had more muscles and Luke was shorter—maybe five-eleven—but they were shaped a lot alike. "Did you play high school football?" I asked Luke.

"Yes ma'am. Quarterback, just like Walker."

"Where'd you grow up?" Martha likes to know all about people.

He hesitated a second, like he wasn't sure. "New York and Florida, mostly."

"Also like me, he was too little to play football in college," Walker added.

Luke gave a mock shudder. "I was too scared. Some of those guys were *big!*" They were laughing as they headed for the pool.

"As glad as I am to hear Walker laugh," I told Martha when they were out of earshot, "I hate to hear him enjoying the single life quite so much."

"Give him space, Mac. He's going to be all right." Without being asked, Martha reached for the bread and started arranging it on a plate. Finally she brought up what we'd both been dying to talk about. "You hear about the murder over at the old Hedrick place?"

I started slicing three bright red tomatoes, sorry for people who had to buy them. "Heard the gossip at Myrtle's, is all. You know any real facts?"

"Yeah, a few. Several of the guys stopped by, and that was all they could talk about. They acted like they'd completely forgotten all those thefts we've been having."

Deputies who bring accident victims by the emergency room have to hang around filling out paperwork. In Hopemore some get to feeling so at home that they pop in for coffee breaks all the time, and let their tongues wag. Martha fills me in, but only when Ridd's not around. He gets upset when we "cozy up to crime," as he calls it.

I set mustard, mayonnaise, and ketchup on a tray. "What'd they say?"

"It was real sad. One of our nurses, Amanda Kent, was beaten to death sometime last night and lay there until they found her this morning. She came from Dublin and had just finished nursing school in Augusta last spring."

"So young!" I wanted to shake her guardian angel until its teeth rattled. Angrily, I sliced cucumber rounds for my vegetable plate. "Did you know her?"

"No, but people who did said she was real sweet." Martha's amber eyes clouded with sadness. "They say she'd been beaten so hard that any one of several blows could have killed her. Whoever did it was either real mad at her or crazy."

"Oh, my!" I felt sick to think somebody like that was still walking the streets.

"Apparently nobody else they've talked to at Hedricks' heard anything, but they say that wasn't odd, because she lived in a garage apartment."

I went to the fridge for a few carrots. As I peeled and cut them into sticks, I remembered, "Back when I was a girl, the Hedrick boys collected antique cars, so they built a four-car garage with *two* apartments over them. Was somebody living in the other one?"

"Yeah, but he left this morning, so they haven't talked to him."

"Sounds suspicious to me."

"Nobody said one way or the other. They were going to canvass the neighborhood to see if anybody else heard anything. Maybe they've found somebody who did by now."

That was all she knew, so we talked about other things, including the thefts, which the police couldn't seem to get a handle on. Antiques were being taken from the town's wealthiest families, generally during parties when a lot of people were away from home. "So far they don't have a single lead," Martha told me, "and I guess they'll stop working on that until they get this murder solved." We don't have a real big police force. A murder like this would stretch it to its limits.

As odd as it would seem later, nobody mentioned the Kent murder again all evening. Obviously during dinner we couldn't talk about murder, not with Cricket sitting there. After dinner we settled down to a game of dominoes, and in our family dominoes are serious business. Even Cricket plays, sitting on Joe Riddley's lap and putting their tiles in place.

Between plays I kept asking Luke questions about his family, but except for saying that his mother died when he was a junior in high school, he slid out from under my questions like butter on a biscuit. I was so busy wondering why that I let him beat me.

"Nobody beats Me-mama at dominoes," Cricket said admiringly.

"I'm a real killer," Luke told him.

We would all remember that.

But now trouble comes to you, and you are discouraged; it strikes you, and you are dismayed. Job 4:5

Four

It was four days later—Wednesday—and the courthouse clock was chiming two when Assistant Police Chief Isaac James strode into our office. I was working on payroll and Joe Riddley was preparing a fertilizer order for the county's largest cotton farmer.

"Howdy, Officer James," I greeted him. We've known Ike since he was so little he had to be held up to put pennies in our gumball machine, but in our office we call the police "officer" and they call Joe Riddley "judge" or "your honor."

"Howdy, Miss MacLaren, Judge Yarbrough."

I've mentioned before that Joe Riddley was a magistrate. Let me pause a minute to explain what a magistrate is and does. When a former chief magistrate asked Joe Riddley to serve nearly thirty years ago, I protested, "You can't be a judge. You aren't a lawyer and we have a business to run. You can't be sitting in court all day."

That's when I discovered that in Georgia, magistrates don't have to be lawyers and they don't sit in court all day. The chief magistrate of a county—in Hope County, Judge Sidney Stebley—gets elected, then appoints other magistrates. After a Superior Court judge approves them and swears them in, they go over to Athens for forty hours' training. Each year after that they go back to Athens, or down to Savannah, for an update on new laws.

Georgia magistrates have two primary jobs: to know the law well enough to decide whether there's enough evidence to sign warrants for search or arrest, and to hear preliminary cases to set or deny bond. Joe Riddley saw magistrates as engines at the front of the legal train and trial judges as cabooses at the other end. (Magistrates can also marry people, but Joe Riddley always claimed that would embarrass him to death. I think he was afraid somebody he married would get a divorce. He'd take that hard.)

Anyway, because he only dealt with criminal cases and let the chief magistrate hear civil cases over at the courthouse, for thirty years Joe Riddley had done most of his "judging business," as we all called it, right in our office—except when he had to go down to the jail for a preliminary hearing. I'd gotten used to law enforcement officers coming in and out of the office, and after years of attending magistrate classes with him, hearing him issue warrants, and listening to him talk about what went on down at the jail, I knew almost as much about being a magistrate as he did. The officers certainly didn't pay a speck of attention to my being there when they were presenting evidence.

❧

That morning Ike stood twisting his warrant around in his hands like he was nervous, so I joked, "We haven't seen you since you came by to pick up that fellow who was trying to sell me the ecumenical counseling center ferns. What was he wanting, drug money?"

"Sure was, Miss MacLaren. He'd stolen those plants off the center's front porch that very afternoon. Lucky you recognized them."

"I'd sold them two days before."

Ike shifted from one foot to another, making our filing cabinets rattle. He's a huge man—played fullback for Georgia—and so dark that at night he and his shadow blend. That afternoon, shadows crept from all four corners of our office as I heard him say, "I hate like the dickens to have to ask this, Judge, but I need a search warrant for Preacher Blessed's apartment."

Joe Riddley looked up curiously from the invoice he'd been checking and shoved his reading glasses up on his forehead. "What you searching for, Officer James?"

"Connection with last Friday night's murder. Here." Ike thrust out the warrant so Joe Riddley could read it. "And here's a tape of our conversation this morning. I know it's irregular, but I'd like you to hear it." Joe Riddley nodded, and Ike pushed a button.

Luke's voice was as clear as if he were right in there with us. "*I feel kind of foolish, and this may be absolutely nothing, but some men in my church thought I ought to come. When you all came by Saturday afternoon and said a woman had been killed next door, I was shocked, but I didn't think I could help. I hadn't seen or heard anything over there the night before. My apartment's on the other side of the house, so I can't see that property from my windows. And if you told me the woman was beaten to death, it didn't register. I'd been polishing my sermon, and I tend to be a little spacy until that's finished. Anyway, I didn't learn she was beaten until last night, when I met with our men's Bible study.*"

"*Nobody in your presence ever mentioned she was beaten to death?*" Isaac's voice on the tape was frankly disbelieving. No wonder. That had been the main topic of conversation at church, in the grocery store, and on the sidewalks for three solid days.

"We didn't mention it—" I started, thinking of Saturday night. Joe Riddley motioned for me to hush. He was right. I knew better than to talk to either one of them when they were conducting official business.

"*No sir. Before church I was busy with the music team, afterwards the high schoolers had a guest speaker that took the whole hour, and as soon as church was over, I joined my dad over at Hilton Head. I didn't hear anybody mention how the girl was killed.*"

"*Must be nice to just work on Sundays, then go to Hilton Head,*" Ike rumbled.

Luke laughed. "*It would be if I did it all the time. Monday's my day off, and since I'll be on a youth retreat over Labor Day, I asked for yesterday off to help my dad celebrate his sixtieth birthday. I didn't get back until nearly suppertime last night, so until the Bible study all I knew was that a woman had been killed—not how.*"

"*I see.*" Ike sounded like he was trying hard to believe him.

Luke's voice grew more confident as he told about what he did know. "*In our young men's Bible study last night we studied Daniel chapter two, where Daniel interprets a dream. We got to talking about how we don't do dream interpretation much these days, but maybe we should, and as a joke I said I'd had a doozy Friday night that somebody was welcome to interpret for me.*" He laughed self-consciously. "*When I told them about it, one of the men said, 'You know, Luke, that woman next door to you was beaten to death that night. Maybe God was showing you something that could help the police.'*"

Even on the tape Luke sounded embarrassed. "*I frankly doubt it. I'd already read over the Daniel passage twice last week, so I figure that was what made me dream.*"

But everybody else in our group thought I ought to at least describe the dream to you, in case it could be of any help. So even though it's probably silly, here goes."

When Luke finished, Ike turned off the tape.

"That's all you've got? Him walking in this morning to tell you about a dream? Sounds crazy, not criminal." Joe Riddley is generally nice about stopping whatever else he's doing to swear out a warrant. I hoped Ike put his crabbiness down to the August heat.

"Yessir, but he didn't mention it Saturday when we talked to the neighbors. He said he was asleep all night and didn't hear a thing. Then he walks into the office cool as you please today saying that since we asked people to tell us anything at all, no matter how silly," Ike rolled the last word around on his tongue, "maybe he does have something that can help. And that bit about the men thinking maybe God was giving him inside information we could use?" Ike heaved a sigh of pure disgust. "You know as well as I do, Judge Yarbrough, that we all wish God would make it that easy. There's something else. Did you hear how he described her? 'Hands raised in supplication?' What kind of description is that?"

"A preacher's kind," I told him.

"Well it's odd this time, because she really was found with her hands over her head in a funny position. Nobody knows that except the police and whoever killed her."

That gave me shivers up my spine. I could see it made even Joe Riddley nervous.

Ike continued, "Preacher or not, Chief Muggins is certain he went next door and beat that poor Kent woman to death."

That's when he told us Charlie Muggins had called a psychiatrist up in Augusta who specializes in studying criminal behavior, who had said that when people claim to dream about a crime, it's usually something they've done and can't bring themselves to confess.

Finally, Ike laid the warrant on Joe Riddley's desk. "We aren't asking to arrest Preacher Blessed, Judge. We just want to look for suspicious clothing, things like that."

Joe Riddley pulled down his reading glasses, cleared his throat, and read the warrant. "You seem to have your papers in order. Raise your right hand. Do you swear . . ."

While they went on with the familiar ritual I'd witnessed hundreds of times, I stood looking out the window, wishing I could kick Charlie Muggins where it would do the most good. When Ike left, Joe Riddley slumped in his chair. "This is one of the few times, Little Bit, when I wish I weren't a magistrate."

❦

I went over to massage his shoulder with one hand. "I need a bowl of banana pudding. Want to go to Myrtle's for pie?"

"I think I'll stick around here." That's when I knew how upset he was.

Over at Myrtle's I ordered pudding and iced tea. Getting upset always makes me crave sweets, and since Myrtle's husband had heart problems, not diabetes, she hadn't cut down on sugar yet. The meringue on my pudding must have had a fourth of a cup.

I was nearly done when I heard somebody say, "Hi, Miss MacLaren. You lost your last *friend*?" Maniac towered over me. His ponytail was lying over his left shoulder, right next to his earring—a small gold bead—and in one hand he held a copy of our weekly paper, the *Hopemore Statesman*.

I motioned him to the other side of Myrtle's coral plastic booth. "Hey, Maynard. Sit down, have a snack, and cheer me up. This pudding is real good."

He slid in, complaining as usual. "We've been so busy I haven't even had *dinner* yet. What's the *special*?"

Myrtle appeared in time to hear him. "Meatloaf with scalloped potatoes, steamed carrots, applesauce, a biscuit, banana pudding, and tea."

"That will be fine, but bring me *unsweet* tea." After she'd gone, he leaned across the table to say glumly, "If you don't *tell* them, they'll bring sweet tea every *time* down here."

"At least you get a choice," I reminded him. "Up north, even if you do tell them, they won't bring *sweet* tea."

"I guess that's *true*." Maniac being agreeable made me grumpier than ever. I hate having to be nice to somebody because I can't tell them what's bothering me.

Myrtle set his plate down in just a minute and after he'd muttered, "Cooked to death, as usual," we ate in silence. I kept taking quick peeks at him when he wasn't looking, because that was the closest I'd been to Maniac since he got home, and he puzzled me. He'd left Hopemore after high school a skinny plain boy who talked and acted like a spoiled mama's boy. Up north, he'd developed into a right handsome young man. Thank heavens, he looked more like his mama than his daddy, with her fine gray eyes and lovely yellow hair. I didn't much care for the ponytail, but at least he kept it clean. In a ray of sunlight through the plate-glass window, it gleamed like fresh straw. If he'd kept his mouth shut, you'd never know he complained constantly and had that affected habit of emphasizing certain words, like he was Big Tom laying down the law to Young Pat and Queen Anne on a coonhunt.

However, Maniac seldom kept his mouth shut for long. As soon as he'd wolfed down his dinner he wiped his lips with one of Myrtle's flimsy paper napkins (she'd cut back on the quality of her napkins since she stopped offering fried chicken) and said in a tone that sounded like it was all my fault, "If I'd known I was going to run into you, I'd have picked up *your* paper when I got *ours*." He looked at the lead article, then held it out to me. "It's got a picture of that woman who was *killed*."

I took the paper, curious. The picture showed a rather plain young woman with a long face and dark hair hanging straight beside it to rest on her shoulders. Her smile was sweet, rather than flirty, and she wore very little makeup. Remembering my Saturday thought, I felt a twinge of guilt. Amanda Kent was definitely no painted floozy. "Did Hubert say you knew her?"

"A little bit. Daddy fixed her *television* the day she *died* and I carried it back that afternoon."

I pretended to be checking the obituaries, but actually I was watching him closely. "Did your daddy say she was rude to you?"

He leaned half-way across his plate and raised his voice. "She was *worse* than rude. I'd hardly set the TV down on its *table* when she said, 'Here's your *money.* Good*bye.*' Then she practically pushed me out the *door.* I'd *hoped* we might have a *chat.* She's been going down to that place on *Freedom* Street—you know, Miss Marybelle *Taylor's house* that they've turned into a *temple* of some sort? She'd told Daddy we'd have to bring back her television by five-*thirty,* so she could get down there by *six,* so I wanted to ask her some *questions.* Heaven *knows* we don't have much *diversity* in *Hopemore.* I wanted to know what goes *on* down there."

"Planning to convert?" I couldn't resist pulling his leg. Maniac wouldn't know a joke if it rose up and bit him.

"Of course not! I've been Episco-*pa*-lian all my *life.* But I thought seeing as how's it's in *town* and all, I'd like to *know* what they *do.*"

"But she wouldn't tell you?"

"She pushed me out her *door!* Rudest woman I've seen in a *long time.*" His eyes blazed with indignation.

Would Maniac consider rudeness reason enough to beat a woman to death? Maybe he could tell what I was thinking, because he turned pink. "Well, I guess I'd better *go.*" He got up and hurried out the door, leaving his paper behind. I decided to scan the obituaries before I went back to see if I'd missed anybody. I could drop the paper by their store on my way.

"D'you eat another dinner as well as pudding?"

I looked up to see Joe Riddley towering over me. "Maniac kept me company. Sit down."

"At least you do your philandering in public." He tossed his cap onto the opposite bench, slid into the booth and shoved Maniac's dishes to the end of the table. "Just milk and chocolate pie, Myrtle," he called when she poked her head from the kitchen.

I handed the paper across the table, pointing to the picture. "Here's that girl who got killed."

I shouldn't have done that. Once Joe Riddley gets a paper I never get it back until he's done. He read the whole time Myrtle was clearing and wiping the table and bringing him his pie. Finally he handed it back to me. "I see Charlie Muggins is entering the November race for sheriff."

Our police chief is appointed by the city council, but the sheriff has to be elected. The current sheriff, Bailey "Buster" Gibbons, was a good friend of ours and an excellent lawman. "Buster's never been opposed in twelve years, Joe Riddley. How could Charlie even think he could beat him?"

"I don't know, Little Bit. Maybe he can. Buster's not as smooth and smarmy as Charlie, and Charlie's made friends in high places since he's been here."

If you have concluded that neither of us could stand Charlie Muggins, you're right. Neither of us had liked him since he was brought in from Dalton six years before as the town's last great white hope. We had some fine officers they could have promoted from within the ranks, but the two obviously best candidates were black. After Charlie came, one moved to Maryland and Isaac James was made assistant chief. At the time, Joe Riddley grieved, "I tell you, Little Bit, I don't know how long Hope County can survive if we keep bypassing our own best people and bringing in inferior ones just because they're white."

Charlie hadn't risen much in our estimation in the years he'd been there, and our fondness for him had hit a new low the past June when his wife—one of our church members—went up to Atlanta and filed for divorce. Martha said that before she left, Luke Blessed brought her into the emergency room with bruises and a broken arm that would have looked a lot like wife abuse if she hadn't sworn she fell off a porch. Luke had also driven her to Atlanta, as I remembered, and refused to say where she was staying.

Joe Riddley ate his pie and drank his milk with a glum look. "You know, Little Bit, Ike James is a good officer. I wonder if Charlie is leaning on him. A quick arrest on that young woman's murder would look good for his campaign."

Later that night Joe Riddley had to go to the city council meeting to report on a weekend feeding program several churches had started for families of children who got free school lunches the rest of the week. He came home mad enough to chew nails.

"Charlie Muggins was supposed to talk about his budget, but all he could talk about was that murder. I tell you, Little Bit, I've never seen Charlie like this about a case. He was so jumpy he could hardly sit still. Left the room three times to call and see if there was any new information, and he claims he's got the entire police force concentrating on the case."

"Pre-election campaigning," I muttered. We were up in the bedroom, where I'd been folding and putting away laundry.

Joe Riddley shrugged. "Could be. But I've never known him to get so worked up about *anything*. Couldn't stop talking about that girl—what a sweet person she was, how pretty she was—he sounded like a twelve-year-old with his first girlfriend. I finally asked him how he'd gotten to know her so well, and he said he'd never met her, but he feels he's gotten to know her real well from her picture. Do you know, he's had that picture from the paper laminated and carries it in his pocket? Kept bringing it out and looking at it with tears in his eyes. Once he waved it around and said, 'She ought to have been safe in our town.'"

"He makes me sick." I headed for the linen closet to put away sheets and towels.

I came back to the bedroom to find Joe Riddley packing for his fishing trip the next day. He pulled me toward him and nuzzled his chin in my hair. "He can make you sick and he can make you mad, honey, but don't let him make you foolish, you hear me? Stay away from that investigation while I'm gone. It's got nothing to do with you." He kissed me.

As soon as he let me go, I went and got the blue shirt he'd laid out to go with his brown fishing pants and replaced it with a tan one instead.

He put back the tan shirt and got back out the blue one. "I don't expect the photographers from *Gentlemen's Quarterly* to make it that far up the mountain, Little Bit, but if they do I'll be sure to tell them my wife thought my outfit didn't match. And don't you try to change the subject. I was talking about that case. You stay out of it, you hear me?"

"I hear you."

The way things turned out, though, it was fortunate we hadn't used the wedding service with the word "obey."

Distress and anguish fill him with
terror; they overwhelm him, like a
king poised to attack. *Job 15:24*

Five

Joe Riddley, Ridd, and Cricket left before daylight
the next morning. I got down to the store about eight and
worked hard all day. Just as the courthouse clock was
chiming four and I was considering what to do for supper,
I was honored by a visit from Walker.

"Those fool cops ought to be shot!" Walker slammed
his fist on his daddy's desk so hard that a stack of invoices
slid to the floor. Walker's always been a pounder, but at
least he pounds furniture, not people.

He flushed and bent to pick them up. "Sorry, Mama.
I know I'm out of control, but this thing's scary. First they
search Luke's apartment, then they haul him back down
to the station twice in two days asking him to clarify his
dream—whether he might have heard or seen something
he hadn't remembered before. I keep telling him he needs

a good lawyer, but he thinks he doesn't need a lawyer so long as he's telling the truth."

"Tell him I said to remember that Bible verse about being harmless as doves and wise as serpents—and take seriously the second half."

Walker pounded the top of my filing cabinet. "Luke doesn't know cops like we do. They're circling him like buzzards! This morning down at the station they asked three times when he last saw the victim. He never *ever* saw the victim!" He crossed the office and pounded the doorjamb. "Why don't they talk to somebody else?"

"They are," I assured him. "Martha said this morning that deputies were down at the medical center interviewing anybody who'd worked with Amanda Kent."

Walker shook his head like he hadn't heard a word I'd said—which, being Walker, was probable. "I tell you, Mama, this town isn't what it used to be. All sorts of weirdos are moving in. You wouldn't believe some of the people I meet selling insurance. Look at Maniac, for instance. He used to be a perfectly nice kid."

"You made fun of him when he was little," I reminded him.

"Well, he *acted* a little peculiar, but at least he *looked* normal. Why'd he have to come home with a ponytail halfway down his back and an earring?"

"Maybe he likes the way they look." I was tickled to be having that argument with Walker. We'd had similar ones several years back, and each been on the other side.

"Maniac's not the worst," he admitted grudgingly. "There's some fellow running a Temple of Inner Peace in the old Taylor house down from my office. Beard halfway to his knees and all sorts of necklaces around his neck."

"Is that any more peculiar than old Amos Pickens used to be, always complaining his roof leaked because of spaceships landing on it? And what about Hector Blaine, who thinks the Confederate treasury is buried on his property and keeps wanting banks to loan him money using that as collateral? We've always had peculiar people around here. They make life interesting."

"So why don't they question them? Luke never killed that girl. I *know* it." Walker flung himself into the red chair by the window—the same chair where he used to read when he finished his homework in elementary school. I could remember when his legs dangled above the floor. Now they stretched half-way across the office.

"They haven't arrested Luke," I consoled him. "They're just asking questions. But she did live right next door. Don't you think it's odd Luke never even saw her?"

"Not particularly. Miss Bessie's driveway is on the other side of the house and so are all Luke's windows. He has no call to go into that side of the yard. Daddy needs to do something. What's the point of being a magistrate if you can't protect people from police harassment?" He folded one forefinger and stuck the knuckle in his mouth. Even as a baby Walker never could do something as normal as suck his thumb. Always bit that knuckle.

"The police aren't harassing Luke, son, and even if they were, magistrates don't protect people from police harassment." Walker knew that as well as I did. He was just desperate.

He slumped lower in the chair, reached down, worked his finger into a little hole in the side of the cushion, and started pulling out bits of cotton stuffing. As often as I stitch that cushion up, Walker always makes another hole so he can pull out tiny bits of cotton and roll them between his fingers.

It's funny about being a mother. No matter how big your children get, when you see them troubled you see ghosts of other times they've been hurt. I looked at my thirty-five-year-old and saw a fourteen-year-old who couldn't get some girl to like him, a seven-year-old who'd lost a fight at school, and a three-year-old whose big brother went biking without him. I wished I could haul him onto my lap and nuzzle the top of his head until he felt better.

"I can't think of a single thing your daddy could do at this point," I told him regretfully. "Besides, he won't be back until Monday."

"He could talk sense to Ike James, that b—"

"Walker!"

"Don't Walker me, Mama. You've been standing up for Ike since we were in high school. You even cheered when he made that touchdown our senior homecoming game. That was supposed to be my touchdown, and you knew it." He glared across the office at me.

I was astonished. "That was seventeen years ago, and Ike had the ball," I pointed out. "And how often do you get to see somebody carry a ball eighty-four yards for a touchdown? He ran like the wind. Nobody came close to catching him."

Walker still glared. "I was supposed to carry in that play. You shouldn't prefer a black boy over your own son, Mama. And now he's about to arrest Luke and you're act-ing like he's one fine cop."

I gave him a stern Mother Look. "Ike *is* one fine cop, Walker, and I will not have racial slurs in this office. If you're going to carry on like that, you go home and cool off."

He flushed. "Sorry," he muttered. "I like Ike. You know that. But he needs to see that Luke didn't do it, Mama. He didn't do it!" He pounded the arm of the chair.

"Your daddy thinks Ike's under a lot of pressure from Chief Muggins to find a suspect. So far he doesn't have anybody but Luke."

"Then find him one. You've done it before. Do it again. Please? I'll take back every single thing I ever said about you—" He trailed off, as well he should.

"*Meddling* is the word I believe you've used, followed by 'Why can't you keep your nose out of other people's business?'"

If I sounded a little bitter, it's because the way my family sometimes talks about me hurts my feelings. I'm not a real detective and I know it, but a few times in the past I'd thought the police had the wrong end of a stick and been able to help them out a little. Just the month before, I'd been over visiting my brother in Montgomery and helped track down a missing child.[*] But do you think my sons were proud of me? You should have heard them carry on when they found out about the Montgomery episode—especially the gun.

Walker held up both hands like he was surrendering. "I'll take it all back, Mama. I swear. Just find out who did this thing. . . ."

"I wish I could, son, but I wouldn't have any idea where to start." I added what little comfort I could. "You know as well as I do that neither magistrate is going to sign an arrest warrant if they don't get enough evidence. Hold onto that and pray they'll find the real killer soon. Remember what your daddy always says—God is a God of justice." Maybe if Walker started praying, he'd at least get his own life back on track.

When he left, I did some praying of my own. I didn't learn who the murderer was, but I did think of a couple of people I might talk to. Just to ask questions.

❧

The obvious first person to see was Martha again. With their daughter Bethany at mission camp and Ridd and Cricket gone, she was working all the hours she could, so about five-thirty I moseyed down to the medical center.

Some people might think small towns have poor medical care, but Hopemore takes pride in our medical center. We've got up-to-date equipment, lovely facilities,

---

[*]*When Did We Lose Harriet?* (Zondervan, 1997).

and a board of directors whom we know personally and hold accountable. We get a lot of fine, bright young doctors wanting to raise their families in a pretty small town and practice medicine like it used to be before insurance companies and HMO's started calling all the shots. It's not unusual for the newspaper to report that our newest physician was at the top of a medical class or voted most distinguished medical student of the year.

We're especially proud of our emergency room, and I glow when I think that our Martha is one of its supervisors. I found her doing paperwork behind the desk.

When she looked up and saw me, she smiled. "Lonesome already?"

"Oh, I miss the old coot, but right now I'm hungry. Clarinda doesn't feed me worth a lick when Joe Riddley's gone. Just cream of chicken soup and biscuits for dinner." I peered around. Except for one examining room, the emergency room was empty. "Seems quiet right now. You free to go eat?"

Martha stood and stretched. "I'd love to." Martha is always in the mood for food. She was half a step ahead of me all the way to the cafeteria.

Martha chose chicken pot pie and a slice of carrot cake with cream cheese icing. "Carrot cake's good for you, Mac," she tried to tempt me. "Has lots of vitamins."

"Humph," I told her. "That's the kind of thinking that keeps us both fat." I took a hamburger and congealed salad, feeling virtuous. Besides, I had ice cream at home.

At the table I let us both get started good before saying casually, "Walker came by and said Luke Blessed is getting all sorts of attention. Have you heard anything about it?"

Martha spoke around a mouthful of cream cheese icing. When her kids aren't around, she's a great believer in the saying *Life is Short—Eat Dessert First.* "Have we ever. They're swaggering around saying they've found the murderer and it's a *preacher*. Some of them love that.

They're all ready to put poor Luke in jail, to hear them tell it."

"The sheriff's detention center," I corrected her. That's the high-faluting name the county gave the new one. "Did they say anything about what evidence they've got?"

"Yes, but you don't need to fool around with this while Pop and Ridd are gone. Ridd will kill us both if you get involved in this, after last month in Montgomery."

I heaved a short, impatient sigh. "If I hadn't been awake for his delivery, I'd swear Ridd's a changeling. He has absolutely no sense of adventure."

"Is *that* what you call it?"

"No, I call it battling evil when it comes after those I care about. Would Ridd like that any better?"

"Not much. But I'm with you, Mac. Working in the emergency room, and seeing what people can do to other people—" She shook her head. "I picture evil as a malignancy that takes hold of anybody who will host it, then grows to consume them. And I know somebody's got to fight it. I just don't think it ought to be you. Especially when Pop's out of town."

"All I want right now is information for Walker. He's pretty worried. Just tell me what evidence they've got—please?"

"Well, Luke went in yesterday telling them some story about having a dream that they swear matches in every detail the way her room looked."

That didn't sound good. How could I compare the tape I'd heard of the dream with the actual apartment? I'd have to think about that later. For now, Martha was still talking.

". . . a flier from our church on the floor near the body, covered in blood. Of course, everything in the place was. Whoever it was kept beating her even after she was dead."

Nurses must have stomachs of cast iron. After Martha said that, she immediately took another huge bite of cake. I looked at my ketchup, shuddered, and pushed the hamburger away. However, I had to protest one thing. "You can't turn around anymore without seeing a flier from our church. Joe Riddley says we're all going to have to up our pledges to pay for paper. Anybody could have left that—or the girl herself could have picked it up."

"They also took hair samples from him, because they found hairs clasped in her hand. Thank God for DNA testing, Mac. If it's not his hair, he'll be home free. It just takes a while to get results."

"By which time the damage done to his reputation, our congregation, and the general kingdom of God could be immense," I pointed out. "You know how papers love a scandal when a preacher is involved."

Martha nodded, swabbing up the last crumb of carrot cake. "Preachers and politicians."

"Do they have anybody else they're looking at?"

She pulled the chicken pot pie toward her. "Maybe. Somebody said she played cards pretty often with the guy in the other garage apartment, and they could have been more than friends. But he's been out of town all week. They'll talk to him when he gets back."

"*If* he gets back. Sounds like a good suspect to me."

"Maybe so." She took several bites then added reluctantly. "They also found the weapon—an old crowbar. It was in the cemetery behind her house, but it didn't have any fingerprints on it."

Her voice sounded as anxious as I suddenly felt. The Hedrick house backed up to Hopemore's pre-revolutionary cemetery. Most towns in this area have one, and it's generally the buffer between white and black communities. If the crowbar was found there, it could imply the crime was committed by a black man. Just a whiff of that to an outside newspaper, coupled with her being found in her nightgown, could have loud and nasty repercussions. We've come a long way in middle Georgia. I dreaded the thought of a setback.

"A crowbar?" I mused out loud. "In Luke's dream it was a walking cane."

Martha was surprised enough to pause mid-bite. "How do you know?"

I was annoyed with myself. I'd come to get information, not give it. "Isaac James came by yesterday and played the tape for Joe Riddley. I happened to be there."

She winked. "Happened to stay and listen, too. But maybe it just looked like a walking cane. Some crowbars are skinny and curved at one end."

"Maybe that's good for Luke. What would he need a crowbar for?"

Martha shrugged. "To beat somebody to death? Look, Mac, I like Luke, and Bethany thinks he hung the moon, but the police think they've got a pretty good case. Until DNA pulls it apart, that's the primary direction they're heading in."

"It all sounds pretty circumstantial to me—a dream, forensics tests still to be made, a crowbar with no prints. I can't see Joe Riddley signing a warrant for arrest unless they get more than that."

"Judge Stebley might, if he weren't in Alaska for three weeks. You know who found the body, don't you?"

I shook my head. It hadn't occurred to me to wonder.

"Ronald Duckworth. Lorine was Amanda Kent's best friend."

"Lorine? Wasn't the Kent woman closer to Rhonda's age?"

"Sure, but that's what I heard."

That was bad. Lorine Duckworth was Judge Stebley's first cousin—their mothers being sisters. She was also one of those women God made in the image of the mosquito. She buzzed and buzzed around something she wanted, then went for the jugular. What Lorine Duckworth wanted, she was used to getting.

For instance, when she was sixteen, she wanted Ronald Duckworth, who'd been hired to paint her

grandmother's house. In those days Ronald was handsome as he could be, a vision of tan muscles and bright
yellow curls up on his ladder. Anybody could have told her
that the muscles would eventually go slack, the tan fade,
and the hair fall out. Some people could have even told
her that a smile of flashing teeth was what God gave the
man instead of brains. A few tried, but Lorine wasn't listening. She was dead set on having Ronald.

Her daddy blustered and her mama cried, but they
were both on hand down at our church one Saturday afternoon to see their daughter married. And although Ronald
was nearly thirty when they got married and she barely
seventeen, Lorine had been running his life—and that of
their only daughter Rhonda—ever since. She'd have run
the church, too, if some of the rest of us had let her.

Rhonda Duckworth looked a lot like her daddy, flat-
out gorgeous. In the past twenty-five years she'd been
Miss everything Hope County had to offer as well as
homecoming queen at the university and a runner up for
Miss Georgia. If she seemed a bit shallow, men didn't
seem to mind. I'd seen her around town that summer with
a young lawyer, an insurance buddy of Walker's, and even,
once or twice, Dr. Holder. Joe Riddley claimed she had no
more sense than her daddy or she'd have left home long
before.

I tackled my hamburger again. Getting cold, it
wasn't very good, but I was going to need sustenance to
follow all this up. "Do you know how Ronald came to find
the body?"

Of course Martha knew.

"Lorine and Amanda were supposed to go up to
Augusta shopping that Saturday morning, but Amanda
didn't come to pick her up, so Lorine sent poor Ronald
down to see what was the matter."

Poor Ronald, poor Rhonda, poor Judge Stebley—anybody in Lorine's vicinity was eventually called poor somebody or other.

"How did Ronald get into the woman's apartment?" I wondered aloud.

"When she didn't come to the door, he looked in her windows and saw something that made him call the police. They broke down the door and found the body. That's when Charlie Muggins raced three blocks with his siren blaring and called in every law enforcement officer in three counties. The deputies say Lorine has practically lived down at the station since, demanding that they do something."

Now I saw why Ike was hounding Luke so. If both Charlie Muggins and Lorine had decided Luke had killed Amanda Kent, poor Sidney might be willing to stretch things and issue a warrant. His life wouldn't be worth living otherwise.

And if Charlie Muggins—who already hated Luke for helping his wife—was campaigning for election and Lorine was out for revenge . . . that's the first time I realized how much danger Luke could be in.

Will they not instruct you and tell
you? Will they not bring forth words
from their understanding? *Job 8:10*

Six

I looked around the cafeteria. "I wonder if any of these people knew Amanda Kent?"

Martha looked around too, and jerked her head toward a table of four nurses near the window. "The nurse with red hair knew her pretty well."

The hair was not only red but curly, even though its owner tried to contain it into a ponytail at the nape of her neck. Her back was to us, so I couldn't see her face.

Martha checked her watch and gathered up her dishes. "I've got to be getting back. You want to come sleep in Bethany's bed tonight?"

"Heavens no. I'll be fine. But I sure would like something to take my mind off Joe Riddley being gone— like talking to that nurse with red hair. Could you introduce us?"

For a minute Martha looked like she was going to refuse. I murmured, "What Ridd doesn't know won't hurt him." Reluctantly, she went to invite the nurse to our table.

I looked her over as she came toward me. Tall and angular in a yellow shirt, white slacks, and sensible nurses' shoes, she had bluegreen eyes, more than a smattering of freckles, and a mouthful of teeth. When she wasn't smiling she had a slight pooch to her lips that made them look fuller than they might otherwise.

I am used to thinking of short people as bouncy and tall people as graceful. This woman was tall but a constant motion of waving arms, bouncing curls, and fluttering lashes.

Martha started introducing us—"Selena Jones, this is my mother-in-law, MacLaren Yarbrough"—then came to a dead stop. I guess she couldn't think of a polite way to add, *An old busybody who likes to poke her nose into other people's business.*

"Oh!" Selena squealed excitedly, rapidly blinking her lashes. "Do you have that plant place down on Oglethorpe Street?"

That's not exactly how I would have described Yarbrough Feed, Seed and Nursery—which has not only the big downtown store, but acres of nursery, feed storage and greenhouses beyond the city limits—but I nodded.

"Oh!" she squealed again. "I've been wanting to talk to you."

With a beginning like that, how could I lose?

Martha left with a quick wave. The girl dropped into Martha's chair, propped her bony elbows on the table, and puckered her forehead in worry. "I've got this draecena— you know?"

I nodded, also knowing exactly what she was going to say next. "It's got these funny little cottony bits all over it, and I don't know what to do. Somebody said I ought to talk to you, that you could save it if anybody could. I can't believe you are right *here!*"

Mealybug. She was right to be worried. She'd do best to throw it in the garbage and pray her other plants hadn't already caught it—but I wasn't about to say that right away. "Well," I said judiciously, "there are several things you can try."

By the time we'd exhausted the subject of mealybug, we were bosom friends. I leaned forward a bit confidentially and lowered my voice. "Did Martha say you knew that poor girl who was murdered?"

She blinked several times like a scared horse. "Yes, ma'am. We knew each other a little in nursing school, and once we got to Hopemore, we did things together sometimes. We didn't work together, of course—she was up in ICU and I'm in pediatrics—but . . ." Her eyes filled with tears. "I can't believe what happened."

I squirmed inside. Martha was right—I *was* an old busybody, stirring up this young woman's grief for my own ends. Then I remembered Luke and Walker. I shoved a napkin her way and asked gently, "Do you have any idea why anybody would do such a thing?"

She dabbed her eyes and shook her head. "Mandy was the gentlest, sweetest person you ever met. The only time I ever saw her mad was if somebody was hurting a patient unnecessarily—like if a doctor got a bit rough with somebody. It was Mandy who blew the whistle on an orderly who was hurting our coma patients. Oh—" She clapped her hand over her mouth. "We aren't supposed to talk about that, but since you know Martha—Anyway, Mandy was usually the most peaceful person I knew."

"Had she ever mentioned being scared of somebody, or worried?"

"Not lately. She'd seemed real happy. She told me just last week that all she wanted out of life was to be a good nurse, marry her fiancé, and be happy. I can't believe she got killed right after that." Her eyes reddened with her effort not to cry, and her nose grew pink.

One word had caught my attention. "She had a fiancé?"

"That's what she called him. I knew she had a boyfriend up in Tennessee, where she went to college a couple of years, but I didn't know they were engaged. I never saw him, but I know they talked on the phone a lot. He must be feeling terrible!"

She pressed her lips together, took three very deep breaths through her nose, and said calmly, "Even if it makes me sad to think of all she missed, I have to remember: it was her karma." She sounded like she was reciting a lesson.

I have never quite understood what karma is, but I knew it didn't mean that Amanda Kent was doomed from birth to be beaten to death. God gets a good bit of undeserved blame from uninformed people of all religions.

Of course I didn't say that to Selena Jones. No matter what Joe Riddley might tell you, I can be tactful when I need to. I hazarded a guess. "I heard Amanda Kent went down to that new temple on Freedom Street. Do you go there, too?"

"Oh, yes! The goswami is wonderful. He's not like a lot of preachers. He doesn't have all the answers, he's real honest about that, but he's seeking peace and helps us to seek, too. Being with him is like—well, you know."

Actually, I didn't. I'd never met a gos-whatever she called him. I shoved over another paper napkin and a pen. "Why don't you give me your phone number? I'll check to see if we have anything else in the store that might get rid of those mealybugs."

"You are so kind!" That made me feel like such a dirty, low-down skunk I couldn't meet her eye, so I organized the dishes on my tray while she wrote down the number. Then she checked her watch and pushed back her chair. "Oooh, I'm late! Thanks!"

She jumped up without looking, knocking a tray passing by. As a cup of cola poured over the edge of the tray onto the floor beside me, I saw it was Dr. Holder's tray.

I dodged the splash while Selena cried, "I'm so sorry! I'll get you another Coke."

She started toward the drink dispenser, but he called her back. "Don't bother, nurse. Actually it's root beer, and I'll get it. Just watch where you're going in the future." As he noticed me, he added a pleasant, "Hello, Mrs. Yarbrough."

Selena covered her face with her hands, stricken. "You know him?"

"He lives on our road. Is he one of the ones Amanda Kent got mad at?"

"Oh, no. He's one of the nicest doctors we've got— takes a lot of care not to hurt patients. Besides, Mandy didn't know him, since she worked nights. She told me a few weeks ago she wanted to meet him, because he's doing research into the alleviation of pain by mind control. Rather than drugs, you know? Mandy said it could be very important for older patients." Selena pressed her palms to her flaming cheeks. "I just can't believe I made him spill his drink. He must think I am such a klutz!"

"Don't worry, honey, he's got more important things to think about."

"I hope so. Omigosh, I'm late!" She hurried out in a flurry of long legs and flying hair.

As I sat there wondering who I ought to talk to next, Selena Jones dashed back. "If you ever want to go down to the temple, they have special yoga classes for senior citizens."

"Thanks, honey," I said, pushing away from the table. "I'll keep that in mind." I didn't think of myself as a senior citizen, but it sounded like as good a place as any to go next.

Seven

I stood on the sidewalk gazing up at a silver moon
and stars. They were hung not in the heavens but from
the eaves of a wide front porch. Beneath my feet I felt a
tremor that some might have thought was traffic, but I
knew was Marybelle Taylor whirling in her grave. If she'd
ever imagined her lovely family home would become the
Temple of Inner Peace, she would never have let them
carry her from First Methodist to the city cemetery.

Yet the house, recently repainted a soft shiny white
with a dark gray porch floor, looked much the same as it
used to when I went there for Garden Club board meetings—except for the moon and stars and a green and gold
sign by the beveled glass front door:

Temple of Inner Peace
Goswami Pandava
Inquirers' Class Friday 7:30–9 P.M.
Sunday Worship 3 P.M.
Personal Council Anytime
Peace Be With You

⌖

I didn't need to do much detecting to know two things: this goswami couldn't spell "counsel" and had spent some of his life in church. He hadn't gotten "Inquirer's Class," "Sunday Worship" and "Peace Be With You" from eastern religion. Thinking back, what Selena had said about karma sounded an awful lot like the way people who don't know much about predestination define it: *Whatever will be will be.* If she'd learned that from him, her goswami certainly didn't have all the answers.

I mounted the steps, skeptical and a little nervous. No matter what was going on in Marybelle Taylor's former home, anything claiming to be religion draws power to it of one sort or another. There was one sort I didn't want to meet up with. And while I could sing Martin Luther's "And though this world with devils filled should threaten to undo us, we will not fear" with the best of them in a pew next to Joe Riddley, it wasn't as easy while climbing those steps alone with who-knew-what behind the door.

Obeying a small sign taped to the glass, *Please Enter,* I turned the polished brass doorknob and shoved. The door swung open with a silent "whoosh" and bells trilled gently overhead. Inside, I was surprised. The entrance hall still smelled of lemon furniture polish and held only a small, expensive-looking Oriental rug and a polished cherry table. I'd expected a statue with lots of arms.

As I stood there getting my bearings and thinking that Marybelle would never have left books and brochures all over her hall table, I noticed pictures she'd never have hung, either: a wimpy blonde Jesus staring into heaven with a pious expression that would make angels sick, a horseback warrior in a feather bonnet raising a spear to an improbably orange sunset, and a bald old man in a yellow sari sitting cross-legged under an anemic looking tree. Apparently this was an equal-opportunity temple.

Since nobody seemed to be responding to the bell, I tiptoed over to look at the materials on the table. Like the pictures, they were a hodgepodge from various faiths. A Koran lay next to New Testament, which was next to rainbow-colored tracts about seeking higher truth and finding inner peace. The purple tract on top seemed to be Bible passages edited curiously. The end of Matthew 6, for instance, should read *Seek first the kingdom of God and His righteousness, and all these things will be added unto you*. It had been edited to read, *Seek the kingdom which is within you, and prosperity will be yours*.

To insure the temple's own prosperity, a hand-lettered sign sat beside a carved wooden box. *Prices marked. Honor System. Please pay for what you take.*

I tiptoed to the arch at one side of the hall. Marybelle's heart-pine living room floor had been covered by a white Berber carpet. In the bay window stood bongo drums and a mahogany stand that looked very like a pulpit. I recognized the shefflera and Benjamin ficus in large brass pots as Marybelle's own, thriving as well amid all that inner peace as they had under her staunchly Methodist care.

On the other side of the hall, Marybelle's walnut dining table for ten had been replaced by six tables for four covered with bright cotton cloths. Where the china cabinet used to stand was a long table with an urn and blue china mugs. A white dry-erase board filled one wall, listing prices for herbal teas and fruit juices in green marker.

I saw all that in far less time than it takes to tell it, for soon I heard someone coming my way and eased back toward the hall table. I was pretending to be engrossed in a thick paperback called *The Science of Self Realization* by the time a man in sandals shuffled through strings of beads hung in a doorway at the rear of the hall.

If I weighed that much, I probably wouldn't pick up my feet, either. He wasn't any taller than I, but nearly as broad as he was tall. Seeking higher truth apparently didn't involve fasting. As he moved closer, I detected a strong smell of fresh garlic.

He wore black pants and a white shirt, with several thick silver chains and charms hanging on his chest. I recognized a cross, a star of David, a yinyang, and a peace symbol. Beneath them his beard flowed almost to his waist, and like his thick curly hair and bushy eyebrows, it was black with flecks of gray.

He gave me one quick look, then bowed his head with both hands at his waist. I found myself looking at a small bald spot, like the soft pink center in a fluffy black flower. "Peace be with you." His voice was deep, the words running together like a hum. "We are not open now. It is my hour for meditation. But may I be of assistance?" With each word waves of garlic overpowered the lemon polish.

I laid down the book and tried to sound eager. "I heard you have a yoga class for . . . senior citizens." You'll understand why the last two words came out hard when you have to apply them to yourself.

"Monday, Wednesday, and Friday mornings at nine." Still without lifting his head he reached for an orange brochure entitled "Higher Consciousness Training for Those Nearing the End of This Life Cycle."

If I hadn't had an ulterior motive for being there, I'd have gone out that door so fast he wouldn't have seen my dust. Instead I murmured "Thank you so much," stuffed it in my purse, and again addressed the fluffy black flower. "I'll think about it. I heard about you through one of your members, Selena Jones, but I'm not quite sure what religion you are."

"We seek the truth from all religions," he said grandly, waving one large hand, "and we have no members, just inquirers. All are members of the One Truth, whether they have begun to inquire or not. Are you inquiring yet?"

I decided to take his question at face value. "Well, yes, I did want to inquire a little. I wanted to inquire about Amanda Kent."

He looked up briefly, a flash of dark liquid eyes, then immediately returned to floor-gazing. "Amanda Kent has departed to a higher, more blessed plane."

"But she was a member—an inquirer—here, I believe?"

He nodded. "Yes, but she has departed now. We remember her no more."

"Surely you *remember* her!" I chided, shocked.

He shook his head. "Remembering the past is not the way to peace. Now I must excuse myself. It is my time for meditation. Come again when you wish to seek truth and inner peace." Again, palms together at his thick waist, he bowed—looking like one of those dolls weighted at the bottom. If I knocked him over, would he spring right back up?

Before he could leave, I urged, "At least tell me if she came here the night she was killed. Somebody said she was coming to the temple that evening."

"She has departed. We remember her no more." He sounded peeved.

I thought of suggesting he get a grip on his inner peace, but he muttered, "Excuse me. I must meditate. Good day." Then he turned and shuffled sedately away.

He hadn't looked at me except for two quick glances. Maybe he felt it was modest not to look at women. I found it merely unnerving.

He pushed his way through the strings of beads and disappeared. I would have found *that* more impressive if I hadn't known the door led only to the kitchen. A whiff of garlic remained in the hall.

I was peeved myself. For one wild instant I considered rolling up his gorgeous hall rug and carrying it off. Would he be as detached about the loss of an expensive carpet as he was about the loss of one of his "inquirers"?

Fortunately, I am old enough to recognize temptation when it taps my shoulder. Besides, the thought of what Chief Charlie Muggins would say as he hauled me before Judge Stebley (or, worse, Judge Yarbrough) was more than enough to restore my sanity. In penance I took out my coin purse and left a dime for the yoga class brochure.

As I turned toward the door, I noticed a small cork bulletin board on one dining room wall. Curious, I tiptoed in. A servers' schedule for the month was posted, and from the times, I concluded the servers worked the juice bar before and after inquirers' class. Amanda Kent was scheduled to work both slots, until ten, the evening she died. She had been neatly whited out for the next three Fridays.

Amanda Kent has departed. We remember her no more.

"I'll remember you," I promised her fiercely.

Since I was so near, I headed back to our store. Our manager would have closed at six, but after talking with the goswami I needed to feel my own red plaid cushion beneath me and rest my arms on my own desk awhile.

To my surprise, I found Walker sitting in his daddy's chair working the computer.

"What're you doing here?" I greeted him, tossing my pocketbook in the corner and sinking into the old wooden swivel chair that's exactly the right height so my feet can reach the floor. That's important when you're five-foot-three.

"Checking today's accounts." He rubbed his eyes and pushed away the papers. "I couldn't look at one more insurance form, so I thought I'd make sure things were running okay with Daddy gone. We sold three truckloads of cotton fertilizer this afternoon. It's time for the final spreading."

"Since when did you get so smart?" Walker has never cared a thing about farming. Ridd grew up wanting to know everything about growing things, and when Joe Riddley offered him twenty acres of land, gladly took them and planted cotton. Walker turned down the acres we offered him. Said he didn't have time to mess with cotton.

"I'm smart enough to know there's new software that could help you all with inventory, if you'll get it."

Surprised, I wondered—for the very first time—whether Walker would have liked to learn the business side of things instead of the agricultural. Why had that thought never occurred to either of his parents before?

"What are *you* doing here so late?" he finally thought to ask.

"Oh," I said carelessly, "I had supper with Martha, then went by that new temple place to see if I could find out anything." I didn't bring up yoga classes for senior citizens. You don't ever want your children thinking you're old. They might start giving orders.

I'd shocked Walker enough as it was. "Don't you be going down there by yourself! You don't know *what* you might run into!"

"I was trying to help Luke, but all I found out was that Amanda Kent went to the temple the night she died and was scheduled to staff the juice bar until ten. Maybe if I get to know some of the others who go there, I can find out when she went home and with whom."

"What's the point of that?"

"To find out who killed her."

He slapped a stack of inventories on Joe Riddley's desk so hard a paperweight shaped like the U.S. Capitol jumped half an inch. "I didn't ask you to find out who killed her, Mama, I asked you to prove Luke *didn't*."

"The surest way to do that is to prove who did." I rested my elbows on my desk and rubbed both cheeks with my fingers. "I wish we could get into her apartment and have a look around. I'd like to get to know her a little."

"You're sick, Mama. The woman is dead."

"The only time you look like your daddy is when you glare, but never mind. We might as well leave the case to Charlie Muggins."

That was playing dirty and I knew it—right on a par with telling a child you're going to leave him somewhere when you've no intention of doing so. Walker, however, always responds well to manipulation. Sure enough. "If it suited him, Charlie Muggins would try to convict a rooster of laying eggs."

"Then can you figure out a way to get me inside that girl's apartment? I really would like to see it before they take all her stuff away and rent it again."

He nibbled his knuckle a minute. "I wrote the policy on that place. I guess I could call the manager and say I need to inspect it since the police finished."

∽

It was twilight by the time we climbed the wooden outside staircase to Amanda Kent's apartment. The huge live oaks that shaded the yard in mid-afternoon now made deep patchy shadows. Beyond the back fence I could see the near edge of the old town cemetery. I'm not a normally nervous person, but I was glad to have Walker along.

Truth to tell, I was glad to have it anyway. When he's not on his high horse, he's good company.

He thrust the key in the lock, opened the door, and flicked on a light. "Here we are, such as it is. The manager assures me it has been well cleaned."

It was clean, but it certainly wasn't cool. As I followed him in, my panty hose bound my legs like warmers and I knew the long sleeves I'd put on that day to work in an air conditioned office were not suitable for an apartment that had been shut up for four days.

I hurried to open both front windows and the double window on one side, then turned to look around. The furnished apartment was one big room with a bathroom and walk-in closet built into the windowless corner. A stove, refrigerator, and short counter stood along the back wall, a daybed against the solid side wall, and a table with four chairs under the double side window. The walls were white and the tweed carpet gray—except for a few big stains over near the bed.

I stepped back to a window, suddenly dizzy. Those stains made Amanda Kent's death real in a way that nothing else had. Even with the windows open, I seemed to smell dried blood. Behind my eyes I saw a girl crouched on the floor while someone lifted his arms and beat, beat, beat . . .

I could scarcely breathe and my stomach was starting to heave. I had to flatten my nose against the screen and inhale deeply several times before my heart slowed. "Dear God, preserve her," I urged softly. I know some people don't pray for people after they're dead, but that minute I felt so deeply for that young women, I just couldn't help it.

Finally I turned to look at the room again, approving the personal touches Amanda Kent had added to make this her home. Beige placemats. Brown-flecked beige drapes. Nubby beige-on-beige throw pillows dotting the stripped daybed.

A long low bookcase divided the eating space from the rest of the room and made a place to set a vase of dried flowers, a lovely golden dulcimer, and a green statue of a fat laughing man. A small rocker near the single daybed was too fine for the rest of the furniture. Had Amanda brought it from home, or bought it with some of her first earnings? Either one, it gave me a pang to look at it. You could tell it had been special to its owner.

Next I noticed, being who I am, that the place was full of houseplants, all needing water. I got a jar from under the counter and filled it at the sink. It felt a bit like a sacrament to move about that girl's place pouring water onto a pothos, spider plant, three ferns, and a rubber tree she would never water again.

"We didn't come up here to water plants, Mama," Walter objected from the door. "What are we looking for?" A tremor in his voice told me he was unhappy to be there.

I put away the jar. "I don't know—anything we can learn about Amanda Kent from the way she's fixed up the place."

"She liked weird art." Walker pointed to a hand-woven wall hanging in soft browns, off-white, and green.

I had noticed a loom placed near one front window. I went over and looked at the piece she'd been working on, in the same shades as the hanging. "I wonder if she wove that and her placemats and pillow covers?" I asked, absently reaching toward a stray fleck of pale blue thread caught on a screw head.

"Let's go," Walker called impatiently. "I have a practice tonight."

I moved on without removing the thread. "Give me five more minutes."

I tried to remember Luke's dream, but it was hard. I'd only heard it once. There certainly was a bed used like a couch here, but no big wing chair—Wait! Bending down, I saw four indentations where a large chair had sat, behind the stains on the carpet. I shuddered to realize why the chair was gone.

Next I moved to the telephone. The police had taken her address book, but I poked around and found a cardboard filing box holding old utility bills. I sat down in the rocker to look them over, and found the telephone number of somebody in Tennessee whom she called at least once a week. I also found another number in the same town, which she'd called once in the past two months, in the evening.

"I'll borrow a piece of paper from this telephone pad," I murmured, tearing it off.

"You can't borrow from a dead woman," Walker reminded me. "Say what you mean—'I'm going to *use* this piece of paper.'"

I pressed my lips together and breathed through my nose while I counted to twelve. I learned to do that around the time Walker learned to talk. Then I said sweetly, "I'm going to steal this piece of paper, Walker. Does that make you feel better?" I copied down the two phone numbers and put the bills back in their file.

What else did I want to see? The bathroom told me nothing except Amanda Kent favored herbal shampoos and few cosmetics. I could have guessed that from her picture. The kitchen told me she also favored herbal tea and brown rice. I could have guessed that, too. The only unexpected thing in her refrigerator, hidden behind a large carton of yogurt and two bottles of root beer, was a package of semi-sweet chocolate chips, half gone. Did she nibble them after a meal of bean sprouts and tofu? Did she feel guilty about having them? Was that why she hid them?

Under one front window a small bookshelf was sparsely filled with medical textbooks, vegetarian cookbooks, and books on improving yourself. I picked up a copy of *The Science of Self Realization* like the one I'd seen at the temple, except this one was worn from frequent reading. There were no novels or mysteries. Apparently Amanda Kent had been a serious young woman.

Walker moved restlessly at the door. "Are you done?"

"Almost." Quickly I opened the closet and peeked in. Rumor was that she had been found in her nightgown. So why was a perfectly good oversized T-shirt hanging on the back of her closet door over a white chenille bathrobe? Had she had a special nightie she wore to entertain in and a comfortable T-shirt to sleep in alone?

"One more minute," I promised Walker over one shoulder. I started opening dresser drawers. All I found were three more T-shirts. No nightgowns at all. Perplexing.

"Mama, you aren't detecting now, you're just being nosy. Come *on!* We're supposed to rehearse tonight, and I'm already a little late." I followed him out the door and down the wooden steps.

In another minute he'd be gone. If I could re-live those next three minutes, would I still ask, "You been up to Thomson lately?"

I could see his shoulders tense up. "No, and I'm not going. Cindy knows where I live. If she wants me, she can come back."

Any mother knows sweet reason seldom works, but those few times it does keeps us hoping. "Coming back might be hard on her pride, after leaving," I suggested. "It wouldn't hurt you to go up to Thomson and say you're sorry. Remember what Granddaddy used to say? 'Always say you're sorry. If you haven't done anything wrong, you can afford to, and if you have, you can't afford not to.'"

He didn't say a word.

We'd reached the ground. I stepped aside to check two mailboxes attached to one wall. Amanda Kent's name was still on one. The other belonged to Gideon Levy.

"Hurry," Walker urged, flapping his hands. "These gnats will eat us alive."

We walked across the leaf-strewn dirt driveway toward my car. Since he hadn't gotten mad yet, I dared to plead, "Ask Cindy to come home, honey."

He took in a quick, angry breath. "It's not that easy, Mama. She won't come unless I give up the band, and the band could be our ticket to everything we've ever dreamed of."

I felt a spurt of anger. How could he be so thick-headed? "Except the dream of raising those two children in a home with both parents there and loving them." I shoved him aside to open my own door. "Not to mention a grandmother who's plumb aching to hug them again."

I was immediately ashamed. Here we were flaring up just like we had twenty years before. One of us, at least, should have learned to control the family temper. I took a deep breath and tried. "I'm sorry, Walker. I have no right to interfere. But remember, parents have to make a few sacrifices while their children are little. When they leave home, you'll have plenty of time to do what you want."

He turned away. At his own car he pounded the top so hard he'd probably need to get a dent taken out. Then he called across the open lot in a voice full of pain, "I have to do this, Mama, and I have to do it now. Music won't wait." He got in, slammed his door, and gunned his engine, waiting for me to pull out ahead of him.

Whatever gets into men at a certain stage of life, it has nothing to do with common sense.

$$\infty$$

Not until I set my pocketbook in the floor of my car did I realize I'd carried out Amanda Kent's paperback. Walker was in such a hurry, I hated to make him let me in to return it, but stealing her book seemed a lot worse than borrowing a sheet from her notepad.

"She won't miss it," I reminded myself firmly.

The courthouse clock chimed eight as I pulled out of the drive and turned onto Oglethorpe. I wasn't ready to head home. I had one more place I wanted to go.

A member of my Sunday school was laid up with a sprained ankle for several days. She might like a little visit. Besides, if Amanda Kent's fiancé had come to town since the murder, that woman would know about it—right down to the label in his shirt.

All I had to do was ask casually, "Did any of that poor girl's family come up last weekend—a boyfriend or anybody?" and I got an earful about how nobody had come to identify her except her poor mother, who was divorced and all alone now that her only child was dead, and would need to come back to pack up everything because the police wouldn't let her take a single thing until they were through.

I steered the conversation away from Amanda's mother and asked again if anybody else had come, like a boyfriend. No, no boyfriend had shown up. Not even her daddy, who lived up in Virginia with a wife almost as young as his daughter.

I wasn't interested in Amanda's daddy, but I found it curious that her fiancé hadn't come. I also found it hopeful. A fiancée who didn't come was at least as good a suspect as a preacher who didn't know the victim. And the fiancé had one more thing to recommend him: he came from out of town.

Eight

Seeing Amanda's apartment made the notion of a murderer in Hopemore very real. I hadn't been nervous about those thefts during parties—although I'd started locking the doors when we out at night, and I'd hidden my grandmother's silver—but that night I found myself dreading staying down our road alone.

I took Lulu inside with me. Not being an inside dog, she wandered restlessly about the kitchen before curling up on a rug near the stove, but I knew I could count on her to raise the dead if anybody tried to come in. I also got the living room fireplace poker and carried it around with me until bedtime. Some people might wonder why I didn't get one of Joe Riddley's shotguns out of the locked cabinet in the den, but I never have liked guns. Things tend to happen too fast and too irreparably when there are guns around.

Joe Riddley called on our cell phone before I went to bed, to say they'd gotten their tents set up and actually caught enough fish for supper.

"We're having a mite of trouble getting Crick down, though. He's so excited about being here, he won't lie down and go to sleep. I don't want Ridd to paddle him, but it may take that."

"Sing to him," I suggested. "That's what Martha always does."

I seldom sleep well when Joe Riddley's away, and that night was no exception. For one thing I kept hearing noises I don't usually hear. For another, Lulu kept moving restlessly around the room. She was more of a pain than a help, but I didn't want to put her outside. Finally I fell asleep about four and didn't wake until well past seven.

I took Lulu back to her pen through a damp, still morning, then stopped on my way back to the house to gather fresh figs for my breakfast cereal. I carried the cereal, juice, and coffee out onto the porch, which I always say is the best room in our house. When we screened it in, we added wicker rockers and indoor-outdoor carpeting in the round part and a hammock and a long table on the side porch. We live out there whenever it's not too hot or too cold.

While I ate, a soft summer storm came down with a hiss, punctuated by thumps on the roof. It was more mist than rain, accompanied by the loveliest fresh breeze. I love the smell of rain-washed air.

I finished my cereal listening to the sweet piercing call of robins protesting they'd had enough rain. Is anything more peaceful than a drizzly summer morning? That day the rain fell so softly I could scarcely see it near the house. Half-way across the yard I could see drops. Beyond the toolshed it was a fine gray mist. I could almost hear the plants drinking it in. I felt so peaceful, I didn't think of murder for nearly an hour.

With great reluctance I picked up my dishes and went inside to try the number Amanda Kent called weekly. I didn't know exactly what I was going to say, but would play it by ear depending on how brokenhearted he sounded.

~~~

He didn't sound brokenhearted at all. In fact, he sounded so shockingly cheerful when he answered that it took me a couple of seconds to realize I'd gotten an answering machine. A pleasant voice with a Tennessee twang told me he was Vic Davis in the biology department and couldn't take my call right then, but if I'd leave my number he'd get back to me "sooner than you expect."

I made myself a cup of tea and dialed the other number. A child answered the phone, so young I couldn't tell if it was a boy or a girl. When I asked for Dr. Davis, the piping little voice called, "Mommy, is Daddy still here?"

"He's down in his study, honey," a woman called back. "I'll get him. You go finish your breakfast."

I heard her faint "Yoo-hoo, Vic, telephone," then a voice came on the line. It was the Tennessee twang I'd already heard. "Vic Davis here. How can I help you?" He sounded about the age of my sons—a man old enough to take charge of his own life and willing to take charge of yours.

"I'm calling from Hopemore, Georgia—"

He quickly interrupted. "Cheryl, honey. Hang up. This is a business call."

"Okay," the child replied regretfully. I heard a click, and hoped she wasn't as good as my children used to be at pretending to hang up, then listening in.

"Who are you and why are you calling me here?" he demanded angrily.

"Excuse me," I said, "but I am calling about Amanda Kent."

He paused then said carefully, "I taught a Mandy Kent several years ago. She moved to Georgia after that. Is that the one you mean? Did she ask you to call?"

The edge in his voice on that last question answered my own question. He knew her all right, but his anxiety made me think he didn't know she was dead—had been wondering why he hadn't heard from her this week. So why hadn't he come down? When Joe Riddley and I were in college, we talked once a week. The few times I wasn't there when he called, he drove two hours to be sure I was all right.

Of course Joe Riddley didn't have a wife and child to lie to before he left.

If Vic Davis had been carrying on with Amanda Kent and stayed married to that sweet-voiced woman, he must be an excellent actor. Could he have come down and killed Amanda Kent, then gone home to prepare himself for this very call?

I was wondering how to find out when he demanded again, "Did Mandy ask you to call me?"

"Not exactly," I admitted. "Somebody else told me she had a fiancé in Tennessee at this number."

His laugh was short and blunt. "Fiancé? I don't know who you are, lady, but you'd better get your story straight. Mandy was my student. I'd advise you to keep your nose in your own business. Now excuse me. I have papers to grade."

He slammed down the phone before I could say another word.

"Hang up on me, will you?" I muttered into the phone. "I'm going to give your name to the police so fast it will make your head swim." But a persistent little question nagged me all the way to work. Did Amanda Kent have any good reason to think Vic Davis loved her, or had she merely deluded herself into an engagement? Either way, she could have made things uncomfortable for him.

Isaac James agreed to meet me in the back office of Yarbrough's at nine-thirty. I didn't tell him what I wanted.

He came into the office peering uneasily behind him. When I invited him to sit down, he perched on the front of our extra chair and cast nervous looks toward the big window in the office door.

"What's got you so jumpy?" I asked, feeling a lot less formal without Joe Riddley.

He rubbed a wide hand over his jaw. "Well, Miss MacLaren, it's like this. Chief Muggins has been very explicit about our not discussing the Kent case with anybody. He even went so far as to say 'particularly not Mrs. Yarbrough.' I'll be in a fix if he finds out I was here."

"Think what a fix you'll be in if you take the wrong person to trial." I leaned back in my chair. "Relax, Ike. Officers aren't coming back here looking for warrants with Joe Riddley out of town. He's got the magistrates over in Jefforson County covering for him, but if Chief Muggins finds out you were here, tell him you forgot Judge Yarbrough was fishing."

"I can try, but he's not likely to believe me. What did you mean about taking the wrong man to trial?"

"You don't really think Luke Blessed killed that girl, do you?"

"Nobody's asked me what I think or don't think, but all the evidence we've got so far points in that direction. Besides, I told you, we've all been warned not to talk about this case—especially with you."

I couldn't help a snort of disgust. "Your officers are running their mouths like NASCAR engines over at the hospital." I stopped and pressed one hand to my lips, appalled. Running my own mouth could cost me my only source of inside information.

He grinned. "I never pay attention to hearsay evidence. Now, what did you haul me over here for?"

I told him about Vic Davis—what he'd said, what he didn't say, and who Selena Jones said he was. "Fiancé, eh?" Ike stroked one cheek with a finger as thick as a hotdog. "But you say he didn't sound like he knew she was dead?"

"Not at all. Of course, he could be a good actor. If he killed her, he's had a whole week to plan that conversation. Apparently Chief Muggins hasn't contacted him yet."

Ike shook his head. "We never heard a word about a boyfriend. Everybody we've talked to says she was a real loner. We've found one or two women she went to movies with, but except for Mrs. Duckworth, she didn't seem to have a close friend in the world."

"Somebody said she played cards with the guy in the next apartment."

Ike nodded. "But nobody ever saw her go into his apartment or let him in hers."

"Is he still out of town?"

He stopped himself mid-nod. "I *told* you, I am not at liberty to discuss this case."

"Well, then, don't discuss it. But you might check on this professor in Tennessee. He's been talking to her on the phone once a week, and he told me in plain words of few syllables to butt out of Amanda Kent's business."

"What did he say when you told him she was dead?"

"I never got a chance. He hung up too fast."

Ike pounded one fist against the other palm. "Oo-eee, I'd like to see his face when he finds out." We exchanged a long look.

"Didn't your sister move up to Chattanooga? How long's it been since you saw her?"

"I was thinking t'other day I was due for a visit." Ike stood. "I've got today and the weekend off. I might run up to Tennessee for the night."

I handed him the two phone numbers I'd gotten. "That first number is the college where he works. I'd rather you talked to him there. He's got a wife and a little girl."

Ike pursed his lips. "That's not good."

"It sure isn't," I agreed. "If you went by the college, you could check it out for your nephew. Who knows? He might be interested in majoring in biology."

Ike chuckled. "In another seventeen years. Still, you can't be looking at colleges too early. Thanks, Miss MacLaren. Now how about if you leave this to me and you concentrate on keeping this business running until the Judge gets back?" He picked up his hat and headed for the door.

"I keep it running when he's here," I informed him tartly. As he started out, I added softly, "Ike? I know you can't discuss the case with me, but if you could come by and give me a good description of Vic Davis's face when he hears your news, I'd consider it a neighborly act."

Nine

Friday afternoon I found Ronald Duckworth in his painter's overalls on the second-from-the-top step of an eight-foot ladder, trying to change a bulb in their porch chandelier. I was there because I'd finally thought up an excuse to go talk with his wife, Lorine.

When I said that Lorine married a painter when she was sixteen, I neglected to mention that Lorine's family owned the biggest sawmill in our part of Georgia. In Georgia, sawmills mean money. The whole family was rich, prominent, and proud. (All except Lorine's cousin Arnie Potts, a pudgy dark boy Ridd's age who ran away to San Francisco in the late sixties to become a hippy. The family gave out that he'd gone abroad to study, but Arnie had worked for us the summer before he left, and he sent me a postcard of the Golden Gate Bridge. I found him a sensitive if spacy boy with more ideals than sense, but the family never mentioned him after he left. He wasn't fit fruit for their family tree.)

It never occurred to Lorine that because she hadn't married money, she'd need to give up having or spending it. Almost as soon as her granddaddy died she persuaded her grandmother to move into a smaller place so she, Ronald, and Rhonda could move into the family house over on Academy Street, down from where Walker later bought.

Since her grandmother obviously couldn't take her furniture, Lorine persuaded her to leave it. Then she persuaded her grandmother's maid to stay to care for it and the yard man to stay to care for the yard. Rumor was, she even persuaded her grandmother to keep paying their wages. How else could a housepainter's family keep two full-time servants?

The house is what Hollywood thinks Tara looked like—big, white, with green shutters at the windows and fat columns supporting wide porches on three sides. The kind of place, in short, that nobody in her right mind would want to keep up. However, nobody in town ever claimed Lorine Duckworth was in her right mind, except Joe Riddley. He maintains that since half the battle with a house like that is keeping it painted, Lorine knew exactly what she was doing when she married Ronald.

To give Ronald credit, he never stopped working after marrying Lorine, and he did good work. He was genial, too. Everybody liked him—except one man he hired and had to let go for stealing. Our family's private nickname for Ronald was The Happy Painter. Joe Riddley also said it was no wonder he was always happy—Ronald probably went to work for the same reason some men take vacations: to get away from home.

So Lorine had both Ronald and her place in society. Talking about money is vulgar, so nobody knew for sure, but we all speculated that Lorine's daddy continued to give her an allowance. How else could she have made so many improvements on that house in the past twenty years? Every bride and club in town wanted to have a party there.

I peered up at the four-bulb chandelier dangling from the twenty-foot ceiling. The dead bulb looked to be about eight inches out of Ronald's reach. "Looks like you could use a twelve-foot ladder," I told him.

I've already said that Ronald Duckworth at thirty had a lean body, a shock of blonde curls, a wide, easy smile, and not much sense. At fifty-six he had the same smile, a small round potbelly, wispy yellow hair over a pink scalp, and no more sense. Seemed to me that a man who spent his life on ladders would know what length he needed.

He looked ruefully at the distance between his hand and the dead bulb. "Sure could, but I didn't bring it home. This old bulb would go out just before Lorine's big Do." His face was pink and damp with heat.

Given how many Do's Lorine tended to have, the chances were good that no matter when a bulb went out it would be right before one of them. I felt a little guilty, though, that the particular Do giving Ronald his present trouble was the Garden Club buffet. I was treasurer of the Garden Club. In fact, the excuse I had for being there was to ask what extra plants Lorine wanted to set around in corners.

Actually, of course, I wanted to ask about Ronald finding Amanda Kent's body. Here I was with a perfect chance to get the information first hand.

I moved over to the ladder. "That looks a little unsteady to me. How about if I hold it while you try going up a step?" He tried the next step, but still lacked two inches.

Ronald and I both knew better than to stand on top of a ladder, but what man can resist a chance to show off? Swaying like a tightrope walker, he carefully balanced his body and stepped up, holding the new bulb aloft in one hand. With the other he grabbed the chandelier. If he'd had a third he could have changed the bulb.

"Sorry I can't come up to hold the new bulb for you," I called up. "Why don't you put it in your pocket until you get the old one out?"

"Good idea." He fumbled for his side pocket, swaying dangerously, and got the new bulb safely stowed. Then he reached up to twist out the old bulb.

I hung onto the ladder for dear life. "I heard you found that poor girl who was killed last week. I'd have had a fit if I'd found somebody like that."

His words were muffled while he stretched up. ". . . awful, Miss MacLaren. She was about the same age as Rhonda, so I kept thinking what if it was Rhonda who'd gotten hurt. It like to put me to bed for a week."

He pitched the dead bulb out onto the lawn. I took note of where it landed, then asked, "How'd you come to go over there in the first place?"

When Ronald didn't answer, I remembered something Joe Riddley once told me. "The only way to talk to Ronald Duckworth is to make statements and let him respond. A direct question plumb flusters him."

"Oh," I said, "I remember. You were doing some painting for her."

He brought out the new bulb and stretched to insert it in the socket. The ladder quivered. I braced my legs and held on tight. "Oh, no, Miss MacLaren, nothing like that. Lorine claimed she and the girl were supposed to run up to Augusta for the day, and Lorine was having a fit because she hadn't showed by noon. So she sent me over to see if anything was the matter. There." He finished the bulb.

I glimpsed a box of bulbs on a nearby green porch rocker. "Why don't you replace the other three while you're up there? Save you time and trouble later." Before he could object, I stretched to reach the new bulbs without letting go of the ladder.

"You were smart to look in the window when she didn't come to the door," I said while he stretched to twist out another bulb.

He pitched the old bulbs one by one to land near the first. "That was Lorine's idea, and she said to call her if I saw anything odd. I found something odd, all right. Her lights were on. Right in the middle of the day! So I called Lorine and told her."

He didn't speak again while he put in the last three bulbs. Neither did I. While he swayed, I prayed, hoping God wasn't too busy with wars and natural disasters to care whether Ronald and I broke our necks.

Finally he got the last bulb in, then he balanced on one leg and fumbled for the first step. When he finally got down, you could have heard me exhale out at the street.

"I need to sit down and rest a minute," I told him. I was trembling all over.

We settled into two of the six green rockers Lorine kept on her porch summer and winter. He pulled out a cigarette and lit it, then tossed it into the yard. "Lorine doesn't like me to smoke. I try not to, but sometimes I forget."

It seemed to me he'd have better luck remembering if he didn't keep a pack of cigarettes in his top pocket, but I didn't say that. I had something I wanted to say worse. "So you thought something was wrong because the girl had her lights on. That must have looked like she was wasting electricity, huh?"

Before Ronald could answer, another voice spoke from the door. "Why MacLaren Yarbrough! I didn't know you were out here!" Lorine came out the screened door, hands on her skinny hips to show off her coral nail polish. It went well with the mint green slacks and matching top she'd probably bought in New York or Atlanta. As always, her dark hair was sprayed and smooth like she'd just come from the beauty parlor.

She turned to her husband. "Ronald, get those light bulbs off our front lawn this minute! And that ladder off our porch! What will people think?"

Ronald rose, shambled out to the lawn, and picked up three bulbs. I started to remind him he'd tossed four, but didn't like to call Lorine's attention to how long I'd been there. He fetched the ladder and headed toward the back without another word. Lorine took his rocker.

I've always thought it was a shame Lorine got her daddy's long nose and close-set eyes along with her mother's thin mouth and pale freckled skin. She'd have looked better with her daddy's mouth and skin and her mother's nose and eyes. But you don't have to be beautiful when you can fly to New York to buy clothes and run by the beauty parlor every morning to get your hair combed out, chipped nails repainted, and color restored as soon as each gray hair appears. I don't usually remember Lorine is plain until I'm on my way home.

"I came by to ask what large plants you need for tomorrow night," I told her, reminding my conscience that that really was *one* reason I'd come.

"How sweet of you," she said, with sugary dishonesty. Lorine and I never enjoyed each other's company. She wanted to be treasurer of the garden club, for one thing. And while she wasn't much more than Ridd's age, she flirted with my husband, for another.

However, I'd been pumping hers, so fair was fair. "Ronald's been telling me about finding that girl who got killed Friday." I figured I might as well say it. She'd probably been listening at the screen.

Thin freckled lids fluttered over her black eyes. "We've been asked not to talk about that until the trial," she said primly. "Ronald knows that as well as I do."

"I asked him to tell me a little about it," I admitted. "I've been out of touch lately."

As I'd hoped, knowing something I didn't loosened her lips a tad. "It was dreadful! When I think about that man beating her to death—" she pressed her palms to her cheeks and shuddered. "Amanda Kent was the sweetest girl you ever saw. A precious child! We were absolutely best friends—shared an interest in spiritual things. Mystical experiences, meditation, things like that." She checked the small gold watch on her wrist. "In fact, I have to go meditate in a few minutes. I'm so glad you stopped by, though."

That was deft and sudden. My mother would have automatically risen, said goodbye, and headed for her car. I fought Mama's good breeding to ask another question. "They know who did it?"

"Oh, yes. That young preacher some of you people at church insisted on hiring. If you remember, I opposed calling him right from the start. Now look what's happened. I was actually in the police station when he came in to confess. I heard the whole thing!"

I widened my eyes and tried to look impressed. "Do!"

She leaned closer and nodded rapidly. "I was in the next office, and—don't you breathe a word of this, now!—Chief Muggins said since Amanda was such a friend of mine, I could listen through a crack in the door. Poor Chief Muggins. Did you know Luke persuaded his wife to leave him? I don't know how he could stand to be in the same room with the man."

"What did you hear?" I asked, wishing I had a concealed tape recorder. Why hadn't I thought of that before?

"Oh, Luke pretended he'd dreamed it—can you imagine?—but he was confessing all right. He knew all about her apartment, what the weapon was—everything."

"I thought he said the weapon was a walking stick when it was really a crowbar." Her eyes narrowed. "Or so somebody told me," I added with a wave of my hand. "It wasn't?"

She tossed her head. "He just said that trying to fool Chief Muggins."

"Did he say why he killed her?"

"That's obvious! He wanted her to come to church. When she told him she was a member at the Temple of Inner Peace, he got furious. Beat her so badly she was almost unrecognizable. Those fundamentalists make me sick."

I wouldn't consider Luke a fundamentalist. Even if he was, I couldn't see the logic in beating somebody to get them to church. I didn't say that. I also didn't say what made *me* sick: Lorine's spreading gossip that didn't make a speck of sense.

I was, however, ornery enough to ask innocently, "I wonder why on earth he'd have gone to see her that late at night? Preachers don't usually go visiting after bedtime."

"Most preachers wouldn't, of course, but Luke Blessed would stop at nothing to get young people to church. Did you know he's been using an electric guitar for the teenagers' service? Anybody knows that's the preferred instrument of the devil."

She sat there like a ravenous hyena licking her chops at the idea of Luke Blessed getting arrested. I longed to ask how she knew the devil well enough to know what instrument he preferred. I also wanted to ask why she thought Luke would have taken a crowbar along on a pastoral visit, to see what reason she could come up with. However, there were things I wanted to know even worse.

For one, "Why did Ronald get so worried when he saw her lights on?"

"Oh, Ronald." Her diamond tennis bracelet flashed as she flicked one hand to dismiss him. "He worries about every little thing. But you know, Mac." Lorine lowered her voice like she was about to tell me something real important. "I think I must be clairvoyant. I'm not a worrier. You know that. But that morning I was worried sick about Amanda. For no reason at all. So when Ronald called, I knew something was bad wrong."

"Why did Ronald call you instead of the police?"

She shrugged. "You know Ronald. Depends on me for everything. But as soon as he called and said those lights were on, I went ahead and called the police. Told them to break down that door if necessary. 'Just get in there and see what's the matter.' I told them."

"I heard you went down to the station with Ronald, too." I prided myself on how that seemed to pop out.

"Not with him, honey, *for* him. That man was a nervous wreck. It was all he could do to climb the stairs to his bed. He stayed there the rest of the day."

From what I heard, Ronald stayed in bed most days he didn't have a painting job, but saying that wouldn't get me very far. "He's lucky he's got you to take care of him," I murmured, squirming in my chair and hoping lightning wouldn't strike me dead.

"He sure is," she agreed vigorously. "Now, about those plants. What I wanted . . ."

Lorine might be a member of the Garden Club, but she never did the flowers for her parties—and seldom paid for them. She had a thousand and one reasons why Yarbrough's or our local florist ought to donate every blessed one. The upcoming Garden Club buffet was a benefit, so members would bring table centerpieces to auction off. What Lorine wanted from me was large plants to group in the corners of her downstairs rooms. By the time she'd finished explaining what all she wanted and I'd finished cutting it approximately in half, I could hear the courthouse clock chiming six.

As I got ready to leave, she asked casually, "You see much of your new neighbor?"

"No, he's mostly with his dad." Then, from her puzzled expression, I realized she didn't mean Maniac. "Oh, Dr. Holder? No, except when he jogs by at night. He often goes for a run after work."

"I'm glad he takes care of himself, as hard as he works. Has he told you about his wonderful research?"

When I shook my head, she gave me the smug little smile she reserves for people who have the misfortune not to be her. Then she leaned close and whispered, although there wasn't another person in sight. "We see a lot of him, because he's been squiring Rhonda lately. He's coming with her to the buffet tomorrow night. In fact, I wouldn't be surprised—but no." She sealed her lips with a coy finger. "That's telling tales out of school." She stood. "And now, Mac, I'm sorry, but I really must go. I'm due somewhere in a few minutes."

As I left the porch, I couldn't help wondering, as Dr. Holder's nearest woman neighbor, whether I had a Christian duty to warn him that if he married Rhonda he'd also get stuck with Ronald and Lorine.

On my way down the walk I saw a gleam in the lawn—the setting sun hitting that last light bulb. I tiptoed across the grass and picked it up so a mower wouldn't hit it. I found myself looking anxiously behind me as I did, though. I didn't want Lorine claiming I'd found Hector Blaine's Confederate treasury lying around on her lawn and stolen it, and if she could believe her preacher killed a woman because she wouldn't go to church, Lorine could believe anything.

I tossed the bulb into a litter bag I keep hanging over the back of my seat and drove home slowly through a glorious evening. Nobody would suspect we had a monster loose. The air around the courthouse square was a lovely pinky gold. Sidewalks and trees shimmered in that wonderful light, and the old brick buildings along Oglethorpe Street softened into something beautiful.

If I'd known how dark things were about to get, I'd have hurried home, jumped into bed, and pulled Mama's George Washington bedspread over my head.

> Is not wisdom found among the
> aged? Does not long life bring
> understanding? *Job 12:12*

Ten

Maybe it was sitting on that hot front porch in panty
hose and long sleeves, or maybe it was spending time with
Lorine, but I could hardly wait for a long bath. Even so, I
found myself nervous about going into an empty house. I
fervently wished Joe Riddley was there to welcome me.
Then, feeling guilty at begrudging him the little leisure
time he ever took, I sent up a prayer that he was having
a good time. For good measure, I sent up another that
they would be able to keep Crick out of the lake.

As I turned the corner into our road, a fuzzy black
cloud erupted from an open back window of the old Pickens place.

A second later Dr. Holder dashed through his front
door and down the steps, clutching his head with both
hands. His hair, face, arms, hands, and bare legs were covered in soot. He wore a red T-shirt and what had once

been light blue sweat pants, cut off to make shorts. They were streaked and gray.

I slid to a stop and rolled down my window. "What happened? Are you all right?"

"I'm not sure yet." He wriggled his head in his hands like he was trying to put it back in place. "This house is going to be the death of me!" As he came toward my car, the only white I could see were his eyes and teeth.

"What on earth have you been doing?" Working a coal mine was a good guess.

"Trying to get that blasted kitchen ready for plumbers and electricians. Tonight I finally attacked the last wall, and found an old fireplace plastered over. I wondered if it still worked, so I put a broomstick up to see if it was clear. The stick got stuck on something, so I took my crowbar and pried around it a little. Next thing I knew, something huge and heavy crashed down—along with half a ton of soot. I'm lucky I wasn't killed!"

"You poor thing!" Not only was his floor likely to be damaged, but soot is apt to work its way all over a house in less time than it takes to tell it.

"I don't know what to do next," he confessed with boyish desperation. "From the sound that thing made landing, I'll never be able to lift it. I don't even know what it is."

I'm a sucker for that tone of voice. In a minute I was standing in his gutted kitchen in my nice clothes, confronting a heap of not only soot but all the debris that collects in a chimney that's not been cleaned for forty years.

"Oh, my!" was all I could say. I'd already seen a faint film of soot on fresh creamy walls in the adjoining dining room and large sooty tracks across a perfectly wonderful Afghan rug in the front hall. Dr. Holder belonged to the one-room-at-a-time school of house restoration, but hadn't yet learned to seal off finished rooms from those under construction.

He picked up a crowbar that had been shiny blue before its recent confrontation. Gingerly he prodded a rusty hump that sat on top of the pile. "Do you have any idea what this is? And why anybody would shove it up there?"

I poked it a bit with one toe. "An old cannon barrel, is my guess, left by either General Sherman or Confederate troops. One of the Pickens boys probably found it in a field and brought it in."

"Why shove it up a chimney?"

"Amos may have aimed it at aliens, or somebody earlier may have aimed it at carpetbaggers. They could have even just felt a draft and wanted to block the airshaft after they stopped using the fireplace."

He kicked it a couple of times. "I can't imagine what I'll do with it except design my whole kitchen around it. I can't lift it, and it's probably left a dent in my good floor." He picked up a broom and headed toward the most distant debris.

I held out a hand to stop him. "Don't sweep, whatever you do! You'll need to carefully shovel this mess into a wheelbarrow and cart it out to some place where you don't want things to grow, but first get heavy plastic and seal off the doorways into the rest of the house, or you're going to find soot even in your linen closet and dresser drawers. You really ought to either store all your nice things until you finish the whole house, or seal off each room with thick plastic as you finish it. I speak from painful experience," I added ruefully.

He wiped his forehead with one forearm, leaving matching sweaty streaks on both. "You know, friends told me to rent an apartment, concentrate on my research, and pay somebody to finish everything before I moved in. I hate to admit it, but they were right. Some days I want to bomb the place and build a nice new house from the ground up."

"You won't get twelve foot ceilings and heart pine floors," I reminded him. "It's going to be worth it. You're just at what Joe Riddley calls 'a sticking place'—one of those places where you've got to stick to the job in spite of yourself." I had a sudden inspiration. "How about if I call Maynard Spence down the road and see if he can give you a hand moving that barrel? If you offer to give it to him for his museum, I'll bet he'll come like a shot—pardon the pun."

His smile was a crescent of white teeth in the soot. "I'd be grateful. I certainly can't move it by myself. I'd love to know how they got it up there in the first place."

"Honey," I told him, "the Pickenses were husky, just not very bright."

When I looked at his sooty phone, and realized that my throat was starting to hurt from breathing the stuff, I told him I'd go home to call Maynard. I left by the back door, picking my way through long unmowed grass and stooping to retrieve a couple of pieces of litter on the way. Generally the site was extremely clean. Maybe having to be neat in surgery made him neat other places, too. He kept glass and plastic in a five-gallon bucket on the porch for recycling and had stacked a pile of cast iron plumbing pipes under a mulberry tree to be carted off. From bits and pieces sticking out of a fifty gallon barrel down at the back fence, I hoped he'd gotten a permit to burn his scrap lumber.

Every house outside the city limits has one of those old burn barrels. Not too long ago we had to burn everything we didn't compost or throw down a handy gully. Nowadays the county picks up garbage from a dumpster at the head of our road and we take recyclables to a center across town. To burn, we have to get a forestry permit. (Hubert Spence calls that government interference in his life, and makes poor Maniac burn every scrap of paper with their name on it—says he doesn't want somebody getting his address off a garbage dump.) Joe Riddley had urged Dr. Holder to get a permit to burn his construction debris because it's too much trouble to haul that much wood away.

I tossed the bits of paper on top of Lorine's lightbulb and drove home slowly, honking at Hubert rocking on his porch. Joe Riddley might be gone, but I still had neighbors. I didn't even bother to take Lulu in.

I washed my hands good—making a quantity of dismal gray bubbles in the sink—and got myself a tall glass of iced tea to get the taste of soot out of my throat before I called Maniac. As I'd predicted, he was delighted to hear about the cannon barrel, and even willing to help move it. "I'll go over *right now.*" In a little while I heard his car start. I wondered if he might be a tad lonely over there with just Hubert for company. Hubert's idea of an exciting evening is rocking awhile, then watching television sports.

My poor clothes might never come clean, and I wanted a long shower instead of a bath. After five minutes in Dr. Holder's kitchen, my hair needed a good wash, too—which was a bother since I was due at the beauty parlor the next afternoon. My new perm would be a frizzy mess until then unless I rolled and dried it.

"Stop fussing," I told myself crossly, stepping under a stream of hot, invigorating water and letting it pound the top of my head. "Nobody's going to see you tonight, and tomorrow you can wear Miss Millie to the store. Most likely there won't be one soul coming in to notice anyhow."

Miss Millie was a wide-brimmed straw hat with a black band and a red peony. I'd bought on a Caribbean cruise we took for our forty-fifth anniversary, and "It looks like a Millie to me" was Joe Riddley's explanation for giving it that name. I hadn't worn the hat since we got back, but tomorrow sounded like the perfect time to introduce Miss Millie to Hopemore.

I was combing out my hair when Joe Riddley called. "You're late getting in tonight." I didn't mind that he was growling. I knew it meant he'd worried a little.

"I had to drop by Lorine's to talk about plants for tomorrow night. Then on my way home, I got in on a little excitement down at the Pickens place." I told him about the cannon, the soot, and sending Maniac off to help.

"Maniac's all right in an emergency." From Joe Riddley, that was high praise.

"Speaking of emergencies, did you all sing Crick to sleep last night?"

He gave a snort of laughter. "No, but Ridd sang *me* to sleep, then he sang himself to sleep. Crick was still bouncing around the tent when Ridd conked out. This morning we found him dead to the world on top of his sleeping bag, though, so I guess he eventually put himself to bed."

"He could have gotten out of that tent and gone wandering off in the woods!" Every single story I'd ever read about children lost in forests scrolled through my memory.

"He's fine, Little Bit. He's too scared of snakes to wander far. Mighty dainty about some things, too. First time Ridd sent him behind a tree to use the bathroom, he came stomping back saying, 'Daddy, there's no bathroom *behind* that tree.' We've had a time convincing him it's okay to use the ground."

"And when you get home Martha will have a hard time convincing him to use anything else," I predicted.

"You doing all right down there?"

"Just fine. Keeping busy, as usual."

"Anybody coming by wanting a beagle pup?"

"No. We've still got two left plus the one you promised Crick."

"Not getting involved in looking for whoever killed that girl, are you?"

That was tricky. Joe Riddley can tell if I'm fibbing, even a hundred miles away. The best thing was to divert him. "I've been up to my ears in cotton fertilizer orders. You would leave when it's time for the last spreading. And did you order potassium? In last week's newspaper column I mentioned that sweet potatoes need it, and we've already had five customers come in for some. We're going to run out if you haven't ordered it."

"I ordered it. Ought to be here Monday."

"That's great. Listen, I'm starving, so I need to go see what's in the fridge. You all have fun, now. I'm fine down here. Love you." I hung up quickly, then was immediately sorry. The house felt very big and lonely without Joe Riddley. I might fetch Lulu in later.

While I ate scrambled eggs and toast, something hit me: this was Friday. What better time to visit the Temple of Inner Peace than this very evening, when all the people who'd been there last Friday were most likely to be there again?

> Can a mortal be more righteous than
> God? Can a man be more pure than
> his Maker? *Job 4:17*

Eleven

Deciding what to wear was a bit of a problem. I had no idea how an inquirer at a Temple of Inner Peace ought to dress. Something long and flowing sounded right, but I didn't own anything long and flowing except a caftan for evenings when it was just me and Joe Riddley—black, patterned with bright flowers. I could see the *Statesman* gossip column next week if I wore that out of the house. So, much as I hated the notion of getting dressed again, I put on a denim skirt and flowered blouse.

As I pulled up panty hose and slid my feet into pumps, it occurred to me that I wasn't the least bit crazy about going down there alone. Our town used to be safe at night, especially for the wife of a magistrate, but with a murderer loose . . .

I tried calling Martha, then remembered it was the evening for her diet meeting.

I considered calling Walker, but suspected he'd have a band practice. Besides, I was a little antsy about calling him after I'd been so meddlesome the night before.

Who else? I know practically everybody in town, but I couldn't think of a single other soul I wanted to invite along. Some people would be scandalized. The others would at least want to know why we were going. I didn't want to tell them.

For the second time that evening I thought of Maniac. Surely he and Dr. Holder had finished doing whatever they were going to do with that cannon barrel. Hadn't Maniac said he wanted to know what went on down there? I headed for the phone.

"Did you get the barrel moved out of his kitchen?" I asked when he answered.

"Oh, *sure*! We just put it on a wheelbarrow and dumped it off the back porch. I'll go by tomorrow with one of the men from the *store* and take it to the *museum*. I can't thank you *enough* for telling him I might *want* it. When I get it cleaned and *polished,* it's going to look *wonderful* on the front lawn. I *think* I can even get . . ." I wasn't really listening, just waiting for him to run down so I could bring up the other thing.

"Maynard." I finally waded in mid-stream. "You were saying you wanted to know what goes on down at that Temple of Inner Peace? I wondered if you'd like to go there with me right now. They have an inquirer's service tonight, with refreshments afterwards."

For possibly the first time in his life, Maniac was speechless. I hurried on.

"I was by there yesterday and picked up a brochure on yoga classes, but before I register, I need to know what sorts of things they teach. You know?"

I hate it when people throw in "you know?" as a way of soliciting agreement when I don't know enough to know if I agree or not. However, I've observed that most people go ahead and agree based on whatever they *think* the other person means. It makes for some very general discussions. This one was no exception.

"You can't be too *careful*, Miss MacLaren," he agreed. "You don't want to get *into* something you wish you *hadn't* or can't get *out* of."

"That's right, Maynard. And with Joe Riddley and Ridd out of town, and Walker rehearsing with his band, well, I wondered if you'd be free to go with me. Pretty soon," I added in case he was still sitting around sooty.

"*Sure. I guess* I could. Let me check with Daddy to see if he *needs* me." In a minute he was back, sounding happy as a bullfrog. "*Sure*, Miss MacLaren. Give me ten minutes, and I'll be down to pick you *up*."

I agreed gladly. His new Saturn would add a sporty feel to an already adventurous evening.

It was nearly eight when we got there. I'd hoped to tiptoe in unseen, but I'd forgotten the chimes above the door. They pealed merrily as we entered. We froze, mortified, while everybody in Marybelle Taylor's living room looked our way.

The room was half-full of people sitting cross-legged on the white carpet, listening to a music group and breathing incense so strong I nearly changed my mind and went home. I was charmed to see Selena playing a long wooden flute. She looked very pretty in a floor-length green dress with wide flowing sleeves. Her red curls lay loose on her shoulders.

A young man—thin almost to the point of emaciation, with a long pale face under a shock of dark straight hair—plucked a dulcimer of light wood. A stocky boy with blonde hair in his eyes gently patted the bongo drums. Selena nodded to me, but didn't miss a note.

The inquirers were mostly women, and all ages. Seeing a slew of high school girls, I wondered if their mothers knew where they were.

I knew most of the older women, of course. They looked away as soon as they recognized me, maybe embarrassed to be caught there. Then they sneaked quick peeks back with tentative smiles of the "I didn't know we had so much in common" variety.

Of course, I may have misinterpreted. They may have been admiring Miss Millie, who perched on my head with her red peony bobbing. I had considered adding sun glasses to complete my disguise, but decided against it. For one thing, you can't disguise yourself when you grew up in a town. For another, I didn't want to hear Joe Riddley laugh his head off when he heard I'd been traipsing around in sunglasses and a Caribbean hat.

Not everybody was looking at me. Most of the young women were eying Maniac, who looked particularly good in navy slacks and a sort of overblouse in creamy linen with large gathered sleeves. His cheeks were pink— whether from embarrassment or from the earlier labor of moving the cannon barrel, I didn't know—and his shoulders filled out his shirt very nicely. Standing behind him, I felt like he was a grown man I scarcely knew.

That was an unsettling idea, considering I'd brought him along for protection.

One of the young men produced a padded folding chair from somewhere, set it against one side wall, and motioned us inside. As we tiptoed in, I saw Lorine Duckworth at the back. She looked as startled to see me as I was to see her.

I was mighty glad to have a chair. Maniac settled easily at my feet, legs drawn up and arms clasped around his knees. Oh, to be that young and flexible again! Maybe I *ought* to consider yoga—or at least bending exercises.

The young man handed us a sheet of pink paper, but I'd forgotten to bring my reading glasses. If that was a bulletin, I'd have to follow the others.

Across the room Selena, eyes closed, was swaying in time to her music. I caught Maniac looking in her direction several times with a puzzled wrinkle on his brow.

After a few minutes to settle in, I began to listen to the music—a kind of wail with a soft beat beneath it. The dulcimer player wasn't as good as Selena, so he let her have the melody and merely played an occasional harmony. Pretty, I thought at the time. After ten minutes I was wishing they'd either stop or come up with a catchier tune. I also wondered why Selena didn't faint from lack of air. That was a long time to play a flute.

It was a long time to sit still, too. My legs were growing stiff from sitting without my feet fully touching the floor. In a perfect world, chair legs and seats would adjust to short, medium, and tall. Out of the corner of my eye I saw Lorine, who'd been there longer, tiptoe out—probably to the powder room. I considered joining her, but just then they finally stopped playing. The anemic-looking man put down the dulcimer, picked up a guitar, and announced, "Let us sing praises to the universe."

Unlike his awkward playing on the dulcimer, his guitar chords were confident and strong. The group clambered to its feet, holding its pink papers. Obediently I stood too, creaky and glad to stretch my legs. I couldn't sing, of course, since I couldn't read the words, but I hummed easily along. The tune seemed vaguely familiar.

Gradually, snatches of words came to me. Not the words this group was singing but words I remembered ...

Memory is a funny thing. Suddenly I wasn't over sixty, I was barely six and spending a hot July week with my grandparents down in the country. My great-aunt Amalia took me every night to a tent meeting where the preacher handled snakes and women jumped up and down yelling during prayers. We sang one song over and over each night as people went down the sawdust aisle for the preacher to touch them on the forehead. When Aunt Amalia went down, I climbed up on the pew to see over the heads of the other grown-ups. When the preacher touched Aunt Amalia, she fell straight back in a sort of trance.

I watched wide-eyed for four nights, until I made the mistake of describing all those wonders to my grandmother. The next evening I sat in boredom in Grandmama's parlor, listening to Granddaddy snore and rebelliously humming the altar call song to myself.

Who'd have expected to find that old tent meeting tune in the Temple of Inner Peace?

When the song finished, the guitar continued to strum softly. I heard a soft clatter behind me and turned slightly to see the goswami coming through a beaded curtain from Marybelle's butler's pantry. Tonight he wore a long flowing white robe with purple bands around the sleeves. His beard was neatly brushed over his chest.

He walked through the crowd with his eyes nearly shut, his arms aloft in blessing. Half-way into the room he started to hum one note. Those who knew what was going on also started to hum. Catching on, I hummed too. We sounded like a power station revving up. When the group started to sway, I swayed with them—until I realized I had no idea what we were doing. For all I knew, I was standing there worshipping a foreign god. I hushed, pressing my lips together to rid them of the tingle that remained.

Beside me, Maniac stood with his head bent. I leaned toward him, concerned that he might be feeling ill, for incense made the room close in spite of the air conditioning. Instead, he was softly reciting an Episcopal service. If there was darkness to hold at bay in Marybelle's former living room, Maniac was working on it.

Up at the podium the goswami abruptly dropped his arms and smiled. Between his soft beard and mustache, his teeth were tiny and creamy white, like pearls. The humming stopped. The guitar kept on for a measure or two then dwindled off, as if the musician hadn't expected to quit quite so soon. People folded themselves back to their seats on the floor. I felt very conspicuous, sitting there like a queen above all those heads and shoulders.

The goswami let the silence stretch like a rubber band while he looked slowly around the room. If he recognized me, he gave no sign. When he had our full attention, he spoke in a deep, compelling voice. "Tonight we speak of the place of the teacher in your lives. The teacher who walks in the shadow of the temple gives you his wisdom, his faith, and his lovingness."

Maniac stirred at my feet and gave his head a quick, impatient shake, but if the goswami saw, he ignored it. Warming up and finding his cadence, he preached long enough for my feet to get prickles and my back a crick. From the way the crowd was nodding you'd have thought he was saying something profound. I was disappointed, though. I hadn't expected a message I'd agree with, but I'd at least expected meat. This was nothing but thin vegetable soup of feel-good platitudes. "The highest perfection of human life is to know peace"? Sounded like couch potato theology to me. "The most important thing in life is to seek knowledge"? I'd known kids like that. Thirty-five and still in graduate school.

Yet the inquirers sat as rapt as coonhounds at a possum tree. I thought of something G. K. Chesterton once said: that when people cease to believe in God, they don't believe in nothing, they believe in anything. The Temple of Inner Peace looked like a good example.

It maybe also proved how hungry people are for oases of calm in this frantic world—and to be loved. The goswami exuded peace and calm, and the whole time he spoke his dark liquid gaze moved from person to person pleading, "I care for you. Won't you care for me?"

At last he stopped. I thought the service was over until Lorine murmured in the back, "What the teacher says, we must remember. What the teacher advises us to forget, we must forget." Trust her to want the last word, even there.

The goswami gave her an approving nod. "What the teacher says to forget, you must forget," he repeated.

His voice changed, like a preacher switching from the sermon to the announcements. "Last week one of our number was translated into a higher plane. We speak of her no more. Others may feel sorrow and wonder why—" Selena started to nod, then checked herself as the goswami continued, "—but *we* do not. We accept the will of the Creator. The Creator knows best." Again he stopped.

Selena nodded twice, as if to deny nodding before, then surreptitiously pulled out a tissue and wiped her eyes, as if she'd gotten dust in them.

She has departed. We remember her no more. The words flitted through my thoughts like butterflies. *I will remember,* I fiercely winged resolve his way.

His eyes met mine and moved on. For the first time I noticed sweat beading his forehead and cheeks. He must be hot in that long robe over his clothes. He fumbled at the side of his robe, drew out a large handkerchief, dabbed his face, and stuffed it back.

As before, Lorine couldn't stand silence very long. "The world may discuss these matters, but we will not," she said fervently. I felt as irritated as I used to when she came to our Sunday school class and had to give all the answers. Several younger inquirers, however, murmured agreement, and what she'd said seemed to galvanize the goswami. He leaned forward and grasped the podium as if he would be propelled out among us if he didn't hang on for dear life.

"The world *loves* fruitless discussions about the past. Do not be drawn into those discussions. Do not speak of this *at all*. I, your teacher, *command* you!" He lightly pounded the podium. Several inquirers jumped. Most exchanged puzzled looks.

Finally he spoke again, his voice lowered to a husky warning. "If you disobey, I am no longer your teacher."

When I looked from him to the others, I saw nervous, uncertain nods.

The goswami let the silence swell, then said gently, "I love you, my children. I want the best for you. This has come to test our commitment to seeking peace. Where do we find peace? In the present. The present is all that matters. What has come and gone is no more. Hear me, your teacher. Never look back. Sink into the peace within you and nurture it, until it controls your every thought and desire. That is the task I set myself, it is the task I set you. That which is past is in the hands of the Creator. We do not concern ourselves with it."

I concern myself with her, I argued fiercely in silence.

His eyes met mine and looked away. "Peace is what matters. Let peace direct your thoughts."

I shifted my gaze to Selena. She looked as rapt as if the goswami were the angel Gabriel. At my feet, Maniac was reciting the Lord's Prayer under his breath.

To my relief, I heard those words so dear to many congregations: "As we close . . ."

"Shut your eyes and feel this present moment," the goswami instructed. "Feel yourself in your own body. Feel your blood rushing through your veins, the incense working its way into your lungs. Feel yourself at one with your surroundings. One with what is beneath you, what is around you. Know the present moment. Seek peace within."

He stopped. The musicians picked up their instruments and began to play softly. He remained at the podium, eyes closed, swaying. Again I was reminded of those plump children's toys weighted at the bottom.

I pretended to close my eyes, but really only lowered the lids a bit. I had no intention of feeling myself at one with a folding chair.

Instead, I wondered if he'd added that last bit just because he saw me sitting there—decided to warn his disciples before I could talk to them.

That thought was followed by another: Was he warning them not to talk because he *knew* who killed Amanda Kent?

My eyes have seen all this, my ears
have heard and understood it. What
you know, I also know. I am not
inferior to you. *Job 13:1–2*

Twelve

Just when I thought I couldn't sit there one second
longer, the goswami made a motion with one hand and
the man with the guitar began a lively tune. Selena
picked up the melody on her flute and the big boy with
floppy hair patted his bongos.

The goswami bowed low, then stood and curved his
hands so his thumbs made o's with his first two fingers.
The light was such that he made faint rabbits on the wall.

"Peace be with you," he intoned.

Those on the floor bowed toward him. "And with
you."

Without another word he strode into Marybelle's
butler's pantry, followed by a gentle clatter of beads. Two
women next to the archway got up and moved toward the
dining room. Soon we heard the clink of cups and soft gurgle of liquid being poured.

As the musicians continued to play, people gradually climbed to their feet, stretched, and ambled toward the juice bar. Just like cows heading for the barn. I stood, too, got my knees working, and looked around for Lorine. She'd already left.

Hoping I could get some information in spite of the teacher's warnings, I waited until the crowd thinned, then got up and approached Selena. "You play beautifully," I told her.

She beamed. "Thanks. I am so glad to be able to use my music for something worthwhile. Until now, it's only been for my own pleasure."

"Your *pleasure* is worthwhile," Maniac spoke over my shoulder.

"This is *more* worthwhile." She fitted the flute into a maroon flannel bag.

"Why?" he challenged her. "*Why* should it be better *here* than anywhere *else?*"

"This is my friend and neighbor, Maynard Spence," I said, hoping to get them to quit picking at each other. Neither of them paid me any mind.

"Playing for worship is holier than just playing—*I* think," she added, as if suddenly aware that arguing wasn't likely to attract anyone seeking inner peace.

"*God* is in *any* good *music.*" Maniac lifted his chin and dared her to disagree.

"Children, children!" I felt like saying, but Selena—although flushed that deep pink that is the curse of angry redheads—didn't answer him again. Instead she turned to me. "Did you come about those yoga classes I told you about? I'm sure you'd find them beneficial."

"I got the information." I patted my pocketbook.

"Would you like some juice or something?" She waved toward the hall like a hostess. I couldn't help thinking how much more appropriate she looked as Marybelle's successor in that house than her leader.

There was a grace and poise about the tall gangly girl that told me she'd been at home in fine houses all her life.

"Yes, thank you," I said quickly, before Maniac could decline for us both. Selena lifted one side of her long skirt and led the way.

I ordered cranberry raspberry juice and Maniac got white grape, then Selena ushered us to a table. Once she'd gotten us settled, she hurried away to speak to other people. I was disappointed, but looked around for somebody else who might talk to me. At the moment, everybody was talking to somebody else. Not one soul even smiled our way. I made a mental note to be nicer to visitors at our next church coffee hour.

Maniac seemed to be brooding over his exchange with Selena. I saw him look her way several times, then look down morosely at his drink. Since he didn't seem inclined to talk, I listened in on nearby conversations. On my left, six high school girls had dragged chairs around a table for four. I expected to hear what young girls usually talk about before school starts—back-to-school sales, classes they planned to take or hoped they could get out of, and boys. Instead, those girls were gushing about the goswami's sermon.

". . . loved it when he said ignorance is something we need to be cleansed of."

"That is so true!"

I noticed them looking our way. Was their conversation for Maniac's benefit? No, for just then a girl at a table to my right said softly but urgently, "I know she's gone to a higher plane, Gideon, but I don't want to *forget* her!"

Intrigued, I turned to see a young blonde woman leaning earnestly toward the anemic-looking dulcimer player, who sat sipping orange juice. That's who the high schoolers were trying to impress. I could see why, too. With that dead white face, fall of dark brown hair over his high forehead, and dark, brooding eyes beneath delicate brows, he could make any young girl's heart flutter.

He caught me looking at him. Two things came together for me in an instant: first, Gideon Levy was the name on the other mailbox at the Hedricks' garage apartments. This must be the neighbor with whom Amanda Kent had played cards, the one Martha had said was out of town and coming back today. Second, the dulcimer he'd been playing looked like the one I'd seen on Amanda's bookshelf the day before.

My suspicion about the dulcimer was confirmed when the girl said, a bit desperately, "All during the music tonight I kept thinking Mandy was in the back somewhere and would come out to play. Wasn't it hard to play her instrument?"

He hesitated, then nodded. "A little. But I try to control those thoughts. We must seek peace." He laid one hand over hers and murmured gently, "Be at peace. Be at peace."

I examined him more closely. He had that slightly seedy look of a single man who lives alone, eats poorly, and doesn't get enough sun. If he was a murderer or a thief, he was a bold one. He caught me looking at him again and stared back until I shifted my gaze.

Why, I wondered, should a young Jewish man be leading singing in a Temple of Inner Peace? For that matter, why should Selena Jones—who looked Irish—be there? Not to mention a WASP grandmother in a Caribbean hat.

The girl beside him lowered her voice, but still protested. "It's not that simple. I keep thinking of things I want to ask Mandy. She was leading me toward the light. Now—"

He squeezed her hand. "Someone else will lead you toward the light. You heard what the teacher said—think about the present, not the past. That's the only way to peace. Take deep breaths and exhale the holy word. Serenity. Serenity. Serenity."

To the cadence of his voice she breathed and murmured obediently, "Serenity. Serenity. Serenity." They

118

stood and moved into the hall, still chanting. The girls at the next table leaned back in their chairs and started talking about sales, classes, and boys.

Maniac spoke beside me. "Sorry to be so *quiet*, Miss MacLaren. I was thinking Miss Marybelle would have a *fit* if she knew how her house is being *used*."

"She probably would," I agreed, "but her cousins in Atlanta didn't want to live here, so they sold it to the first person who wanted it."

"I wish I'd *known* it was for sale." He glared at the high crown molding and long thin windows with their original glass, as if they should have notified him. "I'd have bought it in a *minute*."

"Now how could you buy a place like this?"

He looked down at his drink and flushed.

I was sorry for having pointed out how young he was, just starting out in life, so I added consolingly, "Besides, you were living in New York, remember?"

He sighed. "*I* know. I should have come home *sooner*. But Daddy didn't tell me Miss Marybelle had *died*."

I wasn't paying much attention to Maniac's complaints. Over Maniac's shoulder I saw the goswami plod out from Marybelle's kitchen. He now wore the black pants, white shirt, chains, and sandals he'd worn on my first visit. I wondered if that was his clerical uniform. He looked not unlike a rotund priest or rabbi.

He went to the bar, turned his back to us, and ordered something to drink, then spoke to Selena. She looked at us quickly, then away.

"Your daddy probably didn't tell you when a lot of people died," I said absently, wondering what the goswami had told Selena about us. "He wouldn't think it would matter unless they were somebody important to you."

"But this *was* important," he insisted, looking hungrily at Marybelle's carved mantelpiece. "I'd have *bought this house in a minute!*"

I'd had about as much of his bellyaching as I could take. "How could you have bought this house? Your daddy wouldn't let you sell the farm—or the store."

He hesitated, then shrugged. "I wouldn't have *had* to." He tapped his fingers on the table and asked, "Can you keep a secret?"

I nodded reluctantly. I don't like knowing other people's secrets.

"Do you remember Mama's brother Jimmy? The one who moved to Memphis?" I nodded again, although it had been a long time since I'd thought of Jimmy. He'd been the sharpest, if not the smartest, boy in my class, always waving his hand in the teacher's face to be called on. He'd also been treasurer of any club he joined.

"*Well,*" Maniac said, finishing his drink in one gulp and setting the glass down on the table with a thump, "Uncle Jimmy owned a chain of *jewelry stores*. He never married, and he died two years ago. Same heart defect that killed Mama—their whole family had it. *Anyway*—please don't let it get *around*, Miss MacLaren—but when he *died*, he left *everything to me*." He looked around the dining room regretfully. "I could have bought this house without any *trouble*. I just didn't know it was for *sale*."

Maniac was full of surprises. I looked at him with new respect—not because I was drinking juice with a plutocrat, but because he'd been home six months now and kept a major secret in Hopemore. Except for his new green Saturn, I hadn't seen a single sign that Maniac had money. But now that I thought about it . . .

"Maynard, did you buy the historical museum?"

He shook his head and a little smile flickered at the corner of his mouth. "No, ma'am, the *county* owns the museum. But I sent them a little anonymous *donation* to *fix it up*—in Uncle Jimmy's name—on condition that they hire me part-time."

I laughed out loud. Our staid county council thought they were helping out poor Maniac, when in reality Maniac was helping us all. Remember how I said Maniac wouldn't recognize a joke if it rose up and bit him? He probably laughed himself to sleep every night.

He wasn't laughing right now, though. He sighed and propped one cheek on his hand. "I *always* wanted to live in this house, ever since *high* school. I used to help Miss Marybelle keep her garden—did you know there's a *wonderful* little walled garden in the back?"

For a minute I was a child again, one of five little girls invited to Marybelle's tenth birthday party. Marybelle loved *The Secret Garden*, so for her birthday that year her daddy hired a mason to build an eight-foot brick wall around part of their big back yard, a space perhaps twenty feet square. He also put a blue door in one side wall, invisible from the house and too tall for even grownups to see over. After Marybelle opened her other presents, he solemnly led us out to the blue door and gave her a shiny key. She unlocked the door and led us inside for cake and ice cream. At that time it was only walled-in grass. Marybelle—and, for a time, her friends—spent happy hours digging and planting that little garden. It eventually was so spectacular that it was featured twice in *Southern Living*.

I didn't tell Maniac any of that. What I said was, "Yes, I knew. We used to have Garden Club board meetings out there when the weather was nice."

"It truly is one of the *treasures* of *Hopemore*," he said regretfully.

"Of which there aren't many," I added. I was wondering how to shake him out of his gloomy mood when a voice spoke above us.

"Got everything you need?" As Selena bent nearly double to address me, her wide sleeve accidentally brushed Maniac's arm. He drew it back like a rattler had bit him, but she ignored him completely.

I smiled up at her. "We sure do, except good company. Won't you join us?"

She took a chair and arranged her skirt in a feminine manner I didn't know her generation practiced. "Did you enjoy the service?"

I murmured something polite, but Maniac glared and said sarcastically, "I never knew worship was *supposed* to be *fun and games*."

Again she flushed. "You know what I mean. Did you find inner peace?"

She looked from one of us to the other and sounded so earnest, so eager that we should. I wanted to say, "Oh, yes, honey—I felt more inner peace than ever before in my life," but I knew I'd never pull it off. I took the coward's way out and had a fit of coughing.

Maniac didn't bother to pretend. He shook his head. "Not that I *noticed*. Do you want something to *drink*?"

She shook her head. "No thank you. I'm fine." The way they were so icily polite to each other, you'd have thought they were in a royal court, not a juice bar.

I leaned forward and asked softly, "Selena, was Amanda Kent here last Friday night? Did she pour juice and stay until the juice bar closed?"

She caught a quick breath and drew slightly away from me. "We mustn't talk about that. You heard what the teacher said—"

"I'm not talking about Amanda dying, honey, I'm asking about her life. I saw from the schedule that she was supposed to serve all month. Did she serve last week? Wasn't she supposed to be playing with you all and pouring juice this very night?" I felt like I'd been taking mean pills, but I wanted to shock her into talking.

I didn't succeed. Selena darted one quick look toward the bar, then, "It is not the will of the creator that we dwell on the past. That is not the way to peace."

"It's not *God*, but your *teacher*, who wants your friend forgotten," Maniac said bluntly.

Selena gave him a shocked look. "Please don't speak of Mandy again!"

I expected her to excuse herself and leave, but she didn't. She just sat there looking miserable. I wondered if the goswami had told her to stick to us to keep us from talking to anybody else. Obviously we weren't going to get anything from her.

"*I* won't speak of her again," Maniac assured her. "She was the rudest woman I ever *met*. *I* fixed her TV and took it back, and she practically *shoved* me out the *door*."

The whites of Selena's eyes had turned pink and misty. "You don't understand," she said in a low, furious voice.

"I certainly *don't*," he agreed. He shoved his chair back. "Miss *MacLaren*, we ought to be *going*. I need to check on *Daddy*. I don't like *leaving* him this *long*." He strode from the table and waited for me in the hall, jingling the keys in his pocket.

I turned to Selena. "I'm sorry if he's upset you, honey."

"Oh, he hasn't upset me." Her voice was husky but she gave an airy little wave. "I am learning to rise above the ugly passions of this world. But I hope he finds truth and inner peace. Otherwise he'll die young of a bad heart."

Considering that bad hearts ran on both sides of Maniac's family, it was entirely possible. Instead of saying so, I gathered up my pocketbook. "I need to get back, too, to check on our pups. I forgot to feed and water them tonight."

Selena's face brightened. "You have puppies? What kind?"

"Beagles. Just ready to be taken from their mother."

"Oh! We had a beagle when I was growing up. Are you selling them?"

"Would they let you keep one where you live?" I didn't want some landlord blaming me for her bringing home a dog.

"Sure. I've bought a little mobile home just out of town. I even have a fenced back yard. Could I come see them? How much do you want for them?"

I named a price a good bit lower than Joe Riddley was asking. I always do when I think somebody will give a pup an especially good home. "Why don't you come out tomorrow before three thirty?" I suggested. "I have to leave then for the beauty parlor."

"Don't sell them all before I get there," she begged.

I joined Maniac in the foyer and we started for the door. A basket sat on a little table that hadn't been there earlier. It held a lot of dollar bills, a few fives, and one ten. Maniac pulled out another ten and dropped it in. "To help keep *up* the place," he muttered as those little chimes pealed behind us.

He was still glowering as held the car door for me. I hurried to get in before it filled with gnats, apologizing for being longer with Selena than I'd intended. "She might be interested in one of Lulu's pups. She's coming by tomorrow evening to look them over. She used to have a beagle when she was little."

I thought that might make him smile, but it didn't. He went around to his side without a word, got in, and slammed the door. I gave him a quick frown. I didn't want to ride home in a confined space alone with an angry man.

Alone with an angry man.

Amanda Kent had certainly been alone with an angry man last week about this time.

Who would she have let in at that hour? And why?

You will be secure, because there is
hope; you will look about you and
take your rest in safety. You will
lie down, with no one to make
you afraid. *Job 11:18–19*

Thirteen

Although the halogen security light was blazing
away in our back yard, the shadows looked darker than
usual. I asked Maniac to come with me to the pen while
I fed the pups. He picked up the friskier of the two males
and held it out to the light. "What a *beauty*! If *I* had you,
that's what I'd *call* you—*Beauty.*"

"Want him?" I offered.

He shook his head regretfully. "I don't think Daddy's
up to the *bother* of a puppy yet. But he sure is great." He
set the puppy down and watched it toddle toward its food.

"I'll go in and look under all your *beds,*" he offered.

I waved him away. "I'll be fine once I get inside."

I'd been thinking so much about Amanda Kent all the
way home that by now even Maniac looked like a possible
murderer. Before he could insist, I heard the phone inside.

"Phone's ringing. Goodnight." I gave Maniac a quick wave and hurried in.

"Where the dickens have you been?"

My knees went weak with fear. "What's the matter, Joe Riddley? Is Crick hurt? Are *you* hurt?"

"Hurt that you asked about me after your precious grandson, but no, Little Bit, we're all fine. Ridd's got Crick down by the lake trying to catch fireflies. Where have you been? I've been trying to reach you for nearly two hours. Martha's not home, either."

"Martha's at her diet meeting, and I went somewhere with Maniac."

"Maniac again? Woman, if you're leaving me for somebody else, at least pick somebody I can be proud of."

"There's more to Maniac than you know, honey, but you don't have to worry. He spent the evening talking to a tall red-head."

"Maniac and a red-head? That'll be the day."

"You wait. I'll tell you about it when you get home. But what's the matter? Why are you calling again?"

"Nothing's the matter. I'm sitting here all by myself near the campfire, feeding the mosquitoes and wondering where my wife's off to. Have you been trying to chase down the person who killed that girl?"

He caught me off-guard. "Not exactly."

I heard him slap his thigh. "Ridd was right! Over supper, he asked if you agreed not to poke around in that while we're gone. That's when I realized you never answered my question. Slick, Little Bit. But Ridd warned me, 'She'll do it, Daddy. You know she will.' So I had to call back. There's a killer out there. You sit tight until I get home."

"I'm sitting as tight as I know how, and I haven't done a thing you need worry about. But Walker's real worried, honey. Charlie Muggins has pulled Luke in two or three times asking him more questions, and from something Lorine said this afternoon, I'm afraid Charlie wants to get back at Luke for helping his wife leave."

"Charlie's meaner than a junkyard dog, but he can't arrest a man just because he's mad at him. He'll need some evidence."

"Or another suspect."

"Either one, it's his job, not yours. Now where was it you and Maniac went tonight?"

When I told him, he snorted. "Did you find inner peace?"

"No. I wouldn't become one with my folding chair." I knew he'd appreciate that story, and he did. "I can't just sit around here missing you," I finished, sweetening up the pot.

"Why don't you pack your jeans and come join us? Close the store tomorrow. Ridd and Crick could fish from shore and we could go out in the boat."

No wonder he was missing me. Before, it had always been Joe Riddley and his boys. Now he was the grand-daddy and Ridd and Crick were the team. But the days when I would abandon a nice soft bed for an air mattress on the ground are over.

"No thanks, honey, but maybe we ought to rent a cabin in one of the state parks when it gets cooler. I could do with a week in the woods alone with you."

"Me, too."

As he was about to hang up, he warned again, "Don't go poking around that murder while we're gone. Isaac James won't let Charlie get totally out of line."

"Ike's gone up to Tennessee this weekend, visiting his sister," I informed him, "but all I plan to do tomorrow is work, close early, spend an hour in the pool, and get beautiful for the Garden Club buffet."

"You be sure to lock up real good for that, now," he reminded me—as if I needed it, with a murderer loose in town. "We don't want somebody stealing the TV."

"It's antiques they're stealing, honey. We don't have anything they'd want. But I'll put Lulu inside while I'm gone. And that reminds me, somebody's coming tomorrow to look at the pups."

"Don't give away Crick's. You know which one it is?"

"Of course. The female. I'll take her in the house before the buyer comes."

He paused a minute, then added casually, "This buyer isn't mixed up with the murder, I don't reckon."

Oh, that man knows me well!

"She was Amanda Kent's friend," I admitted, "but she's just coming to look at a pup." It was time to take charge of this conversation before he started nagging me again. "Now you all be careful, Joe Riddley. Don't let Crick too near the water without a grownup. You know how fearless he is. And . . ."

As I'd hoped, that was enough to make him want to hang up. "We're taking good care of Crick, Little Bit. You take care of yourself until I get home. You hear me?"

"I hear you, honey."

I hung up and went to bed with a smile, thinking drowsily, "I do love that man!"

That's a pleasant way to fall asleep.

Fourteen

I thought about Gideon Levy all Saturday morning. Why hadn't he heard Amanda Kent being killed and called the police? The walls between their apartments were probably no more than studs, Sheetrock and paint. Had he, perhaps, killed her himself?

When the courthouse clock chimed eleven and I hadn't had a single customer, I hung the Closed sign on the door and drove down to the Hedrick house. I'm not dumb enough to call on a possible murderer without leaving a trail, though. I propped a big note on my desk saying where I'd gone and also left a message on both our house and our store answering machines. I hoped my biggest problem would be remembering to take those messages off before Joe Riddley got home and heard them.

As soon as Gideon came to the door, I knew I'd waked him up. His eyes were crusty in the corners, he had patchy overnight whiskers, and his hair had been combed with his fingers. He looked younger than he had the night before—no more than twenty, I figured, and skinny as a rail. He'd pulled on jeans but hadn't gotten around to a shirt. His ribs stuck out in a torso as white and hairless as marble. If he got violent, I definitely outweighed him.

As soon as he saw me, he clutched his fists to his bare chest. "Don't worry," I assured him. "I've seen lots of men without shirts. You aren't embarrassing me one bit." He looked kind of dazed, and I realized I hadn't bothered to introduce myself.

I spoke fast, because I didn't want to lose my nerve. "I'm MacLaren Yarbrough. I write a column for the Hopemore *Statesman,* and I saw you last night at the Temple of Inner Peace. Could I come in a minute to ask a few questions?" I'd decided to mention the *Statesman* because chances were good that even if he read the paper, he didn't read the lawn and garden column.

He stared at me like I was a puzzle he was trying hard to solve. His thinking seemed to be taking a lot of effort, but I didn't like to interrupt. Finally he brought out a question. "You related to Walker?"

"His mother." I was surprised, but only that he knew Walker, not that he'd made the connection. Our resemblance is more than coloring. One of his friends in sixth grade told me I looked just like Walker but with more hair.

Gideon continued to give me a drowsy unblinking stare. "Cool. I jam with Walker and Luke. Sometimes. On the guitar." His sentences came out in little chunks of information. He looked like he'd fall asleep again the minute I left.

"You know Luke, too?" I knew it was a dumb question, but I wanted to keep him talking long enough to wake up.

"Yeah. Went to school with my big brother. Crewed together, too, on—" He broke off and muttered, "I forgot. Not supposed to mention that."

I didn't know what it was Luke didn't want mentioned, but he'd given me the foot in the door I'd been needing. "It's partly because of Luke that I'm here. May I come in?" Without waiting for him to think up an answer, I stepped past him into the big dim room.

His blinds were down and a little air conditioner in the side window barely made a dent in the heat. The air was warm, stale, and full of a sweet incense that made me gag. The layout was Amanda Kent's reversed, and a curious combination of expensive and shabby. One corner was filled by a music system that I knew, from what Walker paid for his, had cost several thousand dollars. The television was a big thirty-nine inch. Gideon himself wore jeans that carried a designer label, and running shoes tossed by the door were the kind high school kids have been known to kill for. Yet the gray carpet was threadbare and the only other furnishings in the room were a daybed, an old Formica table with three chairs, an easel, and bright swirly canvasses everywhere. If you'd asked me to title them, I'd have called them Confused #1, Confused #2, Confused #3, and so on, but maybe they were good enough to keep Gideon in music equipment and expensive clothes. I had no idea.

I also had no idea how long I could stand the foggy air and that sticky sweet smell.

He pulled a blue ribbed spread over his bed, tossed a brown bolster against the wall, and motioned me to sit down. He'd had a mannerly upbringing, even if he did live like a hippy. As I'd expected, the bed was still warm.

He dragged a chair over—a cheap kitchen chair with a green vinyl seat and a green vinyl pad for the back—and straddled it, resting his chin on the back and wiggling his bare toes on the worn gray rug. As sleepy as he looked, his toes and fingers were in constant motion, drumming, drumming, drumming. I could see him trying to bring his thoughts together. Finally he gave his head a little shake. "You were at the temple last night. Are you an inquirer?"

Was I? By then I wasn't sure of anything. I needed fresh air worse than I needed to be polite. "Honey, could we open a window? I'm feeling a tad peculiar." Without waiting for permission I went over to the front and opened one. After a deep breath I felt stable enough to return to the daybed. I sat and down and admitted, "I'm actually inquiring into the death of your neighbor, Amanda Kent."

His chair reared back on two legs like a horse, the green vinyl pad between me and his bare chest. "You the police?"

"No, a reporter. Remember?" I aimed for what I hoped was a crisp interview style. "I understand you knew Miss Kent pretty well. Played cards together. So you and she were probably in and out of each other's places all the time?"

He shook his head again, as if trying to clear it. "Uh, no. I mean, sure we played cards. But not here. Mandy didn't go for that. We played on the table out under the tree." I saw a picnic table under a maple.

"And you were both on the music team down at the temple?"

My last word reminded him. "You heard the teacher last night. We shouldn't speak of Mandy any more. The present is what matters. That's the way to find peace." Gideon hadn't found it so far. His fingers and toes still drummed to a rapid tune only he could hear.

"The way to find peace is to find out who killed Miss Kent."

He ducked his head like a tortoise retreating into its shell, tucked one hand under each armpit, and stared stubbornly across the room with stormy dark eyes.

I backpedaled. "Okay, let's don't talk about Amanda. Let's talk about you."

He thought about it a minute, then nodded. "That's cool." He took his hands from his armpits and drummed on the high back of his chair.

"Tell me about last Saturday. I understand from Mr. Ronald Duckworth that you and he found the body."

He leaped to his feet, graceful as a bobcat and about that friendly. "I told you, I'm not talking about Mandy! You want to talk about her, you go somewhere else." He strode to the refrigerator, brought out a can of Co-cola, popped the top like he was breaking my neck, held it high and poured it into his mouth—all with his back toward me.

I spoke to that achingly slender white back. "Luke's in trouble, Gideon. The police think he killed Miss Kent."

He shook his head. "No way. Luke wouldn't kill anybody."

"Yes way." I used little Crick's expression without thinking. "He'll probably be arrested if his friends don't help him. That's really why I'm here. Could you at least tell me what happened to *you* last Saturday? When Amanda Kent was found? It might help Luke."

He thought about it while he finished his Co-cola, crushed the can, and tossed it in an overflowing cardboard box of trash. Finally he spoke as he came back to his chair, lithe as a panther. Or was I seeing animals because of whatever was in the air? I took a deep breath, which was a mistake. My head was feeling distinctly odd.

Gideon seemed to speak from a distance. ". . . dude woke me up . . . was looking for Mandy . . . wife was worried about her, you know? . . . knocked but she hadn't . . . had I seen her. I said no . . . had a ladder, so could we look in her windows . . ."

Window. I needed the window. I got to my feet and walked (weaved would be more accurate) to the open window and took deep breaths of fresh hot air. Behind me, Gideon hadn't stopped talking. " . . . odd. I mean, why not call the manager? She lives in the house up front. But he said all I had to do was hold the ladder. He climbed up real easy, though he's no spring chicken" (I guessed that made me a winter hen) "and peered in the window—"

"Which window was that?" I interrupted, taking another deep breath.

"The side one. His truck was blocking her front ones."

I remembered her apartment and the bookshelf divider. "What could he see?" It was an odd conversation, me talking through the open window and Gideon only a voice behind me. Maybe it made it easier on both of us not to be eye-to-eye.

"Nothing. Not Mandy, anyway. She's got this shelf in the middle of the room that he couldn't see past. Anyway, I asked when he came down, 'What did you see, man?' He said, 'Nothing, but her lights are on.' I told him that was no big deal, these places are dim in the morning because of all the big trees. But he said he needed to call his wife, she said to call her right away if he saw anything odd. Too weird. I mean, if he thought something was wrong, why call his wife?"

"Yeah," I agreed. "Why not call 911?"

"I guess he didn't think it was that weird." His voice dropped to a mutter. "I didn't think anything was the matter, either. I figured she was sleeping late. She worked nights, so she slept a lot in the daytime."

"What happened next?"

"He came up here to call. Told his wife the lights were on. I think she must have told him to stick around, because I'd made myself some coffee by then and he said it sure smelled good—hinting like. I offered him a cup, and before we were done a rescue truck came tearing up the drive. We went down and he told the guys what he'd seen. They went up and knocked, then they broke down Mandy's door." He stopped abruptly.

I turned in time to see him rub one hand across his eyes, as if trying to erase the memory. "What did you do?"

"I went up after them. If something had happened to Mandy, I wanted to know."

"Was Ronald Duckworth with you?"

"No, he stayed down on the bottom step. I forgot all about him after we found . . ." Gideon trailed off. "Man." He pressed a hand to his mouth. "That was—it was—" He started shaking.

I decided then and there he hadn't killed her. He wasn't awake enough to fake those shakes. "Oh, honey, I'm so sorry."

He shook his head and swallowed convulsively. "It's okay. I'll be okay." He took a deep strangled breath and murmured softly as he exhaled, "Serenity. Serenity. Serenity." From the look in his eyes, though, it wasn't enough. That sight would haunt him for years.

Suddenly he blinked and gave me a wide-eyed stare. "I just remembered something else. The first thing that dude asked when he woke me up? Before he even asked about Mandy, he asked if I'd heard anything next door the night before. Wasn't that weird?"

I held my breath. "*Did* you?"

He started to shake his head, but his eyes wouldn't meet mine.

"Did you?" I repeated.

He started to shake again. He shook so hard he held onto the back of his chair. "Don't make me think about that again! I'd found peace. Now it's going away."

"Gideon!" I used my most severe Mother Voice. "What did you hear?"

He fought for control, breathing deeply with his eyes still closed. "It doesn't matter." He seemed to be arguing more with himself than with me. "She's passed to a higher plane."

"We'll all be passing to a higher plane if that murderer isn't caught. *What did you hear?*"

When he opened his eyes, they were wet with tears. His words fell out in choppy, breathless sentences that must have been corked all week. "Probably the whole thing. I was up late. Watching TV. My big brother moved to Israel last winter. Palestinians attacked his town that day. I thought maybe I'd see something on CNN."

"Oh, honey! Did you?" Murder, at the moment, seemed less urgent than his personal terrors.

"Nannh. Nothing but newscasters airing their own opinions." He stopped and stared into space as if watching his own private TV viewing. I waited without moving a muscle. Finally he roused and spoke in a monotone. "I was about to turn it off when I heard pounding next door. Loud. Real loud. So loud I banged on the wall." He gestured limply toward a bare space beside his bed, six inches from Amanda's bed through the thin wall.

"What time was that?"

"Twelve thirty? One o'clock? When I banged, it stopped. I heard a few soft sounds, but nothing like that again."

"You didn't go see what it was?"

He shook his head. "I thought she was doing exercises." Tears spilled over his eyes and onto his pale cheeks. "I heard it all, and I didn't do a thing." He lowered his dark head to his folded arms and sobbed.

Easy words of comfort wouldn't do any good. I let him cry it out. When he got up and splashed cold water on his face, I asked, "Have you told that to the police?"

"Police?" His eyes were drenched with tears, but his expression was blank. "They never talked to me. They got all busy"—he gestured with both hands, lost for words—"so I came on back over here. Then the teacher called and said he wanted to fix up some upstairs rooms for private retreats—put in partitions to divide them, you know?" He pointed to the paintings lying around the room and wiped his eyes on a grubby dishtowel. "I'm really an artist, see? But I don't sell much yet, so, like, I do odd jobs to pay the bills. Carpentry, painting, things like that. He said if I'd come over and work all week, he'd give me meals and a room to sleep in, and I could meditate with him during the evening. That really helped. I felt real peaceful by last night, but now . . ."

What he meant was, now a nosy old woman had come and brought it all back. He was kind enough not to say it.

Later I'd fret about Marybelle's lovely bedrooms being chopped into little cells. For now, I was concentrating on getting outside before that incense got me. At the door I verified what I thought I'd heard. "You stayed at the temple all week and the police never knew you were there?"

"I guess not. They haven't asked me anything."

I left him at the top of his stairs, staring after me with anguished eyes.

I'd talk about all that with Joe Riddley when he got home. Right then I wanted to speed home and jump in our pool. Some people have a prayer closet. I have a prayer pool.

First, though, I drove by the store to ease my conscience that it hadn't burned down while I'd been gone. Walker was standing on the sidewalk peering at the Closed sign. I pulled over to the curb, rolled down my window, and called, "Hey! Looking for me?"

He ambled over to the car, stuck his head in my window, and wrinkled up his nose like a baby smelling its first baby-food jar of peas. "Mama! Have you been smoking pot?"

"Of course not. Whatever gave you that idea?"

"You reek of the stuff. Where have you been?"

So that's what it was. I was ashamed of myself for not recognizing it. I'd suspected I was sniffing it often enough on dirty clothes Walker brought home from college.

Grown up and reformed, he was waiting for my answer with fire in his eye.

"Over talking to Amanda Kent's neighbor. But don't you go running your mouth. I don't believe in drugs, but neither do I believe in turning in people after I've barged in on them, waked them up, and asked all sorts of questions I had no right to ask."

I had diverted his attention. "What kind of questions?"

"Oh, like did he hear anything the night that girl was killed."

"Mama—" Walker started in a warning tone, then lowered his voice. "Did he?"

"Well, yes. If Charlie Muggins has a lick of sense he'll talk to him soon. Gideon said he heard pounding that night."

"That's all?"

"He might remember more now that he's remembered that much. Maybe Luke could talk to him."

"Luke needs all the help he can get," Walker said gloomily. "Things are getting worse. They hauled him back down to the station today and asked him to describe the man in his dream so a police artist could draw him. When the artist finished, Luke said the picture was *him,* not at all what he'd described. Lorine was down there—"

"Lorine's going to be one of Luke's biggest problems. She's convinced he killed her best friend, and she's out for blood."

Walker looked grim. "I'd like to wring her neck. She's already told half the town that Luke's so-called dream killer was really himself. Even Luke has realized he needs a lawyer."

"It's about time. God wouldn't have given us common sense if we weren't expected to use it."

"What I came by to ask, is, if he needs it, could you and Daddy help a little? The way he lives, I don't think Luke can have very much stashed away."

Can you and Daddy help a little? How many times had I heard that sentence in Walker's lifetime? He's always been one of the most generous people I know— with his own money and ours.

"You'll have to ask Daddy when he gets home tomorrow evening."

"I hope he'll see his way clear. This is real important to me." He started to back off, then leaned back in my window. "Oh, and Mama? Go wash your clothes, take a bath, and fumigate that car."

~~~

I was half-way home when I saw a blue light behind me. Joe Riddley accuses me of having a lead foot, but I knew I hadn't been speeding enough to attract attention. Besides, most of the sheriff's deputies give me a lot of leeway. Must be a state trooper. I pulled over and waited. My heart sank as I saw Police Chief Charlie Muggins climb leisurely out of his cruiser and amble my way. Had I broken a law back inside the city limits?

Have you ever carried on a conversation with a chief of police when your clothes reeked of marijuana? I certainly didn't want his head in my window. Joe Riddley would never let me forget it if he had to come home early from fishing to post my bond.

No matter what happened, though, I would not tell Charlie where I'd been. Journalists, I reminded myself, never reveal their sources.

I have failed to tell you that Chief Muggins looks like a cross between a polecat and a chimpanzee. The nose and chin are pure polecat, the forehead and eyes, chimpanzee. Picture him for yourself. I don't like to dwell on his face more than necessary.

He took off his hat as he reached my car, and held it in one hand. That was a mistake. The hat had plastered what remained of his thin yellow hair to his scalp like somebody had ironed it in place, then added a little ridge around his head.

He bent down with a smile like a polecat spying a plump rat. Considering that he was looking at me, that made me nervous. I made motions and called through my closed window, "It won't go down." It certainly wouldn't. I would see to that. "What did I do wrong?"

"Not a thing, Miss MacLaren," he called in. "I saw you pass a few blocks up and wanted you to give Judge Yarbrough a message for me. Tell him we'll be wanting a warrant for arrest first thing Monday morning, bright and early."

"You already know there's going to be a crime committed between now and then?"

"We've had the crime, ma'am. Just need the arrest."

"If you're talking about last week's murder, I thought you were waiting for some forensic tests."

"We've gotten preliminary results, and they're all we need. Good thing, as it turned out, because that's all we're gonna get. We sent the evidence out of state for a DNA test, and the man who was carrying it lost his luggage."

That was a puzzler three ways. First, couldn't they find a place to do a DNA test in all of Georgia? Second, our county budget doesn't run to couriers. Nobody's complained about evidence being sent Fed Ex or UPS in the past. Third, why would anybody carry valuable evidence in checked luggage instead of on his person? This case— or, rather, Charlie's handling of it—smelled worse than a hog sty in August.

However, I didn't smell so good at the moment, myself. I didn't fancy sitting there asking questions until it occurred to him I could open my door. He's slow, but he gets there.

"I'll tell Joe Riddley," I called through the window. "Now if you'll excuse me, I need to be getting home."

"Take care, now. Until we lock up our man, there's not a woman safe in this town."

"Maybe not, but it's not Luke Blessed we need to fear."

"Well, now, Miss MacLaren, why don't we leave that up to a jury to decide?" He stepped back, then put a hand on my door. "Oh. I had a call a little while ago from somebody who saw your car parked over at the Hedrick place. You wouldn't be messing around in this case, would you?"

"Why should I do that when you have it under control? But have you talked to Amanda Kent's neighbor?"

"We're talking to lots of people. Anybody who knew her, in fact. He's on our list."

"Well, he might have something to tell you. Bye-bye." I pulled out nice and easy, leaving him standing by the side of the road.

Fifteen

Our pool has an eight-foot wall around it and bolts
on both gates, and years ago Joe Riddley rigged a mirror
so we can see from the pool anybody coming up the drive.
I'd been swimming for an hour when Selena arrived, driving a green sports utility vehicle that looked too clean to
have been fording rivers or breaking trails through virgin
forest lately. My experience is that most of them are
bought by bullies who delight in pulling in front of people,
changing lanes without looking, or turning left after a
light turns red.

Selena, however, was no bully. She looked apologetic
and pretty as she climbed down, wearing white jeans and
a green-and-white striped T-shirt. I pulled on my pool
wrap, slid my feet into canvas shoes, and went out to meet
her—regretting that I'd forgotten to bring out Miss Millie. I was going to have to entertain with frizzy hair. I'd

141

also forgotten to take Crick's pup inside, and she was by far the cutest of the three. Sure enough, she came gamboling across the pen at once to cover Selena's ankles with licks of love.

"You sweetie," Selena cooed.

"That one's not for sale," I told her regretfully. "Our three-year-old grandson wants her. But either of the other two—"

Selena had already reached for the shyest pup, who stood quivering with a look that said, "I wish you'd notice me, but I'm afraid you won't."

"Beauregard," she murmured, scooping him up into her arms and nuzzling the top of his head. "You look like a Beauregard. Doesn't he?" She held him for my inspection as if I hadn't been feeding and cleaning up after that dog every day of his life.

"Beauregard sounds fine. Dignified, yet whimsical. Will you call him Beau?"

"We'll see." She held him away from her as he wiggled happily and tried to lick her face. "He's adorable! Can I take him today?"

"Sure. Put him in the pen for a minute while I get you a box."

"I brought one," she admitted sheepishly. "I even went and bought him a food dish and a little leash—" She nuzzled him again. "You've got a ball, a rawhide bone to chew, and a bag of puppy food, Beauregard. What do you think of that? Here, Mrs. Yarbrough, if you'll hold him a minute I'll write you a check."

"Put him back in the pen," I repeated. "I'd get him all wet—or the other way around."

Selena and Beauregard were heading to her car when I saw a cloud of dust bucketing our way. Have you noticed how when you are looking your worst, everybody and his neighbor comes to call? This wasn't too bad, though. Just Maniac. He pulled up into the yard, climbed out, and brought me the biggest watermelon you ever saw.

"I thought you might like a watermelon for your supper," he told me, carrying it toward us. "Oh, *hello,*" he added carelessly to Selena, as if he hadn't known she was there.

Who did he think he was fooling? Anybody with eyes could tell he'd changed his shirt and brushed his ponytail before he came. He hadn't been picking watermelons in those shiny loafers, either—or without socks. He'd have been eaten up with bugs. I wondered if Selena found his ankles attractive. She seemed to be staring at them.

"Miss MacLaren said you were coming this *evening,*" Maniac told Selena severely.

"You've been in New York too long," I told him. "Around here, this *is* evening. Carry the watermelon into the kitchen, please, Maynard. And thanks."

When he came back, Selena held up her pup. "See my new baby? Isn't he adorable?"

Maniac looked quickly toward the pen. "Oh, good. That's not the one I wanted. But he's a *great pup,*" he added hastily, seeing fire in Selena's eye.

He reached for the puppy and scratched it under the chin. He pulled back, though, when a tiny pink tongue darted out toward his nose. "No you don't!"

He and Selena both laughed. I had hopes they'd call a truce, but as Selena reached out to reclaim her pet she told him, "His name is Beauregard, after—"

"General P. G. T. Beauregard," Maniac completed her sentence. "I know. Is that because he doesn't take *orders*? That's what Beauregard was most famous for, you know."

She held the puppy under her chin. "No, it's because he's going to protect me. My mama grew up in Charleston, where General Beauregard is still held in high esteem for protecting them during the War."

"*After* the War he fought with *everybody.* Jeff Davis, Joe Johnston—"

"How do you know so much?" Selena's tone conveyed that she didn't expect people who fixed televisions to also read.

Maniac was looking so murderous, I tried to smooth things out a little. "Maynard's the curator of the Hopemore Museum and Historical Society."

"She's never been by," he said with a curl to his lip. "Probably doesn't think we have anything worth *seeing*, after *Charleston.*"

I wished Maniac would stop accenting words. It made him sound so affected.

Selena seemed to think so, too. Her lip curled to match his. "I never lived in *Charleston.* I grew up in *Martinez,* outside *Augusta.* And I *went* to your museum one day, but it was *closed.*"

A quick look of annoyance crossed Maniac's face, then he shrugged. "We're just open *afternoons* right now, but I hope to be open a few days a week after the first of the *year.* Come by again and look *around.* You *might* find it *quaint.*" He paused, then added, "You'll also find an *article* I published last year about Beauregard's *Report on the Defense of Charleston.*" He turned away from her and spoke only to me. "One reason I came *down,* Miss MacLaren, was to ask whether I could rummage around in the *attic* of your *store* someday soon. I'll bet there are all *sorts* of old things up *there.*"

"Old rats, old rafters, and old termites," I told him crossly. Maniac wasn't half this bad with other people. What was the matter with him? "Come back when Joe Riddley's here and ask him. Anything up there is left over from his daddy's and his granddaddy's day."

"I *love* this town!" Selena exclaimed. Beauregard yipped in agreement.

"You *do*?" Maniac sounded genuinely surprised. "*Why*?"

"Because people stay here. People live where their grandparents and great-grandparents lived using the same stuff. Did your ancestors live here, Mrs. Yarbrough?"

Ancestors sounded like somebody from the Middle Ages, but as young as she was, she probably thought my grandparents lived in the Middle Ages. "No, but Joe Riddley's great-granddaddy built this house. We moved in when his parents got through with it."

"Oh, wow!"

If she was pulling out extra stops to annoy Maniac, she succeeded. "Nobody here *appreciates* their history," he informed her. "They use *priceless* objects for *every*day, not *caring* if they *chip* or *break* them. And there's an *utter* lack of *culture.*"

"Pooh!" she tossed her head. "You're no more than an hour's drive from Augusta's art museum and symphony, and there's the Blind Willie Blues Festival up in Thomson and the bluegrass festival over in Lincoln County. And Flannery O'Connor's house is right over in Milledgeville. There's plenty of culture around here. You just have to look for it."

She held her puppy close and crooned, "We'll go hear us some bluegrass music come fall, won't we Beauregard? Yes we will." She kissed the top of his tiny head.

Maniac's nostrils flared. "That *dog* is probably *covered* in *germs.*"

That riled me more than anything he had said so far. "That dog is perfectly clean, Maynard Spence, and you know it. We don't tolerate dirty dogs around here." Lulu, Beauregard's mother, barked from her pen in perfect agreement.

Maniac ducked his head in a quick apology. "Well, she oughtn't to be *kissing* it, Miss MacLaren. I gotta *go.*" He hurried to his car, then came back to thrust a slim book at Selena. *The Prophet,* by Kahlil Gibran. "Read page fifty-six. See if it sounds familiar."

As soon as Selena left, too, I dug out a copy of *The Prophet* Ridd gave me one Christmas, to see what message Maniac was giving Selena. Maybe something from that part about two lovers giving each other a bit of space?

No, page fifty-six dealt with teaching. A third of the way down the page I found what he wanted her to see. "The teacher," said the prophet, "gives not of his own wisdom, but rather of his faith and lovingness." *Not of his own wisdom.* The goswami had left out "not." But would Selena like Maniac better for pointing that out? I doubted it. If Maniac was courting Selena, he had a funny way of going about it.

> For the ear tests words as the tongue
> tastes food. Let us discern for ourselves
> what is right; let us learn together
> what is good. *Job 34:3–4*

Sixteen

If Dr. Holder was courting Rhonda Duckworth, he had a funny way of going about it, too. When I got to Duckworths' at seven-thirty, he was in the dining room surrounded by a group of men discussing Georgia's football chances for the coming year, while Rhonda was in the front hall welcoming guests with her mother. I almost didn't recognize the man she was talking to—a well-built man in a tailored gray suit and polished black shoes—until he turned and I saw the ponytail over one shoulder.

"Maynard Spence!" I exclaimed before I thought. "You clean up real good."

He surveyed the creamy linen pantsuit piped in green that I like to wear to summer parties. "So do *you*, Miss MacLaren." His eyes twinkled. We both remembered that the last time he saw me, I was in my bathing suit with frizzy hair.

Lorine was sending Rhonda so many raised eyebrows and sharp little nods toward Dr. Holder that she eventually excused herself to us and went to join him. He put an arm around her waist, but didn't seem to really notice she was there. Football is serious business around here.

So is the Garden Club buffet. It's our biggest fundraiser all year, held at the end of summer when vegetables are plentiful and member cooks can show off new recipes. We invite anybody in the county who'll come— over a hundred, that year—and people put money under the dish they like best. Members also bring centerpieces to auction off. Nobody who knows me expects me to cook, but in addition to sending all the plants decorating Lorine's corners, I'd brought a blue vanda orchid I'd grown in the greenhouse Joe Riddley gave me one Christmas. To my way of thinking, God never made anything prettier than orchids, and blue vandas are particularly fine. I craned my neck to see where Lorine had put it, but couldn't find it.

"May I get you some punch?" Maynard asked. Was it my imagination, or had he failed to accent a single syllable?

I was about to take his arm when Lorine called across the hall, "Oh, Mac! I need a private word with you."

When Lorine spoke to you in that tone, it was usually wise to head in the other direction. I gave her the same smile I give the dentist when he says I'll need another appointment. "Just let me get something to drink."

"It won't take but a minute and it's very important." She started toward me, but more guests arrived. Lorine, thank heavens, was too good a hostess to ignore them. While she was cooing over something or other, Maniac and I made our escape.

I enjoyed the looks he got as we walked arm-in-arm toward the punch bowl, but I soon released him to seek friends his own age while I drifted from room to room— avoiding Lorine, talking to people, wishing my panty hose were longer, and feeling a little at loose ends without Joe

Riddley. I was used to looking over my shoulder at a party and seeing him across the way. I was also used to his nudging me from time to time to ask, "You want another drink?" I had to trot back and forth to the punch bowl myself when my glass got empty, and it seemed to get empty an awful lot. Swimming always makes me thirsty.

Lorine had the house all decked out, and she'd had Ronald repaint her living room again. One year they painted that room four times. Joe Riddley calculated that over the twenty years they'd lived there, Lorine had reduced the room by three-and-a-half square feet.

This time it was Wedgewood green with cream woodwork and blue, cream and green striped drapes. It also had new sconces she'd found in Savannah, and Lorine was too busy bragging about them—"1800 or earlier, I'm sure"—to remember she wanted to talk to me privately. Lorine cared more about antiques than anybody I knew, with the possible exception of Maynard, and at least Maynard wanted them for his museum. Lorine just liked to own them. She was on a first-name basis with every antique dealer in the Southeast, and had them all looking for the things thieves stole from her house the night a lot of us went up to hear the Augusta symphony—particularly her great-grandmother's jewelry.

While Lorine was bragging about her new sconces, she had poor Ronald showing off a framed letter from an Atlanta dealer assuring them that Jefferson Davis once slept in their guest room bed. If Jeff Davis slept everywhere people claim he did, he'd have slept his lifetime away. However, nobody mentioned that. We are generally mannerly in Hopemore.

Before time to eat, I went looking to see where Lorine had put my orchid. In addition to Lorine's grandmama's table—which seats eighteen—Ronald had set up tables all over the house, out on the porch, and under a tent on the side lawn. Lorine, being Lorine, had had Rhonda hand-write placecards for every single guest. I found my poor orchid stuck in the far back corner of the den at a table for four people I didn't know. I switched it with a droopy arrangement from the mayor's table in the living room, and headed for the buffet.

I loaded my plate with salads and casseroles, made from I couldn't begin to imagine what, and added a nice ham biscuit so I'd recognize at least one thing on my plate. I didn't have to go looking for my placecard. As a member of the board, I'd be at the big table in the dining room. I was surprised, though, to discover Dr. Holder beside me.

From the look on Lorine's face when she came to her seat at the head of our table, she was surprised, too. Rhonda was at a table for six across the dining room, between Maniac and a loudmouth who also serves on the Garden Club board. From the smirk on the loudmouth's face, I suspected he'd switched placecards with Dr. Holder so he could rib Joe Riddley later that his wife was carrying on with a neighbor while he was gone.

You might think Lorine could graciously have asked them to change places, but that particular loudmouth was dating Lorine in high school when she met Ronald, and he's hung on to a grudge all these years. Lorine was smart to just give Dr. Holder a gracious smile of welcome, make sure he knew all his table neighbors, and tuck into her meal.

For a while I was so busy talking to other people I didn't notice that nobody was talking to Dr. Holder. When I did notice and tried to think of something to say, I found it hard when he was wearing a suit and tie. I didn't want to sound too familiar, but when I racked my brain for something that wouldn't sound idiotic, I came up with nothing. Finally I blurted, "Did you ever get rid of your cannon, Dr. Holder?"

His eyes crinkled when he smiled. "Yeah, and after going through that together, I think you ought to call me Drew."

"Fine, Drew. Please call me Mac."

"Mac." He seemed to test the name and approve it before nodding toward the other table. "Thanks for suggesting Maynard. He was great. We wrestled it off the back porch, then he came by this morning with two men to haul it away."

Across the room, the loudmouth spoke into one of those silences that occur at twenty past the hour. Everybody in the dining room could hear him. "Hey, Maynard, didn't I hear you were up to that girl's apartment about the time she got killed?"

Maniac flushed and opened his mouth, but Lorine couldn't resist putting her old beau in his place while bragging to everybody else. "'That girl,' as you call her, was my best friend, so I can't tell you how glad I am they're fixing to arrest that no-good preacher for killing her. I was down at the police station today, and Chief Muggins says he's got an airtight case. When does Joe Riddley get back, Mac?"

"Tomorrow evening," I told her shortly. Withholding that information wouldn't have done Luke a speck of good, but I felt like a traitor giving it.

The loudmouth chimed in again. "Hey, Mac, is Yarbrough the Super Sleuth helping Charlie out with the investigation? Joe Riddley told me all about tracking down that killer over in Montgomery last month." His bray showed what he thought of my abilities. "Me, now," he added, putting an arm around Rhonda's chair. "I prefer tracking down pretty girls."

"Rhonda, honey," Lorine said quickly, "would you tell the kitchen they can put desserts out now?" Those who hadn't gone back for seconds pushed back their chairs, and Rhonda rose to do as she was told. Did that girl ever miss having a life of her own?

While she was still out, a doctor's beeper went off out in the hall. As he rose to leave, I heard his wife say in resignation, "Hey, folks, he was here nearly two hours." We all laughed. Her husband was one of the town's most conscientious doctors, and we were used to his leaving in the middle of things. She called over one shoulder, "By the way, Drew, I haven't had a chance to thank you for making Bert take last weekend off." She added, for the rest of us, "Drew offered to switch weekends on call with Bert so we could go to Amelia Island for our anniversary. Wasn't that sweet?"

Drew Holder didn't say anything, just looked embarrassed. I leaned over and murmured, "And then you got stuck with that murder."

"Yeah. Are you all really looking for whoever killed her?"

You all? If Dr. Holder—Drew—had any idea how often Joe Riddley fussed about me poking my nose where he thought it didn't belong . . . But that wasn't why I didn't reply at once. My short list of suspects might consist only of the professor in Tennessee, but every man in Hopemore was on my long list until the murderer was caught—except Joe Riddley and our two sons.

Drew didn't seem to expect an answer. He just said, "That was the grimmest thing I ever saw. If there's anything I can do to help, tell your husband to call me, will you?"

Lorine couldn't stand it that she couldn't hear what we were saying. She leaned forward and interrupted us. "That certainly was sweet, Drew. Especially with you getting ready for your big conference and all."

"What conference?" someone asked from down our table.

He patiently put down a forkful of green bean casserole. "I've been doing a little research on reducing pain through mind control. We're having a few people down next month to talk about it."

"A few people!" Lorine chimed in again. "A little research! You all may not know it, but Dr. Holder is the foremost authority on this subject in the whole Southeast. This is a very important conference."

He looked so flustered that I suspected Lorine wasn't exaggerating, for once. And to think, I helped him get rid of a cannon in his kitchen!

It was past ten by the time we'd auctioned off the centerpieces and I'd counted the money with our local bank president and sent him to deposit it. I dreaded thanking Lorine for the party. Unless she'd just wanted to know when Joe Riddley was coming home, she still had something to say to me. I suspected it involved my giving away time or money.

I hoped to find her in a crowd, murmur quick thanks, and go, but I found her talking to Drew Holder alone in the back hall. From his pained expression and her earnest one, I suspected she was trying to get free medical advice. He looked very relieved when I sidled up, and moved away immediately.

"I want to thank you for a lovely party, Lorine," I began.

She grabbed my elbow and dragged me to the far end of the hall. "What were you doing over at Amanda's today?" Her cheeks were so pink and her eyes so sparkly she looked closer to pretty than I'd ever seen her—except for the look on her face.

Sulky, my mama used to call that expression. "Honey," she'd say, "you'd better develop a sweet disposition, because with a sulky face like that you'll never catch a husband." Lorine's mama must not have given her that advice.

"I wasn't at Amanda's," I told her in my best not-that-it's-any-of-your-business tone of voice. "I was next door."

Her eyes narrowed and she leaned so close I backed up a couple of steps. "You stay away from there, you hear me? Don't you go talking to Amanda's neighbors or friends or anybody else. You leave that to people who know how to do it."

"If people who know how to do it were the least bit interested in the truth, I might. However—"

"However, nothing." Her whisper was a hiss, and her face looked as long and smooth as a rattler's. "Concentrate on your precious Walker and the mess he's got his life in. Leave Charlie Muggins to do his job. Or you'll be sorry!"

I was so riled up I didn't say another word. Not because I couldn't think of anything *to* say, but because I knew that anything I said would make me ashamed to remember. For once in my life I was about to leave a party without thanking my hostess.

I turned and saw we'd had an audience. Hovering behind me were Maniac Spence and Ronald Duckworth. Except for when he'd been showing around that letter about Jeff Davis, I hadn't seen Ronald all evening. It tells you something about his personality that until then, I hadn't noticed. I could smell him, though. He'd been smoking.

Maniac stepped forward and put out his hand. "Thanks for the *party*, Miss Lorine. But I shouldn't have stayed so long. I don't like to leave Daddy alone this late." Poor Maniac, maybe he couldn't help sounding like it was our fault he'd been having such a good time he hadn't left sooner. Maybe he'd gotten so in the habit of complaining that by now it was the only way he knew to talk. I'd start working on him a little when I got a chance. He wasn't too old to salvage.

I could hear Joe Riddley now. "You've got enough on your plate with Walker, Little Bit. You don't need to take on Maniac as well." But Joe Riddley didn't need to know a thing about it. I'd just put a little bug in Maniac's ear now and then. He ought to shape up nicely.

Drew Holder stood behind him. "I guess our whole road got bitten by the same bug. I came back to say I need to go, too, I'm afraid. Thanks for asking me."

As we passed through the front hall Drew told Maniac, "I really appreciated your coming for that cannon so quickly. Do you really think you can use it?"

"Oh, yes. It's going to clean up splendidly. When it's polished and mounted properly, it will be a focal point on our lawn."

"Was it a Confederate cannon, or one of Sherman's?" I asked.

"Confederate. I wouldn't dare point one of General Sherman's at the heart of town."

We all laughed in a neighborly fashion as we walked together into the stifling heat.

At the top step of the porch Drew stopped and heaved a deep sigh, as if exhaling the entire evening. I expected him to say something, but he only gave us a wave and headed toward his Lexus, which was parked in the drive behind Lorine's powder blue Cadillac.

"Bye-bye, Drew. Be seeing you," I called after him.

If I'd had any idea how soon that would be, and under what circumstances, I wouldn't have sounded so chipper.

> Between dawn and dusk they are
> broken to pieces; unnoticed,
> they perish forever. *Job 4:20*

Seventeen

As we reached the octagon block sidewalk, I turned left. Maniac started to turn right, then checked himself. "May I see you to your car, Miss MacLaren?"

See? A boy with good manners isn't past rescuing from a lot of other bad habits.

"Don't bother," I told him. "I'm just a couple houses down, in front of Walker's. Thank heavens we live in a town where a woman can walk down the street at this hour."

I walked pretty briskly, however, because Academy is a canopy street with huge trees on each side that meet overhead in the middle. That night, every tree looked big enough to hide a killer. It was a comfort when I got in my car to see Maniac waiting to be sure I got there safely. I blinked my lights to show I was in, and he waved and headed home.

I didn't start my own car at once. I was all keyed up from getting riled at Lorine. I thought I'd just run into Walker's and check on how he was getting along without Cindy. His band didn't expect to get home until seven—just in time for Luke to shower, eat, and get to the early service—so Walker need never know I'd been there.

You may wonder why I wouldn't be scared to go into a dark house alone, but Cindy's a nervous person, so they'd installed a topnotch security system and motion sensor lights all over the place. I drove right up to the back patio, got their spare key from under a garden gnome, and started in. Then I noticed that the plants on the deck needed water. I hosed them down good, and it was so bright with the lights that I wasn't even afraid out of doors. Whenever a sensor light went out, I did a little jig and it came right on again. I felt like a movie star, always in a spotlight.

It really upset me to find Cindy had taken her crotons, though. She had several varieties in lovely brass pots, and she loved those plants. She babied them inside through the winter, then put them outside again each spring. If she'd taken them with her, she must think she'd be gone a long time—and didn't trust Walker to save them in case we got a freeze.

Fuming at their foolishness, I let myself in the kitchen door, set Cindy's security system to "home," and turned on a light in every room. I missed the animals. Cindy always had a couple of dogs and three or four cats around the place, but she must have taken them with the children and the crotons. I spared a minute's pity for Cindy's poor mother, until I remembered she was enjoying a summer of my grandchildren's lives I would never recover. Then my pity dried like mud and I wanted to shake Walker and Cindy both.

Walker must be more upset than he let on, though. His house didn't look like he spent one second longer in it than necessary. He must have cancelled the maid, too, because dishes overflowed the sink, dust covered the furniture, and a trail of dirty clothes led from the washer toward the front hall. Grease was congealing on top of a pot of canned noodle soup on the stove, and milk filmed a glass on the kitchen table.

I have never been known for housekeeping, but I did not raise my sons to live like that. Furious with Walker, Cindy, and Lorine all three, I jerked open a drawer, put on one of Cindy's frilly aprons, and got to work. I washed dishes, mopped, dusted, vacuumed, and changed all three beds. I even scrubbed the tub, probably ruining my good pantsuit in the process.

Joe Riddley says there isn't a woman alive who doesn't want her work admired. He may be right. When I finally collapsed on the den sofa for a breather, I thought about staying until Walker got home, just to see his face when he saw his house. I checked my watch. One forty-five. He wouldn't be home for hours yet.

A moment's thought convinced me, though, that was a good thing. Walker, being Walker, might not appreciate what I had done. "Snooping" and "nosy" were words that came to mind. "Oh well," I told myself. "He probably won't even notice the place is clean."

Since I'd gone that far, I figured I might as well throw in a wash. From the number of socks I'd picked up, Walker must be walking around in his last clean pair. I could sneak in the next morning on my way to church and toss the load in the drier, then go back after church and fold it. After being up all night, he wasn't likely to hear me.

I gathered up all the clothes I could find, then I thought to look in the back of his closet. As a boy, Walker stuffed clothes out of sight if they were extra dirty. Sure enough, I found a pair of nice khaki slacks and one of his favorite golf shirts, a pale yellow one that showed up well with his tan. They were all rolled up and pushed far into a corner, so I pulled them out and shook them.

They were covered with stains.

Dark stains dotted the shirt and ran down the pants. Some were blurred and long, like they'd dripped. Others were almost perfectly round, like they'd spattered.

I could not breathe. *How had Walker Yarbrough gotten blood all over his clothes?*

One part of my mind refused to believe what I was seeing, but another remembered that Walker had let Cindy go in June without a word. Was he involved with that nurse? Was that really why Cindy really left? I couldn't help remembering Walker in my office declaring, "I *know* Luke didn't kill that girl, Mama," or how uneasy he'd been in her apartment, or him standing by my car that very day asking me to help Luke. What had he said? "This is real important to me."

I knew that dream might not mean a thing, but the man Luke saw was blonde, taller than him, and muscular. So was Walker. Could my son have done that dreadful thing?

Every fiber in my being denied it, but didn't the mother of even the most hardened criminals deny that *their* Tommy, Jerry, or Mike could ever do such a thing? Just because I couldn't picture Walker beating a woman to death didn't mean he couldn't do it.

I am not proud of what I did next, but I'd do it again in a minute. I balled those clothes back up like I'd found them, stuffed them even further back in that closet, and got out of there. I'd come back when I'd had time to think things through.

~~

Outside, the night matched my find. The breeze was hot and sticky and along the driveway, cedars and crepe myrtles made shadows like furry monsters. The half-moon looked half dead, and it sailed in and out of charcoal clouds against a sky as dark as soot.

When I got in my car, I was shaking so hard I was afraid I couldn't drive. I locked all my doors, which we weren't used to doing in Hopemore, and took off like a rocket. As I reached the street, I read the dashboard clock and couldn't believe it. How could it be only five past two? Three and a half hours had flown while I was cleaning, but I had aged ten years in the last twenty minutes.

Just as I started to pull out into Academy Street, I nearly got run down by a police cruiser racing past. "You know better than to drive that fast without your lights or sirens on," I yelled, scared to death. By then the cruiser was squealing to the curb up the block. Two officers jumped out and ran toward a house.

I followed it and found it parked in front of Duckworths', which seemed to have every light in the house on. That was odd. Neither Lorine nor Ronald were night owls.

Although I was still numb from Walker's, I was still curious, so I pulled in behind the cruiser and cut my engine. Was somebody sick? Had they been robbed? Should I go see?

I knew what Joe Riddley would say. "Don't butt in where you aren't wanted, Little Bit." On the other hand, how could I drive off when something was so clearly the matter? While I was still considering, headlights swept across my rearview mirror and a car pulled in to the driveway. It screeched to a stop inches from Lorine's rear bumper and Dr. Holder jumped out, wearing navy shorts and a white polo shirt. He grabbed his bag and sprinted to the porch. After that I wasn't going meekly home to bed. Somebody in that house might need another woman.

I let myself in the front door—not wanting to bother anyone by knocking—and found Dr. Holder talking urgently to an officer in the front hall. Ronald and Rhonda sat like rag dolls side by side on the living room couch. Ronald looked baffled. Rhonda was sobbing. Not one soul noticed I was there.

"Why was she out in the yard in the first place?" Ronald asked loudly. "In the middle of the night?" Nobody answered him. The officer kept talking to Dr. Holder.

"What's happened?" I asked at the door. I sniffed, and smelled smoke. "Is there a fire?"

Dr. Holder turned toward me, startled and puzzled. The officer, whom I'd known since he was teething, came over and said softly, "Hey, Mrs. Yarbrough. Mrs. Duckworth was killed out in her backyard sometime after eleven."

My heart nearly stopped. It was well after ten when I was watering Walker's plants!

Rhonda spoke, as if arguing with Death itself. "We went to bed. We all went to bed at eleven, right after everybody left. Why would she get up and go out in the back yard in the middle of the night?" She sounded like a Shakespearean actress reciting her lines. Lady Mac-Beth, perhaps, or sad Ophelia.

I went and sat down beside her, putting an arm around her. She trembled like a young wild thing first confronting terror. "Maybe she heard something," I suggested—then rejected it immediately. If Lorine sent Ronald across town to check on Amanda Kent in broad daylight, she'd certainly have sent Ronald to check on strange noises at night.

The officer, however, nodded. "It's possible. Or maybe she wanted a breath of air."

Rhonda raised sopping wet eyes and asked in an irritated voice, "The house is air conditioned. Why should she go outside for air?" I applauded her spunk, and was surprised she could be so bright—especially under the circumstances.

I retracted that opinion a second later when the phone rang beside her. She answered, listened, and said, "She can't come to the phone. She's dead."—and hung up.

"Who was that?" the officer demanded.

"Somebody wanting Mama. He called before."

The officer gave her a frustrated look.

"I need to see the victim," Dr. Holder reminded him.

Rhonda stood up, lovely and graceful as ever. "Come on. I'll show you. Stay here, Daddy." Drew put an arm at her waist to help her out. Nobody seemed to notice or care if I trailed along, through the kitchen and across the latticed back porch.

The front yard was Lorine's—well groomed and showy. The back yard was Ronald's—a hodgepodge of painting supplies and five gallon paint buckets. Ronald's truck sat directly under the glare of a halogen light. Behind the truck a painting tarp lay on the driveway. I knew what it covered, and felt sick to my stomach.

Rhonda led the way to the tarp, stooped, and pulled it back, averting her face. "We couldn't stand to leave her here, so we covered her up." She retreated to where I was waiting near the back porch steps.

Lorine lay face-down on the driveway, looking like she'd decided her bed was too soft and come out for the night. One arm lay gracefully away from her body, the other under her. Her hair was perfect. I could see that much from where I was. She wore a royal blue robe—the kind of thing a woman would put on to run down to the kitchen to see about a few last details, except Lorine usually left kitchen details to her help. Had she thought of something they might have forgotten—meat to be put in the refrigerator, cream left in a silver creamer—and come downstairs, then seen something in the back yard and gone to investigate?

"She could have seen a prowler," I murmured to myself, "and come out to shout and chase him away."

The officer looked around. "Ground won't take prints very well. Too dry."

God forgive me, my next thought was gratitude that Luke and Walker were out of town. Ashamed of myself, I grabbed Rhonda's hand. Hers was trembling. Or was it mine?

Dr. Holder knelt beside Lorine and felt her pulse. I wondered why. Even from a distance I could tell Lorine was dead.

No matter what I thought about her when she was alive, I couldn't help but pity her then, lying with her nose in the dirt for the world to gawk at, poke, and talk about, without her having any chance to talk back. Few of us will be truly ready to meet our Maker, but I've always hoped for time to tie up a few loose ends. Any loose ends Lorine left when she came out that back door would stay loose eternally.

Even though alive she could irritate me more than anybody, I found myself thinking about a few kind things she'd done—heading up a drive to collect toys for children in the hospital one Easter, and opening her house for parties without ever complaining about the wear and tear on her furniture, or the worry and expense of getting it clean. "Give her a pretty mansion, Lord," I begged silently. "She won't be happy with anything less."

Dr. Holder was still examining the body, his long strong hands moving down her torso. Rhonda startled me by calling across to him, "It's her face. It's . . ." She stopped.

Dr. Holder moved out of his own light and lifted the head. "Strangled," he said flatly. "Looks like by a scarf or something, that was later removed."

Rhonda moved closer to me. Her hand was cold and clammy, like a fish pulled from a lake. That made me think of Joe Riddley. I sure wished he was there! But then, if he'd been in town, I would be home by now, so it was just as well he was out of town.

"Daddy had to go to the bathroom," Rhonda confided, although I hadn't asked a thing. "He's got prostrate trouble." I didn't correct her. Given Ronald's present circumstances, the word was appropriate. "Then the phone rang," she went on. "Some man, wanting Mama."

"Who was he?" I asked, thinking it might help her to remember what had happened.

"I don't know. Daddy went looking for her and found her missing from bed, so he went downstairs looking for her. I heard him in the kitchen, so I went to see if anything was the matter. I felt a little hungry, too. I didn't eat much dinner. We both started looking for Mama, but she wasn't anywhere—in the house." Her words lurched, then stopped.

"What made you come out here?" If they thought she'd gone for a drive, it would have made more sense to look out front, where her Cadillac was parked.

"I don't know. After we'd looked everywhere else, Daddy said maybe she'd come out back. So we came out here and found her." She rushed through the last, came to another abrupt stop, then added, "I went back to tell the man, but he'd hung up."

"What did you do then—call the police?"

"No. We thought at first she'd fainted, so Daddy said we ought to bring her inside. But when he started to pick her up . . ." She pressed her hand to her mouth and swallowed hard. "Then I called 911 and Drew. I knew Mama would want Drew."

I couldn't tell whether she'd wanted him herself or not. Rhonda never let her feelings show much, and right then all the feelings she had were for her mother. Even when Drew came over, put an arm around her, and steered her toward the back porch. "Go inside and make some coffee, honey," he told her. "It's likely to be a long night."

⊷

It sure was. No matter where you live, there's a crew of people who have to show up for a murder. For the next two hours they came, silently for the most part, so as not to wake up the neighbors. Our town is good about not making noise on Academy Street.

I stuck around hoping to hear some more about what they thought had happened, but the police seemed as baffled as Rhonda and Ronald. The best guess anybody could make was what I'd originally suspected: Lorine had seen or heard a prowler, thought she could scare him off, and gotten killed instead.

I knew Chief Muggins didn't believe me when I explained as I handed him a cup of coffee, "I was just passing by and saw the doctor coming in."

"I couldn't have stood it without her." Rhonda rested her head on my shoulder.

"You need to go get yourself some sleep," I told her. "Go on up, now. They'll call you if they need you." Obediently she trailed up the stairs.

Chief Muggins gave me a sour look and headed back outside without a word, but I noticed he drank the coffee. I realized I'd probably missed the only opportunity I'd ever get to poison that old goat, but as penance for even thinking such a thing, I ran a sinkful of hot soapy water and washed up all the mugs. No matter what their rank or job, our policemen use a lot of mugs.

"As soon as people start getting up we'll question the neighbors," I heard Chief Muggins tell his troops beyond the back porch. Since one neighbor owned the town's largest industry and another was the bank president, I couldn't fault his decision not to wake them. Anyway, houses on Academy Street are so far apart and back yards so well screened by fences and tall bushes, nobody was likely to have seen or heard a thing.

By the time I dried the last mug my legs were sagging. I'd done more dishes and cleaning in that one evening than I usually did in six months. I couldn't believe the clock on Lorine's microwave. It had only been two hours since I left Walker's.

I refused to let myself think about Walker yet. Instead, I thought about my bed. I could feel that cool pillow touching my cheek.

I picked up my pocketbook and tiptoed out without saying goodnight to anybody. Ronald was sitting on the den sofa looking pitiful and lost. Dr. Holder was trying to persuade him to take a couple of tablets. Chief Muggins was giving orders out back.

I let myself out the front door and carefully pushed the button to lock it behind me. I'll always wonder why I did that. Who would sneak into a house full of policemen? But then, six hours before, I'd thought a woman was safe on Academy Street.

Eighteen

As I passed Miss Bessie's, I slowed to be sure Luke wasn't home. I couldn't believe it when I saw his old white Toyota in the drive. "He must have ridden to the gig with Walker," I told myself. Something, though, made me drive back to Academy Street. Walker's Infiniti crouched like a happy housecat in his drive. How long had he been home?

I drove fast, checking my rearview mirror more than usual, and hurried into my house. Lulu yawned reproachfully from a rug near the stove. "Sorry to wake you," I apologized.

First thing, I called Walker. He answered sleepily. "When did you get back?" I asked.

His answer made ice water run in my veins. "We didn't go. The people heard Luke was under suspicion of murder, so they cancelled. Can you imagine anything sillier?"

Yeah. Inviting a suspected murderer to play in a club full of patrons. I'd have done the same in the manager's place. All I said to Walker, though, was, "So where were you tonight?" Then I waited, my stomach churning like a washing machine.

When he said, "Uh—at home," I'd have known he was lying even if I hadn't just spent three hours at his house. Any sentence Walker precedes with "uh" is likely to be untrue. To be fair, I have never known him to lie to harm another person, or even to get out of something he's done wrong. He lies when he doesn't want the hassle of explaining something, and sees no reason why he should.

"Walker, turn on the light and look around you," I snapped. "What do you see?"

I heard rustles and a click. "Ummm—my bedroom?"

"Do you see anything different about that bedroom?"

Silence. Then, "Did you come over and pick up a little?"

"Pick up a little? I bulldozed my way through three months' filth. In another day or two the rats would have carried the place away. But this is real important, honey. Where were you? We both know you weren't home."

"Mama, this may be hard for you to accept, but I'm all grown up. I don't have to tell you or anybody else where I go at night."

"You do tonight. Lorine Duckworth was strangled in her backyard, just two doors down. Charlie Muggins is going to want to know where every man in Hopemore was between eleven and two."

"Whoa! Do you mean that?"

"Of course I mean it."

"I'm real sorry to hear that. And I'll tell Charlie where I was if he asks. Good night."

"Wait! Did you tell Luke what I said about Lorine pushing the police to arrest him?"

"Yes ma'am."

"What did he say?"

"He said he could forgive her for that—that it's hard to lose your best friend."

"That's nicer than what you said."

"Luke's nicer than I. Good *night,* Mama." He hung up.

≈

Maybe I should have stayed awake and worried, but I was too tired. I fell asleep as soon as I pulled the sheet to my chin.

When I heard a bell, I thought Walker was calling back. I fumbled for the phone, then realized it was the doorbell. Had I even gotten to sleep? I peered at the clock. Six thirty. Who on earth could be at my front door?

I pulled on a robe and ran a comb through my hair, but didn't bother to wipe the raccoon smears from my eyes. Whoever it was, they could take me as they found me.

It was Charlie Muggins, trying to look sorry about bothering me and only managing to look more useless than usual. He had his youngest officer with him, a prankster who used to work for us in high school. That morning he was working to look solemn. I knew he was embarrassed. Me, too. For his sake, I wished I'd washed my face.

"Sorry to take so long coming down," I told them. "People so seldom come to our front door that I didn't recognize the bell."

"Mrs. Yarbrough," Chief Muggins said formally, removing his hat and smoothing what remained of his hair, "I'm afraid I'm going to have to ask you a few questions about last night." He actually had tears in his sunken little chimpanzee eyes. "We're sure going to miss Mrs. Duckworth. One of the finest women in this town. Absolutely devoted to seeing justice done."

Devoted to seeing Luke Blessed in jail, I thought, but didn't say it.

"Fine woman," Chief Muggins repeated when I didn't say anything. "And I am determined to bring her killer to justice. Now Mr. Duckworth has told me that you and his wife had an altercation at the end of her party. He has further stated that the dress you had on when you arrived at his house after the murder was the same one you wore to the party, so I am wondering what that altercation was about and what you did when you left the Duckworth home."

I know it was supposed to be a solemn interview, but something about Charlie Muggins invariably brings out the devil in me. And why was he wasting time interviewing me when he could be out looking for a real suspect?

"Who'd have thought Ronald would notice what I was wearing at a time like that?" I marveled. "Especially since it was a *pantsuit.* Don't *you* remember?"

The young officer ducked his head with a grin. Charlie moved toward my door. "Maybe we'd better come in."

"It's a lovely morning, isn't it?" I said hospitably, taking my favorite rocker.

It was. Mockingbirds fluttered around the birdbath, a purple finch warbled from a crepe myrtle, even the little brown rabbit we called Cottontail Yarbrough was nibbling grass down by the maple. Roses sent out a heavenly scent, while from down the road I got whiffs of dewy grass, honeysuckle, and something burning. Maniac must be burning their week's mail. I hoped Charlie wouldn't notice and cite him. Poor Hubert had been cited three times already that summer for illegal burning.

"What was it you wanted to know?" I felt light and relaxed in spite of not having but two hours' sleep—or maybe because of it. Then, as Charlie Muggins opened his mouth, I suddenly remembered what I should have remembered before: those clothes in Walker's closet and his lack of an alibi. Had Charlie already talked to him? Had Walker told him he'd been home all evening? *Had Walker killed Lorine Duckworth?* I couldn't help remembering what he'd said beside my car the day before: "I'd like to wring her neck." Well, somebody had.

No feeling in the world is as dismal as suspecting one of your children. You feel guilty for even thinking such a thing, yet you know them so well. You keep remembering snips of conversation, expressions of face, until you can't help asking yourself, "Could he have possibly done that?"

Fortunately, Charlie Muggins was only interested in me. "I want to know what you and the deceased were quarreling about," he demanded. It burned me up that he could even *think* I would kill anybody. It also burned me up that the young officer was writing everything down without giving me the warning.

"Ask Maynard," I told them. "He heard us. Lorine was warning me not to look into her friend's murder—that you knew what you were doing. Basically she was telling me to bow out."

"Wise lady. But I can see she made you mad."

"Not mad enough to choke her."

"For the record, please tell me where you were from ten-thirty, when you left the party, until two, when you returned to the Duckworths'."

Ordinarily that would be a reasonable enough request. Just then, though, it felt like a time bomb. "I went over to my son's," I began cautiously. "He was out of town, so I was checking on things—watering plants, things like that." My mind was racing. I wouldn't say Walker was there, but could I make it sound like he was? I was trying so hard to be careful, I nearly missed the gift Chief Muggins dropped in my lap.

"Ridd's?" I didn't even have to nod confirmation. He was already asking, "Where was Martha?"

"She went to her mother's for the night." Please note, that was the absolute truth. Martha had called Saturday morning to say that with everybody gone, she was fixing to run down to Statesboro for the night.

"Anybody see you go in or out?"

"Not one soul. After all, it was after ten-thirty when I left Lorine's."

"How long were you there?"

I didn't mind looking guilty, now. "A lot longer than I intended. I, uh, lay down on the den sofa—"

He leaped to exactly the conclusion I hoped he would. "Fell asleep, did you?" He wheezed a nasty little laugh. "How long did you snooze?" Who ever picked that man for our police chief? He was easier to lead than a sheep.

"I never said I was snoozing," I said, trying to sound indignant.

He gave another little laugh and again smoothed the few strands of yellow hair that remained on his head.

I stared at that hair, mesmerized. Blonde hair. Could it have been *Charlie Muggins* in Luke's dream? Had our chief of police killed Amanda Kent? He was certainly cut up about her death, and while he claimed he'd fallen in love with her picture, he could have just as well fallen in love with her while she was alive. Amanda would probably have let him in late at night if he'd been in uniform, but she might not have been as taken with him as he was with her. Could that have made him furious enough to kill her?

I had the whole story written, but I missed his next question. "Mrs. Yarbrough," he said impatiently, "I asked when you left Ridd's."

"My son's." I tried to sound like I was refreshing my memory about who Ridd was, but on the record, I'd be telling the truth. "Oh—around two. On my way home, I saw lights at Duckworths' and a police car out front. Then I saw Dr. Holder running in, so I went to see if I could be of any help. You know the rest."

I could hardly wait for them to leave, so I could write down my idea about Charlie Muggins as murderer. Joe Riddley should be able to find out if Charlie Muggins had an alibi for the night Amanda was killed. Maybe this case was over.

I wasn't at all sleepy, so I decided to go on to church. I could nap later if I felt like it.

I don't usually go to early service, because most of my friends go at eleven o'clock and I like to see them afterwards and catch up a little. Working six days a week, I don't get around as much as some women. Also, first service is contemporary, which means informal clothes, guitars, drums, and a keyboard. I prefer a pipe organ and Sunday clothes.

I've always been delighted, though, that our church offers people a choice, and that particular morning I was glad it offered *me* a choice. I had so much praying to do, I didn't care what kind of music they had. I was too tired to chat with friends, and didn't feel like dressing up. I pulled on my denim skirt and a plaid cotton blouse, slid on sandals, and set out for church without even panty hose. I felt quite daring. God might forgive me, but if Mama was looking down from heaven, she never would.

I heard the throb of an electric bass as soon as I got out of my car. Inside, music rose like a flower bursting open from sheer vitality. The scene wasn't that different from what I'd found at the Temple of Inner Peace on Friday—a small music ensemble up front, Luke Blessed in jeans and a colorful stole leading praise with his guitar, kids in jeans and sandals standing on the carpet waving their arms and swaying to the beat. The main difference I saw was, this wasn't an equal opportunity service. These people were worshipping Jesus, and weren't ashamed to say so.

Just like on Friday night, an usher hurried forward to steer me to one of several folding chairs set haphazardly around the room. A few older people looked my way with welcoming smiles, much as the women had Friday night, except without embarrassment.

When Luke saw me come in, he threw me a quick, anxious look. I smiled, and he relaxed into a smile of welcome. I hoped he had a good alibi for the night before, and figured on staying around long enough to find out.

The music calmed down in a song or two, and I found myself sinking into a holy peace I never expected to find in that old fellowship hall. The prayers were personal and immediate, and Luke's sermon was excellent. He didn't sound the least bit worried about being arrested any minute for at least one, if not two, murders. He even alluded to that once when he said, "We never know how much we can count on God until we have to. No matter how big your troubles, God is a whole lot bigger."

I followed the crowd out and lingered until he finished shaking hands with other people. Finally it was just the two of us. His eyes were concerned as he took my hands between both of his. "Mac, are you all right?"

"Am *I* all right?" I echoed. "I'm not the one we ought to be worried about."

"Are you sure? Before seven this morning I got real worried about you. Felt like there was something—I don't know—scaring you." His grin was boyish and embarrassed. "Probably something I ate, huh?"

I shook my head, puzzled. "No, I was having an interview with Charlie Muggins around then, and it got pretty scary in places. I must have been sending out help messages." We both laughed.

"Did it turn out all right?"

"Well, he didn't arrest me, much as he'd have liked to."

"Good for you. Hope I have that kind of success."

I couldn't think of any good way to get from there to where I wanted to go, so I said bluntly, "I heard your gig got cancelled last night."

"Yeah." His grin was rueful. "My reputation put them off. Can't blame them, really. A murderer in the band might make some customers nervous."

"That thought occurred to me, too. So what did you do instead?"

"Went to bed. It's been a rough week, and I had the beginnings of a headache, so when Walker called to say the gig was off, I took a couple of aspirin and crawled into bed with a good book. Very soon I pulled up my sheet and slept until morning."

That wasn't good, unless—"Did Miss Bessie know you were there?"

"She may have heard me. We don't see much of each other."

I took a deep breath and asked a sneaky question. "What did Walker do?"

"I don't know. He said he'd probably stick around home. Asked if I wanted to go over there for pizza and a movie, but I really needed sleep."

I was disappointed, but moved on to the next thing I wanted to know. "Walker told me what happened about the police artist's picture. He said you're going to retain a lawyer?"

Luke nodded with an embarrassed little laugh. "Seems silly, doesn't it? But I feel like I owe it to the church to get this cleared up as soon as possible. The kids don't need people wondering if I'm guilty. And frankly, there's some element at work here I don't understand. It sent chills up my spine to see that woman drawing my own picture when I clearly said the man in my dream was blonde, taller than me, and muscular. More like Walker, for instance."

That sent chills up my spine instead. I gave what I hoped was a convincing laugh. "It wasn't, I hope?"

He laughed, too. "Not that I recognized, but the face was weird—I couldn't see it clearly, yet I felt at the beginning like I knew it real well and liked the person a lot. It was. . ." he groped with both hands for an image. "You know how hard it is to really picture the face of somebody you love?"

I nodded. "Sure. I could tell you what Joe Riddley looks like, but if I try to see him in my mind, all I get is a shape and a happy feeling."

"Yeah! That's what I got at the beginning of the dream. A shape and a happy feeling. It was only gradually that I started to feel scared, although he kept smiling. When I got real scared, I woke up the first time."

"But you never recognized him?"

"No, but that whole dream thing was dumb—probably a mixture of reading Daniel and playing in the band. Maybe it *was* Walker I saw, pounding away on Nebuchadnezzar. Who knows?" He bent to pick up his guitar. "I'd better go teach the high schoolers before they climb out the windows. It was good to have you this morning. Feel free to come anytime. And pray I'll have the wisdom to know what I need to do to clear this thing up soon."

He looked so young and vulnerable that without thinking I opened my arms and gave him a bear hug. "Lord love you, Luke, what do you think I've been doing for the last hour?"

"Thanks, Mac. There's one consolation, though. Things can't get much worse."

About that he was very wrong.

A despairing man should have the
devotion of his friends, even though
he forsakes the fear of the Almighty.

Job 6:14

Nineteen

They found Gideon Levy's body that afternoon, but I didn't know it. After church, I never went back downtown.

I spent the day trying not to think about murder. I slept awhile, had a swim, put on a pretty summer dress, fixed my face, and drove to a barbeque place out in the country that makes true southern barbeque—cooked slow over a pit, without sauce.

I got sliced pork, Brunswick stew for Joe Riddley, and coleslaw for me, then stopped by Ridd's garden to pull a few ears of fresh corn and bright red tomatoes. He and Martha live on the edge of town in one of those comfortable bungalows built in the nineteen twenties from a Sears & Roebuck kit. They have a big yard for the kids, a half-acre garden, and live a pretty equal distance from his cotton fields and both their jobs.

Martha's car was in the drive, but I didn't go in. Knowing Martha, she was probably trying to finish canning a bushel of beans before Ridd got there. He'd wind up putting Crick to bed and helping her take the last hot jars from the canner. I appreciate the way they share housework and child care, but I sometimes think Ridd and Martha skimp on relaxation and the little romantic touches that make marriage more fun.

By the time Joe Riddley pulled in about six, grubby and tired, I had Beethoven on the stereo, water boiling for the corn, and the table set on the screened porch with a couple of new yellow rosebuds. Joe Riddley loved roses the way I love orchids.

Ridd's pickup pulled in right after him and Crick called, "Hey, Me-mama, we came to get my dog!" He scrambled down, gave me a brief hug, and ran to the fence. "There he is. That one!" he said, pointing to the wrong pup.

"You wanted the other one, honey," I told him, reaching down to bring her out.

"Not that one, the udder one," he insisted. "That's the one I wanted. I know it!" Like his Uncle Walker, Crick used "I know it" as his final word on any subject.

I looked at Ridd. "Do you care if he gets a male or a female?"

Ridd lifted one shoulder. "Not particularly."

Crick cuddled the pup and giggled when it licked his chin. "You're my dog," he told it, "and your name is Cricket Dog Yarbrough."

The three grownups grinned. Already he had Cricket Cat Yarbrough and Cricket Turtle Yarbrough. "Thank heavens he doesn't know his real name," Joe Riddley muttered, "or we'd have Joe Riddley dog, cat, and who knows what."

Crick and his pup climbed back into the truck. As they pulled off, Lulu nosed around the pen and whined. "It's getting empty, isn't it, girl?" Joe Riddley bent to scratch her behind the ears. "Five down and one to go."

"When you finish smooching that dog you can kiss your wife," I told him. He gave Lulu a final pat and came right over. We walked into the house with his arm around me, like we'd been walking most of our lives.

Inside, he tossed his filthy hat onto my nice clean counter and headed for the shower. I put the corn in to boil and carried supper out to the porch. I also shook the rocker cushions. I didn't want to look at Charlie Muggin's dent while I ate my meal.

The barbeque was delicious, the corn as tender as a baby's skin, and the tomatoes bright red and juicy. Joe Riddley had so much to tell me about the trip—especially about how much Crick enjoyed it—that we'd nearly finished eating before he thought to ask about what had been happening in Hopemore.

I started at the beginning, visiting the Kent woman's apartment with Walker and finding the phone number of the professor in Tennessee. "I'm pretty sure he killed her," I finished. "Ike James is up there this weekend, and he'll come tell us about it tomorrow."

Joe Riddley speared the last tomato slice. "I thought it might be something like that."

"You did not. You had no idea he existed!"

"Somebody existed," he pointed out.

"If it's not him, I have another suspect." I told him about Charlie Muggins. "His hair's the right color and he's the right size."

"Don't get too caught up in Luke's dream," Joe Riddley warned me.

"I'm not, but even without the dream it makes sense. Charlie's wife is gone, the nurse was all alone in town. Maybe they were having an affair. I just don't know how to find out if he has an alibi for the night she was killed."

Joe Riddley thought that over while he ate the last ear of corn. "Wasn't that the night the police officers went to the Braves game up in Atlanta?"

"Maybe so, but are you sure Charlie went?"

"No, but I can find out." He reached for the last pork. "How was Lorine's party?"

I couldn't believe I hadn't told him about that already. "Lorine got murdered, too!"

He stared at me like I'd gone crazy. "Lorine got murdered and you never mentioned it until now?"

I nodded, then I started sobbing like Lorine Duckworth had been my best friend. "Right there in her own driveway—" I wiped my streaming face with my greasy napkin and wondered why I was blubbering then, when I hadn't all day, "—and nobody heard a thing."

Joe Riddley fumbled around in a basket by one of the rockers and handed me a tissue box. I have enough allergies to keep tissues in every room.

He came over and pulled me toward him, held me close until I felt better, then led me to my favorite rocker. He took his favorite right next to it, and we held hands in the growing darkness while I told him the whole story.

"Do they think it's connected with the other murder?" he asked at the end.

"They're so clueless that Charlie Muggin was out here at dawn, sitting in your chair, wondering where *I* was between the party and the time they found her."

"Where *were* you?" He gently squeezed my fingers in his big ones.

I started telling about cleaning Walker's house and following the squad car back to Lorine's, thinking I'd leave out that bloodstained shirt and pants. I finally told him about that, too, though. He'd have to know sooner or later.

He stopped rocking and grew very still. "What explanation did Walker give?"

"I haven't asked," I confessed. "I was too scared. Even being pretty sure the professor in Tennessee killed her, I was scared."

Joe Riddley was never a man to worry when he could act. He stood up and pulled me up, too. "A real bear in the corncrib is easier to deal with than imaginary bears all over the house, Little Bit. Let's go ask him right now."

In five minutes we had put on our shoes, I'd grabbed my pocketbook and he'd put on his cap. In one more minute we were heading to town. We took the back way to Walker's—which is why we didn't see yellow crime tape up again at Hedricks'.

Walker's car sat right where I'd seen it at four that morning, making me think he'd been home all day. Joe Riddley pounded on the back door hard enough to wake the soundest sleeper, which is what Walker looked like when he came to the door. He had on khaki shorts, a Davidson T-shirt, and a stubble that showed he hadn't shaved. He also had creases on one cheek and I could hear a sports announcer's voice from the den.

"Come on in," he invited, standing back to let us past. "I was about to order a pizza. Want some?"

"We've eaten, thanks." Joe Riddley stayed on the deck and held me from going in. "And we aren't staying. Your mother has a question to ask about something she found here last night."

I expected Walker to get the look he had when I found a girlie magazine in his closet when he was ten. Instead he took a step forward and glared. "She had no business being here last night. Get off my case, Mama. I mean it. I don't like to be rude, Daddy, but what's in my house is none of her business."

"I suppose bloodstained clothes wadded up on your closet floor aren't my business?" As soon as I'd said it, I wanted to bite my tongue.

"Bloodstained clothes?" A slow dull flush rose in his cheeks, but I could see anger rising with it. He clenched the fist that wasn't holding onto the door and pounded the doorjamb so hard the frame shook. "Mama, who told you to go messing in my closet? Get it through your head that I am all grown up! I don't need you washing my dishes, laundering my socks, nor poking around in here." He stepped back and shut the door.

"At least he didn't slam it," I said quickly, seeing the look in Joe Riddley's eye.

"I never reared that boy to talk that way to his mama." He raised his fist.

I caught his hand. "He was right. I had no call to be messing around in his closet."

He peered down at me. "You're really scared, aren't you, Little Bit? You think Walker's done something awful. And you don't want to know what."

My teeth started to chatter. "I don't know Joe Riddley. I don't really think Walker would . . . but I saw the stains. Lots of stains. And smears."

He pulled his hand away and knocked again. Walker came to the door and opened it a crack. His face was surly. "Son," Joe Riddley said mildly, "we don't want to butt in on your private affairs. Heaven knows we haven't said a word all summer when we've wanted to say plenty. But if you are in trouble—"

"—any kind at all—" I added hastily from behind his shoulder.

"—and want to talk about it, we're available. We want you to know that."

Walker gave a funny little laugh. "Oh, I'm in trouble all right, but there's nothing you can do about it. Thanks anyway, Daddy." His voice was husky, but if I had even a fleeting hope he was going to tell us everything, I was wrong. He shut the door. Through the glass panes we saw the slump of his shoulders as he padded back to the den.

We didn't say a word on our way home. What was there to say?

The Lord said to Satan, "Very well,
then, he is in your hands; but you
must spare his life." *Job 2:6*

Twenty

I went to bed worried sick about Walker, even though
Joe Riddley kept assuring me he hadn't killed anybody.
After tossing and turning all night, I crawled out of bed
feeling like somebody had beaten me with a thick stick. I
was glad to get to work and find Isaac James at the back
door by our loading dock.

"Mornin', Judge, mornin', Mrs. Yarbrough." He spoke
formally and held his belt with both hands, like it had
gotten too heavy around his waist. I remembered one
young officer saying, right after he got his uniform, "With
everything hanging on my belt, it feels like I'm about to
lose my pants."

That morning, Ike clutched his belt like it carried the
weight of the world.

Joe Riddley pulled the big ring of store keys from his pocket. "Mornin', Officer James. I understand you and my wife have a date this morning."

"Did you see him?" I asked eagerly.

Isaac's dark eyes told me the answer before he spoke. "Yes ma'am, I saw him. He has an alibi for the night of the murder. Went to a faculty party with his wife and didn't leave until after midnight. No way it was him."

"Oh." Now I knew what a balloon feels like when somebody pricks a hole in it.

Isaac held out a white piece of paper to Joe Riddley. "And Judge, I need a warrant for arrest." Ike looked utterly miserable.

As Joe Riddley fit the key into the lock, the court-house clock chimed eight. "You're starting mighty early, Officer James."

"Yeah, well, I knew you got here around now and I wanted to get this over with. I also wanted to come myself. It's your young preacher. I'm awful sorry."

Joe Riddley went through the door and kept walking, like Ike had said something unimportant. I trotted after him, glad my legs could still move when the rest of me was numb. Ike followed as Joe Riddley unlocked our office and hung his cap on its nail exactly like it was a normal morning. It was when Joe Riddley sat down that I knew he'd heard what Ike said. He sat down heavy.

"Let me see what you've got." He held out one hand and Ike handed him the warrant. Joe Riddley scanned it and laid it down on his desk. "Officer James, do you seriously believe you have enough to go to trial?"

Isaac shifted uneasily from one foot to the other. "Chief Muggins believes we do, your honor. The hairs we found are consistent with Preacher Blessed's. His description of the place matches very closely, and his fingerprint was on a flier from your church—"

"Luke and the youth group put those fliers all over town!" I burst out before I thought. "And you know as well as I do that 'consistent with' doesn't mean identical, it just means they're in the same segment of the population." Both men ignored me, as they should. I wasn't supposed to be there, after all.

"Given the nature of the crime, Judge, Chief Muggins is asking that you deny bond."

"Oh he is, is he?"

"Yessir." They exchanged a long look.

Joe Riddley sighed and reached for his pen. There wasn't a thing he could do except sign the warrant.

I walked Ike out, nodding to a few employees who were beginning to refurbish the shelves. "You know Luke didn't do it, Ike."

"I can't talk about that, Miss MacLaren."

"At least tell me about the man in Tennessee," I coaxed, stopping him at the open loading dock. "I had such high hopes it was him. Maybe we can break his alibi."

Isaac tucked the warrant into his hip pocket as if he found it as distasteful as I did. "I did myself, but that alibi will stand. I talked to people who were at the party. He was there."

I nearly had a crick in my neck from peering up at him. "How did he act when you told him she'd been murdered?"

"Seemed real surprised, and a little guilty—"

"Maybe he arranged that alibi. Maybe people are lying for him."

Isaac shook his big head. "No ma'am. I think he was feeling guilty about how relieved he was. When he finally started talking, he sounded like a man who'd gotten rid of a pest. Said she'd been in his class five years ago and he admits they got involved, but he swears he loves his wife and ended the relationship with Ms. Kent when she left the college. He claims he hadn't seen her for two years. He also swears he was never her fiancé."

"She still called him several times a week."

"Yes, ma'am. I reminded him of that, but he said for years he's just been an ear on the line. He said Amanda Kent would call about a doctor hurting his patients or people in a coma getting scratched and she'd be crying all over the place. He said she wanted a daddy more than anything else. He also said that lately she'd seemed to be a lot happier."

"Did he think that could be because she'd gotten so involved in the temple?"

"He was concerned about that temple. Said Amanda was giving them way too much money. But he said he'd wondered if she was beginning to get interested in somebody else."

I rubbed a rough thumbnail against my skirt. "It wasn't Luke Blessed. He didn't even know her."

Ike looked down on me with pity. "At least Chief Muggins is only charging him with the one murder. We have information he visited Levy Saturday afternoon, and we know they had a fight a few weeks ago. Somebody broke a window."

The hair rose on the back of my neck. "What Levy?"

"Fellow who lived in the other garage apartment, next to Amanda Kent." Isaac was obviously surprised I hadn't heard. "Somebody killed him Saturday night."

"*Gideon?*" I felt like somebody had socked me in the stomach. "*Dead?*"

Isaac nodded. "That was the name."

Luke wasn't the only one who could have talked to Gideon Saturday afternoon. I'd told Walker Gideon had information about the Kent murder.

My knees gave way. I stumbled back a couple of steps and collapsed onto a stack of peat moss bags. "Why haven't I heard about this before?" I fanned my face and Isaac stepped away to give me more air.

"You all right, Miss MacLaren?"

"No, but tell me what happened."

"I don't rightly know, but it sounds like this town was really hopping Saturday night. The station was buzzing when I got back yesterday about three. They'd just discovered Levy's body, but thought he'd been killed the night before—about the same time as Mrs. Duckworth. You know about that, I understand?"

I nodded. "Two murders in one night." It didn't seem possible.

"And a robbery over to the mayor's, too, during the shindig at the Duckworths'. Somebody got his entire collection of civil war stamps and letters."

I didn't care beans about the mayor's stamps and letters. I was picturing Gideon Levy, and feeling sick. "How did they kill him, Isaac?"

Isaac hesitated. "Choked him, just like Mrs. Duckworth. That's one reason Chief Muggins didn't charge Mr. Blessed with those crimes. They were clean, quick killings. Miss Kent, now, she looked like somebody wanted to wipe her from the face of the earth."

❧

"I don't know what's happening to this town," I told Joe Riddley when I got back to our office.

He didn't even look up from his computer. "It's not the town. It's one sick person."

"Or two or three. They had another robbery Saturday night, during our Garden Club buffet, and there's been another murder. Gideon Levy, the boy I talked to Saturday morning."

Joe Riddley didn't say a word. What was there to say?

I slumped into my chair. "Well, whoever it is, it's certainly not Luke. Can we go see him?"

"I'll go down after dinner." He pretended to be fascinated by whatever was on his screen.

"He's going to need a good lawyer, but Walker thinks he can't afford one. Can we help?"

Finally he looked my way. "We can't do that. The magistrate who signed his arrest warrant can't pay his lawyer."

"Somebody's got to, Joe Riddley. You don't for a minute think that young man killed anybody, do you?"

Joe Riddley reached for his cap. The way he stood up, I realized that before too many more years, my husband was going to be old. "I need to go out for a while, Little Bit. Maybe the church ought to start a legal defense fund."

I knew what he was really saying. As soon as he'd gone, I dialed the church office. Maybe the magistrate who signed the warrant couldn't pay for Luke Blessed's defense, but there was nothing to prevent his wife from making a substantial anonymous donation.

Joe Riddley didn't come back to the office all morning. I looked out the window a couple of times and saw him personally slinging heavy bags of topsoil or cow manure into somebody's van. Once I saw him maneuvering a forklift of sod toward a waiting truck.

We drove home to dinner together but didn't talk. We ate so little that Clarinda grumbled, "You folks getting too old to need a cook. Just get yourselves some bird food and be done with it."

I wasn't worth diddley squat at work that afternoon. The only thing of value I accomplished was calling church members and a few special friends to tell them about the Blessed Defense Fund, which I soon abbreviated to "a fund to help Luke with legal expenses." The other sounded like church war work—which, I guess, in a way, it was. War against ignorance, prejudice, and evil.

An awful lot of people said they'd send in a check right away, but there were some who were reluctant to contribute. "I don't for a minute think he did it," one woman told me, "but I don't like for our church to get mixed up in something sordid."

"Seems to me like you'd be more comfortable around Pharisees," I muttered—after I hung up.

I tried calling Walker, but didn't find him in his office—or expect to. You don't sell much insurance sitting behind a desk, and Walker is the best insurance salesman in town. There probably weren't five houses in the county he hadn't called on at least once.

"No, he's not here," said the woman who runs his office. "He's out trying to drum up some new business. By the time he pays accidental deaths on both that Kent woman and Lorine Duckworth, he's going to have a bad month."

"He carried both of them?" It was fortunate I was already sitting down.

"Oh, yes, ma'am. Lorine and Ronald had standard couple's policy, and Miss Kent took out a policy for her mother."

"You don't think of young people buying life insurance," I said tentatively. "That must have been some selling job Walker did."

She gave a hollow laugh. "That's what he said when he heard she'd been killed. 'And it took me three visits to convince her to buy a policy for her poor widowed mother.' He never expected to have to pay out on it, you see."

Surely Walker wouldn't kill anybody on whom he'd written a life insurance policy. But he'd never mentioned knowing her. Why not?

Also, Amanda Kent was killed by somebody who'd gotten very angry. Walker sometimes got so angry he scarcely knew what he was saying. Had he gone off a deep end and finally pounded a person instead of a wall? If she'd let him in three times to talk about insurance, she might have let him in for other reasons. With Cindy out of town—

I couldn't stand my own thoughts. I grabbed my pocketbook and left the office. "I'm going on home and swim," I told Joe Riddley when I found him out back watering bedding plants. "You come later in one of the trucks." Before he could object, I went.

"Lock your doors," he called after me.

It was getting to be a habit. Neither Joe Riddley nor I believed for a minute that Chief Muggins had the murderer behind bars.

> If only my anguish could be weighed
> and all my misery be placed on the
> scales! It would surely outweigh
> the sand of the seas. *Job 6:2–3*

Twenty-One

I didn't even get my bathing suit on before Joe Riddley called. "That girl who bought the pup called here. I said you'd call her back. She sounded upset, but didn't say why."

I almost didn't recognize Selena's voice it was so husky and strained. I could tell she'd been crying. No wonder, losing two friends in two weeks. "I'm sorry, Mrs. Yarbrough, but I can't keep Beauregard," she said. "Could you please take him back?"

I was puzzled. I'd have sworn that match was made in heaven. "Well, sure, honey, if he's not satisfactory—"

"Oh, no, he's *very* satisfactory. I hate like anything to give him up, but I'm moving back home with my folks tomorrow, and my baby sister is allergic to dogs. May I bring him in the morning?"

I made a quick decision, hoping it was a good one. "Why don't I come out right now and pick him up? I'm taking the afternoon off anyway."

Maniac was mowing the grass as I passed. I beeped, and he waved for me to stop. "I've decided to take that puppy after all," he said, leaning in my window. "Daddy says he'd *enjoy* having a pup around. Can I get him tonight?"

"I'm sorry, but Cricket took the male. You can have the female, or you might want the one Selena took—she's returning him. I'm fixing to pick him up right now."

"*Beauregard?* What *happened*—didn't he *protect her* well enough?" Oddly, he sounded more surprised than sarcastic.

He'd also given me a horrible new idea. Selena Jones was one of just two members left on the temple's music team. Was somebody picking them off one by one? Did they know a secret somebody was afraid they'd tell? Did the same person kill Lorine, fearing Amanda told her the secret, too?

If Selena was asking herself the same questions, no wonder she wanted to get out of town. I hoped she wasn't in danger until I got there.

I nearly asked Maniac to come, too, but I didn't. I still wasn't convinced Luke's dream meant anything, but with the professor in Tennessee out as a suspect, I was leery of blonde men in Hopemore.

Besides, Maniac was giving me a distinctly funny look . . . Oh. He was waiting for my answer. "Apparently not. Come down when you see my car."

On my way to Selena's I started naming all the blonde men I knew, but it was hopeless. Hopemore is full of sandy-haired men with light blue eyes.

I might have known, since I was in a hurry, that I'd get stuck behind at least one tractor, two logging trucks, and a spell of road work. The workers burned up outside while I sat guiltily in my air conditioned car, waiting for the single lane sign to turn from Stop to Slow and wondering why the Georgia highway department chooses the middle of summer to work on roads. You'd think we had six feet of snow all winter. By the time I reached Selena's, I was fit to be tied. And I'd forgotten a box for the pup.

Her little place looked a whole lot more peaceful than I felt. The green mobile home under tall oaks was more like a cottage. An old fashioned pink rose grew up a trellis at one end. Healthy pink geraniums spilled over an old iron wash pot by the door. A white porch swing hung from a low tree branch. It looked like a place you could rest in after work—if you weren't terrified of being murdered.

I heard Beauregard yipping inside as soon as I got out of the car. Selena peered out a window, then hurried to let me in.

In decorating, as in clothes, Selena's taste ran to green, cream, and yellow. Her living room was cheery with cross-stitched samplers and hand-worked throw pillows. The mistress, however, looked sodden and scared. Her eyes were full of tears, her cheeks streaked with them. Her hair was damp in front, like she'd wept through her fingers then shoved them through her tumbled fiery curls, and a wadded green and cream afghan on the couch made me think she'd been huddled under it before I arrived.

Beauregard backed against the couch and trembled, still yipping. I bent to pick him up. "You can't have forgotten me that quickly," I scolded. "If you smell carefully you'll get a whiff of your mama." He wiggled with joy and licked my nose, then squirmed to be put down. As soon as he reached the floor he scampered over to Selena and leaned against her leg. She picked him up and cuddled him under her chin.

"I heard about Gideon this morning," I told her gently. "The assistant police chief stopped by our office and told me. That's awful."

She nodded, and tears spilled onto her freckled cheeks. "It was. I found him."

"Oh, honey, how dreadful! Why? How?"

She grabbed a tissue and blew her nose. "He was so late for music practice before the service that Norman—the drummer—and I said . . . said we'd go over and . . . and kill him."

She sat down abruptly on the couch and pulled the afghan around herself and Beau. Beau wiggled to get his head out, then rested his chin on her hand.

"We thought he'd overslept again." She sounded like she was repeating a story she'd already told. "He sometimes did. But he didn't come to the door—even though we called and *called*." As if that would summon him back to life. I thought of Rhonda, insisting Lorine had no reason to go outside, as if that meant she could not possibly be dead.

"How'd you get in? Did you have a key?"

She lifted a dangling thread from the afghan and wound it round her finger. "No, we got the manager. She didn't want to bother him—said people deserved a little privacy. But I think she was already afraid something bad had happened. Because of Mandy—you know?" She swallowed convulsively, then went on as if plunging downhill. "She opened the door, then she stood back and Norman went first, and I was right behind him—"

She stopped, pressed her hand to her mouth, and burst into tears.

I held her, smoothing her hair, until she grew still. "Have you eaten all day?"

"I didn't feel like it. I fed the dog," she added virtuously.

"I knew that already, honey. A pup who hadn't been fed would have let me know at once." I was rewarded with a watery smile.

I put on a kettle and rummaged in her cupboard for tea. I also found cheese, crackers, and an apple. Selena didn't say a word the whole time, but she gratefully drank, ate, and fed Beauregard stray crumbs.

"I don't know how I can give him up." She stroked the little head on her lap and held a speck of cheese toward the eager pink tongue. "He already seems like a part of me."

"Maybe you won't have to." I took a green chair across from the couch and leaned toward her. "Selena, I know your teacher said not to talk about Amanda's death, but he hasn't told you not to talk about Gideon's. I fear they may be related. I also wonder if they're connected to the temple."

"No!" She made a quick little motion, but I went right on.

"Two of the three people killed this past week were in your music group, honey. Is it possible that they knew—maybe even you and Norman know—something somebody else doesn't want known?"

She knew what I was saying. "No. The teacher isn't like that. You don't know him."

"No, I don't," I admitted, "but I do know my own preacher. He's been arrested for murder and I know he didn't kill anybody. And you've lost two special friends. I want to do everything I can to sort this out. Will you help me?"

She started to shake her head, but Beauregard looked up as she looked down. She bent to kiss him, then nodded. "I don't want anybody else to die. I know I must accept it as the will of God, but I can hardly stand it!" Tears spilled over onto her cheeks.

"I don't believe for a minute that murder is ever the will of God," I said angrily. "Murder is the work of evil, not goodness. I think God weeps to see it."

She looked at me with puzzled eyes. "That sounds a lot like my priest back home."

I reached over and patted her knee. "It's possible we both might be right. Will you tell me a few things about Gideon?"

She hesitated, then nodded. "Yes, ma'am."

"Then finish eating while I think about what I want to know."

She obediently nibbled cheese and crackers and sipped tea while I thought.

"Somebody said Luke Blessed quarreled with Gideon. Do you know about that?"

She paused with her cup half-way to her mouth. "It's Luke who got arrested?"

Her casual use of my own preacher's name surprised me. "You know Luke?"

"Sure. He goes"—her voice faltered and she swallowed hard—"*used* to go over to play gin rummy with Gideon all the time. I think they knew each other before they came to Hopemore. They never said that, but they mentioned things that made me think it."

I held my breath on my next question. "Did Luke know Amanda, too?"

She wrinkled her forehead as she sipped her tea. "I don't think so. Mandy worked nights and slept days, mostly, and she wouldn't go up to Gideon's. They played cards under the tree—usually in the late afternoon while Luke was at work."

"Did you know Luke and Gideon had a quarrel a couple of weeks ago?"

"They bickered all the time. It didn't mean anything."

"But do you ever remember a big fight, with a broken window?"

She shook her head vigorously. "It wasn't really a fight. Gideon was telling Luke about some of the goswami's teachings, but he didn't tell them very well and Luke said they didn't make sense—that Gideon was looking in the wrong direction for inner peace. Gideon said Luke was narrow-minded, and he got mad. Jumped up and down and yelled, and finally he threw a baseball at Luke. It missed and went through the window. That's all." She added defensively, "Gideon was like that. He flew off the handle sometimes."

I could think of at least one explanation. "Did you know Gideon used drugs?"

She hesitated, then admitted, "The teacher says some drugs can help us attain a more spiritual state. He only gives them to those who are training for the priesthood, though. He doesn't deal or anything. And we are supposed to only use them in very private places, like at home or in the temple."

In the temple. Where Gideon had spent the past week creating small cells for meditation. I didn't mention that. Instead, I asked, "Who all is studying for the priesthood?"

"We aren't supposed to say," she said primly. "It's a secret rite."

"Selena, I am not trying to pry, I am trying to help. If you won't help too—"

"Gideon and Mandy both were," she said quickly. "I can tell you that much."

"And you?"

She looked at her hands. "Just this past month. I wasn't sure of my call before then."

I still wasn't sure of it, but I didn't say that. I didn't say anything, in fact. I was too thinking about how her information changed the picture—and not for the better. It was one thing to imagine the goswami killing his flock because they knew a secret he wanted to keep. It was a whole different thing to picture somebody wiping out the temple's novice priesthood. To some people's way of thinking, a preacher would be the most likely suspect for that. And they would argue, once Luke got into the killing habit, why not add Lorine to his list? She led the opposition when he was called to our congregation, and had opposed everything he'd tried to do since. I wiggled my head to dispel those thoughts.

"Mandy and I wouldn't use drugs." I knew from her tone that Selena thought that's what I'd been thinking. "The hospital would fire us. The teacher said we could attain blessedness without them."

Poor Mandy attained blessedness all right. The hardest way imaginable. I leaned closer to Selena. "Tell me anything you remember about the night Amanda was killed."

Selena froze with her mug halfway to her lips. I could see her battling her scruples about disobeying her teacher. I didn't say a word, just prayed she'd make the right decision.

Beauregard made it for her. He whined, and when Selena had picked him up and cuddled him, she looked at me over his head and asked, "What do you want to know?"

"Did Amanda work in the juice bar until it closed?"

"No, only until nine-thirty, then she asked me to take over for her. Said she had to get home before ten." She started trembling so hard that Beauregard got frightened and whined. She cuddled him close and cried, "I wish I could have stopped her!"

I covered her trembling hands with one of mine and stroked the anxious pup with the other. "Don't blame yourself, Selena. There was no way anybody could know what was coming. She didn't say why she had to go home early?"

Selena started to shake her head, then got a surprised look on her face. "Yes. Yes, she did. She said she had to meet somebody. In fact, she looked so excited I thought maybe her boyfriend had come down."

She sighed and lifted brimming eyes to mine. "It doesn't seem fair, Mrs. Yarbrough. Mandy was usually serious, but that night she just glowed."

I thought that over. "Somebody else said today she'd been happier for several weeks. Do you remember that?"

Selena nodded at once. "Yes, she had. Since June or so. Maybe it was because she was finally finding inner peace."

I pushed away a sudden thought of Walker, wifeless since June. "Did she go home alone that Friday night?"

"Yes. Usually she and Gideon walked together, but that night he was worried about something and left right after the service." That jived with what Gideon had said Saturday.

"She wasn't going to meet her boyfriend from Tennessee, Selena. I know that for a fact. Could she have been meeting another man?"

"No." Selena shook her head quickly. "I don't think so." She played with the pup to avoid looking at me.

"Maynard said she didn't want him in her place," I said thoughtfully, "and Gideon said they only played cards under the trees. Selena, did Mandy not like men? Even the man in Tennessee said he hadn't seen her for years. I find that puzzling."

Selena took a deep breath and looked up at me with pain in her eyes. "Mandy was raped her first year of nursing school. She went out running one night and three men jumped her. She . . . they . . . after that she wouldn't be alone with any man."

That explained a lot. But it didn't explain one important thing. "So who would she have let into her apartment late at night wearing only a nightgown?"

Selena shook her head. "Nobody, Mrs. Yarbrough. That's what I can't understand. Mandy would have died before she let a man in her place dressed like that."

Except Amanda *didn't* die before she let a man in her place. She died sometime after.

Twenty-Two

After our little talk, I couldn't drive off and leave Selena alone. She didn't protest when I told her to pack a bag, bring Beauregard, and come stay with us overnight.

"Have you told the medical center you are quitting?" I asked while she packed.

"No. I just called in sick today. I'll tell them tomorrow."

"Let it go a day or two," I suggested. "Maybe you'll feel differently by then."

I'd forgotten I'd invited Maniac to come down when I got home. He arrived before we'd gotten her bag out of her car.

He hurried to help. "Let *me* carry that."

Selena held Beauregard up to her chin and looked at the ground. I suspected she didn't want Maniac to see how soggy she looked.

He noticed right away, however. Maybe he wasn't as inexperienced around women as I'd supposed. "Are you all *right*?" he asked, gently stroking Beauregard's head with his free hand.

She nodded.

"Are you *sad* about giving up the *pup*?"

"Maybe she won't have to give it up," I told him. "Come on in with that bag, Maynard. Selena's staying with me tonight."

"What's *happened* to her?" Maniac asked bluntly without moving.

"The young man who got killed yesterday was her friend, remember?"

"Oh. I'm *sorry*." One hand hovered near her, but didn't touch her.

He sounded so concerned, though, that she looked up at him, then dropped her lashes and nuzzled Beauregard again. She would never be beautiful, but with sunlight filtering through the maple tree and dappling her hair, she was very striking. Still stroking the pup, Maniac stood looking down at her—for although she was tall, he was several inches taller—and for all the attention the two of them paid me, I could have been at my office. I didn't mind. I was fascinated to see Maniac paying attention to a woman.

Of course, if he wound up marrying somebody I introduced him to who was hooked on the Temple of Inner Peace, both Joe Riddley and Hubert would have my hide, but I could cross that bridge if Maniac ever got to it.

"Why don't you all put Beauregard back in with his mother and sister?" I suggested. I headed on into the house, thinking maybe they could do with some privacy.

Poor ducks, they didn't have the vaguest idea what to do with it. They came in a few minutes later arguing as usual. ". . . you *ought* to at least *think* about it," Maniac stormed.

She lifted her chin. "I *have* thought about it, and I'm sure I'm *right*. The teacher is the most sincere man I *know*."

This was dreadful. Not only was Maniac accenting words, Selena was, too.

"You can be *sincere* and sincerely *wrong*," Maniac insisted stubbornly.

She turned away. "Mrs. Yarbrough, may I go to my *room*? I'm a little *tired*."

"Sure, honey." I took the case from Maniac and waved him toward the door. "Can you see yourself out?"

"I *came* to look at a *dog*," he reminded me impatiently.

Selena sniffed. "I'd *pity* any dog *you* raised." Chin in air, she followed me upstairs.

I showed her our guestroom and the bath next door, then left her to settle in. I found Maniac hanging over the dog pen, where Lulu was giving her returned son a delighted welcome. "I'd like to throttle that gos-whatever he is," he muttered. His eyes were so stormy that I was glad the goswami was nowhere around.

"Please don't," I begged. "We've had our quota of violence in town for the month." I reached down and scooped up the female pup. Lulu barked anxiously. All this coming and going was hard for her to understand. Me, too, if you came right down to it.

"I like *this* one better *anyway*," he told me, rubbing the pup's head gently. "I'm *still* going to call her *Beauty*." She stuck out a soft little tongue and licked him in approval.

I sold her to him gladly. It might do Maniac good to have at least one female who thought he was wonderful.

He started toward his car, but I called him back. "Wait, Maynard. I want to ask you something."

He heeled as obediently as one of Joe Riddley's dogs. I wondered how to ask what I had to say. Finally I blurted, "Why do you accent words so much? I noticed you didn't do it with Dr. Holder the other night. You talked perfectly normal to him."

He bit his lip and flushed. "Habit. I had a teacher who talked that way in third grade, and I thought he was wonderful. I started copying him, then after a while it got to be normal. When I got to college and worked on toning down my southern accent, I stopped emphasizing words, too, but whenever I get back down here, I slip right back into it along with the accent." He ducked his head and rubbed out a weed with one toe. "It's pretty annoying, huh?"

"Pretty," I admitted. "That and—er—so much complaining detract from the fine man you've become."

I wondered if I'd gone too far, but he grinned. "I have been pretty bad, haven't I? Daddy said last week that if I don't stop grousing about living down here he's gonna put me on the next train north. And you know what? I discovered I don't want to go. I must be finding my roots or something."

I suspected the "something" had red curly hair, but I didn't say so.

He sighed. "The problem with the way I talk, though, is I don't even *know* when I'm *doing* it."

"Right now." I touched his arm. "How about if I touch you like that if I hear you and am close enough? Would that help?"

"Sure—if you're close enough. What if you aren't?"

"I'll wink."

He threw back his head and laughed. "Joe Riddley will throttle *me*—and that sentence needs an emphasis."

As he drove off, I accepted a hard fact: our little neighbor boy was all grown up into a sometimes charming man. I was going to change, too. I'd no longer call him Maniac. He was Maynard.

Joe Riddley came home walking so heavily up the back steps I thought he was carrying something. I was surprised when all he set down on the counter was his cap.

I was busy pulling out the ham and potato salad Clarinda had made for dinner and we hadn't eaten. It was a good thing we had so much left. It hadn't occurred to me when I invited Selena to spend the night that I'd have to feed her. Thank goodness I had Ridd's tomatoes, cucumbers, and carrots to add to the ham and potato salad. With a package of frozen biscuits and honey from Ridd's hives, we'd be fine.

"Evenin', Little Bit." Joe Riddley's voice was as leaden as his feet. "I stopped by to see Luke on the way home, but he was talkin' to his lawyer."

"Luke has a lawyer?"

He sighed. "For all the good it will do him. Walker called Jimmy Newton."

"Wait Newton? He's never handled a murder case in his life." A hulking high school classmate of Walker's, Jimmy had gotten a college degree based on his football skills and a law degree based on his daddy's connections. He specialized in civil cases where it was in the client's interest to continue the case indefinitely. Jimmy Newton was the best procrastinator you ever saw. His childhood nickname was Wait-a-minute, shortened to Wait.

Joe Riddley gave me a sour nod. "That's what I told Walker when I stopped by his office after I left the sheriff's detention center, but Walker says Wait is a good buddy of his who will give Luke a good price."

"Luke doesn't need a good buddy or a good price, he needs a good lawyer!" I started for the phone.

Joe Riddley put out a hand to stop me. "Little Bit, who are you calling?"

"Walker, to tell him to get Luke another lawyer."

"Walker won't listen. He says Wait is a good man."

"Being a good tight end in high school doesn't make him capable of defending Luke."

"Walker won't listen," Joe Riddley repeated. "Believe, me, I tried." He finally noticed what I'd been doing. "Why're you makin' so much supper?"

Before I could answer, Selena came down the back stairs. "May I help, Mrs. Yarbrough?" Joe Riddley brightened up considerably. I introduced them, then sent Joe Riddley up to wash and Selena out to the porch to set the table.

Joe Riddley liked the young woman. I could tell by the way he didn't notice what he ate while he asked a string of questions. He finally asked the one I'd been dying to ask but hadn't yet dared. "How'd a girl like you get mixed up with that temple place?"

Selena tilted her chin, but Joe Riddley, mopping up honey with his biscuit, didn't look threatening, just interested. She relaxed. "I grew up Episcopalian, but in nursing school I got out of the habit of going. Not that churchgoing is a habit—" she added hastily.

"Sure it is." Joe Riddley finished his biscuit and reached for another. "Faith, now, that's not a habit, but going to church is like flossing your teeth. You keep doing it regularly, you don't even think about whether you will or not. You neglect it a week or two, and you've got to make the decision every time. Gets hard to decide to do it."

Selena looked at him like he'd said something wise. Maybe he had. After so many years, it's hard to tell whether somebody is smart or just normal. Anyway, she waited a minute to see if he was finished, then went on. "The first Sunday afternoon I was here, I walked around town to get acquainted. When I saw that house, I fell in love with it."

Hope stirred in every one of my matchmaking genes, but I didn't give it much living space. You can't make a successful marriage out of nothing but love for the same house.

"When I saw people going in and realized it was a kind of church, I went in, too. I'd just broken up with a boyfriend—he kept giving me orders, and I can't stand that" (I made a mental note to tell Maynard) "but I still liked him a lot. I was real confused. The teacher spoke that day about how the most important thing in life is inner peace. That is so true. He also said they needed people who played instruments for their music team, so I signed up."

"I see." Joe Riddley reached for a third biscuit and poured more honey on his plate. If Selena stayed very long, I'd have to let out his pants. He chewed thoughtfully for a minute, then asked, "Have you found this inner peace?"

"Not exactly," Selena admitted, "but I'm working on it. It can take a lifetime."

"Don't work on it too hard." Joe Riddley washed down his biscuit with iced tea. "A redhead like you—looks to me like you'd want a few sparks now and then to keep life interesting. Maybe even hard decisions to wrestle with. Time enough for peace when you're dead." He shoved back his chair. "Want to come help me feed the dogs?"

They went out to the dog pens together like cronies. I suspected Selena was going to find more inner peace feeding dogs with Joe Riddley than she had in past weeks. But I couldn't help worrying. Was she next on somebody's list?

What I feared has come upon me;
what I dreaded has happened to me.
Job 3:25

Twenty-Three

I didn't like to tell Selena she'd be safer working
than hanging around our empty house, so I just suggested
that keeping busy at the hospital might take her mind off
things. She agreed so fast, I wondered if she were nervous, too, about being left alone. Early Tuesday morning
we drove our two cars and Ridd's truck into town like a
small parade.

It was an hour until Yarbrough's opened, so nobody
else was around. Joe Riddley had business out at our
greenhouses, so I went alone into the office and read the
Augusta Chronicle and the *Macon Telegraph*. Both had
front page stories about Luke's arrest.

Quickly I turned on the computer and typed a hasty
letter, then grabbed my pocketbook and scribbled Joe Riddley a note: *Running errands. Be back soon.*

After I'd taken Clarinda to our house, I went to see Luke. The sheriff's detention center let us talk in a private room with a guard at the door. When Luke came in wearing the navy jumpsuit the county provides involuntary guests, I joked, "Your clothes match your eyes."

I was trying to cheer him up, but I should have known better. Luke sounded far more cheerful than I felt. "Yeah, and the place is air conditioned with better food than I cook at home. I may stay."

"Don't say that," I begged. "We want to get you out of here as fast as we can. Have you called your parents?"

He bit his lower lip. "It's just Dad. I don't want him knowing unless he has to."

"It's on every front page in the South, hon. You know how papers are about preachers. I just know he's packing to come. Give me his number, and I'll call and tell him I'll find him a place to stay. I'd offer our place, but we've got somebody with us right now."

"He could stay at my place—the rent's paid until the end of the month—but you don't have to call him. I'll do it later."

I decided it was time for some plain speaking. "Luke, are you ashamed of your family?" He blinked twice, startled. "Last Saturday Gideon Levy"—I knew from his swift intake of breath that he'd already heard about Gideon, but I didn't stop—"said he's known you for years, that you and his brother—"

"Were college roommates." Luke nodded. "There's nothing secret about that. David's going to be heartbroken about Gideon. Me, too. He was a swell kid. Mixed up, but sweet."

"He sure was," I agreed. "Did you get to see him Saturday to find out what he knew about Amanda Kent's murder?"

He shook his head. "Walker told me to and I went over, but he wasn't home. I thought I'd go back Sunday evening." He rubbed his eyes to erase whatever he was seeing. "I was too late." I rubbed my own eyes, but I couldn't erase what I was seeing: Walker going to Gideon's instead.

Pushing back my dread, I filled Luke in on what Gideon had told me, then added, "He started to say something about you and his brother crewing, but he broke off and said 'Luke doesn't want me to talk about that.' What was he not talking about?"

Luke flushed. "It's no big deal. My dad has a sailboat. And speaking of Dad, I'll call him tonight or tomorrow. Don't worry about it."

Why did I have the feeling he was adroitly changing the subject?

Two could play that game. Being a parent, I believed his dad would want to come at once, whether Luke wanted him or not, and I'd just realized where I could get the number: it would be listed as Luke's next of kin at the church office. Having settled that to my satisfaction, I moved on. "I hear Walker got you a lawyer, Jimmy Newton."

"Yeah." He was squirming again about something. I was pretty sure I knew what.

"Don't worry about how you're going to pay him. The church set up a fund for that."

Luke flushed an even deeper red. "You all didn't have to do that."

"Somebody had to," I said firmly. "Now, this is going to sound real nosy, but would you give Jimmy permission to release to me copies of any evidence he has? Maybe there's something your friends can do to help him defend you."

"I'll be glad to give you permission to see anything you want, but you don't have to go to all that trouble. I'm sure, uh, Mr. Newton will do anything that's necessary." He still seemed more dismayed than worried. Maybe he was too young to realize how much trouble he was in.

"We'll all be doing all we can," I assured him. "You just eat right and be patient."

"I'm also trying to figure out what God wants me to do in here. I've been talking to some of the other guys, and did you know there's not a preacher in town who visits this place on a regular basis? There's also not a Bible study, prayer meeting, or even a support group for prisoners' families in this whole town."

I couldn't help sounding a bit impatient. "You can come back to visit, but we want you out for now. Would you please sign this?"

He scribbled his signature above where I'd typed his name. Full of purpose I sent him back to his cell and headed toward Jimmy Newton's office.

Back when my boys went through their dinosaur phase, Walker used to be fascinated by the stegosaurus because it was immense but had a brain the size of a walnut. I've always wondered if that was what first attracted him to Jimmy Newton. Jimmy stands six feet four in bare feet and must weigh close to three hundred pounds. I guess he isn't a total dummy—he finished law school and passed the bar—but I have yet to observe any sign of active intelligence except in his choice of an office.

That's in the old First National Bank, a lovely building of soft red Georgia brick designed by an architect named Choate who designed a lot of banks around here in the nineteenth century. Nowadays those old banks are used for antique stores, insurance companies, and lawyer's offices. Jimmy's had high ceilings, long windows, and a terrific view of the courthouse square.

When I got there he had his feet on his desk, a wet cigar in his mouth, and his ear glued to the phone. He waved me to a brown leather chair and blew out a cloud of smoke that nearly asphyxiated me on the spot, then said cheerfully to whoever was on the other end, "Don't worry about a little thing like that. We can delay for at least another six months."

He pointed to an old humidor filled with peppermints. I tried one, but it tasted like tobacco, so I spat it into a tissue. Jimmy finished his conversation, swung his feet off the desk, and asked genially, "What can I do for you today, Miss MacLaren?"

"I've come from seeing Luke Blessed."

He didn't say a word for the time it took the courthouse clock to chime nine. Then he nodded. "Fine man, Luke Blessed."

I thought that was a preamble, but Jimmy was done.

"He's in a bit of trouble right now, Wait," I pointed out.

"Yeah. He sure is." We sat in silence some more.

I wanted to scream. Instead, I did what I'd come for—handed him Luke's letter. "Some of us want to do anything we can to help."

That was stretching things a bit, since "some of us" only included me, myself and I, but it was important for Jimmy to think there was a committee. Jimmy liked committees and served on a lot of them—which may have done a lot to account for Hopemore's reputation as the slowest-moving town in middle Georgia.

Jimmy read the letter like it was some ancient scroll he had to translate from the original hieroglyphics, then looked up. "So what can I do for you, Miss MacLaren?"

"Let me read the police report, for starters. We need to know what evidence the police have."

Jimmy nodded. "I'll do that, as soon as I get it."

"You don't have it yet?"

"No ma'am. I just got retained yesterday afternoon, and I've been real busy. I thought I'd go over and pick up everything sometime after dinner."

I leaned over his desk. "Wait, my preacher is in jail. Our church needs him out real bad, so he can run the youth program." Jimmy was active in his youth program in high school. I hoped that might strike a chord.

212

It must have, because he pushed back his chair and hauled himself to his broad flat feet. "Golly, Miss MacLaren, I could run over and get the reports right now, if you like."

"Why don't I drive you? Then we can come back here and make a copy. No need for you to walk in this heat." I had an ulterior motive. Jimmy would pass two blocks' worth of stores, including a barbershop and Hubert's appliance place, on his way. I didn't want him stopping to get a haircut or buy a television. Remember, I'd known Wait Newton all his life.

I had to be sneaky, though. It wouldn't do for Chief Muggins to see me dropping off Luke's lawyer and waiting to pick him up. "I've got to get something from the Bi-Lo," I told him. "Stand on the corner when you're done. I'll be right back."

I bought a magazine at the grocery store and waited in the parking lot until I spotted Jimmy coming out to the sidewalk with the papers he was entitled to, then went to get him. I drove him back to his office and made the copies myself, since his secretary was up to her ears in typing— probably requests for continuance.

When I left with my copies, Jimmy was lighting another cigar. By the time he finished it, he might get around to reading the papers he'd picked up. If he didn't have a few other cases to continue first.

⊷

I went back to the office, tossed my note to Joe Riddley in the wastebasket, and called the church office. The secretary gave me Luke's dad's phone number and the latest figures on Luke's defense fund. I had no doubt Jimmy Newton could continue the case long enough to use it all, but hoped we'd have Luke free long before that.

A woman answered the telephone. "Luke?" she asked eagerly.

"No, I'm a member of his church," I explained. "I told Luke I'd call his dad and help him find a place to stay if he plans to come to Hopemore."

"He's on his way," she told me. "His plane left over an hour ago."

"Plane?" Hopemore's not real close to an airport. "Where's he flying into? Do we need to meet him?"

"That won't be necessary. It's the corporate plane, and Mr. Blessed will be met by a car and driver. He should arrive by noon." Her voice softened a little. "How *is* Luke?" She sounded like she knew him well.

"I saw him just a few minutes ago, and he's doing as well as can be expected, but I know he'll be glad to see his father."

"I hope so." She didn't sound at all as sure as I had.

I was puzzled, but there wasn't anything I could do except wait—and read the papers Jimmy Newton had given me.

Every little noise made me start until I realized what was making me nervous. I didn't want Joe Riddley finding me reading police reports.

I retrieved my note, smoothed it out, and put it back on his desk. Then I carried my copies over to Myrtle's. At that time of day the place was empty except for a big table of retired men up front who met there every morning to shoot the breeze and eat breakfast—in that order of importance. I holed up in a back booth with a Co-cola, scrambled eggs, grits, and biscuits. "And bring me some real butter," I added crabbily. "I know you've got some back there somewhere."

After reading the police report's detailed description of Amanda Kent's injuries, though, I shoved back my eggs and grits unfinished. I didn't think I'd ever want to eat again. What would make anybody that angry with another human being?

The official description of what she was wearing was a little different from the gossip: a green floor-length nightgown with long sleeves, bra, and underpants. Underwear? That was puzzling. So were fourteen tiny cuts on her arms and legs, "as if from a small sharp knife." The medical examiner could offer no explanation for them.

Reading about how she had held her hands—curved above her head, with the thumbs pressed against the first two fingers—struck a chord. I tried it with my own hands, and remembered where I'd seen it. That was how the goswami held his hands when he blessed the group after the service. Was Amanda blessing her killer?

"Hands raised in supplication," Luke had described it in his dream. That looked bad. How could he possibly have known?

I turned to the transcript of his dream and compared it line by line with what I remembered. Finally, I turned one page of paper over and made two columns:

Like	Unlike
a bed used like a couch against one wall	lamp with a *dark* shade (white)
doorway across room from bed	TV in one corner (was a stereo)
big chair (with high back?)	weapon = *walking cane* (tire iron)

victim had dark brown hair

hit so hard I saw blood spurt up all over

person collapsed forward

two hands raised in supplication

beating and beating

Luke had gotten almost every detail right. One thing puzzled me, though. Where on earth had he been standing in his dream? The wing chair was nearly against the wall. To have been behind the chair looking at the door, Luke would have needed to stand inside the wall between her place and Gideon's.

Or inside Amanda Kent's head.

I thought about that awhile, and I remembered Luke worrying about me on Sunday at exactly the time Charlie Muggins was sitting on my side porch. Why'd he do that? I was getting an idea that scared the socks off of me. Maybe it was time to talk to Martha again.

One thing I haven't mentioned. In addition to being an emergency room nurse, a mother, and a bean canner, Martha is one of the best Bible scholars in town. She teaches an adult class at church that has grown so much it meets in the fellowship hall, and leads an interdenominational women's Bible study that's run for nearly ten years. If anybody could answer my question, it would be Martha. With Crick just back from a weekend away and Bethany due home from camp any day now, I suspected she'd be home.

I hurried back to the office, glad Joe Riddley still wasn't back. With my hands shaking—I wasn't sure if it was from excitement or fear—I punched in her number. It took her so long to answer, I knew I was bringing her in from the garden.

While I waited, I wadded up my note and threw it away again.

"This may sound crazy," I said when Martha came on the line, "but what do you know or believe about clairvoyance and ESP?"

"How do you mean?" She sounded puzzled—as well she might. I hadn't led up to the question, just popped it on her.

"You know, getting messages from somebody else without words. Knowing what they are thinking. Is that really possible? Or is it evil fooling us?"

Martha is utterly unflappable. "Sure it's possible. It's only evil if the intent of the message is to deceive or harm. If it's there to help, it's called getting a word of knowledge. It's listed as one of the gifts of the Spirit in First Corinthians twelve."

I grabbed a Bible Joe Riddley kept on the shelf and quickly found the chapter. There it was, in verse eight: *To one there is given through the Spirit the message of wisdom, to another the message of knowledge by means of the same Spirit.*

"You mean the Holy Spirit might tell me what you are thinking, if I needed to know for some good purpose?" It sounded pretty spooky—not one of those things our church spends much time talking about, I can tell you that.

Martha chuckled. "Sure. But you'd have to stop talking long enough to listen."

"Can it happen while you're asleep?"

"It can happen anytime the Spirit decides to make it happen. Some people get the gift for a specific situation, while others seem to have it a lot of the time. If you're talking about Luke, he does seem to have an uncanny ability to know when someone else is in pain. Did you know that the night Cindy left, he showed up on Walker's doorstep with his guitar and a pizza, saying, 'I had a feeling you might need cheering up'? And when Miss Bessie fell in July, Luke went home from the office within fifteen minutes, worrying that something was the matter with her."

I hadn't known either of those things. "What about his dream the night Amanda Kent was killed? Could he have been getting a message then? It certainly didn't do her any good."

"I have no idea whether that was a word of knowledge or just a dream, and even if it was a word of knowledge, it might have a different purpose than we think. Either way, I'm just saying that Luke sometimes seems to know when other people are getting hurt."

"Would people testify to that? Would *you*, if you had to?"

"Sure, but what jury would acquit him based on his having a spiritual gift? Get real, Mac. You'd better come up with something they're more likely to believe—like the real murderer. But don't you dare tell Ridd I said that."

"Joe Riddley, either," I agreed, "but I'm going to do my best."

I hung up with more questions than answers. "Instead of giving Luke a word of knowledge about Amanda's beating," I fussed out loud to God, "why didn't you stop the beating? What was Luke supposed to do with that knowledge so late? And how on earth is anybody supposed to convince a jury he knew about her apartment because you told him? Looks like you could make things a tad easier."

Our preacher told a story once about a medieval saint who grumbled to Jesus about how he was treating her. She was told, "This is how I treat my friends."

"In that case," she retorted, "I'm not surprised you have so few of them." That morning I identified completely with the saint.

I've learned, though, that God can handle my grumbles and even my anger. I wasn't struck by lightning. I didn't get an answer, either. But I did get a phone call. From Maynard Spence. Scared to death.

"Miss MacLaren, I think Selena's been kidnapped!"

Terrors overwhelm me; my dignity is
driven away as by the wind, my
safety vanishes like a cloud.
Job 30:15

Twenty-Four

Kidnapped?" I felt like time had stopped. "Why? Did you see somebody drive away with her?"

"No, I think she's in the little building behind Miss Marybelle's."

"The garage?"

"No, a new building. I don't know what to do. I hate to call the police in case I'm wrong, but if they're hurting her—" He broke off, then added, "I thought, since Selena was staying with you . . . I can't stand here talking. I've got to get back. Can you come?"

"I'll meet you in Marybelle's alley," I said, not knowing if this was real danger or a fool's errand.

Joe Riddley sometimes says, "MacLaren doesn't stumble into trouble, she runs headlong into it." This was one of those times. I was so terrified for Selena that I grabbed my pocketbook and headed out. I went back only

218

for a second to retrieve my note once more, smooth it as best I could, and leave it on Joe Riddley's desk again. I ought to just get it printed on wood, like an old school hall pass.

I got to Marybelle's in more like three minutes than five and parked near the mouth to her alley. Her house was up past two other backyards. I'd done that walk often as a girl. I didn't see Maynard when I got there, though. I was peering around anxiously, wondering where to find him, when he slithered down from a huge magnolia that pretty much filled the space between Marybelle's walled garden and her garage. I winced when I saw how big that tree had grown. It was planted to commemorate Marybelle's birth, a month after mine.

"What's happened?" I demanded.

"Shhh." He put a finger on his lips and tugged me down toward the next garage. "We'll be okay here," he said softly. "We can see if they come out again."

I looked around anxiously for a kidnapper. "Who? The goswami?"

"Him or the other man. I don't know who *he* was. I just saw the top of his head. He had on a white painter's cap. That's his green van in the alley." He jerked his head, and I saw just the end of an old green van with no windows in the back. Maynard was still babbling. ". . . carried out two big boxes, then they came out of the kitchen carrying a long skinny bundle and took it into the shed. In a minute they came back without it and went back in the house. I'm afraid it's Selena and they're going to take her away somewhere!"

I looked around for a shed, but didn't see one. Maynard was so flushed and sweaty, I feared he'd just gotten too much sun. "Selena went to work this morning," I pointed out, trying not to sound as exasperated as I felt at being dragged all that way on a silly chase. "What makes you think that bundle could be her? And what are you doing here anyway?"

"I had a television to deliver this morning, and I always drive by this house when I can. As I passed, I saw Selena going up the steps. I thought maybe she'd like to have coffee, so I parked and went to find her. Those dumb little bells rang when I went in, but nobody came. I figured they must be having a meeting, so I left my car out front where she'd see it and ran around here to take a quick peep at the walled garden. I wanted to see if that teacher fellow was taking care of it. But when I tried the garden door, it was locked. Miss Marybelle *never* locked that door."

"Not after she grew up." As girls we'd considered the garden wasn't secret unless it was locked.

Maynard grabbed my arm so hard I'd probably have a bruise. "So I climbed the magnolia to see inside, and the garden is gone! They've put a building in there! And while I was in the tree, that's when they brought out the bundle. Thank goodness they didn't see me. I don't know what they might have done. I'm just sure it was Selena!"

I stared at that brick wall in astonishment. It looked just like it always had. The door in the side wall even had a new coat of blue paint. It also had a shiny padlock. "What kind of a building? It can't be very big—nor very high. Does it have a roof?"

"Yes, a flat one, but no windows. And it takes up almost all the space. They dug up all Miss Marybelle's roses!"

I appreciated his grief. Marybelle's roses had drawn visitors from several states.

We contemplated the blue garden door from behind an oak leaf hydrangea. Maynard started toward the door, but I held him back. "It's locked. Besides, you can't barge into somebody else's shed without a search warrant. Let me go talk to the goswami."

I hurried down the alley, around the corner and up the steps of the temple, trying not to pant from all that exertion. Sweat trickled down my back, and I was sure my hair was frizzing.

Those irksome bells trilled as I opened the door. In a moment, the goswami padded out from the kitchen. He didn't look like a man who'd just locked a woman in a shed. He looked like a man who'd been interrupted mid-drink—or maybe mid-snack. A couple of drops shimmered like little prisms on his beard, and again he smelled of garlic. Also again, he refused to meet my eyes. Bowing, hands at waist, he showed me his little pink bald spot.

"Hello. I'm the woman who came about yoga last week."

"I remember." His voice was deep and gruff. "You came Friday night. Are you an inquirer?"

"Actually I'm inquiring about a friend. Selena Jones. She came in here, and hasn't come out. I wondered . . ." I stopped, to give him a chance to look guilty.

He merely shook his head without looking up. "Selena is seeking peace. She does not need to be disturbed."

"But she is still here?"

He moved slightly, putting himself between me and the staircase. She must be in one of those meditation rooms Gideon spoke about. "Selena is seeking peace," he repeated. "Leave her alone."

I permitted myself one short puff of angry air. "Very well, I'll see her later." I started for the door, then turned back to ask boldly, "She's not in any danger, is she?"

"She is in no danger. She is seeking a higher plane."

As I crossed the porch and headed back down the steps, I could feel his eyes boring into my back until I reached the sidewalk.

When I got back to the alley, Maynard hurried to meet me. "What did he say?"

"He acted like she's upstairs, and says Selena is seeking a higher plane, whatever that means."

"That's what he said happened to Amanda Kent when she died!"

Maynard was right. I'd completely forgotten.

"We'd better get the police," I decided reluctantly, "but Charlie Muggins would never come for me. You go. I'll stay here. Take my car, it's closer. And talk to Isaac James if you can."

He snatched by keys and sprinted down the alley. I was left standing in the August noon heat surrounded by flies, mosquitoes, and bees.

I felt pretty conspicuous hanging around. You never could tell who might be looking out a window. I could go back to my car, but then I might miss something. Maynard might even bring the police down the other end of the alley and I'd never see them come.

I crept toward the magnolia tree and peered up it. I was wearing a brown pantsuit and square-heeled pumps, and I grew up climbing that tree. Could I still do it?

The wide branch near the alley was lower than my head. I tucked my pocketbook behind a convenient clump of weeds next to the garden wall, grasped the branch with both hands, and walked my feet up the trunk. It was a lot harder than it used to be. After incredible effort I slung one leg over the branch, then hung there half up and half down. What the dickens was I supposed to do next? Unlike bicycle riding, you could apparently forget how to climb a tree.

I swung back and forth a couple of times, wiggling this way and that, until I finally managed to get up. After that, the tree was so big and its branches so broad, it was easy to climb part-way up and find a perch. I hoped those thick shiny leaves concealed me. I didn't want the goswami seeing me after all that trouble—or anybody else, for that matter.

Looking down, I could easily see over Marybelle's garden wall. Sure enough, her lovely plants and narrow brick paths had been replaced by an ugly particle board building with a flat green roof that neighbors, looking down through leafy branches, might mistake for grass. A soft whir probably meant air conditioning.

What could the building be for? A big meditation room? An indoor swimming pool? Maybe even a workout room—although the goswami obviously didn't work out. Whatever they used it for, I would have bet my back teeth it was built without proper permits being pulled. The Garden Club would never let them fill in Marybelle's garden without a fight.

I sat in that tree for ages, worried to death about Selena, looking at that dull green roof. Maynard had had time to get to the county line. My lower anatomy was numb, my legs ached from hanging down, and one of my feet was asleep. For the first time I began to ask myself how I was going to get out of that tree now that I was in it. They'd probably have to call the fire department.

I heard the back screen door slam. In another minute I saw the top of a man's head as he unlocked the blue door and went in. I recognized the cap. Ronald Duckworth. What on earth was he doing there? Was that who Maynard had seen?

I heard the gentle hiss of a well-oiled door, then a thud as it closed behind him. He stayed nearly fifteen minutes. When he came out and hurried back to the house, he left the blue door unlocked behind him.

I forgot all about what I'd said to Maynard about not barging in without a search warrant. All I could think about was that unlocked door and the possibility that Selena was trussed up in there. I unkinked my joints as well as I could and began a painful descent.

When I got to the bottom branch, I was still ten feet from earth. Sure the branch was only five feet above ground, but my eyes were another five feet above that. I peered down all those feet and wondered: How *did* one get down from a tree?

I remembered. You sat down on the branch, slithered out on your bottom, swung down by the knees holding on with your hands, and skinned the cat. Right. Sure.

No way.

I looked from the ground to the blue door. In order to get through the blue door I had to get to the ground. To get to the ground, I had to—

"You'll never ever have to do this again," I promised myself. I hugged the trunk of the tree and slowly squatted until I was kneeling, then I held on with both hands and—

You don't want to know. It wasn't pretty, but it got me down in one piece—if you didn't count the skin and swatches of pants I left on the branch. I dusted my poor skinned palms, considered the ruin of my best brown slacks, and shook my bones to get them realigned, then I crept toward the blue garden door. Thank goodness it wasn't visible from the house.

I opened the door wide enough to slip through and pulled it shut after me. My fingers felt for the inside bolt Marybelle used to have there. It was too rusted to move. I abandoned it and turned. Right in my face was a gray metal door with another open padlock.

I tried the knob. It turned easily and the door swung open into the shed. "Selena?" I called softly.

There was no reply.

Without windows, the far corners of the shed were dark. In the light from the door all I could see was the end of a table, a couple of vases and, to the left of the door, a long soft roll of something. "Selena?" Still no answer.

I was fumbling for a light switch when I felt something hard in my back. You don't need practice to recognize the barrel of a gun. You don't need much to recognize the smell of garlic.

Without a word I was shoved into darkness. Then I heard the door slam and the padlock click shut.

God has turned me over to evil men
and thrown me into the clutches
of the wicked. *Job 16:11*

Twenty-Five

At first I was so shocked I just leaned against that
door, scared to pound on it in case a bullet came soaring
through. Finally I thought to turn on the lights.

Long florescent bulbs flickered on and I saw rough
wood walls, shelves to the ceiling on three sides, two long
tables running down the middle, and stuff stacked on the
shelves and tables. Some of it was wrapped, but what
wasn't wrapped was old—old and valuable. It didn't take
a genius to know this was where the thieves were storing
all those stolen antiques. I saw several things I recognized from friends' homes, including—on top of an open
box—the mayor's prized stampbooks.

It looked like the goswami hadn't been studying theology after all. He, in conjunction with Ronald, had been
studying how to strip Hopemore of its most valuable pos-
sessions.

I was so mad I forgot for a minute why I'd wanted to get in the shed in the first place. Then I noticed a long limp roll lying in front of the shelves. Maynard was right—it could be Selena! I hurried over, kicked it gently and exhaled with relief when it felt soft all the way through. It must just be a rug they'd stolen from the mayor's. He had several worth taking.

Among the stolen items were four ladderback chairs. I sat down on one to consider my predicament. Sure, I was locked in with thousands of dollars of stolen merchandise, but all in all, I felt pretty smug. The place was cool and relatively clean, and any minute now Maynard would be coming back with the police. All I had to do was wait.

Unless, of course, the goswami decided to come back and shoot me. He'd probably looked out and seen me go in, gotten rattled, snatched up his gun and shoved me in the shed without thinking. By now he'd be realizing he couldn't keep me there indefinitely.

In fact, he might be on his way back to solve that problem.

I got up and shoved one of the tables against the door. It was heavy, all covered with stuff, but that was all to the good. I shoved the second up against it, then set my chair facing the door behind the second table. By my watch Maynard had been gone forty-five minutes. He'd be back soon—if he came at all.

My shock at finding Ronald Duckworth mixed up in all this made me doubt Maynard for a second or two, but I knew I'd go crazy thinking he wasn't coming back, so I made myself think about Ronald instead. He'd always seemed a simple, friendly fellow. How had he gotten himself into this mess? Did he need money? Want some of his own to keep up with Lorine's daddy? And all that time, I'd been wondering if Ronald knew Lorine attended the Temple of Inner Peace!

Then I had a dreadful thought. Had *Ronald* killed her, because she learned too much?

Muffled and far away I heard the courthouse clock chime twelve. I hadn't eaten much át Myrtle's and was getting awful hungry, but there wasn't a thing in there to eat. There wasn't a thing to read, either, unless you counted the mayor's civil war letters, and I wasn't in the mood for history. The present was enough war for me.

I heard a click at the door, then a grunt. The door gave a little, but the tables held firm. "Miss MacLaren? Oh, Miss MacLaren, it's me, Ronald Duckworth. Let me in." He sounded so urgent and sympathetic, my gallant rescuer. Thank goodness I had seen him leaving earlier. Otherwise I'd have flung that door open in a minute.

"What do you want?" I called.

"To let you out. There's been a dreadful mistake."

"There sure has," I agreed, "but I don't think I'll come out yet, thanks. Call the police and tell them where I am." I heard conversation, then silence.

After that I didn't hear a thing for fifteen minutes by my watch. I had plenty of time to do the thinking about Amanda Kent I'd been wanting to do, but all the time I was a bit distracted, straining to hear one single sign that Maynard was faithful and remembered where I was.

Amanda must have stumbled onto this little secret her teacher was keeping. From what I'd heard, she had too much integrity to let him get away with it. He—or, maybe Ronald—went to her house that night. Maybe even took her home after the service.

No, she'd been in her nightgown, so he'd come after she'd gotten ready for bed. She'd have let in the goswami. She trusted him, even if she disapproved of what he was doing. She might have let in Ronald, too, as the husband of her best friend.

Either of the two were strong enough to have killed her. And the only person who could have seen the murderer leave was Gideon. Was that why the goswami kept him at the temple that next week, to be sure he hadn't seen anything? Was that why Gideon was later killed, because he remembered he had?

But why would Lorine send Ronald to find the body? She must not have known who the killer was.

Everything seemed so clear that I wished I had a pencil and paper. I'd be sure to forget details later. But I didn't have my pocketbook. It was still hidden out by the alley.

Suddenly the lights went out and the air conditioner died. They had cut my power.

~

I thought my eyes were taking an awfully long time to adjust, until I realized the shed was built too solid for light to come in. Ronald built it, of course. He always was a meticulous carpenter. I even knew how he'd put it up without the neighbors suspecting: one summer he'd built Rhonda a playhouse in her grandparents' yard while her granddaddy lay dying. Ronald considerately pre-cut all the pieces and screwed them together, so the old man wouldn't be bothered by a hammer. We'd thought that was sweet of him.

I have never liked the dark. It was particularly dreadful that day, because no matter how brave I tried to be, I couldn't help imagining all sorts of furry creatures running around on the floor. I pulled my feet up one rung on the stool and whispered a line of George MacDonald's over and over: "The dark still is God. The dark still is God."

I didn't dare speak above a whisper, because I didn't want to miss a sound that might clue me in to what was going on outside.

What was going on was the gurgle and splash of something pouring. Were they going to try and flood me out? No, I recognized the smell. Gasoline. They were going to burn down the shed.

At that point my prayer life became very simple. *Oh, God, oh, God, oh, God!* I didn't mind dying as much as I minded burning. A tiny burn sends me howling for the aloe plant. "Let me die quick from smoke inhalation," I begged.

I had all sorts of regrets. Joe Riddley might never know where I'd gone. If they didn't find my body, I wouldn't get to use my half of the burial plot we'd already paid for. I'd never see my grandchildren grow up, or know if Cindy came back to Walker. And after I'd figured out exactly who killed Amanda Kent, nobody would ever know.

I have to admit I did a little crying around then. Pure self-pity, but I figured I deserved a little pity and there wasn't anybody else around to offer it.

All the time I was praying, regretting and crying, somebody else was splashing and gurgling gasoline around the building. It must be Ronald. The space between the shed and Marybelle's garden wall looked too narrow for the goswami to fit.

<hr />

"Hey, what are you doing?"

"*What* are you *doing*?" One of those two voices was pitched to a high squeal. I heard a scuffle, pounding feet, a heavy thud, and more pounding feet. A distant door slammed.

"Maynard, help! I'm locked in. Get me out! Hurry!" I yelled as loud as I could.

At least one car roared away. Maybe two. Had Maynard driven off?

No, for he called breathlessly, "Miss MacLaren? Is that you? The goswami got away! And I can't find a key! Is Selena there, too?"

"No, just me. And don't worry about the goswami, just get me out of here. The door's locked and they've poured gasoline all over the building. See if there's an axe or something in the garage—and whatever you do, don't strike a match!"

There was another silence, then Maynard called in relief. "Mr. Duckworth! Am I glad to see you. I need your help. Mrs. Yarbrough's locked in here! Do you have a key?"

Ronald must have shinnied over the garden wall while Maynard was chasing the goswami.

"Why no, but maybe there's one in the garage."

Silence again, then "Let me use it," Ronald said to Maynard, then called, "Miss MacLaren, stand clear of the front. I'm taking the wall down."

Great. All I needed was Ronald Duckworth coming in with an axe.

But Ronald had no idea I'd seen him earlier. The only chance either Maynard or I had was for me to put on a convincing act. "Oh, Ronald, I'm so glad to hear you again," I called loudly. "I was afraid you'd gone off and forgotten me. I'm moving to the back now. Go ahead and swing."

The wood splintered with his first blow. When daylight splashed through, I knew how excited God must have felt right after the words "Let there be light."

Two more blows and I could see Ronald working up a sweat swinging the axe in the narrow space between the shed and the wall. Maynard encouraged him from out of sight.

"It's mighty hot. Let Maynard take it awhile," I called.

Ronald hesitated, but Maynard grabbed the axe and swung it with awkward but powerful strokes. In just a few minutes he had a hole big enough for me to crawl carefully through. I went on my hands and knees, avoiding splinters, and stood up—grateful for Maynard's help. I didn't mind a bit that the scent of flowers and fresh grass was mixed with gasoline fumes. No air ever smelled so good. No sun ever shone so bright, no sky was ever bluer.

"I'm right glad to see you," I greeted them with a wobbly smile. "I thought we were about to have roast MacLaren on the menu."

"We were going to let you out," Ronald said reproach-fully. "The teacher and I came to let you out, but you wouldn't come."

"Have you seen Selena?" Maynard interrupted breathlessly, wiping his sweaty forehead with his bare forearm.

"She's not in there." I didn't have time to talk about Selena yet. First I had to persuade Ronald he was safe.

"I'm so glad you came back," I told him warmly. "I'd have let you rescue me when you came the first time, but I knew Maynard was on his way, and I was afraid that dreadful man would hurt both of us before he got back."

"What dreadful man?" Ronald's pale lashes fluttered in confusion.

"The teacher."

"Oh, he's not dreadful, just a shade peculiar."

I pointed to a puddle of gasoline. "He was going to burn the shed down."

"Oh, no, Miss MacLaren, that wasn't the teacher, that was Pete."

"Pete?" Maynard and I asked at the same time.

"Yeah. He used to work for me, but lately he'd been—uh—"

"Stealing antiques," I said grimly.

"Oh, no, Miss MacLaren! Those things are—"

Again he stopped. Then he reached over and gave me a comforting pat. "I don't know why Pete was pouring out all that gasoline, but it must have been a mistake. You say the teacher's gone?" he asked Maynard.

Maynard nodded, looking as confused as Ronald sounded.

"Well, we were having us a little business talk, but I guess it's over now. I'll just go get my Co-cola." Ronald turned back to the house and swung across the lawn like he hadn't just confessed to being one of a ring of antique thieves.

I was about to say that to Maynard, when I had another, dreadful though. If Selena was in that house, Ronald must not be allowed to get to her before we did!

I hobbled after him as fast as I could. "Maynard," I called over my shoulder, "come in a minute. I need to use the little girl's room. Would that be all right, Ronald?"

"I don't see why not," he answered, sweet as pie.

The three of us trooped across Marybelle's back porch and into the kitchen. It looked so normal that for a second I expected Marybelle to come through the butler's pantry to offer me a glass of tea. I swallowed a lump in my throat. I owed it to Marybelle to see that her lovely house was restored to its former dignity.

Leaning against the kitchen table, I asked, "Ronald, would you get me a glass of water? I'm feeling a little faint."

"I'll get it," Maynard began, but Ronald was already moving to the cabinet. He brought out a glass and poured cold water from a plastic jug in the refrigerator. When he handed it to me, I jiggled his arm a little so water splashed all over the floor.

"Don't worry, Miss MacLaren. You have a right to be a little nervous. I'll get a mop. The rest room is in the hall." He pointed, then headed for the back porch.

"Come on!" I hissed to Maynard, tugging him by the arm. I stopped at the powder room and pointed him up the stairs. "Look for Selena!" By the time I got back to the kitchen, Ronald was placidly mopping.

In a minute Maynard was back, breathless. "She's not here."

"Who?" Ronald handed me my glass of water, his face as pleasant as ever.

"Selena Jones, a friend of ours. Maynard saw her come in here this morning."

"I saw her upstairs this morning, but she left while the teacher was showing me what he's been doing up there. He's doing a little remodeling, and wondered if I might want to help, since the fellow who was doing his work got killed the same night . . ." His lower lip wobbled and he didn't finish the sentence. He didn't need to. We all knew what he meant.

While Ronald carried the mop to the porch, squeezed it onto the bushes, and propped it against the back wall, I did a little thinking. "Call the hospital, Maynard, and see if she's there. Maybe she left the temple while you were guarding the shed."

He dialed and asked for her, then drummed his fingers on the countertop and jiggled his feet like he was about to break into a jig. Ronald came back and leaned on the counter, drinking a Co-cola that must have been lukewarm by then. He didn't seem to notice.

Maynard's face widened in a smile. "Selena? It's Maynard. Maynard Spence." How many Maynards did he think she knew? Ronald and I eavesdropped shamelessly, but he didn't notice.

"Listen, uh, I wondered if maybe you're free for lunch. You did? When do you get a break? Great. How about if I come over for a cup of coffee then? Great. See you then."

He hung up and said, unnecessarily, "She's already had lunch, but she gets a break at two. I'm going over to meet her."

It seemed to me like we had a few loose ends to tie up first—a shed full of stolen antiques, for instance. Ronald Duckworth, for another.

The second took care of itself. He started for the door. "I guess I'd better be going. Services," he cleared his throat and tried again, "services for Lorine are Wednesday. I'd count it a favor if you all would be there."

"Sure, Ronald," I said. I let him go. I knew where he lived.

Besides, I had unfinished business with Maynard. "Why didn't you bring the police?"

"Isaac James wasn't there and Chief Muggins said he'd need a search warrant, so for me to find Joe Riddley. I looked all over town, but I never could."

"He's out at the greenhouses," I said wearily. "Chief Muggins knows to ask the store manager. Did you tell him you thought the goswami was holding a hostage?"

"I sure *did*. I told him the *goswami* had kidnapped a *nurse friend of mine ...*"

I lightly touched his elbow and he noticed what he was doing. "Sorry. Anyway, I told him she was locked in a shed, but he didn't believe me. It's a good thing, isn't it, the way things turned out? But he was really obnoxious. Said I'd gotten a lot of funny ideas living up North, that things like that don't happen in Hopemore. Finally I decided to come back and bust open that shed, but I saw that man sloshing gasoline on the door of the garden wall—look!"

The backyard was in flames. At least the shed was. Ronald must have crept out and set the shed on fire while we weren't looking.

It burned to the ground before the fire department got there. I wasn't surprised, with all the gasoline on those wooden walls. The best the firemen could do was leave the place a sodden mess, including my pocketbook.

I was real sorry about those antiques. Maynard was even sorrier. The way he danced around and yelped, I felt like tying him to the trunk of the magnolia and gagging him.

I was sorry about my pocketbook, too. I'd just gotten it in July, when my old one was snatched in Montgomery. And my credit cards had warped in the heat. I'd have to go through the trouble of duplicating all my stuff again. At this rate, the driver's license people would be wanting to tattoo my license on one arm.

I was glad it was Isaac who came to investigate the fire instead of Chief Muggins. He believed me about the antiques. He was skeptical, though, when I explained about the goswami killing Amanda Kent, and downright bullheaded when I told him about Ronald Duckworth. "You didn't actually see him carrying stolen goods?"

"No, but—"

"And Maynard can't testify it was *Ronald* he saw carrying them. Maybe Ronald had another reason entirely for being in that shed when you saw him. You know how Mr. Duckworth is. A little simple, like. He probably didn't notice a thing that was in there except whatever he went in for."

"Yeah, right." I wasn't going to get anywhere down that road, so I tried another. "Do you think you'll ever find the goswami?"

"Sure. His prints are being run through the computer right now. If we get a match, we'll find him. I hope when everything cools down that the arson squad finds enough antique bits and pieces to nail him, too."

The fingerprints astonished us all. The goswami was Arnie Potts—Lorine's cousin who'd gone to San Francisco back in the sixties. No wonder he kept ducking and turning that pink bald spot my way. He was probably scared to death I'd recognize him.

His prints were on file, but just for minor offenses. In the beginning he'd been arrested for non-violent sit-ins and political protests. Later he'd been arrested for stealing food, loitering, and once, stealing a car to get a friend to the hospital. They were the crimes of a hopeless man, not a prosperous goswami.

Arnie hadn't always been a goswami, though. Over the years he'd been in trouble for impersonating a Catholic priest, a rabbi, and a faith healer. Poor Arnie. It looked like he'd been seeking inner peace all his life. I figured that once he went eclectic in his faith, he decided Benjamin Franklin was right: God helps those who help themselves.

He'd never discovered the real truth, that God helps us most when we finally admit we *can't* help ourselves.

> I have become a laughingstock
> to my friends, though I called upon
> God and he answered—a mere
> laughingstock, though righteous
> and blameless! *Job 12:4*

Twenty-Six

Selena was distraught at the news that her beloved teacher had stolen antiques and skipped town. I was afraid she'd never speak to Maynard or me again after she heard about our being the ones who found that out. Instead, she went up to her room for an hour and came down calm and composed. "Just because the man was flawed doesn't mean his teaching was flawed," she said, her chin tilted bravely. "He gave me a lot that was good. I'm going to remember that about him and let the Creator take care of the rest."

Joe Riddley gave her a nod of approval. "If everybody in the world came to that conclusion, Selena, we'd all be happier."

Joe Riddley certainly hadn't found any inner peace. I was glad Selena decided to go with Maynard to a movie in Milledgeville that evening so we could be alone. They were barely out of the driveway before he started fussing.

"'Running errands. Be back soon.' What kind of message is that, Little Bit? There I was, thinking you were picking up the dry cleaning, and you were getting locked in a shed, nearly burned up, and I don't know what all."

"I didn't expect to get burned up when I wrote the note," I pointed out.

"And you don't have one shred of evidence that Arnie ever killed anybody. The hairs that Kent woman was clutching were light and straight, not dark and curly. Don't say he wore a wig, either. If he had, she'd have had a wig in her hands, not a few hairs."

We were sitting in our favorite rockers on the porch, watching fireflies pulsing and listening to night birds calling. "I'd rather talk about happier things, honey. Our grandchildren, or plans for that weekend in the mountains you suggested."

"All right," he agreed gruffly. "Which do you want to talk about first?"

I thought a minute. "I guess first I wish we could think of some way to get a sample of Ronald Duckworth's hair."

He gave a disgusted snort. "The poor man doesn't have much to spare, but I guess you could go by and say you'd like a souvenir of the man who rescued you."

"He wasn't rescuing me, Joe Riddley. He'd have murdered me if Maynard hadn't come right then."

"You're wrong on that one, Little Bit. Ronald Duckworth's no murderer. Hasn't got enough sense, for one thing. He's too nice, for another. He'd be apologizing the whole time. Oh—you're wrong about Charlie Muggins, too. He went to the Braves game with the rest. He didn't kill that nurse, either."

He reached above my head to turn on a porch light he'd installed down low over my favorite chair. Usually when he turned on that light I reached up and gave his arm a grateful squeeze. Putting a light at my height was one of the ways Joe Riddley had showed lately that he loved me. That evening, though, the bulb flared and went out. I felt just like that bulb.

He stomped into the house and came out empty-handed. "Only thing we've got in the whole place is three-way bulbs. That lamp won't take a three-way bulb."

He needn't sound like it was my fault. I wasn't the one who wanted the place lit up like a Christmas tree. "We'll get sixty-watt bulbs next time we go to the store," I told him.

"Yeah." He sank heavily into his rocker, next to mine. We sat there silent for a minute, then he reached over and gently touched my cheek. "You scare me, Little Bit. I don't want you out of my sight again."

Amanda Kent's mother crept into town that evening to pick up her daughter's things. Selena and Maynard saw a light in the apartment on their way home from the movie and went to see who it was. Selena came home wondering where she could put Mandy's loom if she bought it.

"Put it in our living room until you know what to do with it," Joe Riddley offered. "It'll improve the tone of the place." He and Maynard went and brought it right back in his daddy's truck. She and I exchanged a sad smile as we watched the men putting it in the living room. Mandy's weaving was still on it.

Before we went to bed that night, Joe Riddley remembered something he'd forgotten to tell me. "Luke's dad got to town around noon, and he dropped by the office after he visited the jail. Name's John. Brought a lawyer with him, too—one who's retained by John's company."

"Company?" I was too busy putting antibiotic ointment on my tree-climbing scrapes to be paying much attention.

"Yeah. Seems the Blesseds manufacture boats for big cruise lines. John himself goes in for yachting in a big way. He's offered us a cruise on his sailboat whenever we want it. Sixty-five *foot* sailboat, Little Bit."

I was so astonished, I couldn't say a thing. I remembered, though, Luke saying, in an off-hand way, "My dad has a sailboat."

Joe Riddley laughed, but not like anything was funny. "Here the whole town has been putting nickels and dimes together for Luke's defense, and his daddy could buy all of Hopemore without denting his bank account."

No wonder Luke was embarrassed when I told him about the fund. I was embarrassed, too, now. But being rich wouldn't get Luke out of jail.

Joe Riddley said he didn't want me out of his sight, but he'd gone down to the greenhouses when Charlie Muggins dropped by our office the next morning. I wished I had one of those bells under my desk like bank tellers have, so I could touch it with my toe and Joe Riddley could come running. Charlie was obviously set to enjoy himself.

"I hear you nearly got barbequed, Mac." He plopped himself into our red plaid visitor's chair like he'd been invited to sit down.

"Got saved, too—no thanks to you. If that nurse had been in the shed and gotten burned up, you'd have been in big trouble this morning."

He picked one front tooth with a freckled hand. "Instead, I'm sitting pretty. Solved that rash of thefts we've been having. You can read all about it in next week's *Statesman*. They even got a picture of me with the mayor." He buffed his nails against his jacket.

"What do you mean *you* solved it? Isaac James brought you the whole case on a platter, and Maynard and I did most of the solving."

"Yeah, well, I'll tell that to Walker. He's not a happy camper this morning, with all those claims he's got to pay. I'll be sure to tell him he can thank his mother."

I hadn't thought about poor Walker. Seemed like his summer was getting worse and worse, no matter how much I worried and prayed.

Charlie stopped grinning all of a sudden. He leaned closer, and looked at me with his deep-set little chimpanzee eyes. "If you know what's good for you, you won't go meddling in what doesn't concern you. Especially not these murders. I'm taking care of that. If you get in my way, bad things could happen."

I was utterly speechless. Was he threatening me in my own office?

He stood and set his hat on his head. "No need to mention to Joe Riddley that I stopped by. Don't want him to think I'm sparking his wife."

"Don't worry about that," I assured him. "Joe Riddley knows you aren't my type."

When I got over being furious, I got depressed. Everybody in town seemed to be laughing at me, and Charlie was right about one thing. Not much good had come out of Maynard's and my visit to Marybelle's. Sure, people found out what happened to their antiques, but they all got burned. And Arnie got away without anybody really knowing what all he'd done—or if Ronald was in it with him.

One part of me was resolving never to try to solve a crime again. The other was resolving not to mention Ronald to anybody but Joe Riddley until I figured a way to get a sample of his hair.

Charlie wasn't the only one who got his picture in that week's *Statesman*. I badgered Joe Riddley to sue them—I couldn't believe how quickly they'd gotten a reporter over to the temple fire, and never knew when he took that picture of me with splinters in my hair and rips in my clothes. People are never going to let me forget it.

~

Luke was still in good spirits, in spite of the fact that national papers now carried stories with titles like "Multi-millionaire Shipbuilder Protests Son's Innocence." He'd gotten a Bible study going, had several of the guys jamming with guitars (under strict supervision, of course), and even had one profession of faith. "I once told God I'd do anything, go anywhere," he told me happily, "but I never imagined he'd send me to jail."

"You think *God* sent you to jail?"

"Either sent me or is using it for my benefit. I wasn't real sure about coming to Hopemore. I'd envisioned going to a mission field, maybe, or an inner city church. A pleasant little town like this didn't sound very exciting. Don't get me wrong—I like it here—" He sounded anxious not to offend.

"Honey, if it gets much more exciting around here, I may move to Atlanta where it's nice and quiet. But I know what you meant. I'm just having to adjust to the idea of having a St. Francis in our midst."

He blushed and looked down at the table between us. "It sounds pretty arrogant, doesn't it? But at least I know why I was sent to jail. Whether I stay in or get out, I'm hooked on prison ministry. And hey—just like Chuck Colson, I'll know it from the inside out." He nibbled his lower lip. "Even if I have to go to a harder, rougher place than this, Mac, there's going to be a purpose for it." Finally he looked up at me. "I know that. I want you to know it, too."

"Yeah." I was too scared of that possibility to even think about it, much less try to wonder what good might come out of it. Instead, I changed the subject and told him about the woman I'd talked to when I called his dad.

"Muriel," he said immediately, "Dad's private secretary. She's always been my buddy. Since Mother died, I've always suspected Muriel writes every letter I get from Dad, then makes him sign them. I'll call her tonight to let her know I'm okay."

"At least he's sticking around when you need him," I pointed out.

He gave me a repentant grin. He could tell from my tone what I think of young people criticizing their parents. "Yeah, he has. And the very best thing that's come out of this mess is, I'm getting to know him better. We've never sat down in my whole life to talk for an hour without his having to answer a phone or leave for a meeting. Here we can."

Go to jail and bring your family together. Maybe later I could propose that the county put that on a sign out front. Right now I just wanted to get Luke out.

∽

John Blessed wasn't too bad, if you could get past those three-piece suits and shiny shoes. He was all over town, interested in everything that was going on. He spent one morning in the cotton fields with Ridd and another at the greenhouses with Joe Riddley. I was delighted to see he had Charlie Muggins running scared, too. Everywhere I went I saw officers interviewing people, beating the bushes for evidence against Luke. The only problem I could see was, they weren't looking for evidence *for* him—or against anybody else. An open mind is a concept Charlie Muggins never grasped.

John had too much energy for my taste, though. We had him to dinner at our house a couple of times—nighttime dinner, with silver and candles and Clarinda's sister waiting table—and he left me totally exhausted. Wanted to know every thing there was to know about our business. I told Joe Riddley we'd better watch out, or Mr. Blessed would be plotting a hostile takeover.

He couldn't get Luke to let him bring in a high powered criminal team, though. "Mr. Newton's doing everything that needs to be done," Luke insisted.

"Yeah," Joe Riddley grumped when I told him about that conversation, "Wait's moving at his usual lightning pace, filing requests for continuance."

It seemed to me like Joe Riddley was grumpy most of the time. I wondered if he was going through a change of life that hit men after sixty.

~⚭~

Although Selena stayed subdued, she was ready to go home by Saturday. "Another nurse wants to rent my spare room," she told us, "so I feel safe. Besides, if it's my fate to die, I'll die wherever I am."

Joe Riddley snorted, but didn't say a word.

While she finished packing, I went up to her room to sit on the bed and ask a couple of questions that were bothering me. "Selena, when you used to go to Amanda's, did you ever see a green nightgown?"

Selena finished putting a stack of blouses in the suitcase, then shook her head. "I don't know when she got that. Usually she slept in T-shirts."

"She didn't have a green robe or anything?"

"Not that I know—" Her face changed, and she sank onto the bed beside me. "Her happy dress! A long African thing she found in a boutique in Atlanta. It was green, with embroidery around the neck, sleeves, and hem. She loved it. I don't think she'd have slept in it, but she wore it a lot in the evening." She looked at me, puzzled. "But why would anybody call it a nightgown?"

"Some man wrote it down that way, and it stuck," I said wryly. I was thinking it might make a difference in who the murderer was if Amanda had been dressed for company instead of bed. "Would she have worn it for entertaining?"

"Maybe, if they weren't going anywhere."

Neither of us said anything for a few minutes. Selena's eyes were pink and misty and I felt pressure in my chest at the picture of Amanda hurrying home and getting all dressed up to wait for—whom?

Finally I asked my second question. "Was anybody else studying for the temple priesthood besides you, Gideon, and Amanda?"

Her answer nearly frizzed my perm. "Lorine Duckworth may have been studying privately with the teacher. She spent a lot of time either with him or meditating upstairs, but she never came to priesthood training meetings after the Sunday service." She got up and continued emptying drawers. I sat and thought.

Had Lorine known what Arnie and Ronald were up to? Or was she just passing the time of day with her cousin Arnie? She'd certainly attended the service that night I'd seen her. I'd thought she was visiting, like I was—maybe in memory of her best friend Mandy—but she could well have warned him about my being there. Was that why he'd warned his inquirers not to talk?

I tried out a hunch. "Is the temple where Lorine and Mandy became such good friends?"

Selena turned, surprised. "I didn't know they *were* friends. Mandy never said so. In fact, she once said she questioned whether Lorine was sincere about seeking peace."

Something clicked. "Did you always call Amanda 'Mandy'?" Gideon had, too, I remembered. And Vic Davis. But in my hearing, Lorine never had.

Selena looked puzzled, as well she might. I was jumping around like a cricket. But her answer was what I expected. "Everybody did, except the teacher. He was very formal. But she hated Amanda. That's what her daddy called her."

If Lorine hadn't been friends with Amanda Kent, why had she claimed she was?

So she could go to the police station instead of Ronald. So she could hang around hoping for developments. So she could direct the search for a suspect away from her cousin the goswami, or her husband. She knew what Ronald and Arnie were up to, all right.

"Did Ronald come to the temple?" I asked.

"Not that I know of. Just her." Selena laid a hand lightly on my shoulder. "Mac," she said, her eyes earnest and pleading, "if you're trying to pin the murders on the goswami, please don't. Stealing is terrible, but he wouldn't have killed anybody—especially not Lorine. He was the gentlest man I ever met. And he told me once she was the smartest woman he knew." She sighed. "I'm sorry I never felt toward her quite like I should."

"Don't worry about that, honey. Lorine didn't bring out the best in any of us."

After that, Selena and I didn't talk any more about the temple. I hated to see her go, but felt sure she'd be okay now that Arnie was gone and somebody else was living with her. She even promised Joe Riddley that she'd try the Episcopal church.

I rode by her place one evening and saw her sitting with Maynard in her swing while their pups romped on the grass. From the way both were waving their arms, it looked like they were back to arguing as usual.

> Who can see any hope for me? Will
> it go down to the gates of death?
> Will we descend together into
> the dust? *Job 17:15–16*

Twenty-Seven

Once the fire had cooled down and they could sift through the ashes, they found enough remnants of antiques to justify claiming they had all been destroyed in the fire. Poor Walker.

I tried a couple of times to convince Ike that Arnie was probably the murderer, but he said Charlie Muggins had him busy on other cases. Joe Riddley made it clear he was through discussing murder, too. After a few days of fuming, I decided maybe Martha could help me think things through.

Clarinda had to go to a family funeral in Wrens one day and wouldn't be there to fix dinner anyway, so I let Joe Riddley go down to Myrtle's and I met Martha at the medical center. It was chicken salad day at the cafeteria, and their cook made terrific chicken salad.

"What are they saying about Arnie?" I asked when we'd carried our trays to a private table.

She was surprised I needed to ask. "That he stole all those antiques and kept them behind his house until he could sell them. They also say somebody found out Amanda Kent attended our church once, and signed a visitor's card. They plan to use that to show Luke could have known her, even if he says he didn't."

"Nobody has suggested that Arnie might have killed Amanda Kent?"

She looked up from her plate in surprise. "He couldn't have. He was here all that night."

I couldn't believe what I was hearing. "Here? Why haven't I heard that before?"

"I guess I forgot. It didn't seem important."

"Important?" I was flabbergasted. "Are you positive he was here?"

"Sure. He developed chest pains after the service and Lorine was afraid he might be having a heart attack, so she brought him in. It turned out to be indigestion, but Lorine insisted they keep him all night for observation. She stayed until he was admitted, which was going on when I went off duty just after twelve."

"He couldn't have sneaked out later for a while?"

Martha laughed. "In a hospital gown? I think someone would have noticed."

My whole theory was falling apart, and all I could do was eat chicken salad with peach and cottage cheese on the side. The cottage cheese tasted like I felt: bland and lumpy.

"What a frown, neighbor! You look like you've lost your last friend." Dr. Holder stood by our table holding his lunch tray. Dressed in a charcoal suit, white shirt, and natty red tie, he was hard for me to think of as "Drew."

I craned my neck to look up at him and shook my head. "Not a friend, a theory. I was trying to pin the Amanda Kent murder on the leader of the Temple of

Inner Peace, but Martha blew that to smithereens. Says he was here at the hospital that night."

Dr. Holder nodded. "I examined him the next morning myself." He moved on, then came back. "Maynard told me about the trouble you had over there, by the way. I'm glad you're okay." He grinned. "Joe Riddley needs to hang a cell phone around your neck."

Martha chuckled. "Joe Riddley needs to buy her a leash."

I didn't feel particularly charitable toward either one of them, but I moved my pocketbook from the next chair. "Would you like to join us?" Under the table, I felt a jab.

"Thanks, but I've got people waiting for me." He headed for a table across the room.

I glared at Martha. "What did you kick me for? I was just being polite."

She leaned over the table and spoke softly. "Do you know who's at his table over there? Some of the most important doctors in Georgia, getting ready for Dr. Holder's symposium next week."

"The one on thinking pain away?"

"Don't sound so skeptical. It's nothing new. Women use Lamaze for childbirth, for instance. Dr. Holder has some new techniques he claims make it possible to reduce the amount of anesthesia given to elderly surgical patients, which also reduces a lot of the risk. He's been researching it for years, and it sounds wonderful."

"I'm willing to be impressed." I sucked the last of my Co-cola through my straw and softly played the drugstore blues. "And to think—he's a neighbor of mine."

"They'll be sure to put that in his biography." Sassy thing, she didn't crack a smile.

"Speaking of inflicting pain instead of curing it," I said after a minute or two, "Selena said once that Amanda blew the whistle on some orderly here who was hurting coma patients. What was that about?"

Martha frowned. "I'm surprised she told you. We tried to keep it very quiet. The name wasn't even released, except to supervisory personnel."

"But since I do know, fill me in. What happened?"

"One of the orderlies was amusing himself by making little cuts in coma patients to see if they would flinch."

I grimaced. "How horrible!" Something stirred in my mind, but I couldn't make it sit still long enough to pin it down. Meanwhile, Martha was still talking.

"It was. Heaven knows how long he'd been doing it— or would have gone on doing it—if Amanda Kent hadn't noticed the cuts and gone to her supervisor. They set a watch, and one of the doctors—Dr. Holder, in fact— caught him in the act."

"What happened to him?"

"He was terminated, of course, but the hospital lawyer advised us against giving that as the cause. We could get a lot of bad publicity if it leaked out, and we wouldn't have a leg to stand on if he took us to court. None of the patients complained—obviously."

Here was someone else who might have had grudge against Mandy. "Is he still in town?"

She looked down at her plate. "I shouldn't say, Mac."

"Please, Martha. It's important."

"It was that young man who was murdered last week. Gideon Levy."

"Amanda Kent wouldn't play cards with somebody who'd been hurting her patients!

"She wouldn't have known who it was. I told you, we kept it very quiet."

Gideon might have known who blew the whistle, though. When he'd described the noises he'd heard—with those tears in his eyes—was he actually describing what he *would* have heard if he hadn't been killing Amanda, instead? Had Arnie really called him to come spend a week at the temple after Mandy was killed? Or was that Gideon's idea of the perfect hideout?

On Tuesday morning the next week, Ronald Duckworth knocked on our office door and addressed Joe Riddley. "I appreciated you all coming to Lorine's service. I wanted to stop in and see how Miss MacLaren's doin'."

"She's doing fine," Joe Riddley waved my way, "as you can see for yourself. How're you doin'?"

"I do all right until evenin'." Ronald turned his painter's cap in his hands. "Then I get to missin' Lorine. You know how it is, Judge. You live with somebody all those years, you miss 'em when they're gone. Rhonda and I rattle around in that big old house."

"Sit down and visit a while," I offered, feeling like it was time I got into the conversation. Joe Riddley shot me a warning look, but I ignored him. If I could get Ronald to lean his head back against the chair cushion, he might leave a hair.

Ronald obligingly sat down in the red chair, but leaned forward with his hands clasped between his knees. I swiveled my chair to face him. "Maybe Rhonda will get married and bring somebody else into your house," I comforted him. "Dr. Holder's a fine man."

He shrugged. "Lorine had her heart set on that match, but Rhonda says she might like to move to Atlanta and become a model."

"She'd make a good model," I agreed. Rhonda's vacuous stare would look natural on the Bi-Lo magazine rack by the check-out counter.

I leaned forward so our knees almost touched. "You know, Ronald, I keep thinking about Amanda Kent. Being Lorine's best friend, I guess you knew her pretty well."

"I didn't know her at all, Miss MacLaren. Never laid eyes on her, that I know of. Lorine claimed they were best friends, but they must of done all their visitin' away from the house. Neither Rhonda nor I ever saw her."

"So why did you go looking for her that Saturday morning?" I didn't dare look at Joe Riddley. He's not at his most attractive when fire's coming out his nostrils. When Ronald didn't answer, I tried a statement instead. "You were playing a hunch, I guess."

"I told you before, Lorine sent me," Ronald reminded me patiently. "She said the Kent woman was supposed to pick her up, and got all het up because she didn't come, so she told me to get over there and look for her. Told me to ask the girl's neighbor if he'd heard anybody over there the night before, and we ought to look in a window if she didn't come to the door."

"Lorine told you to talk to the neighbor." I felt like a psychotherapist.

"Sure. Said I shouldn't be going up to a young girl's apartment without another fellow along." He ducked his head and grinned. "It was silly, but Lorine was jealous, like."

Seemed to me Lorine was just wanting to make sure Ronald had a witness.

But was Ronald telling the truth about never seeing the girl? I tried to trick him. "I really liked the way she'd decorated her apartment in all those bright colors."

"I never saw her apartment 'cept through the window. Looked like she'd used candlelight white on the walls. I didn't notice anything else."

Trust a painter to notice not just that the walls were white, but *which* white.

Before I could make statements out of any more questions, Joe Riddley started talking football. In a few minutes Ronald pulled himself to his feet and started fixing to go. "Don't go gettin' locked in any more sheds," he advised me from the door.

"Don't bug the poor man, Little Bit," Joe Riddley warned when Ronald had gone. "I'd stake this store he doesn't know any more than you do about that murder."

"I'd still swear it was him who poured gasoline around that shed."

Joe Riddley reached for his cap. "Come on. I want to see for myself."

We drove straight to the alley behind Marybelle's and parked next to the garden wall. I wasn't real crazy about poking around back there. For one thing, it was still filthy. For another, it made me shiver to think how easily my own bones could have been found there. But he made me go right inside the walls and around the whole shed, and he showed me something I wouldn't have believed: the space between the two walls was plenty big enough for Arnie to pour the gasoline himself.

Joe Riddley hit his cap against his leg a couple of times. "Even if Ronald was conspiring with that fellow, I don't think there's anything we could do about it now except hope he's learned his lesson."

"He had to have set the shed on fire," I pointed out. "Who else could have?"

"I don't know!" Joe Riddley so seldom raised his voice that I took a couple of steps back. "I don't know anything, Little Bit," he said, more softly.

"Except Luke never killed anybody," I insisted.

"We can't even prove that. There's not one bit of evidence to help him. Even the evidence they had got lost in airline luggage. Did you hear about that?"

"I heard. Smelled pretty fishy to me."

"To me, too." He slapped his cap against his thigh so hard I thought he'd rip his twill pants. "Little Bit, I'm thinking of giving up being magistrate. I'm tired. Dead tired of it. Used to be, I felt like I was helping make this community a more decent place to live. But this crowd who're running things nowadays—they're not concerned about decency. All they care about is furthering their own ambitions. I'm getting tire of fighting 'em."

I knew he was talking about Charlie Muggins and his buddies on the city council, but there was no point naming names out there in the open. Anybody could be standing in the alley beyond Marybelle's oak leaf hydrangea, listening to us.

"Who'd take your place, honey?"

He shook his head and heaved a deep sigh. "That's the only thing that's kept me from turning in my resignation already. I can't think of a single competent person in town who has both time and inclination."

"Maybe Ridd—" I started.

He shook his head sharply. "I wouldn't wish this on Ridd. He's got enough on his plate with school, the farm, and the kids."

I touched his arm. "Then it looks like you're stuck, Joe Riddley. Until God sends you a successor."

"I wish God would hurry. And right now, I'm ready to get out of town. Want to ride with me up to Augusta? I need to get a few things—"

"Light bulbs," I reminded him.

"Yeah, and we could get you a new pocketbook to replace the one you ruined out here. Might even take in an early movie. But so help me, if you so much as mention these murders, or Luke, or *any* of this on the way there or back, I'm going to put you out of the car. You hear me?"

He meant it. On the way up something occurred to me. "Joe Riddley, maybe we could at least go by and talk to the psychiatrist Charlie Muggins called about Luke's dream. Maybe he'd admit that some people have dreams that ..."

I stopped. Joe Riddley was slowing down and putting on his signal to pull over.

One thing people learn who stay married very long: when to talk and when to hush.

≈

Joe Riddley shopped for light bulbs while I bought a new pocketbook, then we had supper and saw an early movie. We didn't get home until nearly ten.

While he put away his purchases, I went out to bring in some sheets Clarinda had washed and hung out before she left for the funeral. We love the smell of sheets that have dried in the open air. To my dismay, I found that

Lulu had dug out of her pen and run away. That poor dog had been grieving since Selena took Beauregard away. Chances were she'd gone looking for him. I hoped she hadn't gotten as far as the highway.

"You want to go looking for her, or fold laundry?" I asked Joe Riddley, who'd already turned on some game on ESPN. Few things make Joe Riddley grumpier than having to leave a game once he's started it, so I thought he'd offer to fold the laundry while he watched. Instead, he frowned and hauled himself to his feet.

"Do I want to go find the dog or send my wife out into the dark with all the trouble we've had around here these past weeks? That's what I call a real choice, Little Bit. I'll go find the dog." He changed his old soft slippers for working boots, found a leash, took his big flashlight, and stomped out, slamming the screen door behind him.

I hurried out barefoot, thinking we could at least go down the drive together, but he was walking fast. "Have fun," I called after his back.

"Humph," he replied without looking back.

It was one of those gorgeous nights we get right before fall—warm and still, the sky freckled with stars and a sliver of moon low in the west, like God tossed out a fingernail paring. I stayed in our backyard enjoying cool damp grass between my toes and taking deep breaths of honeysuckle and cotton dust—which smells good if you've grown up with it. Down near Hubert's fence, longleaf pines stood like crisp brushes against the sky. I've always liked pines. My daddy used to say they are the nicest color: money green. But Joe Riddley won't have a pine near his house. Says they are too brittle, likely to crack in a storm some night and kill you before you wake up.

I wandered over and sat down in our creaky old swing. For years I'd been after Joe Riddley to climb up and oil that thing, but he claimed if it was noisy, I'd smooch instead of talk. That night I just swung lazily and watched one or two fireflies twinkle among the lacy leaves of the maple Joe Riddley's daddy planted to celebrate our wedding. I wondered if ants think fireflies are stars, then that made me wonder if what we think are stars are really just enormous fireflies in a gigantic garden. Once I get to imagining things like that, I'm apt to moon on for a while.

I was called back to myself by our dogs setting up a yowl in their pen. An old possum must be prowling just outside their fence, but with everything that had been happening lately, I suddenly felt nervous enough to hurry back into the house and latch the screen.

I turned on the radio real loud and decided to make brownies for when Joe Riddley got back. We both love chocolate. One of our favorite refrigerator magnets says, "I'd stop eating chocolate, but I'm no quitter."

When I looked at the stove clock to time the brownies, I saw that Joe Riddley had been gone an hour. Even stopping now and then to call a dog, it doesn't take that long to walk up to the end of our road and back. Surely he wouldn't have gone looking for Lulu up the highway—or would he? Maybe the night had bewitched him, too.

More likely, though, he'd found Lulu quickly and stopped in at Hubert's to finish watching that silly game without my helpful commentary. In a few more minutes I checked from our side porch and sure enough, Spences' lights were still on. I waited another few minutes, then decided to call. If Joe Riddley was there, I'd tell him I was going on to bed.

Maynard was out of breath when he answered, and emphasizing words again. "*No*, Miss MacLaren, I haven't seen Joe Riddley at *all*. Daddy and I watched a French film together—a *wonderful* film I couldn't *believe* they carried in *our* video store—then Daddy went on up to *bed* and I've been sitting in the living room looking over some stuff Miss *Bessie* brought by today. That's why I'm so out of *breath*—I had to *dash* for the *phone* before it woke *Daddy*. There's whole box of *pictures* and another of ladies' *underwear—marvelous* additions to our little collection. There are camisoles, petticoats, even—"

I didn't have time for Miss Bessie's underwear. I didn't even have time to remind Maynard about emphasizing words. I could smell my brownies about to burn. "Sorry to bother you, Maynard, but I've got to go. Talk to you later. Bye." As I took out the brownies, I felt sorry for poor Hubert. French films and antique underwear? Do!

Those brownies smelled so good I thought I'd just have one with a little glass of milk while I waited for Joe Riddley to come back. Then I thought I might as well have another. I was reaching for a third when I heard a car barrel down our road and tires scream into our drive. I got to the back door as Ridd's pickup screeched to a stop.

Ridd never drives fast. Never. It is a family joke.

He pounded up the stairs and through the door I held open for him, his face white and his breath coming in short gasps. "It's Daddy, Mama. He's been shot."

Have the gates of death been shown
to you? Have you seen the gates of
the shadow of death? *Job 38:17*

Twenty-Eight

My knees buckled like Joe Riddley was the starch
holding me up. "What happened? Where is he? *How* is he?"
I leaned against the counter so I wouldn't slide to the floor.

Ridd held the doorjamb, looking as weak as I felt. "I
don't know. Martha called and said rescue was bringing
him in. He got shot in the head. They don't know if—if"
He stopped talking and gasped for air.

That stiffened my spine. I picked up my new pocketbook. "You drive."

As we rounded the curve before Hubert's I saw a
blaze of lights on the road. On one side was a field of pines,
on the other the fenced watermelon patch. Sheriff's
deputies swarmed all over the place. One waved us over to
the far right side of the road, but Sheriff Gibbons recognized Ridd's truck and came immediately to the window.

Joe Riddley always joked that Bailey Gibbons went into law enforcement because he looks like a bloodhound, but Buster's a terrific lawman. Until Charlie Muggins' recent bid, he'd never been opposed in an election. That night his jowls sagged and his sad face looked drained. He and Joe Riddley had been friends since kindergarten.

Ridd rolled down his window, and the honeysuckle smelled as good as ever, no matter what was going on. "Is this where it happened, Buster?" I saw a dark stain in the dirt under the glare of all those lights, and felt my heart skip two beats.

"'Fraid so, Mac. Hurry to the hospital. I'll come soon as I can. Drive careful, now."

Usually he wouldn't need to warn Ridd. Ridd drives more like a little old lady than I ever will. That night, though, he didn't even slow down at the tracks to save his shock absorbers. The only thing I said the entire trip was, "Why on earth didn't they call *me?*"

"Martha tried. Your line was busy and she didn't want to waste time going through the operator, so she called me instead." He didn't add what I suspected: Martha needed to talk to Ridd anyway, and thought I'd need his support getting to the hospital. She was right on that.

When we got to the medical center she was the first person I saw. She hurried to hug us both, looking as worried as I felt—which was pretty bad. "They've been able to stabilize him."

I joked, from habit. "Honey, I've been trying to stabilize him for forty years. You all think you can do it in five minutes?" Then I started crying. I'd barely stopped when Walker got there.

I hadn't seen him since he shut the door in his daddy's face. I could tell he was remembering, too, because the next thing I knew he'd caught me up in a bear hug and was talking between sobs. "I killed Cindy's crotons, Mama. That's what the stains were. I got so mad at her I hacked them to death, but I didn't know the sap would stain my clothes. I was too embarrassed to tell you, and now Daddy ... Daddy ..."

Crotons. Why hadn't I thought of that? Their sap dries to look exactly like bloodstains unless you know what it is, but *I* should have known. I also should have had more faith in my son.

Feeling guilty—and at the same time more relieved than I would ever let him know—I hugged him back. "Have you called Cindy, honey?"

"No." He sniffed and wiped his eyes. "I drove up there on Saturday night—that's where I was when you were at the house—but she wouldn't come home unless I promised to cut back on the band. We had a big fight, and—how's Daddy, Mama?"

I told him what I knew, ending with, "Daddy's in God's hands, Walker, but I want you to do us all a favor. Call Cindy right now and ask her to come. Tell her you need her."

His face was blotched with tears and his eyes swam with them. "I do, Mama. I do need her."

"Then go call her." I gave him a push and he stumbled toward a phone.

I could hear him from where I stood. "Cindy, it's me, Walker. Daddy's been shot, honey. He's real bad. I don't know—" His voice broke, then spoke again in hope. "You will? Really? Oh, honey." He turned and gave me a thumbs up, then turned and hunched close to the phone. I moved away so I couldn't hear any more.

"Mac?" I turned and saw Drew Holder, dressed not for work but in yellow jogging shorts and a gray shirt. He had a large dark smear on his chest. When he saw me looking at it, he crossed his arms over it. "I found him," he told me gently. "I'd gone for a run and saw him lying in the road. I ran home to call 911, then went back and did what I could until they got there. We're going to save him, Mac. I swear it. We are going to save the judge!" He took my hand in both of his, and his were trembling. If anybody could save Joe Riddley, I knew he would.

As he left, I murmured to Martha, "That man's hand-some no matter what he wears. You ought to have seen him the night a cannon fell down his chimney. Covered from head to toe with soot, and still gorgeous."

She nodded. "He even looks good in bloody surgical scrubs." She stopped, and neither of us felt like joking any more. The blood Drew had on him right then was Joe Riddley's.

When they finally let me in to see him for a minute, I hardly recognized him. His skin was an ugly gray and he looked shrunken and *old*. I hated watching him labor so hard to breathe, and couldn't help remembering the last things we'd said.

"That's what I call a real choice, Little Bit. I'll go find the dog."

"Have fun."

"Humph."

Anger spurted up inside me. "Why didn't we say something important, hon? Something I could hold on to right now? You can't go off and leave me with nothing more than 'That's what I call a real choice—I'll go find the dog.'"

Joe Riddley certainly wasn't having fun.

"You have to make it, honey. You just have to!"

He didn't move.

They took him into surgery about midnight. All night—that once gorgeous night—we waited and prayed on the world's hardest chairs. With Cindy and the children on their way, Walker teetered between worry about his dad and elation. Ridd slumped in his chair like it had finally dawned on him he was just two old parents away from being an orphan.

Eventually Sheriff Gibbons came in. "Looks like an accidental shooting, Mac. No sign of a struggle or anything, just one clean shot from down the road. Probably somebody doing a little night hunting out of season. Must have gotten scared and took off. Tomorrow we'll look in the woods for tracks, but it's been mighty dry. The only clear print we got on the road was the toe of Doc's running shoes where he knelt beside him." Bailey slapped his leg with his soft hat, then added, "We were fortunate the doc found the judge when he did. He could have laid there all night."

"I'd have gone looking for him before that," I informed him indignantly. Then, embarrassed to sound sharp when he was doing so much, I asked, "Did you find Lulu?"

"Lulu?" he repeated, puzzled. "Your little beagle?"

"She'd escaped from her pen looking for her pups. Joe Riddley was looking for her when he got shot."

"People know your dogs by sight," Buster told me. "Somebody'll bring her home."

Why hadn't I thought of that before I send Joe Riddley out?

⌇

Dr. Holder came out wearing light green scrubs and, sure enough, looking as handsome as ever.

I felt too weak to leave my chair. "Is he going to be all right?"

"He's come through real well so far. The bullet entered to the side of midline and grazed the back of his head. We don't know yet what impairment of function there will be."

Midline? Impairment of function? Was Drew using that hospital jargon to talk about *my husband*? Joe Riddley ought to be there helping me get through that ordeal, not lying on a gurney somewhere while doctors looked across him and talked about the side of his midline and impairment of function.

Dr. Holder seemed to know exactly how I felt. "I am sorry, Mac. So very sorry."

I patted his arm. "You've done what you could, Drew. Are you his surgeon?"

"No, but I asked to assist. After finding him, I wanted to be there." I thought of something Hubert once said about Vietnam: "Once you save somebody's life, they kind of belong to you."

"Please tell us all about finding him," I begged. "I need to know."

He rocked a little from foot to foot. "I had a flashlight, and saw something up ahead on the road. I thought a tree branch had fallen, but when I got closer, it was Judge Yarbrough, lying face-down."

"Face down?" Walker demanded. "You mean they shot him from behind?"

The doctor looked as wretched as we felt. "Yeah. I didn't notice a shot, though, so it must have been while I was down circling a field."

I winced. It must have been while I was creaking in that old swing. It would have drowned out a shot all right. Was that what had set our dogs to yowling? That thought made the hair rise on my arms.

Drew was still talking. " . . . to be sure he still had vital signs, then ran as fast as I could back to my place to call rescue and get my bag. Your place was closer," he added apologetically, "but I needed my bag. I did what I could until rescue got there, then rode with him to the hospital."

"Thank God you were there," I said fervently.

He touched my hand. "A friend of mine used to say the human body is a frail boat, Mac, but we are guided by an expert boatman."

"Amen." I felt like we had prayed.

They took Joe Riddley up to intensive care before dawn. I watched the sun rise that morning from his hospital window, treasuring his every breath. Breath and faith were all I had right then. Joe Riddley had gone into a dark, private place without me.

> He thwarts the plans of the crafty, so
> that their hands achieve no success.
> *Job 5:12*

Twenty-Nine

Joe Riddley didn't wake up.

The nurses were kind enough to let us stay right in intensive care most of the time, and Martha brought me clean clothes so I could change in the nurses' lounge. That's one of the nice parts of living in a town where everybody knows you.

Joe Riddley was shot on Tuesday night. On Wednesday, just as supper carts were rattling in the hall and Ridd and I were beginning to get sick of the sight of one another over his daddy's still form, Isaac James and Ronald Duckworth came in together. "How's he doin'?" Ike asked softly, rocking back and forth on the balls of his feet.

I shook my head. "Not too good." We stood looking down at the wax model of Joe Riddley somebody had left in the bed. I wished I knew where they'd put the real one.

"I hate to bother you at a time like this," Ike said hesitantly, "but I wondered if you could talk to us just a few minutes." I thought he looked a little harried—but didn't we all.

"I'll be right back," I whispered to Ridd, then suggested to Ike, "Let's go down to the ICU waiting room."

As we left, Ronald turned to say politely, "We'll bring her right back, Judge."

Joe Riddley didn't answer.

Ike muttered in my ear, "I've been trying to ask Ronald a few questions all afternoon, but haven't gotten very far. I thought, maybe, you being a friend of his wife and all . . ."

"I'll try." No need to bother correcting his notion about me and Lorine. "What do you want to know?"

"Just follow my lead and if you can help, please do."

When we got settled, Ike leaned forward with his hands clasped between his knees. "As Mr. Duckworth here knows, we've got a new development over at the Taylor house. We got a call this morning from a neighbor that somebody in a green van was trespassing in the Taylor backyard. When officers got there, they found a man trying to break in the back door. He was nearly hysterical that the shed had burned, and when they asked him to go downtown with them, he told them he hadn't done anything wrong, he just worked for Mrs. Duckworth and was looking for Mr. Potts to get his last paycheck. Mr. Duckworth, you saw the man this morning. In what capacity did he work for your wife?"

Ronald sat rubbing his dry palms together, looking miserable. Poor Ike, he must not have discovered that Ronald was allergic to head-on questions.

"Who was the man?" I asked Ike.

"Ex-con with a record a yard long. Grand theft, burglary, assault, three convictions and ten years served. Name of Pete Goodbody."

"Pete!" I turned to Ronald. "You said Pete locked me in the shed."

Words tumbled out of Ronald like pecans out of a shelling machine. "He sure did. Arnie and Pete and me were talking in the kitchen, then he left, but he came right back and said he'd found some woman nosing around the shed, so he'd locked her in. Arnie was real mad. He asked who was it, so Pete described her and Arnie suspected right away it was you, because he'd just seen you. So we went to let you out—but you wouldn't come."

He sounded so indignant I nearly defended myself—until I saw Ike's face. I would not give him the satisfaction of laughing at us both.

"You think he stole the things in the shed?" I asked Ike.

"Claims he didn't. Claims he was merely Mrs. Duckworth's driver and he thought all the things in the shed were legitimate antiques he was delivering for her shop." Ike said the last word carefully. When I met his eyes, a lot of things made sense. In spite of me, I couldn't help admiring Lorine's daring, but I now had a few doubts about the size of her heavenly mansion.

I turned to Ronald. "I wonder why he thought Lorine had a shop."

He spoke earnestly, with pride. "She didn't yet, but she was planning to open an antique business." His eyes grew worried. "She made me promise not to tell until she got enough antiques, but I guess now . . . since she . . ." He stopped and looked at his hands.

I laid my hand on his. "I'm sure it's all right to tell now."

His eyes met mine anxiously. "And she didn't know Pete had stolen the things. He probably told her he'd bought them."

I'd believe that when possums sang. How could Pete Goodbody know who would be at any particular party, or how long they were likely to stay? And Lorine would have recognized any antique stolen from Hopemore. She was also smart enough to make sure she had a watertight alibi for every single robbery. I wondered how she really planned to dispose of the things—and where. Not in middle Georgia, for sure.

"She shouldn't have hired him." Now that Ronald had started talking, he wouldn't stop. "Lorine always believed the best of everybody. I guess she thought giving him a job would help him go straight. But Pete steals all the time. He worked for me last year, and I had to fire him. He stole paint, buckets, he even stole my favorite ladder. You know, Miss MacLaren, you get to be friends with a ladder when you're on it a lot. I sure miss that one. It creaked just a little, a real friendly sound almost like a little song, and—"

I didn't want to spend precious time away from Joe Riddley hearing about friendly ladders. "I guess Arnie had to be in on the robberies," I said to Ike.

"Arnie isn't a robber," Ronald said indignantly. "He called me and told me all Lorine's things were in the shed and we needed to talk about what to do with them. If he'd been a robber, he'd have just left and taken them with him."

I wanted to believe that. Whatever his problems, Arnie had meant a lot to Amanda, Gideon, and Selena. But ... "I sure wonder why he'd let her store the things in his shed."

I trailed the sentence like a cast line. Sure enough, Ronald took the bait, still leading Lorine's cheering squad. "It was Lorine's shed. She bought Miss Marybelle's house! But she put it in another name so people wouldn't guess, before she was ready to open her shop."

If Marybelle ever found out Lorine had bought her house, she'd die.

Then I remembered. She was already dead.

"You must have built the shed," I prompted him.

"Yeah. She told me what she wanted and I built it at night, after work. She made me be real quiet, so I wouldn't bother the neighbors. Lorine was always considerate."

"I wish she'd been considerate enough to leave Marybelle's garden alone," I said angrily.

Ronald leaned over and patted me. "She made me plant every one of the roses over in our back yard. They're doing fine."

Mama always said if you can't say something nice, don't say anything at all. I sat there quiet, remembering the Friday night I went to the temple when Lorine tiptoed out just before the goswami appeared. She'd probably considerately alerted him I was there. I also remembered how she'd considerately prompted him to warn the inquirers not to talk to me about Amanda Kent's death. Amanda must have discovered what was going on. Did Lorine kill her?

And did Arnie kill Lorine?

The very idea made me sick. Arnie had been a pudgy, idealistic boy. From what I'd seen and heard since, he'd grown into a pudgy, idealistic man. What would make him kill? What would even make him let Lorine get away with stealing?

Ronald answered my last question before I asked it. "Lorine let Arnie rent that house real cheap. He was her cousin, you know, and she always did have such a soft heart."

Right. Such a soft heart she set it up so Arnie, not she, would get in trouble if the antiques were found on his property. But Arnie had probably yielded, as so many do, to the temptation that he could accomplish a lot of good by looking the other way when people he knew were doing bad.

"But why would Arnie pour gasoline all around the shed?" I demanded.

Ronald didn't say a thing, so I rephrased it. "I guess he wanted to scare me."

"No, it was Pete," he said obligingly. "Arnie saw him, I guess, because he ran out yelling 'What are you doing?' By the time I got out there, they had both driven off and Maynard was looking for an axe." He leaned over and patted my hand. "I asked Pete about that today when I saw him. He said he wasn't really planning to burn you down. He just wanted to threaten to do it so Arnie and I would pay him what Lorine owed him."

I had one more question for either Ike or Ronald. "Do you think he came back and burned down the shed?"

Ike shook his head. "Goodbody claims he has witnesses that he went straight to Jefferson County after he left the house. We also have a witness who saw Arnie Potts's car come down the alley while the shed was burning, back up, and drive away."

He had to have known the things were stolen, then. Known and decided it was easier to start over than pick a treacherous way through the unraveling. *That,* finally, sounded like the Arnie I knew. He always preferred what looked like the easier way.

"I wonder who burned down the shed, then," I said.

Ronald shrugged. "Nobody knows."

I looked at him suspiciously. "What did you do when you left the house? Picture it in your mind. You went walking out the back door . . ."

Ronald closed his eyes and pursed his lips, like he was trying. Then he got a stricken look. "I lit a cigarette. But then I remembered Lorine doesn't like me to smoke, so I threw it over the wall."

~

Isaac stayed a minute or two after Ronald left. "Thanks. I hated to bother you right now, but I couldn't get him to answer a single question all afternoon. He didn't act like he was refusing to cooperate, just wouldn't say anything to the point."

"Joe Riddley discovered long ago that direct questions fluster Ronald. You have to make a statement and let him respond."

"I wish I'd known that four hours ago," he said wistfully.

"I have one more question. I know Arnie couldn't have killed Amanda Kent, but do you think he killed the other two?"

Isaac shook his head. "To tell the truth, I don't have any idea. But there's no other violence on his record. Just impersonating religious leaders, things like that."

"Arnie's always been seeking peace," I said sadly, "he just looks in the wrong places."

Ike grinned. "I guess he's still seeking. We haven't found a trace of him. Before I go, may I pray with you and the Judge?" We bowed our heads and Ike said the nicest prayer. I hoped wherever he'd gone to, Joe Riddley could hear it.

As we walked to the elevator, I grumbled, "So I sat in that hot, dark shed all that time for nothing, when I could have been drinking cold Co-colas and renewing my acquaintance with Arnie? And all those antiques burned up because Ronald wanted to please his dead wife. It's a comedy, Ike. Except nobody's laughing."

"I'll tell you something that *is* funny," he offered. "Ronald's looking for insurance papers on Lorine's antiques. He says he's afraid she never took out a policy, though, because she didn't have a very good head for business."

We laughed so hard we both had tears streaming down our cheeks. When we stopped, the tears kept coming. I held out my arms and Ike gave me a bear hug. I didn't care who saw us or what they thought.

"When we get home, will you come see us? We drink tea and sit on the porch a lot in the evening, and Joe

Riddley's going to be needing company." Black folks and white folks don't do much socializing yet in Hopemore, but there was no good reason we couldn't start.

"I'll come," he promised.

I had one more happy thought. "Lorine and Charlie Muggins were thick as thieves. This ought to put a stick in his waterwheel."

"Chief Muggins will be doing some pretty fancy contortions this next week," Isaac agreed with quiet satisfaction.

> ... the land of deepest night, of deep shadow and disorder, where even the light is like darkness. *Job 10:22*

Thirty

Around noon on Thursday Walker came in, very agitated. "Luke's trial date's been set." He bit his lip and I saw he was blinking back tears. "I wish he hadn't told anybody about that stupid dream." He pounded the door jamb, then threw me a hangdog look. "Sorry, Mama. But can't you do something?" He caught my glance toward Joe Riddley. "I know Daddy needs you, but Luke does, too. I'll sit here day and night if you'll find out who did it." Like I said, Walker always was generous where his friends were concerned.

"Am I interrupting?" Drew Holder stood at the door, stunning in a navy blazer, tan pants, and striped tie.

"You look magnificent," I greeted him. As I took his hand, I felt strength flowing into me.

He gave me an embarrassed little grin. "My conference starts Monday, so I've been up in Augusta doing a television interview. How's Joe Riddley?"

I looked toward the bed and shrugged. "Bright and lively, like always." There was no change, of course. Joe Riddley lay there like a perfect illustration of what a hospital patient ought to look like.

He put an arm around me. "You're great, Mac. Hang in there." He turned toward Walker. "Thanks for that nice letter you wrote."

Walker shuffled his feet and shot me an embarrassed look. "I wanted you to know how grateful we are that you turned up in time to save him." Walker writing thank-you notes? Wonders would never cease.

Drew looked embarrassed, too. "I'm glad I could be there." Why do men have such a hard time admitting they've done something their mothers would be proud of?

When he'd gone, Walker turned back to me. "Mama, can't you help Luke?"

"I don't know what I can do from here, honey, but I'll try to think of something."

As soon as Walker left, I called Jimmy Newton. I hung up five minutes later feeling like a snail had crawled all over me.

"Why Miss MacLaren, how are you? How's the judge? I'm sorry to hear that. Reverend Blessed? Yes, the date is set, and we're going to do our best to beat this thing. To be totally honest, it doesn't look real good, but I'm going to delay as long as I can, and make the jury look real hard at their evidence. And we can certainly line up some fine character witnesses from your church. I don't think they'll come in with murder one."

When he paused for breath, I said bluntly, "You think he did it, don't you, Wait?"

He hesitated just a fraction too long for my liking. "As his attorney I am bound to consider him innocent, Miss MacLaren. However, it's going to be tough. Real tough."

"What about the dream?"

"I don't think we'll introduce the dream. I don't want to muddy the waters."

"That's what a defense attorney is for, Wait—to show reasonable doubt."

"I'll have to conduct the case as I think best, Miss MacLaren. See you in court."

I turned from the phone and said to Joe Riddley, "Unless somebody besides his lawyer goes to bat for Luke, he's as good as jailed for life." Then I reached over and patted him. "But don't worry, honey. I'm not going to get involved in this thing. Not right now, when you need me."

I sat down in the visitor's chair, crossed my ankles, looked out the window, and wondered how long it would be before I went stark raving mad.

∽

It looked like we were finally going to get some rain. We desperately needed it. We hadn't had any since that little morning shower a week and a half before. Between two dark clouds the sun shot one long dart of thick yellow light. It streamed through Joe Riddley's blinds and striped his bedclothes like jail bars. That was fitting. Joe Riddley was as much a prisoner as Luke. Would either of them ever get out?

"Where are you?" I demanded, pounding my fist lightly beside him on the bed. That felt so good, I knew why Walker liked to pound things. "Come back," I fussed. "I need you. Walker needs you. Luke needs you!" I laid my head down beside him, arms across his legs. The only sound in the room was the distant chiming of the courthouse clock. Two o'clock, and all was definitely not well.

"God," I whispered, "help Luke. You know I'm stuck here, but *please* help Luke!"

As I lay there with Joe Riddley utterly still, I had what I thought was a revelation. Maybe you'd call it the product of forty years of marriage. Maybe you'd call it inventing reasons to do what I wanted to do anyway. Whatever it was, as surely as if he'd opened his eyes and spoken, I knew Joe Riddley wanted me to get out of that hospital room and find out who killed Amanda Kent. Even if he fussed at me for meddling in things, I knew what he'd say when he finally woke up, if he found out I'd sat the whole time beside his bed. "What good did that do, Little Bit? Why didn't you get off your duff and do something?"

"I don't know what to do," I told him. "Besides, when I'm here, I can't think of anything besides you, and I can't go off and leave you by yourself."

You know the poem that says God works in mysterious ways, his wonders to perform? That afternoon he sent me an unlikely angel.

I heard a soft sound at the door and Hubert stood there, his mouth hanging open. "Is Joe Riddley better? Can he talk to you?"

"Hello, Hubert." I turned back to the bed and said loudly. "Joe Riddley, Hubert has come to see you." I tiptoed to the door and whispered, "He can't respond yet, but talk naturally. We hope he can hear us, and maybe soon he'll start talking back."

Hubert tiptoed to the bed and bent down with his face just above Joe Riddley's. "Hello, buddy. This is Hubert here. I thought I'd come see how you were gettin' along. Looks like we're gonna finally get a little storm this afternoon."

Joe Riddley lay there without moving except when his chest went up and down.

"MacLaren looks good," Hubert told him. "Not bad at all, considering."

Considering what? I looked in the mirror, and I did look a little seedy around the edges. I had an idea. "Hubert, could you stay here for a couple of hours? I'd love to go home and take a bath." Maybe on the way, I could think of something to help Luke.

"I'd be glad to!" Hubert stood up straighter. I wondered how long it had been since anybody asked him to do them a favor instead of offering to do him one. Mama always said one of the best tonics in the world is to be needed.

I picked up my new pocketbook and bent down to give my husband a kiss.

"Don't get wet, now, " Hubert warned as I left. "It's starting to spit out there."

"I won't. And I'll be back soon."

"We'll be fine right here, won't we, old buddy?" Hubert asked Joe Riddley, then turned back to me. "I'll keep talking. Maybe he'll wake up."

That could work. Joe Riddley might wake up to shut up Hubert.

Hubert was right. It was spitting rain when I got to the car, and raining hard when I got downtown. By the time I reached our cut-off, though, the shower had passed. "That little bit of rain won't do any good," I pointed out to God.

I was a little nervous about being home alone, even if it would only be for a couple of hours in broad daylight. I was nervous about driving down our road, too. It would be my first time since Joe Riddley got shot.

As I passed the Pickens place I was glad to see Drew's car. He must have gone straight home after leaving us. Rhonda Duckworth waved from a porch rocker. She looked quite at home. Ronald might not know everything there was to know about his daughter.

Mist rose from Hubert's cow pond like steam on tea with milk. Once past Hubert's and to the piney woods, I rolled down my windows and gulped in deep breaths to clear my lungs of hospital air. As I got to the spot where the deputies' cars had parked two nights before, I couldn't help stopping and getting out for a minute. The rain had washed out the stain, so I couldn't tell exactly where it had been. Since there wasn't a soul in sight, I demanded loudly, "Okay, trees, who was the skunk who shot Joe Riddley and left him?"

Back in the woods I heard one faint bark. As I turned back to the car, I heard the bark again, then a whine. Did it sound familiar? I cocked my ears and took a step toward the verge. "Lulu?" I called, not believing my ears. "Lulu?"

I heard a whimper, then a series of squeals. "Lulu!" I cried. "I'm coming, honey. Where are you?"

In our part of Georgia, rain turns the soil to a muddy mass of clay that sticks to shoes and turns the shoulders of roads into squishy slicks. As I headed toward the sodden blackberry bushes that bordered the pines, mud sucked my shoes so hard they were pulled off my feet a couple of times, so I stepped barefoot into mud and had to shove a sticky foot back in my shoe. However, I wasn't about to give up. Still calling, I finally reached the squishy pinestraw beneath tall cinnamon trunks. "Lulu? Talk to me, pet." She whined.

I found her lying next to a large tree, burrowed deep into heavy, rain-soaked pinestraw. She lifted her head and whimpered, then dropped her chin wearily. The leash was on her collar, so Joe Riddley had found her and was heading home when he got shot.

I picked up the leash and tugged, but she didn't move. "Come on, girl. Let's go."

She whimpered, but didn't budge.

"Come on, Lulu!" I tugged hard.

She yelped in pain.

I pulled away the pinestraw and was very nearly sick. Her back left leg was a black, bloody mess. "Oh, Lulu! What happened?"

I was scared to lift her, afraid of hurting her. Fortunately, I was wearing a skirt that buttoned all the way down the front. I unbuttoned it and slid it underneath her for a sling. "Don't cry, baby, don't cry," I murmured as I struggled to get her back to the car.

It was hard to open the back door with her limp and heavy in my arms. I was trying to work the handle when somebody said behind me. "Let me help."

Drew Holder stood there, soaking wet. He must have been out running and gotten caught in the rain. I didn't look too good either, standing there in my blouse, slip, and muddy shoes, but he didn't seem to notice as he stood back to let me deposit Lulu carefully on the back seat. She growled deep in her throat.

"Don't get close. She's hurt," I explained. "I've got to get her to the vet."

He pulled a cell phone in a plastic bag from the waist of his jogging pants and handed it to me. "I'm on call, so I brought it along. Want to let them know you're coming?"

I didn't know the vet's number, so I called Walker. Cindy answered the phone on the first ring. All of us did, those days.

"Pop's the same," I reassured her quickly, "and Hubert's with him, but I found Lulu in Hubert's woods and she's hurt. Is Walker there?"

Things were still awkward with Cindy. I hadn't seen her but once since she'd gotten back. She'd hugged me and said how sorry she was, but I could tell she was embarrassed. Since then she'd been keeping Crick so Ridd and Martha could be at the hospital.

"Walker's not here," she said at once, "but I'll call the vet and meet you there. Tad can watch Tiffany and Crick for a little while."

"Thank you. She looks real bad." I couldn't keep my voice from wobbling. The coonhounds are pen dogs, but Lulu's my baby.

"I'll be there before you are," Cindy promised.

I handed Drew's phone back with a little laugh. "I guess I'd better go put on another skirt."

He closed my door. "I'd suggest clean shoes, too."

As I roared down the road, I said fervently, "Thank you, God, for good children and good neighbors."

Cindy was there when we arrived, just as she'd promised. She looked thinner, and more grown-up than she used to. Troubles affect some people that way. She was also very competent. She carried Lulu in and soothed her while the vet did an examination, and not once did I see that young woman flinch.

Walker came just as the vet was about to tell me what he'd found. "She took a bullet, and it's very infected. I'm sorry, Mac, but I'm going to have to take off that leg just below the hip. It's a miracle that she's still alive."

Poor Lulu.

"Mama, a beagle with three legs can't chase rabbits," Walker said in the pompous voice my boys always use when telling me what to do. "Maybe you ought to have her put down. You'll have your hands full enough with Daddy when he gets home."

We looked at each other. Each knew what the other was thinking. *If* he got home. And that could be ages. Taking care of a recuperating dog wasn't something I could do from a hospital room.

Then I looked through the door at that little tan and black head on the doctor's examining room, and Lulu looked straight at me. She was the most intelligent dog we'd ever had, and one of the most loyal. I couldn't destroy all that for one bad leg.

"We'll manage," I told Walker. "Maybe she could go to Ridd's for a few days."

Cindy stepped up and surprised me. "I'll look after Lulu."

Walker looked at her in surprise, too. "Thanks, Cindy." He turned to me and added proudly, "Cindy's got a lot more experience with animals than Ridd or Martha."

When I thought about that later, I realized it was true. I'd tended to think of Cindy in terms of mint juleps and after-hunt balls, but she'd spent her life around horses and foxhounds. In the next few weeks she showed us all that she knew not only how to tend a sick dog, but how to train one. Lulu came home knowing how to cope with life on three legs, and Cindy went up several notches in my book.

Walker went up a few notches that very evening. He thought of something that would have worried me later. "Did you save the bullet?" he asked the vet.

"I threw it away. Did you want it?"

Walker's lips set in a grim line. "They never found the bullet that hit Daddy. This may have come from the same gun, so we ought to take it with us."

It couldn't help much. It was a twenty-two, a very common gun in our county. Anybody who hunted squirrel, rabbit, or possum had one. Joe Riddley had a couple—one from his boyhood and one he'd bought later.

Later that night, Sheriff Gibbons and I agreed that if whoever shot Joe Riddley had also shot Lulu, he or she knew what he had done and might try to finish it.

Buster decided to put a deputy on Joe Riddley's door. I didn't sleep a wink all night.

> Who cuts a channel for the torrents of
> rain, and a path for the thunderstorm?
> *Job 38:25*

Thirty-One

I was dragging considerably by the time Ridd got
there the next morning.

"Why don't you run over to our house for a shower
and a nap?" he suggested.

"What I'd like right now would be a bath in my own
tub. I was on my way home last evening when I found
Lulu—"

"Walker told me. That was great! And he said Cindy
went over to the vet's early this morning, and she's doing
well—Lulu, not Cindy."

"Cindy's doing better than you realize."

Since Ridd apparently hadn't noticed the deputy in
the hall, I didn't bring that up. He settled his long frame
onto the recliner, unfolded his paper, and said, "Take your
time. I'll be right here."

Being at home wasn't as wonderful as I'd thought it would be. I kept worrying that Ridd would go downstairs for coffee with Martha just when the deputy was away using the bathroom. I couldn't imagine why anybody would shoot my old coot in the first place, but what if whoever did came back to finish the job?

Instead of a long bath I took a quick shower, put on a skirt and knit top, and fixed my face in record time. I was almost ready to leave when the door bell rang. Who could that be? Nobody came to our front door. Nobody but Charlie Muggins.

This time it was Drew and Rhonda, flushed from running. With a pang, I realized I never had gotten around to having Drew down for supper. Now it would be awhile.

"How can you run on such a hot, sticky morning?" I greeted them.

"Drew had the day off," Rhonda said, as if that were reason enough.

"Hi, Mac," Drew said apologetically. "We didn't want to bother you, but I saw your car and wanted to see how the dog is."

While I told him, Rhonda peered over my shoulder and spotted Selena's loom in the middle of the living room. "Is that real? Do you weave?"

"I wish," I told her. "That belongs to a friend of ours. We're just holding it for her."

"May I see it? I've always wanted a loom." Being a golden-haired princess, she didn't wait for permission, just glided past me.

Drew jogged in place impatiently by the door, more aware than Rhonda that I wanted to be on my way. Finally he went over and tugged her arm. "Mac wants to get back to the hospital, honey." Absently he reached over with his free hand to pull the little blue thread caught on a screw head, then gave me a rueful grin. "Compulsively neat. What can I say?"

"I've been meaning to do that," I assured him, "I just hadn't gotten around to it. Do you hire out? I could use you around here." I spread my hands to indicate the minor clutter that's always been part of our lives.

He rubbed the thread between his fingers, stuck it in his pocket, and grinned. "I'll let you know when I have a free day."

Rhonda came reluctantly leaving the loom. "Do you think your friend would teach me to weave?"

"I don't know if she even knows how, yet. She just bought the loom from—um—somebody who didn't need it anymore."

Drew tugged her arm. "Come on! You can buy a hundred looms another day, but today you still owe me a mile."

Laughing, she followed him out. Her hair gleamed gold in the sunlight.

Ridd called me on the cell phone on my way back. "Daddy's awake! And he's asking for you!"

I hurried back to find Joe Riddley's doctor and four nurses surrounding his bed. My husband looked at me with a puzzled expression. "How's Jake?"

Jake is my only brother. He lives over in Montgomery and had open heart surgery in July. "Jake's fine, honey." I put one hand on his shoulder to quiet him and one on my heart to quiet *it*. "How do you feel, Joe Riddley?"

"I'm fine. You go on back over to stay with Jake. He needs you worse'n I do."

For a terrified second I was afraid Joe Riddley had gotten a word of knowledge about Jake. Then Ridd stepped close and murmured, "He thinks it's July and he got hurt driving over to Montgomery to bring you home."

"Oh. Has anybody tried to set him straight?"

"Not yet," said the doctor on my other side. "He's only been awake a short time."

"Talk louder," Joe Riddley complained. "I can't hear you."

"Ridd was telling me you're a little confused, Joe Riddley. It's August, and Jake's fine. You've had a little accident and are in the Hopemore Medical Center."

"Hopemore? Why'd they bring me all the way back here?"

"The accident happened in Hopemore, honey. You got shot on Tuesday."

"Is this Thursday?"

"No, it's Friday."

"Did the car go off the road?"

"You weren't in the car. You were out for a walk, looking for Lulu."

"Lulu oughtn't to be out. She's just had her pups." He breathed heavily and moved one arm restlessly.

The doctor touched me lightly. "Let's let him rest a few minutes. We'll call you when you can come back."

I spent the rest of the morning and early afternoon alternately talking sense to Joe Riddley's nonsense, pacing the hall, and talking with the deputy on duty. I could only see Joe Riddley for a few minutes at a time, because he got so agitated at what he couldn't remember. Worse, he couldn't move his legs.

Walker arrived about two, went in for barely two minutes, and came out wild. "Mama, he's crazy! Doesn't know where he is, or why he's here, or even what month it is. And he can't wiggle his toes!"

"I know, honey. The doctor says he may get a lot better, but they don't know yet. His brain has been damaged. We'll just have to wait and see."

If I sounded cool, calm and collected, that was because I'd been dealing with it for a while. Inside I was running down long dark corridors screaming, "Joe Riddley, come back! Honey, where are you? Come back!" The way I was pacing the hall, the medical center was going to have to replace its carpet when we left.

"But he'll walk again, right?" He pounded the back of a chair several times.

"We don't know, so calm down. We're in for a long haul."

Martha came just then. "What's that deputy doing outside?"

Walker noticed him for the first time. "Visiting, I guess."

"Uh, no, he's been assigned to make sure nobody unauthorized comes in," I explained. "Sheriff Gibbons wants to make sure whoever shot Pop doesn't try again."

"Dear God!" Martha gasped. It wasn't an oath, but a prayer.

"Yeah," I agreed. "But between me and the deputy he ought to be safe enough."

She put a hand on my shoulder and spoke in what Crick called her Nurse's Voice. It was a lot firmer than her usual gurgle. "You're dead on your feet, Mac. If you don't get some rest, we'll be admitting you, too. That won't do Pop a speck of good. I'll stay until after suppertime. You go get some rest. I'd suggest you go to our house, but Bethany got home and she's got a slew of girls over there practicing cheers. Walker, could she—"

"I'd really like to go home," I interrupted. "I can't imagine anything nicer than a nap in my own bed."

"Then go. I promise not to leave Pop alone for a second. But hurry. We're going to get more rain, and this one looks like the granddaddy of all storms."

<hr />

There are a few disadvantages to living in the country. On the two-lane road out of town I got caught behind an eighteen wheeler, which in turn was caught behind an old red tractor trying to make it to cover before the storm. We crept along at fifteen miles an hour while a steady stream of traffic came the other way. The sky was dark-

ening steadily into a deep, growling gray. Before I got
half-way home I turned on my lights.

It was a comfort to see lights at both Drew's and
Hubert's. Somebody would be near if I needed them. Why
I ought to need anybody, I couldn't say, but I felt very jittery. The electricity from the storm must be getting into
my bloodstream.

By the time I reached our driveway, the storm was so
close that all the trees in our yard were frightened into
stillness. The sycamores had turned up their leaves in
surrender, and the halogen light in our back yard had
come on, thinking it was dusk.

I dashed to the back porch just as the storm broke.
Hugging my goosebumps in the chilly breeze, I stood
watching water fall in a sheet so solid that a sudden gust
of wind made it bulge. Lightning flickered like strobe
lights, while thunder rolled in from the west. The thunder and lightning made me feel very safe. Who would
come out in all that?

Still, I not only locked the doors, but stuck chairs
under all the doorknobs before I climbed the stairs and
put on my nightgown. The temperature must have
dropped twenty degrees, so I climbed in under both the
thermal blanket and the bedspread.

Tired as I was, I still couldn't fall asleep with all that
thunder. I felt like I was stuck in a basement while
kitchen help rolled barrels across a cement floor overhead. Rumble. Rumble. Rumble. One barrel crashed off a
counter and rolled down a long hall to oblivion. Another
rolled toward me from a long way off, closer and closer in
a wave of noise, then abruptly headed in another direction. A whip cracked. Several barrels crashed to the floor.

Obviously I wouldn't sleep until the storm moved
away. On my night stand I saw the book I'd taken from
Amanda Kent's. I flipped on the bedside light, propped up
on a couple of pillows, and started the first chapter, but
it was so complicated that my mind grew heavier and

heavier as my eyes flitted from underlined phrase to phrase. "... save human society from spiritual death ... cycle of transmigration ... easier and more comfortable way of life ... human body is an excellent vehicle ... rare and very important boat ... on this boat there is the service of experienced boatman ... deeply rooted banyan tree ..."

The storm lessened. My head bobbed. Already half asleep, I laid the book on Joe Riddley's side of the bed and slid down under the covers. Lulled by rain thrumming on our tin porch roof, I slept. I also dreamed.

I was on a huge sailboat with a crowd of men. I recognized Joe Riddley, Ronald, Charlie Muggins, Maynard, and Drew. We rocked back and forth as huge waves slapped the side of the boat, but the men were laughing and knocking at them playfully. Maynard used a burning board. Drew used a sooty crowbar. Joe Riddley used an arrest warrant, which was soon limp and useless. Charlie used his hat. Poor Ronald had only a very narrow paintbrush.

"We're going to drown!" I yelled as a wave crashed over the deck. "We ought to call for help."

"I've saved the pups." Maynard held open his jacket and I saw two pockets, with a pup's head peeping out of each. Each had a blue bow around its neck with threads dangling where the pups had chewed them.

Drew took a cell phone from his waist and handed it to me. "Here. Use this to call. But we won't feel any pain. I've been working on that."

I heard a shout, coming from the water itself. "I saw what you did. I saw what you did." Lorine bobbed angrily on the waves, pointing at me. Beyond her, I saw Gideon Levy and Mandy Kent.

"Don't forget me," Mandy called, waving as she bobbed further away.

"I won't," I promised, waving back. She blew me a kiss.

"Don't get in my way, Mac." Charlie Muggins elbowed me in the side and headed forward. "I've got to get the

*preacher." For the first time I noticed Luke, holding onto
the bowsprit for dear life. I knew if I didn't stop Charlie
he'd push Luke in.*

I shoved past Drew, nearly knocking him over.

*"Don't hurt Drew," Lorine yelled at me. "He's a very
important man."*

*"I know that," I called back angrily. "He's my neigh-
bor. And you're supposed to be dead."*

*"I am," she said matter-of-factly. "You'll have to get
your plants home yourself."*

When I woke up, it was that last exchange I remembered. Me telling Lorine she was supposed to be dead, and
her pointing out I'd therefore need to get my plants home
myself. That was so exactly like Lorine, it made me smile.

It also reminded me that I'd never retrieved the
plants I sent over for the buffet. My subconscious must
have been prodding me. There was a small truckload of
them, and Ronald and Rhonda didn't need to be taking
care of them. As I reached for the pencil and notepad I
keep by the bed, I peered at the digital clock to see how
long I'd slept. Its face was dark. Power lines must be
down. I hoped the medical center had its generators up
and running.

In the little bit of light coming though the window,
my watch read six o'clock. The worst of the storm was
over. Only a gentle rain drummed on the roof.

I still had time to do a little thinking about Mandy
Kent. Three weeks ago to the hour she was going to the
temple to serve at the juice bar.

"I will not forget you," I promised, genuinely grieving. It was not the face from the newspaper I spoke to, but
the face from my dream. My feelings for her had been so
vivid in the dream, I now thought of her not as Amanda
Kent, but as my friend Mandy.

> In the midst of his plenty, distress will overtake him; the full force of misery will come upon him. *Job 20:22*

Thirty-Two

I pulled on a cotton robe, slid my feet into slippers, and padded downstairs. When I got to the kitchen, I heard the whir of the refrigerator coming on. I felt a tad hungry, and since our power tends to be erratic after storms, I got out a cast iron griddle and fried some bacon and eggs while the electricity was working. I also sliced one of Ridd's tomatoes, made toast, and spread it with some of his honey. I even made myself a cup of tea. I don't drink hot tea in the summertime as a rule, but it was chilly after the storm.

The whole time I was cooking, I was thinking about my dream. St. Augustine says one of the marvelous things about memory is that we can forget something, yet remember we've forgotten it—even if we don't remember what it is. That's how I felt about the dream. There'd been something—*something*—that if I could just get hold of, I could solve all the mysteries of Hopemore. But there was no use trying to stare it in the face. It was like a doe that used to graze in Hubert's pasture. If you looked straight at her, she ran. You had to pretend to be looking at something else and watch her out of the side of your eye.

Leaving the griddle on the stove and my cooking things in the sink, I carried my supper onto the porch. Whatever it was, it would come to me eventually.

While I ate, I enjoyed the light breeze, the fresh, sweet air, and rain still pattering on the leaves. By the time I finished, I had goosebumps again, but the pattering and the breeze were too nice to give up. I went back in for a light jacket and a pad and pencil so I could do some thinking. As I sat down, I reached up to flip on the light over my chair.

Not until it didn't come on did I remember about the burned-out bulb. That made me so sad I almost couldn't stand it. *Oh, honey, did we ever fight about something as silly as light bulbs?*

If he'd been there, though, we'd have fought about them again, because when I went to the pantry for one of his new ones, that silly man had bought clothesline instead.

"The clothesline is perfectly good, just sagging a tad," I fumed aloud as if he were just behind me. "What got into you these last few weeks? Now I'm going to have to sit in the dark, because the only bulbs in the entire house that would fit my light are too high for me to reach."

Fussing at him made me feel better—as if he were well enough to take it.

Suddenly I remembered the bulb from Lorine's lawn, the one I'd tossed in my car litter bag. Was it the bad bulb, or one of the good ones I'd had Ronald replace? That seemed like a hundred years ago.

I squished through the rain and across damp grass to my car, admiring huge gray clouds scudding westward. I decided to bring back the entire bag. It was time I cleaned it out anyway.

Just as I got inside, the phone rang. I jumped an inch and ran to answer it without closing the back door. After bacon, the kitchen could use some airing anyway.

"Hello?" I was terrified it was Martha, telling me something bad had happened.

"Mac, are you okay?"

"Luke? Where are you?" I could have laughed out loud. It wasn't anybody from the hospital.

"Same old home away from home."

While he talked, I slipped off my soaked slippers and rubbed my feet back and forth on the sink rug to dry them.

"I asked them to let me make a call, and when I told them who I was calling, they didn't even make me call collect. Listen, are you okay? I've been thinking about you all afternoon and wondered if anything was wrong."

"I'm snug as a bug in a rug. Just ate eggs and bacon. You should have been here." I'd meant to sound cheerful, but it came out forlorn. There was something about having Luke on the line that made me want to break down and cry. I knew I couldn't. If I did, I might never stop.

Instead, I dumped the litter bag onto the counter and started tossing used tissues and old receipts into the garbage can—checking to be sure none of the receipts were for things under warranty. Joe Riddley was bad about throwing away receipts we'd need later when we took something back.

"I wish I could have been there," Luke joked, "but I'm a little confined today." We both laughed, but we weren't fooling anybody. I couldn't help remembering another Saturday evening just a few weeks ago, when we'd joked over dominoes. Why don't we know to appreciate times when we laugh simply because we are happy?

"How's Joe Riddley?" I could tell he had transferred his worries now that he knew I was all right.

"He's finally seen fit to wake up." I gave him the day's report and tried to make it funny that Joe Riddley couldn't remember what month it was, but the notion that

Luke thought there might be something wrong bothered me. He sensed that.

"I think I got a crossed signal, Mac. Don't let it worry you. But I'm going to pray extra hard for him this evening. For you, too. This has to be as hard on you as on him."

"You got that right. He gets waited on hand and foot, but I . . ." I choked up too much to joke any more. "Listen, I need to go. But I'll talk to you later. Thanks for calling."

I hung up and rested my head against the cabinet, wishing I was in a different time and place where I didn't have to go back to the hospital and a very uncertain future. Who was it who said you don't get a rehearsal for life?

"Get on with it," I told myself sternly. "Clean up your dishes and go on back." I looked down and saw I still held one receipt. It puzzled me. Eight penny nails? a crowbar? floor sweeping compound? Nobody who lives in a house as old as ours needs to buy those things. We have sheds and a barn full of that stuff. And when were we in Dublin? Joe Riddley certainly wouldn't drive that far to buy something he could get downtown.

Then I saw the date. Ridd must have bought the things that afternoon he borrowed my car to take Crick shopping for camping supplies. I wadded the receipt up with a frown. Ridd seldom will let anybody do something for him. Borrowing my car occasionally is about his limit as far as we're concerned. He should have just come by and gotten the nails and stuff he needed.

I was about to wad it up to throw away when a voice spoke at the door. "Hello, Mac. Everything okay?" Drew Holder shook his head to clear raindrops from his hair.

"Everybody in town is worried about me tonight," I told him. "Luke just called."

"The preacher who killed Mandy Kent?"

"The one they *claim* killed Mandy Kent. Did you know her?"

He looked surprised. "What makes you think that?"

"Her friends called her Mandy. And at the hospital the night Joe Riddley was shot, you said something about us being boats with a good pilot. That's like something I read this afternoon in a book of hers."

I expected him to nod and say he'd known her at the hospital. Instead, he flushed.

That's when I remembered where I got the receipt I was holding. In Drew's back yard, the night the cannon fell down his chimney. The receipt was dated the day after Amanda Kent was killed. One word stood out: crowbar.

Drew would have had an old crowbar. He'd bought Amos' place lock, stock, and barrel, and the Pickens family had been packrats since the days of Noah. Why did he need to buy a new one that particular Saturday?

It's amazing how much understanding you can get in half a second. I remembered things I'd seen, snips and bits I'd heard, even what seemed odd in my dream: Lorine wasn't accusing me, she was pointing to Drew beside me.

Drew—who had killed Amanda, Lorine, and Gideon. I was sure of it. I thought I even knew why. I just wasn't sure I'd live long enough to tell anybody. *Dear God, what do I do now?* I moved back slightly toward the phone.

He came further into the room. "You're looking for whoever it was, aren't you? I was too busy to read last week's *Statesman,* but I was spreading it out to do some spackling this afternoon and saw that write-up on you. It mentioned the mysteries you've solved. Very impressive, Mac. Nobody told me I lived down the road from Sherlock Holmes."

"Sherlock Holmes was skinny," I reminded him, backing slowly toward our round kitchen table, "and he'd never have gotten himself locked in a shed and nearly incinerated."

"He'd never have come back here alone and left his back door open, either." Drew fumbled in his pants pocket and brought out something hidden in his hand.

Please, God. Please! "No, that was dumb. But I have such good neighbors."

"Had such good neighbors," he corrected me gently. "Mac, I really hate to do this, but I have to." He held out a hypodermic syringe and stepped toward me.

God! I dashed behind the table. Thank goodness Joe Riddley's granddaddy had five children and needed a big one. I couldn't see if there was anything in the syringe or not, but plain air would be deadly.

He eased toward me. I eased away. *God, can I get all the way around and out the door?* Maybe, if I kept him talking. "You ready for your conference next week?"

"Yeah. People are coming from all over for it. My discoveries will revolutionize geriatric surgery." His face blazed with pride.

How you have fallen from heaven, O morning star, son of the dawn!

Was that the Bible, or a poem? I didn't know, but I knew it was talking about Lucifer, the fallen angel.

Drew inched nearer. I inched away.

God? I took another baby step. "Except they don't always work, do they? You tried them on coma patients and they didn't flinch. But when you cut Mandy Kent with a scalpel, did she tell you it hurt? Did she also figure out you'd been the one cutting her patients?"

A dark flush stained his face and he forgot to move. "It was her idea to be the last research subject. She said she had a low pain threshold, so she'd be an ideal subject to show how well they worked. But she wasn't concentrating that night. She was all caught up in something that pseudo swami had said at the temple. She spent too much time down there." He lunged across the table to grab me, but I jumped back out of reach. *God! Help me!*

I was panting, but I tried to sound as sympathetic as I could while focusing my entire attention on that sharp little point. "That must have made you pretty mad."

He stood erect and stretched his arms high over his head. I made myself look at his eyes, not the hand with the needle. Joe Riddley said when you're shooting a bear, always watch the eyes. I figured it applied.

He relaxed and started around the table again. "You can't imagine how mad it made me. Mandy didn't just say it hurt when I cut her, she threatened to wreck my conference. Said I couldn't tell people I could wipe out pain if I couldn't. She threatened to announce that the methods only work for people with high pain thresholds. She was utterly wrong, but she'd have ruined me!"

The flush on his cheeks deepened. It was not at all becoming. Neither was the flare of one nostril.

"But why'd you take a crowbar to her place that night? She wasn't tearing out any walls." As soon as I asked, I knew. "You hit her with it to see if it hurt."

"Yeah. That's a different kind of pain than a cut. Affects the body differently."

I knew he could go berserk when enraged, but the idea of him hitting people to test his theories made me so disgusted I couldn't help taunting him. "Mandy spent not just too much time at that temple, she spent too much money. Or that's what her boyfriend told me."

His eyes flickered. "Boyfriend?"

"Yeah. A professor up in Tennessee. They started their affair when she was in college. Didn't she tell you? He's a lot like you—about the same age, a professional man. The kind of man Mandy trusted. The kind she fell in love with. She must have found you especially attractive—a kind doctor concerned with alleviating pain. Why didn't anybody ever see you together?"

We continued to take tiny dance steps as we talked. He was panting for breath. "We were careful. Nurses and doctors don't fraternize much at the Hopemore Medical Center. It's an old fashioned place with old fashioned morals."

"Yeah. Morals like expecting people not to kill the people they love."

I had gone too far. His eyes grew stormy. "She *said* she loved me, but she'd have wiped out years of research without a qualm. 'I can't let you do it, Drew,'" he mimicked in a high voice. "'I can't let you say it if it isn't true.'"

"What about Lorine?" I was half-way around the table now. Only one more half to go. "Why did you kill her?"

"Rotten luck." He took a long, bold step and I scurried out of reach.

"Rotten luck?"

"Yeah. She'd been at the hospital late that night and saw me coming down Mandy's steps. She told me right after the buffet."

"Was she trying to blackmail you?" I tried to see out of the corner of my eye how far it was to the back door. Too far. Much too far. And if I ever got there, could I reach my car before he caught me? He was in excellent shape. I wasn't. I really did need to exercise.

My mind had wandered, but fortunately I'd said something that tickled him. He chuckled, and for an instant looked like my friendly neighbor again. "Oh, no. Lorine really believed your preacher killed Mandy. She said she knew I had a good reason for being there, but she was afraid other people might not believe me. She also said the police were going to interview the fellow next door to Mandy's, because he knew something."

I felt a stab of pain. *Oh, Gideon, did I lead Drew right to you?*

"So you choked them both. I've heard that murderers generally use the same weapon every time, but you're real versatile." I'd meant to be sarcastic, but his ego was so big, he took it for a compliment.

"Yeah, well, whatever works." He feinted to the right and stepped left. I was ready. I'd already seen it in his eyes.

"What did you have to burn?" I edged a bit further around. "Didn't I smell smoke at Lorine's?"

He grinned, but nothing was funny now. Sweat poured down his face. "You scared the living daylights out of me that night, asking if there was a fire. Lucky nobody else noticed. I'd been burning the scrubs and gloves I wore, in case I'd gotten hairs on them."

"Weren't you burning the next morning, too?" I took another baby step. We'd gone three-quarters of the way around the table, and I had my back to the stove.

"I didn't have time to finish. I didn't expect them to find her until the next morning." He made it sound like Rhonda and Ronald had shown bad manners. "The things hadn't burned all the way, so I had to add more wood and kerosene."

On the last word he stepped back, put both hands against the table, and lunged. The heavy old table skidded across the floor and pinned me against the cabinet. The sugar bowl shattered on the floor.

But he'd been left off balance. In one movement I squirmed into the corner between the stove and the sink, grabbed up the iron griddle, and brought it down flat against his head.

He crumpled across the table.

The syringe dropped from his hand and skittered harmlessly across the floor.

> As I have observed, those who
> plow evil and those who sow
> trouble reap it. *Job 4:8*

Thirty-Three

Oh, God, did I kill him? I forced myself to touch his wrist. His pulse was beating strong.

I had to wiggle a bit to get out of the little bit of space he'd left me, and when I crawled out from under the table I had sugar all over me, but I dusted off my palms and knees and tried to decide what to do next. I felt like grabbing my pocketbook and hightailing it to my car, of course, but who'd believe me if Drew woke up and went home?

Tie him up. That's what I needed to do.

But with what?

Joe Riddley's new clothesline. *Thank you, God, that he bought clothesline instead of light bulbs.*

I dashed to the pantry and ripped that plastic covering with my teeth. Shaking so hard I could hardly make my fingers work, I pulled Drew's hands behind him and tied them together. He nearly fell back on me, so I dragged up a chair and shoved him into it. Then I snaked the clothesline around his leg and tied it to one leg of the table, and did the same on the other side. He still didn't look secure to me, so I tied one end of the clothesline to Joe Riddley's grandmother's pie safe—which was oak and so heavy it took three men to lift it when we put in our new floor—and the other end to a pipe on the water heater. That ought to hold him.

When I finished, my legs buckled. I barely made it to a chair. *Okay, God, what do I do now?*

Call somebody.

Who? Not 911. They'd call Charlie Muggins', and he'd *never* believe me. He didn't mind arresting a preacher, but he'd never suspect a doctor.

You didn't suspect him, either, my conscience reminded me.

"He was short," I objected. "Luke said the man was tall." But I'd never really believed that dream. Even now it was odd to realize how true it was. Hadn't Luke said he wore a green outfit, maybe golfing clothes. They weren't golfing clothes, they were surgical scrubs. Why hadn't I thought of that sooner?

Because he was handsome, nice, and your neighbor, my conscience jeered. Good Lord, did I stereotype people as much as Charlie Muggins? That was a humbling, disgusting thought. Someday I'd think about it. Right now I needed to call somebody.

It took me nearly a minute to remember Sheriff Gibbons' number, and I had to punch it three times before my trembling fingers would get it right. As soon as his dispatcher was on the line, I begged, "Mable, could you send Sheriff Gibbons down to Judge Yarbrough's house? This is his wife and I ... I need him here right away."

"I'll give him the message."

How could she sound so cheerful and normal? How could the sun be gleaming through clouds as if nothing awful had ever happened in the universe?

"Oooh." Drew lifted his head, then let it fall back to the table. When he tried to tug his hands apart and couldn't, he lifted his head again and peered blearily at me. "Mac? Somebody's tied me up. Can you let me loose?"

"I tied you up," I told him grimly. "You tried to kill me. Don't pretend you've forgotten. Just sit still 'til somebody gets here."

"My head aches." He put his forehead on the table and moved his head restlessly back and forth. I couldn't feel a shred of pity.

He looked up again and peered across at me disbelievingly. "Remember at the buffet when that man asked if Supersleuth Yarbrough was on the case? I never dreamed he meant you."

"Why not?"

"Oh, you're a woman. And older . . ."

Prejudice again. Stereotypes run deep and deadly in all of us, and we don't even know they're there. Every one of us divides the world by race, age, sex, or profession into those we count worthy and those we do not. Every one of us.

I was almost glad Drew kept talking. I'd rather listen even to him than my conscience.

". . . then I saw that paper today, and realized it was you he meant, not the judge."

The judge?

Ice water flowed in every vein in my body. "You shot Joe Riddley?"

He lifted his shoulders in a little shrug. "I'm the one who saved his life, remember?" He gave an unpleasant little laugh.

I wanted to throw myself on him and tear his flesh with my bare nails. Instead, I held on to my chair.

"You didn't kill him," I said. "Why not?"

"The dog barked. He bent down to calm her, so the bullet hit his head instead of his heart. Then she ran at me, so I shot her, too. She fell. I thought I'd killed them both." He shook his head to clear it. "I've always been a lousy shot."

"You could have fired again. You had plenty of time." I didn't know why we were talking like that, but I couldn't seem to stop.

"When I bent over him, he was still breathing . . ." For the first time I saw him falter. Was there still a good man in there somewhere? A good man who'd been too willing to host the malignancy of evil?

"'First, do no harm,'" I remembered. "The Hippocratic Oath. That's what saved him, wasn't it?"

Hope flickered in his eyes. "*I* saved him, Mac. I ran back to my house, called the medics, and worked like a Trojan over him until they got there. I didn't really want him to die. But he stood between me and my work."

His voice dropped to a wheedle. "You don't know how important this work is. It can be of enormous benefit to people who can't take anesthetics. Old people, sick people. I helped Joe Riddley. I can help more people if you'll let me go. I'll leave Hopemore. Go to another town. Please? Don't let all I've worked so hard for go down the drain!"

The whole time he was talking he was straining at those knots on his wrists. I hadn't tied them well enough to hold much longer. Once he got his hands free—

I did something I never thought I would ever do. I got Joe Riddley's keys. I went to his den, unlocked his gun cabinet, took out a shotgun, and loaded it. Then I carried it out to the kitchen and sat down across the room from him with it across my knees.

"You wouldn't shoot me, Mac." Drew gave me a teasing smile, but he continued to work the knots. "I'll bet you don't even know how to use that thing."

"I don't like guns," I informed him, "but at the age of ten my granddaddy taught me how to load one. After that I earned all my spending money shooting rats on his poultry farm. I won't kill you, but if I hear another peep out of you until Sheriff Gibbons comes, so help me, you'll wish I had."

The sheriff didn't come for days and days—or maybe it was five minutes. Drew and I sat in silence, and I did a lot of thinking before I heard a car in the drive.

No, it was two cars, one after the other. I went to the back door to see who else had come.

"Mac?" Buster Gibbons climbed out of his cruiser, looking worried.

Ike James climbed out of another cruiser. "Preacher Blessed got a message to me that I ought to get out here. Said he was worried about you. Why've you got that gun? Are you all right?"

Before I could do more than shake my head, Maniac's Saturn screeched into the drive. "You all come in," I told the three of them, "and we'll have a party."

Ike's car was closer to the back porch, so he came in first. He stopped at the door, staring at Drew. From there Drew looked a bit like a spider in a web. I'd probably tied a few too many knots.

Maynard peered around Ike, not saying anything.

Sheriff Gibbons pushed past them both and stood for a minute not saying anything, then he asked, "You and the doc here been playing some kinky games, Mac?"

"Mac's made a dreadful mistake," Drew spoke quickly. "She mistook me for an intruder, and—" He shrugged as well as he could with both hands tied.

"I'm awful glad to see you, Buster," I said with as much dignity as I could muster wearing a robe and jacket, standing barefoot in a mound of sugar with a shotgun on my arm. "You too, Ike and Maynard. This man tried to kill me."

"Nonsense!" Drew barked a laugh.

The sheriff held up one hand. "Wait a minute, Dr. Holder. Let's see what Mac has to say."

It took a while to explain. They didn't believe me at first, especially Maynard. He couldn't believe a nice man like Dr. Holder could kill three people. I had an advantage over Maynard. I'd been there when nice Dr. Holder tried to kill *me*.

"The biggest problem I see," Buster Gibbons told me, "is that we don't have any *evidence* to tie him to these murders you claim he committed. I can take him in for attempted assault, on your testimony—"

"Attempted murder," I corrected him hotly. "See that empty syringe? I haven't touched it. It's got his prints all over it."

Ike James still looked unconvinced. "Whatever we call it, his lawyer will claim he came down as a good neighbor to give you something to calm you down after all your worry over Joe Riddley, and you got jittery and over-reacted."

I decided to go ahead and play my Ace. "I think you all can get evidence to convict him of Kent murder, but you'll have to override Charlie to get it. There are people who will testify that Amanda Kent liked older men, medicine, and helping people. She'd been talking about her fiancé a few days before she died. I think you can connect Drew to her apartment by a piece of string in the pocket of the pants he wore running this morning. Red ones— probably in his dirty clothes hamper. It's light blue string." Drew tugged against the ropes, but could not free himself. "Rhonda and I both saw Drew take it off a screw on Amanda Kent's loom. I saw that thread on the screw when the loom was still at her house. Walker saw it, too, and Selena may have. See if it matches cut-off sweatpants Drew's got. I last saw them covered with soot one night— the night the cannon fell. Maynard, did you notice them?"

Maynard nodded. "I sure did. I wondered why anybody would cut off good sweat pants."

"I'll bet he ripped them on Mandy's loom and had to cut them off." We talked as if Drew was not there, but he was—eyes hot with fury and disbelief.

"You could check her apartment for his prints, too," I told Isaac, "especially the refrigerator. She had bottles of root beer in there, and he likes root beer. Also you could check with the hospital laundry to see if somebody put bloody scrubs in the laundry the Saturday morning after the murder. He may have even gotten her blood on his car leaving her house. He may not have taken time to clean up thoroughly, because a neighbor had pounded the wall."

"If there's blood, we can find it," Ike acknowledged.

As far as I was concerned, Drew's glare was as good as a confession.

I went on listing things I'd had time to think of before they arrived. "Ask Dr. Bert Nelson when Drew offered to let him have the weekend off to go to Amelia Island. I'd bet it was Saturday morning. Drew wanted to be on call when the body was found. And there's a receipt somewhere here—" I peered around, wondering where I'd dropped it. Drew and I both saw it at the same time, lying on the table. He lunged for it with his head, but Ike got there first. "That shows he bought a new crowbar the day after the murder. I can't believe Amos didn't leave one. Somebody may be able to testify that the murder weapon came from Amos's, or maybe forensics can match it to the Pickens place."

Sheriff Bailey Gibbons is a country boy. That crowbar convinced him. "Old Amos would have had one, right enough. He had at least one of everything."

After that I had to turn so I couldn't see Drew anymore. If looks could kill, I'd have been burnt to cinders in my own kitchen.

The Lord blessed the latter part of
Job's life more than the first. *Job*
42:12

Thirty-Four

While Buster got on his radio and called for deputies, Maynard eased toward the door. "If you don't need me any more, I'll be getting on back home. Selena's coming for supper to meet Daddy."

I walked him out. I always like to be polite—even if I've got a murderer tied to my kitchen table.

"Thank you for coming," I told him gratefully. "There's something I've been meaning to tell you, but I haven't had a chance. Selena broke up with her last boyfriend because she doesn't like somebody giving her orders. I thought you ought to know, in case you really like her."

He just beamed. "I like her, all right. The minute I laid eyes on her playing the flute at the temple I said, 'Maynard Spence, there's the woman you are going to marry.'"

"Don't rush her, now," I warned.

304

"I won't. We've got all the time in the world." He gave me a little wave and sloshed through the soggy yard to his car.

Going out, he passed the cruiser coming to take Drew away.

~~~

Ike offered to run me to the hospital, and I decided to let him. I felt like a wet dumpling, and wasn't sure I could drive. Ridd or Walker could come for my car later.

We drove past Hubert's watermelon field and house without saying a word. I'd put my window down to enjoy the unseasonal cool air and to thank God I was alive to feel it. There's nothing to make you appreciate simple things like almost losing them.

As we came abreast of the cow pond place and I saw the Pickens place on the curve ahead, I wondered out loud, "Who can Sheriff Gibbons get to sign Drew's arrest warrant?"

Ike steered around a puddle left from the storm. "Judge Stebley came back from Alaska as soon as he heard about Judge Yarbrough."

"I wish we'd caught Drew before he shot Joe Riddley," I said wistfully, looking at that dark, empty house.

Ike nearly swerved off the road. "He did that?" I nodded. "And you didn't shoot him before I got here? Any jury in the county would have acquitted you."

"I was sorely tempted," I admitted.

"Did he say why he did it?"

"He thought Joe Riddley was looking for Amanda Kent's murder."

"And all the time it was you."

I smiled, but I didn't think it was very funny. "That's what he said, too."

"I wish I could find the gun. I'd add those charges so fast it would make his head swim."

"Me, too."

Something came back to me. "I remember one day he stood by my car and lobbed a rock into Hubert's pond back there. Maybe ..."

Ike pushed his big foot down hard on the accelerator. "I'm gonna drop you off at the hospital, then I'm off to arrange a pond draggin' first thing in the mornin'."

We didn't say anything else until after he'd turned onto the highway, then he spoke so softly he could have been talking to himself. "I never could understand why Chief Muggins thought your preacher did it."

I considered telling him about Luke taking Charlie's wife to the emergency room and on to Atlanta, but I didn't. I figured I ought to work on my own prejudices before I blabbermouthed about somebody else's. Instead, I said, "Lorine pushed him a lot, I think. And by telling him she was Mandy's best friend, she implied she knew things she didn't."

Ike was surprised. "Why would she do something like that?"

I told him what Drew had said about her seeing him coming out of Mandy's apartment. "Drew said she didn't suspect him—just thought he'd been too near the scene at the wrong time—but I think she must have worried that he might have done it. Otherwise she wouldn't have fastened on Luke so fast and encouraged Charlie in that direction."

"Which wasn't hard to do," Ike said sourly. "I've never seen the chief so worked up about a case. You'd have thought he was out for revenge or something." He gave me a quick look, but must have seen that horse wouldn't run. "I wonder why Mrs. Duckworth would want it to be her preacher instead of the doctor?"

"Because she wanted Drew to marry Rhonda. But don't worry about Rhonda," I added, sensing what he was going to say. "I wouldn't be surprised if she didn't wind up in New York as a famous model."

I'd forgotten to say anything about the evidence in the burn barrel, and that took the rest of the trip. He said he'd go back out there in the morning to secure anything that was left.

As he let me out at the door, he asked, "You gonna be here all night?"

"Yeah." I smiled. "Night and day until he's ready to come home. In some ways, it's a relief. As far as Joe Riddley's concerned, it's still July. Maybe he and I can live through August all over—and have it better next time."

Luke got out of jail that same evening—but not really. His heart was so touched by what he'd experienced, he started a Sunday afternoon service down there and several programs to support spouses and children of inmates. He also kept up his weekly Bible study, and encouraged some of our adults to participate. Ridd got so involved that Crick started calling Thursday evenings "the night Daddy goes to jail."

Luke got other groups in Hopemore to sponsor programs to reach children and youth before they get in trouble. Next thing I knew there was a community football program for elementary and middle school children. We sponsored one team, coached by Ike, and Walker's insurance company sponsored another, coached by Walker. I dropped by a game one afternoon and it felt like old times. Those men were having as much fun as the kids.

"Do you still think God sent you to jail?" I asked Luke some weeks later. The whole idea that a loving God might do such a thing was disturbing to me, yet a whole lot of good had come out of it.

Luke shook his head. "I don't have the faintest idea," he admitted, "but you know what I learned inside? Not to try to second guess what God is doing until I get the big

picture, and not to give God instructions. I used to get up
and pray each morning, 'Here's what I want you to do,
please.' In jail I learned to wake up and say, 'Here I am.
What do you want me to do?' Hopefully some day we'll be
where we can see exactly how everything fit together for
good in that situation. All I can do right now is follow the
little bit of good I can already see."

He grinned. "But remember when I told you I could
stay there forever? I lied. I get up every morning and walk
three miles, just to prove I can. And I'll never fuss about
no air conditioning, because I can't stand to close my windows. Freedom is such a blessing!"

We've had some blessings in our own lives, too.
Walker's hung up his guitar during football season, and
his son is on his team. He's got a ways to go as a husband
and father, but he's making a good start.

Joe Riddley is getting better, very slowly. His legs
still aren't strong, but the doctors think he could eventually regain some use of them. He has hand tremors, too,
and the doctor claims he's had personality changes
because he often says inappropriate things. I tell him Joe
Riddley always did say inappropriate things. His memory
has improved some, but it's erratic. Too erratic for him to
continue as magistrate. He got his wish. He got to retire.

Judge Stebley came by the office one morning and
sat in our red plaid chair with his knees primly together.
You'd never know, looking at that handsome head with its
iron gray hair and lovely blue eyes, that he was related to
Arnie Potts and Lorine Duckworth. He got the family fea-
tures Lorine must have wished she had.

"MacLaren, I've been wanting to talk to you," he
began a little awkwardly. He wasn't looking at me, but at
the old oak filing cabinet to my right.

"What about, Judge Stebley?" I asked.

He cleared his throat. "Well, you know Joe Riddley isn't going to be able to be a magistrate the way things are."

I leaned forward and put a hand on his arm. "You don't have to worry about hurting his feelings. He'd been wanting to retire before he got shot."

"I'm not worrying about hurting his feelings. I've already talked to him about this."

I was surprised. "So what's worrying you?"

He finally looked right at me, with a smile both on his lips and in his eyes. "That you'll turn me down when I ask you to serve in his place."

For maybe the second time in my life I was speechless. "Me? A magistrate?"

"You a magistrate. You've been to the training classes with him, you probably know the job as well as either of us do. And folks trust you, MacLaren. I've talked this over with several people in town, and we'd be honored if you'd accept my appointment."

That's how I became Judge Yarbrough. Walker claims it was the cheapest appointment the town ever made. We didn't even have to change the sign over our door.

As for me, I feel it is an honor and a privilege to follow Joe Riddley as magistrate. Of course, it wasn't so pleasant when I got involved with Hector Blaine and the Confederate treasury mess—but that's a different story . . .

If you enjoyed *But Why Shoot the Magistrate?*, you'll also love the first book in the MacLaren Yarbrough series,

When Did We Lose Harriet?
by Patricia Sprinkle

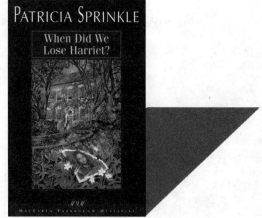

A teenage girl has been missing from her Montgomery, Alabama, home for six weeks. She may be a runaway, a crime victim, or both. What's amazing is other people's lack of concern. Just one person cares that she's gone: a spunky amateur sleuth on the sunset end of sixty.

Armed with razor-sharp insight, a salty wit, and tenacious faith, MacLaren Yarbrough follows a trail of mysterious clues in search of answers to questions that come hot and fast and that grow increasingly alarming. How did a fifteen-year-old girl come across a large sum of money? Why did she hide it instead of taking it with her? Where is she now? And who is willing to kill to keep MacLaren from probing too far? Search with her to find the answer to the ultimate question, *When Did We Lose Harriet?*

Softcover 0-310-21294-4

ZondervanPublishingHouse
Grand Rapids, Michigan
http://www.zondervan.com

A Division of HarperCollinsPublishers

We want to hear from you. Please send your comments about this
book to us in care of the address below. Thank you.

ZondervanPublishingHouse
Grand Rapids, Michigan 49530
http://www.zondervan.com